Forgotten

Forgotten

by

Marc Liebman

A Josh Haman Novel

www.penmorepress.com

Forgotten by Marc Liebman
Copyright © 2015, 2019 Marc Liebman

ISBN-978-1-946409-72-0(Paperback)
ISBN 978-1-946409-73-7(e-book)

BISAC Subject Headings:
FIC014000FICTION / Historical
FIC032000FICTION / War and Military
FIC0012000FICTION / Action and Adventure

Editor: Chris Wozney

Address all correspondence to:

Penmore Press,
920 N Javelina Pl,
Tucson, AZ 85737

or visit our website at:
www.penmorepress.com

Books by Marc Liebman

Big Mother 40
Cherubs 2
Render Harmless
Forgotten
Inner Look
Moscow Airlift
The Simushir Island Incident

DEDICATION

This novel is dedicated to those U.S. and Allied men and women who became POWs. Some came home alive; unfortunately, many did not.

AUTHOR'S NOTE

Forgotten is a work of fiction. At the end of the Vietnam War, many believed the U.S. left people behind. Chuck Norris starred in three *Missing in Action* movies, and Gene Hackman starred in one —*Uncommon Valor.* All helped perpetrate the hypothesis that Nixon in his haste to get the Treaty of Paris signed didn't press the North Vietnamese hard enough on the POW issue.

Feeding the fire was a fair amount of intelligence suggesting that there may have been Americans left behind, most of it laid out in a book titled *An Enormous Crime* by Bill Hendon and Elizabeth Stewart.

During the war, many Americans were known to be taken alive, yet they never appeared on any POW lists. It took years before their fate was known. To this date, we still don't know what happened to some of them and may never know.

The historical context behind the plot of *Forgotten* is:

The North Vietnamese were less than forthcoming about who those they held captive.

Cuban intelligence officers who interrogated American servicemen were extremely brutal and killed several.

On November 29, 1969, Politburo Resolution No. 194 changed the way U.S. POWs were treated. Still, for the remainder of the time they were in captivity, our men were poorly fed, given minimal medical attention even when needed, and were still tortured.

After the war, the Pathet Lao, Khmer Rouge and the Vietnamese People's Army routinely sent troops into Thai territory, ostensibly chasing "bandits." In reality, they were after those opposed to their regimes or who wanted to escape.

The "Golden Triangle" produced and still produces large amounts of opium.

The Students for a Democratic Society were at the peak of their influence as an organization in the U.S. Their leaders, the late Tom Hayden, who became a California State Senator (and his wife Jane Fonda), the late Dave Dillinger, who became a professor at Vermont College and Goddard College, and Bernadette Dohrn, who spend years as an adjunct professor of law at Northwestern University, still affect American politics from the far left.

Add an interesting mix of characters and voilà, you have the plot of *Forgotten*. I hope you enjoy reading the book as much as I did writing it.

Marc Liebman

August 2015, 2019

Table of Contents

Prologue:
REVOLUTIONARY ACTION

Wednesday, March 29, 1967, 2346 local time, Northbrook, IL

A blacked-out sedan slid to a stop outside a storefront with the four service logos that indicated it was a U.S. Armed Forces Recruiting Station. A single desk light, left on by one of the recruiters when he'd departed, dimly illuminated the space.

Despite the all-black attire, a passerby would have easily identified the figure as a shapely woman. She had a mason jar in each hand and a brick under her armpit. Each jar had a rag sticking out of the lid. She stopped a body's length from the large picture window, where the light from inside the recruiting station faded out and the shadows began. She carefully put down both Mason jars on the cement sidewalk, then she hurled the brick, underhand like a softball pitcher. The plate glass window cracked with a satisfying sound before shattering glass left a gaping hole. With a butane lighter, the woman lit the first Mason jar and lobbed it into the recruiting center. It smashed on one of the steel desks, spreading an exploding mixture of soap and gasoline.

The second jar landed to the left of the first one. By the time the woman got back in the car, the recruiting station was a blazing inferno.

Fifteen minutes later, the stolen Ford Fairlane slid to a stop in a shopping mall parking lot, well away from the stores. In one practiced movement, the bomber pulled a .45 caliber pistol out of a shoulder holster and put it to the temple of the driver. Brain, blood and bone splattered the driver's side window.

She walked across the lot to another car, a steel-gray Volvo 123S with red leather seats, unlocked it, and drove away. It took her two hours to get back to the University of Wisconsin's Madison campus. Once inside her studio apartment, the driver dialed the phone number of a fellow student. She knew he was a night owl.

"Bill, it's Julia. Want to fuck?"

"Now?"

"Yeah, now. I need a good fucking."

"Be right over!"

Around four in the morning, Julia ushered the young man out of her apartment. He couldn't get it up a third time and therefore was of no further use. Still dissatisfied, she masturbated until she had another orgasm, then fell asleep.

After her alarm went off at seven, Julia watched a breathless TV commentator's top of the hour story on the fire-bombing of a military recruiting station in Northbrook, Illinois. Fire department investigators said the fire was started by a "napalm-like" mixture. A communiqué released by the Revolutionary Wing of the Students for a Democratic Society had claimed responsibility. The organization, he reported, was opposed to the war in Vietnam.

In another story later in the Chicago station's broadcast, a newscaster announced that a young female had been found shot to death in a Deerfield mall parking lot. The police had no suspects for either the fire or the murder.

Satisfied with her night's work, Julia Amy Lucas turned off the TV. She had just turned twenty-one and this was her first act as a member of the Revolutionary Wing of the Students for A Democratic Society. What surprised her was how much she liked it.

Chapter 1
SHOOT DOWN

Thursday, October 22, 1970, 1410 local time, Gulf of Tonkin

At thirty thousand feet, Randy Pulaski could see where the country of North Vietnam ended and the Gulf of Tonkin began. Above the A-7B Corsair II's clear Plexiglas canopy, puffy cumulus clouds dotted the azure blue sky. It was, he thought, a great day for flying. A thousand feet to his right and five hundred feet above, his wingman flew in loose formation. When Randy rolled into a three g right turn, his wingman—call sign Power House 307—began a similar three g turn to the left. The scissor maneuver let them search the sky below and behind for MiGs and surface-to-air missiles.

Randy felt his G-suit bladders around his legs and mid-section suit inflate to keep blood from draining from his head as he held the sixty degree banked turn. When he passed astern of the other A-7, both airplanes reversed course to start another horizontal scissor. Without the eight thousand pounds of bombs he'd dropped on the target and less than fifty percent of its normal fuel load, the Corsair handled like, well, almost like a fighter. Even though the A-7 didn't have the thrust to weight ratio of a MiG-21, Randy was confident he could out-turn the Soviet-designed plane and stay in the flight long enough to get a shot with his two

3

twenty-millimeter cannons. In his mind, a MiG-19 was a greater threat because it turned better than the '21' and had a better thrust-to-weight ratio than the A-7. So far, he'd not seen a MiG on his first or now, halfway through his second, combat deployment.

Randy eased the stick back to increase the g's and added a bit of power to keep the airplane from decelerating as he looked for the smoke trails made by surface-to-air missiles. The loud, strident, hard-to-ignore tone in his earphones caused him to look at the radar warning system display. It told him a missile was heading toward him from eight o'clock low. The beeps changed to a high-pitched warble when the Fan Song target acquisition radar for the SA-2 missile locked onto a target.

"Sam, *SAM*, *SAM!* Power House flight, break left NOW!"

Randy didn't need to be told twice. He shoved the stick left and forward as he fed in left rudder to make sure the nose was pointed down in a sixty-degree dive. The strobe on the radar warning system display showed the bearing line to the missile. He was about to find out if he or his wingman was the target.

There was not one, not two, but three SA-2s snaking up at him at Mach 2 plus. His A-7 was headed straight at them at about .9 Mach, trading altitude for airspeed. About a quarter mile from the closest missile, Randy pushed the stick to the right to barrel roll out of the closest SA-2s cone of maneuverability. The roll, if done at the right time, would break the beam riding missile's lock on his airplane.

The first missile snaked left and right as it headed skyward, searching for another target. Randy's altimeter said he was passing twenty thousand and then nineteen when the second corkscrewed by less than half a mile away. He was looking for the third missile when he heard a whump and the A-7 shook. When he rolled wings level and pulled out of the dive and headed east toward the Gulf of Tonkin and safety, the controls worked normally.

Seconds later, the yellow master caution light glowed brightly. *Fly the airplane first!* Now down to about fifteen thousand,

Randy eased back on the stick to trade airspeed for altitude. If the engine failed, he wanted as much altitude as he could get to give him the best chance of gliding to the gulf.

Randy looked at the engine gauges as the Pratt and Whitney engine unwound and the A-7 slowed as if it had hit a wall. He pulled the toggle switch to deploy the emergency power package to give him the electrical and hydraulic power needed to control the jet. After trimming the airplane for its best glide speed of two hundred and twenty knots, he jettisoned his two external fuel tanks.

In the training command, instructors drilled into his head that when the shit hits the fan aviate first, then navigate, and then communicate when you have a plan. Randy felt he'd done the aviating because he had the A-7 under control. In Naval Aviator parlance, getting "feet wet" over the Gulf of Tonkin before punching out was the navigation plan. If he ejected over the gulf, the chances of being picked up were close to 100 per cent unless he landed in a swarm of sea snakes or a shark decided he was dinner.

With the emergency power package working as advertised, Randy eased the throttle into the position for an air start, turned on the igniters, and pushed the starter button. Behind him, he could hear the igniters clicking over the whine of the starter. When he didn't hear the soft whump of the engine lighting, Randy again went through the memory items on the emergency air start checklist. The fuel system main and boost pumps switches were on and the throttle was in the start position. Just before he pressed the starter again, he looked at the fuel pressure gauge. It read zero. No wonder the engine is not starting—it wasn't getting any fuel. Shrapnel from the missile must have cut the fuel line.

Randy was about to key the mike when his headset crackled. Shit, he hadn't told anyone yet he had a problem. "Power House 310, this is 307 in trail behind you. You're streaming fuel pretty badly. I've already let Hammer 700 know that you've taken a hit from a SAM. You just fly and I'll keep everybody informed."

Shit, why didn't I hear his transmission? Because, asshole, you were too busy aviating!

"Power House 310, this is 307. The bottom of your plane looks like Swiss cheese. The speed brake is gone along with one of your main landing gear doors. There's hydraulic fluid all over the side and belly and you are losing gas in a big way. I don't know what will happen if you try a restart."

"307 this is 310, I already did. This bird is a glider. It is going to be close." Randy looked at his altimeter. It showed eight thousand feet and he was about five miles to go to the gulf. He felt as if he was a sitting duck.

"Roger that. SAR helo is on the way. You should be in the water in less than ten minutes."

If I make it! It is not a matter of if I am going to eject, but when. Randy pulled the chart on his kneeboard and stuffed it into his flight suit's pocket outside his left boot. Then, he put his kneeboard into his helmet bag and pushed it as far back into the corner of the cockpit as he could.

The cockpit was quieter than usual. Randy heard the gyros whining above the wind noise. The lights on the master caution panel told him that his utility hydraulic system had failed and all the engine gauges were pegged at zero. *Tell me something I don't know!*

Whumph Whumph... The A-7 rocked and Randy looked at the black puffs made by exploding anti-aircraft shells. *Shit!* Any turn will cost precious altitude. The line between the green of the land and the blue of the water was getting closer. Randy guessed the coast was three miles away. He was down to five thousand feet and was going to ride his dying A-7 as long as possible.

A string of red golf balls went by the nose. Their size told him they came from a 57mm gun. Randy scrunched down, hoping to avoid a chunk of shrapnel.

*Whumph Whumph Whumph **BANG!*** The airplane rolled from the impact. Another light came on. The number two hydraulic system died.

FORGOTTEN

*Four thousand feet. Going feet wet now, NOW, **NOW!***

BRRAAPP! Out of the corner of his eye, Randy saw the outboard section of the right wing that folds ninety degrees to reduce the space the airplane takes up on the deck of a carrier fly off. The A-7 rolled hard to the right and he applied full left stick. The rate of roll slowed noticeably but did not stop as the A-7 started to spin like a bullet. With nothing but blue water below, it was time to get out while the getting was good.

As the rolling airplane approached wings level, he let go of the stick, pulled his feet off the rudder pedals and reached back to pull the face curtain. The canopy blew off with a bang and milliseconds later he left the airplane when it was in a forty-degree left bank. The gyro controlling the rocket motor in the Martin Baker ejection seat shot him straight up. Once the drogue chute stabilized the seat, he was "kicked" out. When the parachute opened, Randy guessed he was about two thousand feet above the water, facing west. Fear tingled his body when he realized he was going to land about half a mile from shore, just beyond the surf line. Randy yanked down on the seaward riser to try to steer the parachute out to sea. All it did was accelerate his rate of descent.

During survival training, instructors taught the students to take their gloves off because the leather palms got slippery and made it difficult to release the parachute harness. Randy stuffed them into a pocket and crossed his arms just before he hit the water.

As he sank, Randy pulled down on the Koch fittings and felt the parachute harness come off. When he kicked to the surface, he could see the chute drifting away. Sharp tugs on the toggles on his life preserver led to a loud hissing as carbon dioxide inflated the bladders around his chest and then up around his neck.

So far so good. He was floating and wasn't going to be pulled under by the forty pounds of his survival vest, G-suit, boots, and flight suit.

Zip, zip, zip. Smack. What the hell is that? Randy stopped pulling the lanyard connected to his raft and paddled around to face the beach. Instinctively he ducked as tracers flew over his head. Short rows of geysers of water appeared on both sides and in front. *Shit, they're shooting at me!*

Randy felt a tug on his waist. Thinking it was a sea snake or a shark, he felt down and found the lanyard to his survival kit. When he got the yellow raft to him, Randy debated for a second before he climbed in, thinking it would be easier to paddle it seaward than swimming with all his gear.

Getting in was just like training—grab the handles on the sides and pull yourself in from the narrow end. Once inside, roll onto your back and look up. In the raft, he pulled off his helmet. Now, along with the splashes and the spouts of water, he could hear the gunfire.

Paddle first or communicate? With both arms, he paddled as fast as he could away from the trees. He watched an A-7B spit tracers from its two twenty-millimeter cannons at the tree line. As the jet flew by, the geysers stopped.

The sixty seconds of peace and quiet let him get out his PRC-90 survival radio. Not worried about being overheard, he made sure the radio was on and keyed the mike. "Any station, this is Power House 310, in the water. I am about a half-mile off the beach. Anyone copy."

"Power House 310, this is 307. We have a visual on you and have two other A-7s overhead with ordnance. The helo is about ten minutes out and advises no smoke, copy."

"310 copies." *Paddle, dummy.* Randy dropped the radio in his lap, shed out the earpiece and stuffed it in his ear. He keyed the mike to make sure that he could hear a side tone and then started paddling the raft, narrow end first, toward the safety of the gulf.

At the top of the swells, Randy could tell the surf was winning, drawing him closer and closer to the sand. Desperately, he paddled faster because that beach was the first step toward a stay in the Hanoi Hilton.

"Power House 310, this is Clementine 26. We have a visual on you."

Tracers reached out to the helicopter which Randy recognized as an H-2 Sea Sprite. As he watched the helicopter approach, Randy heard a humming sound and saw bursts of tracer chew up the trees just inside the beach. The ring from the shore stopped.

Paddle, dummy!

The H-2 passed over him at a hundred feet and instead of turning and coming to a hover above him, it headed out to sea. On the top of the next swell, he could see men wading through the surf and coming toward him. He looked down and saw the bottom just a few feet below.

"You bastard, you fucking cowardly bastard. If I ever get home, I will find you and rip your fucking head off!"

Randy could see the faces of the men aiming their AK-47s at him. They were less than fifty feet away. He keyed the mike. "Powerhouse 307, they are about to get me. Tell my wife I love her and I WILL return. And have someone court martial the cowardly bastard flying the helo."

The same day, 1453 local time, North Vietnam

Randy shoved his PRC-90 into the front right pouch of his survival vest and looked at the two North Vietnamese soldiers. An upward flip of the AK-47's barrel toward the shoreline was an obvious gesture telling him to walk to the beach.

When he got to the sand, Randy raised his hands in surrender as six more men emerged from the tree line with their weapons pointed at him. A gesture of unzipping told him to take off his survival vest and G-suit. Both were yanked out of his hands and the contents dumped out, inspected, then dropped into a wicker basket. One soldier knew to compress the vest's manual inflation valve and hold it against the spring to deflate the two bladders of Randy's Life Preserver, Aviator Model 2.

His Smith & Wesson revolver and the thirty spare rounds in an elastic bandoleer stitched into the inside front pockets of his survival vest were handed to the man supervising the search. Three gold stars on the man's shoulder boards told Randy he was an officer.

Rifle gestures encouraged Randy to keep his hands above his head as one North Vietnamese soldier roughly patted him down.

As he was poked and prodded, Randy resolved he *would* live through his stay in the Hanoi Hilton. He wasn't sure if he was madder at the coward flying the helicopter, or being shot down, or being captured, or all of the above, or just scared.

The soldier standing in front of Randy jabbed the barrel of his AK-47 into his gut hard enough to make him gasp, then made a motion for him to unzip his flight suit. Randy peeled back the Velcro tabs around his wrists, unzipped it down to his crotch and shrugged out of the sleeves.

Another wave of the barrel of the AK-47 told him to take off his bright blue turtleneck. The cotton jersey was yanked out of his hand, inspected by another soldier and then tossed onto the pile of his "stuff." Another jab in the side. Randy held out the bottom of his undershirt and the soldier nodded. Off it came. He was down to his jockey shorts and the flight suit was down around his boots.

Another soldier unbuckled his Navy issue watch. The timepiece with its black dial was easy to read at night and accurate, but it wasn't as stylish as the Rolex Submariner he'd left in his stateroom safe.

Also in his safe back on the ship was a woman's Rolex President he'd bought in Hong Kong at the China Fleet Club as an anniversary present for his wife, Janet. The thought of not being able to give it to her in person made him momentarily sad, but now his job was to survive and maybe escape.

One soldier threw his blue jersey and t-shirt back into his chest as a signal to get dressed. Now, in addition to being drenched in seawater, his clothes were full of sand. As soon as he zipped up his flight suit, the North Vietnamese soldier grabbed his hands and tied them together. A second, thick rope was looped around his wrists and then his neck. He was like a dog on a leash with a choke collar.

Randy looked around the column. Ahead were two men with AK-47s. The two immediately behind motioned for him to face forward. Before he turned around, Randy saw two more soldiers carrying a bamboo pole with his flight gear looped over the wood like pieces of meat. He assumed the basket hanging from the pole contained the contents of his survival vest.

Including the officer, Randy counted eight armed men versus one unarmed man—him. Getting shot while escaping wasn't a good option, so it was time to watch and observe. *Even if I got away, then what?*

So far, no one had spoken a word to Randy. Nor had they beaten him. POW debriefs described how U.S. pilots were being beaten, jabbed with pitchforks, even stoned while they were being led into captivity.

When would that come?

Saturday, October 24, 1970, 0846 local time, Hanford, CA

The morning sun beamed down directly on the Pulaski's back porch, warming Janet as she enjoyed a cup of coffee. After marrying Randy, she'd quit her job as a hospital administrator, not wanting to make the daily thirty-five-mile trek back and forth to Fresno. To keep busy, she worked as a substitute teacher.

The doorbell's four tone chimes surprised her. Janet tied her robe as she headed to the front door, thinking it was kids from one of the local schools asking her to buy something as part of a fundraiser. She was a sucker for those pitches because she remembered the days when she'd done the bell ringing.

Instead of one or two children, three adults stood on the doorstep. The only one she recognized was Wendy Hancock, the wife of Randy's squadron commanding officer. She'd met Wendy at squadron functions Randy insisted she attend. Such events were, as Randy put it, "command performances"; junior officers and their spouses were required to show up.

One officer had wings over several rows of ribbons, signifying he was a captain, and the other had a cross on the sleeve of his dress blues. Wendy reached out and touched her arm. "Janet, may we come in? We have news that is not terrible, but it is also not great."

Janet stepped back and reached for a chair behind the door to steady herself. Seeing the slight stumble, the aviator gently took her other arm. "I'm Captain Bill Charbonneau, and I work in the headquarters, Naval Air Forces, Pacific Fleet. Father O'Mara here is one of the base chaplains. Mrs. Pulaski, is there someplace we can talk?"

Janet was glad that Captain Charbonneau didn't go through where he fit into the Navy's organization. After almost a year of marriage, most of it was still a mystery to her. She knew Randy was in Attack Squadron 153, known as the Blue Tail Flies, and was part of Air Wing 19 that deployed on a World War II era carrier called the *U.S.S. Oriskany*. Randy referred to the ship as the "Toasted O" in reference to the 1966 fire that had killed forty-four sailors.

"Yes, yes there is. The house is a mess, but we can sit in the living room. May I get you some coffee?" Actually, it wasn't messy. On Friday, a bored Janet took the time to clean up the clutter and tidy so she wouldn't have to do it over the weekend, but it was military wife etiquette to apologize for anything less than white glove inspection clean. She took her favorite spot on the short leg of the L-shaped couch. Wendy Hancock sat down next to her.

Father O'Mara remained standing; Charbonneau took a side chair. He looked solemn, ands his words were somber. "Mrs. Pulaski, I have the duty to inform you that your husband, Lieutenant Pulaski, was shot down on October 22nd. That's the really bad news."

Janet rocked back. Wendy Hancock reached put to press the top of her hand gently.

"The good news is that your husband was seen to eject from his A-7 and land in the water. He was in contact with his squadron mates via radio. An unsuccessful attempt was made to rescue him before he was seen taken prisoner. His last radio communication was *"Please tell my wife I love her and I will be back."*

"Captain Charbonneau," Janet demanded, "do you know where Randy is now? Was he hurt?"

"No, he did not say he was hurt. While I cannot reveal where he was shot down, I can tell you it was along the coast several hundred miles south of Haiphong. We know it will take them a month or so to move him to one of the prisons where they hold our pilots. The trouble is, the North Vietnamese do not honor the Geneva Conventions by telling us whom they have captured, so it may be months before we get any information on him."

Charbonneau's primary duty was to track Naval Aviators who were thought to be prisoners of war and monitor their treatment. He routinely told his boss, a vice admiral whose title was Commander Naval Air Forces Pacific, that the data he had was at best seventy per cent accurate.

He was sure of four facts. Fact one: the numbers were inaccurate. Charbonneau had evidence some aviators were killed by the North Vietnamese soon after they were captured. Some ejected safely and were killed when they landed in the trees or were badly injured and subsequently died.

Fact two: he knew the POWs were being tortured, beaten, starved, and deprived of the basics—food, sanitary living conditions, and medical care.

Fact three: what little information the North Vietnamese provided was often deliberately misleading.

Fact four: the activities of anti-war protestors, namely Tom Hayden and Jane Fonda who visited North Vietnam, were hurting, not helping, the POWs.

"What is going to happen to Randy?"

"Normally he'd be taken to a North Vietnamese Army base and interrogated before being transferred to one of their prisons."

Janet took a deep breath. "They're going to torture him, aren't they?"

"Mrs. Pulaski, I am not going to lie to you. There is a very high probability your husband will be tortured and beaten. They usually don't kill POWs during interrogations, but they do beat the crap out of them."

Charbonneau actually had detailed knowledge of the interrogation techniques used by the North Vietnamese based on the debriefings of three men—Navy Lieutenant Robert Frishman; Air Force Captain Wesley Rumble; and Seaman Doug Hegdahl—released in August, 1969. All three had been held at a satellite camp outside Hanoi the POWs dubbed "the Plantation." Hegdahl was let go because the North Vietnamese thought he was stupid. The North Vietnamese didn't know he had memorized the names of 256 POWs along with their units, dates and method of capture, dates shot down and other personal information. Many names on Hegdahl's list had not been given to the U.S. by the North Vietnamese.

"Do you have any idea of when my husband along with the other POWs will be returned?" Janet had to bite her tongue not to say, "POWs from this godforsaken, illegal war."

"To be honest, no. The North Vietnamese are using the POWs as hostages to get concessions at the Paris Peace talks."

Why wouldn't they? They want the U.S. to get out of Vietnam. "So you are sure he is not dead?"

"As of the time of capture, yes. We have no idea of what has happened since."

"How'd he get shot down?"

"The only details I can give you are that his A-7 was damaged by a Soviet-supplied surface-to-air missile. Lieutenant Pulaski tried to reach the Gulf of Tonkin, where our rescue percentages are close to one hundred per cent. He ejected right after he crossed the beach and landed in the water less than a half mile from shore."

Charbonneau knew more details, but that was all he was allowed to say.

Wendy Hancock took the captain's statement as a cue. Her husband had been in squadrons where pilots died, but this was her first experience of a squadron member being shot down. As a commanding officer's wife it was her responsibility to make sure the wives looked out for each other. "Janet, we have a support group at Lemoore for the wives of the men who are either missing in action or prisoners of war. I suggest you join it. It will help you get through this. I'll give your name to the group."

"O.K." Janet was polite, but inside she was seething. *Don't expect me to join. The last thing I want to do is join a group of patriotic, gung-ho Navy wives.*

Captain Charbonneau changed the subject. "Mrs. Pulaski, one more thing. Your husband's pay and allowances will continue as long as he is held prisoner. He will be automatically promoted if he is eligible and you can continue to enjoy commissary and exchange privileges as well as free medical care until such time as his status is changed."

"You mean until he is declared dead?"

"Yes." Charbonneau paused. "Right now the Navy is assuming that your husband is alive. I can assure you that he won't be declared dead until all the prisoners of war come home and are debriefed. Then, the Navy will wait five years before it will officially declare him dead. So the short answer is that I don't think he will be declared dead any time soon, especially since we know he was taken prisoner alive."

"Thank you, Captain, that is so… comforting to know. I appreciate your efforts, but if you'll all excuse me, I need to be alone."

The chaplain pulled a card out of his pocket and stepped forward. "Mrs. Pulaski, if you need to talk, here is my phone number. Remember, prayer helps. Randy will need God's help and your prayers to survive his ordeal in North Vietnam."

"Chaplain, I am not the most observant Catholic in the world, but I agree. Randy will need all our prayers." Her voice was polite, but her eyes were bright with unshed, bitter tears.

Sunday, October 25, 1970, 0745 local time, North Vietnam
When the column stopped for the night, Randy was lashed to a tree. His hands were freed so he could gulp down a watery soup

that was his dinner. After the guards went to sleep, he wiggled enough to loosen the rope so he could his slide his butt forward and lean his head back against the tree. Despite being exhausted and uncomfortable, he pushed aside the thought of poisonous bugs crawling all over him and fell asleep.

The spicy smell of food being cooked over an open fire and stinging from the chafed skin caused by the course hemp rope around his wrists woke Randy. His irritated skin was red but not bleeding.

Breakfast was a ball of cold sticky rice covered with a brown, spicy paste. The same stony-faced soldier who'd brought him dinner waited while Randy gobbled down every grain of rice, then he took the bowl.

The rope holding him against the tree was removed and looped around his wrists then his neck. A sharp tug on the rope meant it was time to start walking.

Randy remembered looking at the cockpit clock when he'd ejected. It had said it was two-thirty. On the *Oriskany* out in the gulf, night came about six-thirty so he figured they'd walked along a wide trail for three hours before stopping. At two to three miles an hour, he guessed he was now about six to nine miles inland.

When he woke, Randy felt as if he was beaten up. He was sure the soreness in his back, neck, and arms came from the ejection and his frantic effort to paddle away from the shore, not the walk. The swelling from the bruises from being hit by a rifle butt added to the pain he felt. Each time he moved, the smell of sweat, body odor, and seawater filled his nose.

He guessed he'd been walking about two hours when the column entered a large clearing on the edge of a tar-covered gravel road. Randy ignored his growling stomach as he looked at the sky for planes.

The crunch of boots on gravel interrupted his study of the contrails that laced the blue sky. Out of the corner of his eye, he saw three men approaching. Without saying a word, the first one rammed the butt of his rifle into Randy's stomach.

Gasping in pain and doubled over, Randy raised his head and hissed, "You fucking son-of-a-bitch..." A searing pain in his lower back from another blow sent him sprawling. Randy closed his eyes as he let the pain subside. The stench of stale tobacco caused him to look toward the smell and open his eyes. All he saw was the face of a North Vietnamese officer a foot away from his. "Lieutenant Pulaski, let me officially welcome you to North Vietnam."

The smiling officer spoke in English with little trace of a Vietnamese accent. "I am Colonel Tan Quang Duong of the People's Army of Vietnam. You are now my prisoner and your interrogation starts this afternoon. Therefore, you should start thinking about how you plan to answer my questions. Answer them to my satisfaction and you will be sent to a prisoner of war camp with your fellow war criminals. Or, you can be like some of your hardheaded comrades who had a pain-filled experience that went on for weeks. The longer you resist, the longer you are in my care. It is your choice. I must tell you I have begun to enjoy taking out my frustrations on American pilots, especially Navy ones. They seem to be the most stubborn."

The same day, 1136 local time, Hanford

The sweet garlic smell of Hunan beef filled the room, but the white containers were still half full. Only the bottle of Merlot sitting on the coffee table was empty.

Janet had spent most of the day sitting exactly where she was now—in the middle of the couch, feeling numb and staring at the TV. Her knees were drawn up against her chest and her arms wrapped around her shins as if she was trying to protect herself against more bad news.

It had been twenty-four hours since Wendy Hancock and the two Naval officers had knocked on her front door.

Janet kept coming back to the same conclusion. It could be months or years before she found out whether Randy was alive or

17

dead; meanwhile, she was stuck in the middle of nowhere in Hanford, California. Hanford's claim to fame, other than being the seat of government for Kings County, was that it was the subject of a William Saroyan short story. There was nothing here for her! What should she do? *Goddamn this fucking war!*

Tuesday, October 27, 1970, 0947 local time, North Vietnam

The night before, Randy had fallen asleep wondering how a nighttime low in the seventies that felt so good when you were in a warm bed curled up with your warm wife, felt so damn cold when you huddled alone, barefoot and damp.

His home was now one of two cages, each about six feet square and made from three-inch-diameter bamboo poles spaced about four inches apart. Nine large poles, two of which were a "door frame," were set well into the ground. A roof made from a sheet of corrugated metal protected him from the sun, but not the rain, or the wind.

The cage was where he ate, slept, peed and defecated. A steady monsoon rain made it easy to figure out which way the water flowed, so he knew where to hunker down so that what left his body washed away.

Each time Randy peed, he tried to write NM 307—the side number of his A-7—in the ground. He never had enough urine to complete all five figures.

Meals were all the same—rice or rice noodles, vegetables, broth and, if he was lucky, a small piece of meat, usually fish.

Each session, as Duong liked to call them, started the same way. The fat colonel's two assistants, whom Randy named Heckle and Jeckle after the black magpie cartoon characters, and who were probably sergeants, tied his hands and elbows together. Then they shoved a bamboo pole between his elbows and back. On the way to the interrogation room, Heckle and Jeckle half dragged, half led Randy around the inside of the compound. Duong called the lap "exercise." By arching his back, Randy relieved some of the pressure on his shoulder joints, but it was difficult to walk and hold that position for more than a few minutes.

Duong had poles of all diameters: the thin ones were about one inch, the thickest ones were closer to six. The colonel enjoyed getting his face close to Randy's to watch his prisoner's face contort at the excruciating pain caused when Heckle or Jeckle twisted or lifted the pole. When Randy passed out from pain or the beatings, Heckle and Jeckle used the pole to drag him to his cage.

Sometimes the pole was pulled out when he was tied to a chair, other times it was left in as he sat on a stool or was lashed to the concrete wall. When the pole was pulled out, the relief was instantaneous and Randy flexed his shoulders to make sure that none of his muscles were ripped or torn. On more than one occasion, Randy felt as if his shoulders were about to be dislocated and wondered what would be more painful, popping them back in or having them pulled out.

The fat colonel had another favorite set of toys—rubber hoses of varying shapes and thicknesses. Some were filled with sand. Others were hollow.

Randy concluded that Duong wasn't very sophisticated. He just liked hitting people and causing pain. After the first few beatings, Randy would get to a certain level of pain and it would level out. More, and he would pass out. Less, and it was just that, pain.

Survival school and the mock POW camp had given Randy an inkling of how much pain he could endure. He was determined he was not going to give in to Duong. He'd already told him his name, rank, religion, and serial number, all of which were on his dog tags.

This morning he stank more than usual because Duong, frustrated with Randy's non-answers, had had his soldiers pour a bowl of urine over him every two or three hours.

It had just added another putrid layer to the odor surrounding him. He was still wearing his flight suit, cotton flight deck jersey, and the underwear in which he'd been captured. One more unpleasant smell was not going to cause him to give in to Duong. It was a battle of wills, and so far it was as good as he hoped for, i.e. a draw.

Deep in sleep fueled by exhaustion, Randy didn't hear the latches being pulled off. As he was dragged to his feet, Colonel Duong yelled, "Pulaski, my government says we should not beat or torture our prisoners, but I disagree. You are all war criminals and we need to beat you until you confess to your crimes. You stink like all Americans, so if I must treat you better, try this as a bath!" He signaled to Heckle and Jeckle, and Randy staggered under the impact of water from a fire hose. He started laughing.

Duong waddled up to the cage. "What is so funny, American pig?"

"I like your sense of humor, Colonel. Last night your men pissed on me, and now you are giving me a bath!"

Duong's eyes opened as his anger grew. He swung the hoses he'd been hiding behind his back as hard as he could. Randy saw the blow coming and used his forearm to absorb it. The tail of the hose slammed into the small of his back and he could feel the burning sensation as his muscles started to swell. His bruises now had bruises on top of bruises. Duong stood on his toes and glared. "I am not done with you, Pulaski."

Friday, October 30, 1970, 1522 local time, Laos

At this altitude, Laos looked like the island of his birth, except that from ten thousand feet over his homeland, you could see the blue waters of the Caribbean to the south and the Gulf of Mexico to the north. Over Laos, all you could see were more mountains and more jungle. The only easily recognizable landmark was the Mekong River that divided Thailand from Laos, and it was well to the west. Fro ip here, Laos, Vietnam, and Cambodia were indistinguishable. Country borders were just lines on a map.

Raul Moya surveyed the hilly terrain passing below at 275 knots, his right hand on the throttles that controlled the two Pratt & Whitney R-2800 radial engines of the A-26. From his co-pilot's seat on the right side of the cockpit, Raul could see the shape of a second A-26, glossy black, five hundred feet behind and a hundred feet above.

Moya had begun flying as a co-pilot in 1959 when he joined the *Fuerza Aérea de Liberación*—the air force for the rebels that had invaded Cuba. He'd already had a private pilot's license and just under a hundred hours of flight time.

Comrades on the ground had been desperate for close air support. He and his pilot had made strafing run after strafing run until they were out of ammunition. On the third of the Bay of Pigs conflict, ground fire had knocked out an engine. Before they'd made it back to their Nicaraguan base to exchange planes, his comrades had surrendered.

In the ten years that followed, Raul had flown cargo planes all over Africa for airlines with CIA contracts. When the agency offered him a chance to fly the B-26 in Laos and Cambodia, he leapt at the chance.

This was one of forty B-26Cs pulled out of mothballs in the Arizona desert to be re-furbished in Van Nuys by a company called On Mark. The Air Force had re-designated A-26Ks Counter Invaders.

For the $577,000 per plane conversion cost, On Mark removed the belly and tail turrets to reduce the plane's empty weight. Eight fifty-caliber guns were installed in the nose, along with four racks to carry rockets and bombs on each wing. Its large ordnance load, along with its speed and maneuverability, made the A-26 an excellent close air support airplane.

The U.S. Air Force 609th Special Operations Squadron crews had flown the A-26Ks to Nakhon Phanom in Thailand. They'd attacked targets along the Ho Chi Minh trail until November 1969, when A-26s were transferred by Air America, their employer, to an airfield near Vientiane, the capital of Laos.

Along with ammo for the machine guns and four thousand pounds of bombs, Raul's plane was carrying two pods, each with four Zuni air-to-ground rockets, under each wing.

"Ramrod 31, this is Nail 555, we have work for you."

It wasn't unusual for the Air Force forward air controllers to assign targets. Before they'd taken off, Raul had had no idea where or what the target would be. He'd been ordered to lead his flight of two A-26s northeast for a hundred miles and contact Nail 555. So here it was… Showtime.

"Ramrod 31 and playmate ..." The lack of background noise told him that Nail 555 was flying the newer twin turboprop OV-10 designed specifically for the forward air controller mission. The OV-10 had a big bubble canopy and shoulder-mounted wings. When he'd gotten a chance to sit in the back seat of the armor-plated tub, Raul had thought he was sitting in the center of a glass jar.

Raul's co-pilot, Sander Renquist aka "The Swede", gave him a thumbs-up. He copied the description and location of the target, the roll in heading, and the nearest safe area in case they had to bail out.

Renquist didn't like his given name; his blond hair and blue eyes had given rise to the nickname, which he preferred.

"Nail 555, copy. Give me a canopy flash." The OV-10 pilot rolled his airplane back and forth several times.

Renquist keyed the mike on the yoke. "Ramrod 31 has a tally on Nail 555 and the target. We're coming around to three-five-zero. No need to mark the target."

From ten thousand feet the target was obvious: a dozen trucks moving down the Ho Chi Minh trail. It was rare to see this many out in the open. Either the North Vietnamese Army in the south needed the supplies desperately enough to risk being spotted, or it was a trap, or both.

Out of the corner of his eye, Raul watched "The Swede" set up the armament panel so he could shoot the five-inch diameter rockets first. The rockets with their forty-pound warheads would leave the pod in half-second intervals, starting with the inboard pods, and when they emptied he'd pull the trigger again and the outer pods would fire. As the Zunis streaked toward the target,

Raul jinked erratically as he dove to drop the eight five-hundred pounders hanging in the bomb bay.

"Am marking a truck parked under some camouflage netting for Ramrod 38."

Raul pushed the throttles to full military power and rolled the A-26 into a sixty-degree bank. As his wingman acknowledged the information on the second target, the A-26K entered a thirty-degree dive. Raul liked to get the airplane near its maximum speed of 370 knots to make it harder to hit. He felt "The Swede" adjust the throttles so that they didn't exceed forty-two inches of manifold pressure. The props were already set at 2,400 rpm when his co-pilot pushed the mike button.

"Ramrod 31 is rolling in hot."

Gentle pushes on the rudder and slight movements of the wheel took the A-26 in and out of balanced flight and made it harder to track. "I count only three guns, probably thirty-seven millimeters, shooting at us." "The Swede" sounded calm, almost bored.

'Only' three 37mm guns! You, my friend, have never been hit by one. I have, and I'm lucky to be here.

The lead truck filled the gun sight and Raul mashed the trigger. As soon as the first rocket left the rack, he raised the nose gently so the sixteen Zunis, assuming they ran true, would explode along the line of trucks.

"Opening bomb bay doors." Raul shifted his finger to the bomb release button and pressed it.

Four thousand pounds lighter, the A-26 jumped. He rolled into a steep bank and pulled the yoke back. The drag from the bomb bay doors diminished as they closed.

Renquist used the handle on the canopy to pull forward against the g forces and crane his head around. "Good hits. Five of the trucks are burning and several more are on their sides—"

BAM! Chunks of metal flew around the inside of the cockpit, accompanied by smoke and the smell of burnt explosive. Renquist slumped over.

BAM! WHUMPH! The A-26 yawed to the right. The engine instruments were going crazy. Raul pushed hard on the left rudder and leveled the wings. The A-26 was slowing but still climbing.

A red light flashed in front of him. *Fire!* Leaning forward so he could see around Renquist's head, Raul saw flames coming out of the right engine nacelle. He pulled the mixture lever for the right engine back to idle cutoff to cut the flow of 145-octane fuel.

The phrase *"Dead foot, dead engine"* ran through Raul's mind as he kept the nose straight by pushing left rudder. He turned off the right engine's fuel pumps and yanked the T-handle to fire the carbon dioxide extinguisher. Next, he pulled the right prop control lever into the feather position. He saw the prop slow, then come to a stop.

Good. He reached out and touched Renquist's neck. He felt a pulse. A quick examination showed there was blood covering the left side of his body. How long he would last was anybody's guess, but he had to get the A-26 on the ground fast. The nearest runway was at Lima 36, near the Vietnamese-Laotian border and less than fifty miles away.

"Ramrod Three One, you've got a small oil fire under the right engine, but other than that you look good. You took thirty-seven-millimeter hits to the right wing, lower fuselage, and just aft of the right engine. If you want, I can slide under you and take a closer look."

"Please do. Am heading for Lima 36. The Swede is in a bad way."

"Roger that. I'll stay with you and give them a call. Nail 555 said we clobbered the target. It must have been a fuel dump, because flames shot into the air. You got at least a dozen trucks."

"Thanks." Raul trimmed the A-26 to take out the control pressure and keep the airplane wings level. Battle damage assessment was nice, but it wasn't worth squat unless he landed the plane. The transit to Lima 36 gave him time to double-check his actions, and he found that the only thing he'd missed was the armament panel. By flipping the necessary toggle switches, the guns were in the safe position and the armament panel shut down. If nothing else, it meant there would be no juice to the wires in the wings, so if he crashed on landing it would be one fewer source of sparks to ignite the high-octane gas that filled the wings.

"Ramrod Three One, Lima 36 radar contact. Ambulance and fire trucks are standing by on the north end of the runway. Winds are calm, straight in approach approved. You are cleared to land. We show you about ten miles out at four thousand. No need to acknowledge."

Raul eased the throttle back on the left engine and trimmed the nose forward to descend. A gentle turn to the left got him aligned with the runway, a thin black line between brown areas of dirt and the green of the jungle.

He kept the A-26 at one hundred and fifty knots to stay above its minimum single engine maneuvering speed. Ramrod Three Eight's pilot communicated, recommending a wheels-up landing. He didn't think the right main mount would come down properly. That was O.K. It wouldn't be Raul's first time. He'd made a wheels-up landing during the Bay of Pigs invasion.

"Lima 36, be advised Ramrod Three One is going to land wheels up."

Raul kept the plane on his desired track by trimming nose down as he pushed the flap lever down to the full position. Once he heard the flaps start to go down, he eased off a bit more power. The airspeed indicator paused at one hundred and ten knots. As he got to a half mile, more power came off. By the time the A-26 crossed the runway threshold at fifty feet, the plane had slowed to just over ninety knots.

Raul had started to close the throttle with the A-26 in a slight nose up attitude when he heard a loud twang. The airplane rolled uncontrollably to the right; instinctively he tried to counter with the yoke. Everyone on the ground saw the left aileron come off the airplane, followed by a portion of the left flap.

The A-26 was in a twenty degrees right bank when Raul heard and felt the wingtip contact the runway. The screech of tearing aluminum hurt his ears. He thought he was about to die when the drag of the shredding right wing caused the nose to pitch down. He looked straight at the ground as the barrels of the eight fifty-caliber machine guns in the nose dug into the asphalt. His last thought before he blacked out was how rough the asphalt looked.

Excruciating pain in his left hip woke him up. His groggy brain registered the sound of dripping liquid and the smell of high-octane aviation gas.

The overhead hatches to the cockpit were flopping loosely, so Raul unstrapped and crawled out. As he did, the pain in his hip and back made his eyes water. He forced his brain to ignore the searing stabbing sensations as he crawled back to the cockpit and felt Renquist's neck. He was still alive, so he pulled the lever that released his co-pilot's seat belt and shoulder harness. Once he was free, Raul looped his arms under Renquist's armpits and heaved. He felt the dead weight move slightly, so he pulled again. He could hear the flames licking the left engine and knew he had seconds to get Renquist out of the plane. He tugged again, and a sudden end to the resistance caused both men to roll over. Raul screamed in agony. Two firefighters wearing silver reproof suits picked both men up and started running.

A bone-shuddering, teeth-jarring BOOM knocked all four men down. Raul watched the A-26 burn for a small eternity, then, he looked over at Renquist, who had come to.

"We made it. Good job." Then "The Swede's" eyes rolled back into his head.

Saturday, October 31, 1456 local time, North Vietnam

A grinding sound made by a failed downshift caused Randy to look toward the compound's opened gate. There was a bad upshift and the vehicle jerked forward; the crunching of gears caused Randy to wince. *How hard is it to let the engine come back down to idle before you pull it into the next gear? Didn't they teach you do double clutch? It's Shifting a Non-synchronized Manual Transmission 101.*

The truck stalled and lurched to a stop, and the driver made no attempt to restart the engine. Heckle and Jeckle ran to the back of the truck and opened the tailgate.

Company.

A shape in a familiar olive drab flight suit did what Randy thought of as "the manacle shuffle" to the edge of the bed and stopped. The hood ver his head was pulled off, revealing a pale, dirty face. The man's name tag had been ripped from his flight suit.

Once the American was on the ground, Heckle looped a rope around the man's neck and pulled the noose tight. Jeckle was standing off to one side twirling a section of pole, which he proceeded to jab into the newcomer's back. The man, whose hands were bound in front of him, turned and gave the North Vietnamese soldier a dirty look before he was herded toward the empty cage next to Randy's.

The new prisoner's survival vest, G-suit, helmet and boots were tossed out of the back of the truck. In response to Heckle's shouted instructions, two soldiers scooped up the flight gear and headed toward the interrogation building. The driver ground the starter and ground the gears, and the truck lurched in the direction of the barracks.

Randy shifted positions so that his back was close to the other cage. It would allow him to talk to the newcomer in a hushed tone. "Who are you?"

"Richard O'Reilly. You?"

"Randy Pulaski."

"When did you get shot down?"

"October 22nd. You?"

"This morning. I was hit along the trail on a road recce by what I think was a fifty-seven-millimeter round. The A-7 started coming apart, so I ejected."

"I got hit by a SAM. What squadron are you in?"

"None. I am, or was, the air operations officer for the CTF-77. I was flying one of VA-146's A-7s. You?"

"VA-153." *Shit, this guy's a commander. The air ops slot usually goes to a post CO tour commander.*

"Off the Toasted Oh?"

"Yeah."

"The gooks beat you up?"

"Once or twice a day. There's a colonel by the name of Duong who likes to use hoses."

"Shit."

Randy paused and remembered his training from SERE (Survival, Evastion, Resistance and Escape) school. Find an area of common knowledge and probe to make sure he is not a plant. "Yeah. Where are you from?"

"Chicago."

"Me too. I grew up in Beverly on the south side. Where'd you go to school?"

"The Academy. Class of 53. You?"

Randy sat up. "Purdue. Uh oh. Get ready for fun and games. Here they come."

Heckle and Jeckle took Randy first. As they tied him to a chair, they pulled his elbows so far back he thought his shoulders would pop out of their joints. O'Reilly was led past him to another room. Duong whacked Randy four times, then he left the room, smiling as if to say, "I'll play with you later."

Randy let his head hang and closed his eyes. Thinking about Janet helped him relax and relieved the strain on his shoulder muscles. He was drifting off to never-never land when he heard the familiar sound of a hose hitting flesh. and a drawn out "OWWWWWWW!" He moved his head slightly. Duong had left the door open.

Smack. "OWWWW!"

"What was your mission?"

"Go to hell."

Smack, whap.

"OWWWWWW!"

"What plane did you fly?"

28

Smack. "OWWWW!" Randy heard what almost sounded like a whimper. "My name is Richard Aloysius O'Reilly. Commander, United States Navy. Serial number 635406—"

Randy heard four sounds he recognized as a cotton hose that Duong used to hit faces. A few seconds of silence was followed by the sound of water splashing to the floor.

"What mission, what plane?" Duong's voice resumed, like a snake hissing. When he received no answer, there were two more loud smacks from the canvas hose.

O'Reilly screamed. Two more smacks were followed by silence, and again Randy heard water being poured.

"Tell me, or the beatings will continue."

"You promise not to hurt me?"

"It depends on what you tell me."

"I flew A-7s…. I was a test pilot for a new weapon called the AGM-78… Standard Anti-Radiation Missile. It is specifically designed to destroy surface-to-air missile sites."

"You already have one of those. I am told you call it the Shrike." Smack.

"OWWWWW! No! This is a new weapon… faster… longer range… bigger warhead. I was with an A-6 that used two of them to destroy radar vans… two different missile sites… then I was shot down. I was dropping bombs on the site when my plane was hit. You can check it out."

Randy could scarcely believe what he was hearing. *He lied to me. He said he was on a road recce.*

"I will get someone who knows about missiles to question you. If you have lied, I will beat you until you cannot move."

Randy feigned sleep as he heard Duong's boots get closer. The Vietnamese officer smacked him on the leg with the canvas hose.

"Tell me your mission."

Randy jerked his head up. "I am Randy Pulaski, Lieutenant, United States Navy, serial number 748203. That's all I am required to tell you."

"Stupid American." Whap. The hose raised another welt. "You

will be beaten until you tell me what I want to know." Smack.

"Fuck you…"

Randy awoke in his cage. He had been dumped in a heap with his head at an awkward angle. He groaned as his sore joints moved; the swollen welts stung from anything that touched him. In the cage next to him, O'Reilly was sipping a bowl of soup.

"I guess I missed dinner." Randy winced as he sat up.

"They'll be back. They have to feed us."

"Only if they follow the Geneva Convention." Randy tried to find a slightly less uncomfortable position. He wondered if O'Reilly had really coughed up the secret sauce on the new AGM-78. For the moment, he was going to give the commander a pass. Maybe the guy was feeding disinformation.

Wednesday, November 4, 1970, 0958 local time, North Vietnam

Duong left the two Americans alone for three days in a row, enough time or the swelling to start to go down. Randy's wounds turned a sickly pale yellow-brown, or black and blue. His hypothesis was that Duong was awaiting instructions from Hanoi.

A shout caught their attention. The gate opened and a small truck entered the compound and stopped in front of the office. Both Americans saw two officers, one wearing a Vietnamese uniform, the other Russian, dismount and enter Duong's headquarters. Randy pushed himself up against the bamboo poles that made up the walls of his cage.

"Something's about to happen. The Soviets are here."

The appearance of Heckle and Jeckle confirmed his suspicions. He grimaced. "Let the beatings begin. They'll continue until morale improves."

The two Americans were slammed down, bound, dragged tot he office, and secured to two chairs bolted to the floor. When the guards were satisfied with their rope work, Duong and the new arrivals appeared. The new Vietnamese officer stood to one side while the Russian studied the table where Duong's favorite hoses were displayed in a row. Then he addressed the two prisoners.

"I am Major Nikolai Gorov of Soviet Air Defense Forces. I am here as advisor to our Vietnamese comrades. I understand you Americans have new missile that defeats our radars. True?"

"True." O'Reilly spoke before Randy could say, "Don't tell them anything."

"Tell me about missile."

"It is called the AGM-78. It has a range of more than fifty nautical miles. Even if you turn off your radar, it will remember where the emitter was located. Unlike the Shrike which goes stupid if you turn a targeted radar off, the Standard ARM continues to the emitter."

"Don't tell the fuckers any more!" Randy's words got him several belts with a canvas hose. The pain was terrible, but what made him see red was the awful certainty that O'Reilly had given away two of the weapon's secrets.

"How do you know this?"

"I was the test pilot for the project."

"Interesting."

"Stop! Don't be a traitor!" Randy yelled.

Gorov turned to Duong. "Shut him up." After the fourth hit with the hose, Randy pretended to be unconscious.

O'Reilly volunteered, "I'll tell you more, if you don't torture me."

Gorov lit a cigarette and sat on the table. "Either you talk or we beat it out of you. No matter, we'll get it. If needed, we take you to Soviet Union."

"I'll talk."

Randy listened, making mental notes. O'Reilly explained how the A-6 crews flew SAM suppression missions. After the A-6s shut down the radars, the A-7s bombed the sites. And he knew how the missile worked.

A bucket of water was dumped on Randy, then both men were led back to their cages. Randy waited until their jailers were out of earshot, then he turned on O'Reilly. "You fucking traitor. You gave away the store on the ARM. They'll figure out a way to counter it, and more of our friends will die or be captured—"

O'Reilly cut him off. "Lieutenant! Watch your tongue, or I'll have you written up for insubordination."

"Fuck you!" Randy still couldn't believe that O'Reilly had recited information on the missile without including data that would mislead the North Vietnamese. "Have at it, Commander! I dare you to tell them *why* I am being insubordinate. I'm ashamed to be in the same compound with you. You didn't even try to resist. A couple of belts from a canvas hose and you're buddies with the commies."

"Lieutenant, there's more at stake than you realize—"

"Like what?"

O'Reilly didn't answer.

"That's what I thought, you don't have an answer. If I ever get out of this hellhole, I'll make sure the whole world knows that you rolled over and gave the Soviets everything they needed to know about the AGM-78. You disgust me."

Randy was about to continue when he saw Major Gorov and Duong headed their way, followed by Heckle and Jeckle. Manacles were placed around O'Reilly's ankles and his wrists were handcuffed. A chain connected both restraints.

"Commander O'Reilly, you come with me to Hanoi. There you will be treated well," Duong said, then looked at Randy. "Until you cooperate, your life will be hell. You understand hell?"

"Major, go fuck yourself and the horse you rode in on. O'Reilly, I hope you rot in hell, you fucking traitor."

Monday, November 16, 1970, 1510 local time, Las Vegas, NV

Having driven to Las Vegas from California, Janet methodically set about accomplishing her four-day plan. On day one, she drove around middle class neighborhoods and made a note of the location whenever she found a gap between two legitimate addresses with non-sequentially stepped numbers. Next, she rented a post office box for six months so she would have a mailing address.

In the evening, she filled out the papers needed to document that she was a citizen of the State of Nevada, using a number between those of real houses. Unless someone drove down the street or checked county records, the address would pass for real.

On day two, Janet stopped by the office of the Nevada Legal News and filled out the ad form, notifying residents of the State of Nevada that she was changing her name from Janet Williams Pulaski to Jamie Elizabeth Symonds. She checked the box that would give her a new birth certificate. She paid cash for the ad. It would run for three consecutive weeks, along with the affidavit that would be filed with the Clark County Court.

On day three, Janet picked up copies of her ad so it could be shown to the judge if he required a hearing. If not, the court order changing her name would be mailed to her post office box. Once that arrived, she'd come back to Las Vegas and pay for several certified copies of the court order approving the name change.

Tuesday, November 17, 1970, 1227 local time, North Vietnam

The large raindrops made a rattling sound as they hammered the cage's galvanized steel roof. To Randy, it looked it as if there was a half-inch of water covering the spongy ground. If this much rain fell in his native Chicago, the mud would be ankle deep and cars would be stuck in flooded streets. Here, no one seemed to be affected by the incessant rain.

Being shoeless didn't bother Randy. In fact, he liked the feel of the cool, silky mud between his toes. When they brought him back to the cage, he stuck his feet through the bamboo and enjoyed letting the rain rinse them off. Holding his wooden bowl out of the cage, he collected the fresh, sweet tasting rain.

He had lost track of the days. He kept his mind busy by making a mental map of the camp so someday he could pick it out from an aerial photo. Each day, he added a detail he hadn't memorized before.

Randy estimated Duong's compound was about one hundred

yards wide by two hundred yards long and surrounded by a ten-foot high stucco wall that ran between the buildings. By its architecture he was sure it was a French army base. The two-story building on one short side of the compound was a barracks. On the other end, Randy guessed one of the row's smaller structures was an armory. Opposite the gate was a series of sheds on either side of Duong's headquarters. He watched men in one shed repair vehicles. The others were empty.

Attached to the headquarters was the small building with which he was intimately familiar. Colonel Duong's interrogation room had no windows and no visible door. The only door was the one that opened from the colonel's office.

Randy wondered why the camp had not been bombed. From the air it should be obvious it was a military base. Every day, he expected to be blown to bits by exploding five-hundred-pound bombs, yet none came. Somehow, the compound never made anyone's target list.

He wanted to scratch out NM 307 in the dirt so that someone flying over the camp would notice. It was an impossible dream; Duong would not let him walk without being poled. His home was now a cage, just like an animal in a zoo.

He picked up the tin bowl that held his lunch and fished out a piece of meat from the rice. It tasted like pork. He knew he was losing weight, but not how much; but prolonged weight loss meant he would get physically weaker. When he'd punched out, Randy had been a healthy, fit, five-foot-eleven and a hundred and eighty pounds. He doubted he weighted over 165 now. But from reading Korean and World War II POW debriefs, he knew that staying mentally strong was the key to survival.

Every morning he inspected his body. Some welts had turned black and blue. Others were a sickly yellow. His joints ached from being tied up in odd positions for hours. His fingers were stiff and swollen from being smacked repeatedly by Duong's rubber hose. Still, the damage was superficial, and as long as he didn't get sick or suffer any internal injuries, he would survive. He'd never thought he would thank the Navy for giving him all those shots.

When he saw the two sergeants approaching with a pole, Randy quickly swallowed the rest of the stew. It was time for more fun and games with Colonel Duong.

Heckle and Jeckle tied his hands tightly behind his back. Satisfied that Randy was under their control, they lifted the three-inch diameter bamboo pole to bring upward pressure on his shoulder joints, then started toward the headquarters building. Randy grimaced at the pain, but by now he had been "stretched" enough to know that if he stayed on his toes it wouldn't hurt as much.

Inside the interrogation room, Heckle and Jeckle surprised him by untying his hands before they pulled the pole out. When a large wooden chair slammed down behind him, Randy took it as a cue to sit down. Heckle tied his hands behind him and to the armrests, while Jeckle secured his ankles to its legs.

Well, this is different. What is Fatman going to do now?

In SERE—survival, escape, resistance and evasion—school and JEST—jungle escape and survival training—he'd been taught how to win mental victories by making his captors look bad without their knowing it. It was a way to keep one's morale up. The example the instructors used was the photograph of the *U.S.S. Pueblo's* crew showing their middle fingers. It was time, Randy decided, to turn the tables. "Colonel Duong, where'd you learn English?"

"In your country. My father was the deputy ambassador and insisted I go to an American school. Ten years ago, my father was promoted and we came home."

"So you traded Washington DC for this place?"

"I am doing my duty as a soldier."

"Have you been to South Vietnam?" Duong's eyes flickered and confirmed Randy's suspicion that Duong had never seen combat. Now he was sure that Duong's father had used his influence to get his son this secure posting far from the killing fields in South Vietnam.

Duong's smile looked forced. "Did you have a good lunch?"

"You should fire your cook."

"Funny man." Duong took the pole that was leaning against the wall and slammed the end into Randy's stomach. Randy retched. After the second blow, he threw up what he had just eaten. With vomit dripping down his chin, he looked at Colonel Duong. "It didn't taste any better the second time."

Duong used his favorite hose to slap Randy's right inner thigh. The American closed his eyes, trying to let the flash of pain pass, then he felt it come down on his left thigh. Two more blows to each leg and tears were streaming down his face. Duong finished with a canvas hose slap that left Randy's left cheek stinging and the room spinning. "That will teach you to be a comedian. Now, tell me again, how do you avoid our surface to air missiles?"

"I didn't tell you. That's why I'm here." Randy needed time for his brain to will the pain away. Both legs burned and the back of his head hurt where the stitched hose had struck him.

"Your airplanes dodge them all the time. How?"

"Because the people who shoot at them are bad shots." He closed his eyes, knowing what was coming, but not where. The next blow struck his nose and right cheek. He tasted blood.

"You are going to be tried as a war criminal."

"So try me. Do I get a bath before I go before the judges? If I do, it will be worth it. They won't want to see me as I am now."

Wham, smack. Two more blows and more pain. Randy was just starting to reopen his eyes when he saw a blur to one side. He felt the impact on the side of his head, and then water was splashed all over him. The room spun and his stomach churned. Vertigo in a chair! What was left in his stomach started to make its way to the surface.

He didn't resist and directed the stream in Duong's direction. In college, Randy's friends had joked, often with pride, about who could throw up the farthest after drinking too much. He'd never participated, because getting that drunk would have put his Navy ROTC scholarship at risk. Now he wished he could aim the emesis at Duong's face.

"Tell me what I want to know!"

"I don't know anything."

Duong slapped a pad of paper and a pen down on the wooden top. "Confess to bombing our women and children and the beatings will stop."

"I can't confess to something I didn't do."

"You are Catholic, you confess your sins all the time. This is just one more. You sinned by bombing our hospitals. You bomb innocent people."

"The only thing I will do is confess to murdering you if I ever get the chance." *Likewise, I will confess to beating the shit out of that helo driver who abandoned me.*

Duong laughed. "You won't. Nobody knows or cares where you, not even my government. They have not given me orders on what to do with you. The helicopter sent to rescue you flew away without trying to pick you up. That tells me your own government doesn't care about you."

"My government knows. And they care. My government also knows that you are not treating me in accordance with the Geneva Convention."

"The Geneva Convention does not apply to war criminals. You proved that by hanging Nazis. You are no different. Like them, you kill women and children. You bomb our hospitals."

"You sound like Jane Fonda!"

"Who is she?"

"An American actress who opposes our involvement in this war."

Duong stood up and stepped back. "Ahhhh, smart woman."

"See, I told you something you didn't know."

Wham. Blackness.

Water again woke him up. Randy wasn't sure how long he had been out, but now he was on the floor. His elbows were pulled back and tied to his ankles. There was a rope around his neck; he could see the end of the pole in front of him.

Duong squatted down in front of him and pushed Randy's forehead back. "We will see how long you like this position. Every few minutes we will lift you up higher and higher. I assure you, the pain will be excruciating. If you struggle, the rope around your neck will tighten and choke you. You will slowly hang yourself. Or you can tell me what I want to know."

Duong stood up and signaled. His men slowly raised the pole. Randy could feel the tension from the ropes increase, and the pain started as his muscles strained. "Kill me and you get nothing."

"I get to watch you die in agony. That is my satisfaction."

Wednesday, November 18, 1970, 1026 local time, Hanford

Between katas, Janet wiped the sweat from her face. She'd been working out for nearly an hour. The back of her sweat-stained shirt had the big Peace sign that Randy had called "the footprint of the American chicken." On the front, it said, "Make love and peace, not war."

She heard the sound of a truck squeaking to a stop in front of the house. It occurred to her that there might be a Christmas present sent by Randy's parents.

The doorbell rang. Janet finished the kata with a muted shout and draped a towel around her neck before she headed to the door. A UPS driver was pulling a wooden box on a dolly up the steps.

"Hi, Mrs. Pulaski. I'm very sorry that I have to deliver to you." His name tag said he was Terry Jones.

"Do you know what's inside the box, Terry?"

"Yes, ma'am. I deliver one of these every few weeks. It contains your husband's personal effects. The Navy calls these things 'cruise boxes.' The keys to the locks are in the sealed envelope taped to the top. I am so sorry that this arrived just before the holidays."

"It's okay, Terry. My husband was shot down and taken prisoner. With any luck, he'll be released when the war is over."

"Mrs. Pulaski, that's a relief. I spent a year in-country as a Marine up in I Corps area as a truck mechanic before I got out, so

I know what it can be like over there." Terry Jones went back to his truck and returned with a clipboard. "Ma'am, I need you to sign these forms, then I'll put the cruise box anywhere in the house you want it."

Janet scribbled her name on the form. Her signature was, by design, illegible. "Please, take it into the third bedroom. There's space in the back of the closet."

"Yes, ma'am, you show the way."

Janet turned and smiled to herself, knowing that Terry Jones was going to get a good glimpse of her sweaty backside under her thin jogging shorts. Every job had its perks, she supposed. Once the box was nestled in the closet, Janet led the UPS man back to the front door. The keys went in her nightstand drawer.

Janet resumed her workout. Later, she would go through the box and have another good cry.

Sunday, November 22, 1970, 0923 local time, North Vietnam

As he did every morning, Randy took inventory of what he could see in the compound. The only new items were two small, mud-splattered trucks that looked as if they'd been designed in the forties by G.M. or Ford as pick-up trucks. Three letters—G A Z— were stamped on the tailgate. He filed the letters away in his memory banks to research when he got back to the U.S.

He was trying to figure out which American company would have given the basic truck design to the Russians when Heckle opened the cage door. This time he didn't have rope or a bamboo pole, only handcuffs. *That's interesting.*

Randy stepped out of the cage and watched Heckle close the steel loops around his wrists. A rope with a slipknot was put over his head and drawn tight. Heckle jerked the rope as the signal to follow.

Instead of heading to the interrogation room, Randy was led into the barracks. Inside, Heckle pushed him into a room and pointed to a typewritten note on top of a pile of clothes.

Lieutenant Pulaski,

Today we have a visitor. Please take a shower and shave. Leave your clothes in the shower room. My soldiers will wash them and return them to you later today. A towel, a razor and shaving cream have been provided.

Enjoy the shower.

Colonel Duong

Why is the Fatman being nice? What am I missing? What the hell, I'll enjoy the shower! First one since I was captured.

Randy stood under the water, not caring whether it was hot or cold. He luxuriated in the feel as he soaped and rinsed three times, knowing he was going to be clean.

On a small shelf above the sink, a Gillette razor with a single double-edged blade and a can of shaving cream waited. He preferred an electric razor, but with a month's growth on his face Randy wasn't going to turn up his nose. The razor bumped, pulled and scraped as it cut through the whiskers; thankfully, he managed not to cut himself. On board ship or at home, showering and shaving took ten minutes. Today, he made it last the better part of half an hour. *Duong didn't give me a time limit.*

Before Randy got dressed, he used the mirror to examine the bruises on his back and sides. Most of them had faded.

With the towel wrapped around his waist, Randy held up the coarse black clothes. They looked more like loose, one-size-fits-all pajamas than pants and shirt. The underwear was only slightly softer than the outer garments.. *Maybe they'll give me is a straw hat and send me to work in a rice paddy. Then I'll look like a member of the Viet Cong!*

He'd just finished dressing when Heckle entered and pointed to the floor under the sink. Randy slid his feet into a pair of black rubber sandals lying there.

For the first time since he'd climbed into the A-7 on the *Oriskany,* Randy felt clean. He wondered if they were trying to soften him up. Heckle handcuffed him and put the same dirty rope they been using since he arrived around his neck.

Inside the interrogation room, there was the usual table with Colonel Duong's favorite hoses in a neat row, and a heavy wooden chair. His G-suit, torso harness, and survival vest were hanging on the wall. Underneath were his boots with the socks neatly draped over their tops. It looked as though they'd been cleaned.

Randy was directed to sit down. Jeckle unlocked the cuffs, pulled his arms around back and tied them together. Another rope went around his chest, binding him to the chair. Two more hemp ropes secured his legs to the chair legs. When they were finished, Heckle and Jeckle took up their position in the corners behind Duong's desk.

Randy tried to relax his body and prepare his mind for the ordeal to come. The door swung open and two men entered the room—Colonel Duong and, by his uniform, a Soviet Army officer. Randy estimated that the dark-haired, blue-eyed Russian was in his thirties, five-ten, and a muscular hundred-and-eighty pounds.

He walked around Randy as if he were inspecting a prize pig. Then he put his fists on his hips and, arms akimbo, bent forward so that his face was only a foot from Randy's.

"I am Major Pavel Uglov of GRU. You know GRU?" Uglov emphasized the three letters of the Soviet Military Intelligence Agency.

"Hi, I'm Lieutenant Randall Pulaski of the United States Navy. My friends call me Randy."

The Soviet officer stared at him. Randy stared back, trying not to reveal his fear. Pilots who flew this area were warned that, if captured, they might be tortured by Soviet officers. Intelligence officers on the *Oriskany* had never confirmed that captured U.S. pilots and back-seaters of electronic warfare aircraft were ever sent to the Soviet Union for interrogation; they simply said they didn't have enough information to have an "official" opinion.

Was this the first step on his way to the Soviet Union and disappearing into a gulag? Or would they simply kill him after they got everything out of his brain by means of drugs and torture? Having the GRU involved in his interrogation added a whole new dimension. *Maybe I should have told Duong more.*

"You Polack?"

"No. I am an American. My father came from Poland."

Uglov slapped Randy across the face. "Polish army full of cowards."

"That's your opinion."

"I say they cowards. You coward, too?"

"You can believe what you want."

Smack! A backhanded blow followed that left both cheeks burning.

"Colonel Duong says you think you are funny man."

"No, I am not a comedian."

"What is comedian?"

"A man who makes you laugh. I don't think there is anything funny about having the shit beat out of me on daily basis in clear violation of the Geneva Convention."

"Geneva Convention is for cowards. Like Poles."

Randy didn't answer.

"When did your father go to America?"

"After World War II."

"Was he in army?"

"Yes." When Poland had been about to fall in 1939, his father had been ordered by the government to go into neutral Romania. From there, Tomasz Pulaski and the eighty members of his platoon had made their way to Greece and then Egypt, where they fought in North Africa and Italy as members of the Polish 3rd Carpathian Rifle Division. When Germans invaded Poland, Tomasz had been a platoon leader; by 1945, he was a battalion commander. When the division was disbanded in 1947 he emigrated to the United States rather than return to Communist Poland. In 1948, after settling in Chicago, he became a U.S.

citizen.

"Where he fight?"

"North Africa and Italy."

"In Free Polish Army?"

"Yes."

"He deserted his homeland. He coward."

"No, he didn't. He preferred democracy to living under Stalin."

"So you not like Russians?"

Randy was never sure whether his father hated the Germans more than the Russians or vice versa. Many of his father's friends had been among the 21,857 soldiers massacred by the Soviet Secret Police (in those days known as the NKVD) and buried in mass graves in the Katyn Forest. The Germans killed more of his father's friends during their brutal occupation. While Randy was growing up, his father and other members of the Free Polish Army living outside Poland had done what they could to force the Communist government to tell its people the truth about the Katyn massacre.

A well-documented report, released after a Congressional investigation led by Representative Ray Madden of Indiana, concluded that Stalin had personally ordered the executions. Still, the Soviets refused to admit to the mass killing.

"Don't know. Never met one." *My dad wouldn't let one in his house.* After he'd joined the Navy, his father had told him about some of the barbaric things the Soviets had done to his family in Lodz, Poland, after the war. He was inclined not to like Russians.

"Why you not tell Colonel Duong what he wants to know? Your war over."

"I can't tell him what I don't know."

"You lie. You lie like coward Poles."

Randy just stared at Uglov and saw he was making the Russian uncomfortable.

Uglov leaned forward so that his face was inches from Randy's. "I make you talk. North Vietnamese government says I should not torture you. My government has no such policy. We beat prisoners until they tell us what we want to know. You like beating?"

Again, Randy said nothing. He was trying to force his mind not to imagine what the GRU officer was going to do to him.

Uglov wrinkled his nose and pulled back. "I could smell you when I came. You stank. You needed bath."

"We agree on that. I just had a shower." Randy sniffed loudly and wrinkled his nose. "You could use one."

The GRU major whirled around and drove his fist into Randy's chest. "Do not make fun of me, Polish scum."

Randy forced himself to breathe, hoping the shock to his solar plexus wouldn't stop his heart. *Uglov is dumber than dirt if he thinks he can get me angry by insulting my Polish ancestry.* Two words, "mental victory," made him smile.

"What so funny?"

"You."

"You will not be laughing. I have ways to make you talk."

"Like what?"

"I cause you pain."

"Colonel Duong does that every day."

Uglov held up a black leather case the size of a large book. "I use drugs."

"That will be a change."

Uglov held his balled fist in front of Randy's face. "Or I beat you. Or pull out fingernails. Cause you much pain."

"Go ahead. If you kill me, then what? I can promise you two things. One, my government will hunt you down and treat you like the war criminal you are. And, two, one day the Poles will kick you Russians out. And when they do, the land and air of a free Poland will be a lot cleaner."

Uglov's eyes went wide. "You fucking Polack. I make you squeal like cowardly Polish pig you are."

The GRU officer apparently didn't like hoses. He preferred the palm of his hand and his fists. Twenty minutes later, an unconscious Lieutenant Pulaski was dragged to his cage.

Wednesday, December 2, 1970, 1228 local time, Lemoore, CA

The monthly POW/MIA wives' luncheon was held at the Lemoore Officer's Club for two reasons. One, it was central for the wives who lived in the towns surrounding the base. Two, given the growing anti-war sentiment, it was easier to protect the wives from heckling protestors.

This was the first meeting Janet attended. After pinning on her name tag she looked around, feeling lost, uncomfortable, and very alone. She recognized no one, and her initial reaction was probably the opposite of what the association intended.

She was about to leave when she realized, in a flash, how many women here had their lives in limbo. Most were her age, with a sprinkling of those in their thirties and forties. It dawned on her that Lemoore-based squadrons had been flying combat missions since the mid-1960s.

"Hello, Janet, I'm Helen Starkey. Welcome to the POW/MIA luncheon." A good-looking brunette with a soft, southern drawl held out a gloved hand.

"Hi, I'm Janet Pulaski."

"Well, I'm glad you came. I'm here to welcome you, introduce you to the others, and answer questions. Hopefully, you'll join us. We do two important things. We support each other so we don't lose our minds while our husbands are in captivity, and we lobby the government to keep the fate of our men in the forefront of the minds of our political leaders. Quite frankly, the media doesn't find the POW issue compelling, and neither do most politicians. Funny, isn't it, how none of their sons ever go missing in action—or even assigned over there."

"So I hear." Janet wasn't sure she wanted to let the mental wall she'd built come down.

"We're all in the same never-never land boat. My husband was shot down over North Vietnam in March of this year. His squadron mates saw him be taken prisoner. We wives have to talk about what we're going through, because bottling it up inside lights an emotional time bomb of unknown power and duration. In short, we'd go nuts!"

"I'm sorry for your loss." Janet held her breath, then the words just started coming out. "Randy was shot down. I was told he was captured, and that's about it. It's been a rough few weeks."

"Honey, I know what you're going through. Every day, we have to deal with the hash of anger, depression, loss, and confusion."

"Amen to that."

"Do you have kids? The profile we were given by Wendy Hancock didn't mention any."

"No, no kids. We've been married less than a year and decided we'd wait awhile before we started a family."

"Sounds like us." Helen put her hand on Janet's arm. "Let's go sit down close to the front. The acoustics in this place are terrible, and today we have a packed house. Each month someone from the Navy or the Pentagon comes to talk to us. This week it's Captain Charbonneau. He tells us more than he is supposed to, I think. Truth isn't always easy to hear, but I prefer facts to being given the runaround. The last guy from the Pentagon was a civilian from the POW/MIA office, and he was so vague he pissed us all off. We all signed a letter that went to CNO telling him never to send him back. CNO called our chapter president to apologize."

Janet followed Helen to a round table for six that quickly filled. Besides Helen, Janet learned that she was sitting with the wives of two lieutenant commanders, a squadron executive officer, and a lieutenant. It was understood that wives of squadron COs and XOs were expected to set an example and lead.

Interestingly enough, squadron affiliation seemed to matter more than rank. Helen mentioned that her husband's squadron, VA-163, were known as the Saints.

Salads were already on the table. The main course was a choice of chicken, salmon, or filet mignon. While the food was not five-star, Janet's choice of grilled salmon was well seasoned and delicious. And, she reflected, she wouldn't have to wash the dishes afterwards.

The welcome from the other four women was genuine. None of them had known each other until they were forced to share the common bond of having a husband who was either rotting in a North Vietnamese, Laotian, or Cambodian POW camp, or was MIA. Unless their names were on Hegdahl's list, the status of most men was unknown.

The room became very quiet as Captain Charbonneau walked to the podium. Janet looked around and saw two officers in dress blues standing close to the door of the dining room. Another officer, whose rows of medals showed that he had flown combat missions in Vietnam, began setting up a slide projector.

"Good afternoon. For those whom I have not met, I am Captain Charbonneau from the AIRPAC staff, and I am responsible for analyzing the intelligence we get on prisoners being held by our enemies in Southeast Asia. Today, I am going to talk about the raid on the Son Tay POW camp. As you may know, the so-called arms experts called it a total failure. I will tell you as much as I can about what happened, as well as the positive effect on the POWs that we have *already seen.*"

He paused to let his last words sink in. "What I am going to share with you today has not been released to the media. If this briefing were being given to your husbands, it would be classified Top Secret. So please, do not discuss what I say in public. However, the Chief of Naval Operations has personally directed me to communicate what I can without compromising our most sensitive sources of information.

"If you are asked if you were briefed on the Son Tay raid, your response should be that all you know is what you have read or seen in the press. The Navy, if asked, will say that while I was here I talked about the raid in the most general terms. So, if any of you cannot or are not willing to keep what you are about to see and hear secret, please leave. I hope we do not have any leaks, because if we do, the Navy will clam up, which no one in this room wants to happen."

His last comment was greeted by nervous laughs all around the room. No one stood up to leave. Charbonneau nodded to the lieutenant commander, who put the first slide in the projector. It was titled "Operation Ivory Coast—the Raid on Son Tay, November 20—21 1970." Across the bottom of the slide, the words "Top Secret, Specially Compartmented Information" were printed in red.

The next slide showed a map of North Vietnam with dots, names, and arrows. Some pointed to Son Tay, and others to Hanoi.

"For some time, we have been watching the North Vietnamese move our POWs. They taken small groups of two to six to larger camps. One was Son Tay, located about thirty miles west of Hanoi. We've known about Son Tay since 1968. The official estimate of the number of POWs held there was fifty-five."

Another slide was put up on the screen. It showed the arrows from Yankee Station in the Gulf of Tonkin, as well as ones from several bases in Thailand. "Navy aircraft from the *Ranger* and the *Oriskany* flew strikes, as well as a simulated mining mission into Haiphong Harbor. We know from the reaction of the North Vietnamese that the diversionary tactics overwhelmed their air defense system. This enabled the raiders to fly undetected from Thailand to Son Tay."

A photo appeared on the screen. It showed an HH-3E that had crash-landed in the middle of the compound. "This is Son Tay the day after the raid. So... what happened?"

The captain looked grim. He'd flown A-4s in Vietnam, first as a squadron commander on board the *U.S.S. Constellation,* then as a wing commander deployed on the *U.S.S. Kitty Hawk.* But for the grace of God, he might have been a prisoner in that godforsaken place.

"Because of the difficulty of getting real-time intelligence out of North Vietnam, the President knew there was a chance there were no POWs at Son Tay, or, worse, that we would kill some in a firefight. Those risks were accepted as a price of the mission. The

President and everyone involved wanted to send a strong message to the North Vietnamese that there is no safe place in Vietnam, that we can and will fly, and land, anywhere in their country *at will.*"

Charbonneau took a drink of water from the glass next to the projector. "When our men arrived, there were no POWs. We estimate that we were a month too late. Based on intelligence we gathered at the camp, the POWs had been moved to what we know—thanks to Seaman Hegdahl, Lieutenant Frishman, and Air Force Captain Rumble—as "the Plantation.""

The next slide showed a large, squat, ugly building. Charbonneau stepped off to the side. "If you think the Ho Loa complex looks like a prison built in the late 1800s, that's because it was. The French started building the Maison Centrale in 1886. This is where we think eighty percent of the Americans are now being held."

Charbonneau nodded his head, and two more pictures of Ha Loa popped up side by side. "We call it the Hanoi Hilton. These photos were taken by RA-5s off the carriers, drones as well as RF-8s. The ones that follow have never been seen in public." The lieutenant commander put a grainy photo on the screen.

"The officer in this photo is Lieutenant Colonel Robert Risner of the U.S. Air Force." You could hear the collective intake of breath. A man wearing gray-and-black-striped pajamas and sandals gazed up at the airplane, clearly wanting his gaunt face to be photographed. Another photo appeared, taken from another angle on another day. "This is Commander Bill Lawrence. Both men knew they would be severely beaten for looking up at a reconnaissance plane."

Charbonneau let the audience examine the picture. "So, ladies, despite the media's claims that we don't have adequate intelligence, this is proof that we do. What we don't have is enough. When we get photographs of the men in the camps, we do our best to identify them. This is one of the ways we build our list of POWs. We had similar pictures of our men at Son Tay and decided to stop photographing the prison because we didn't want to give the North Vietnamese hints that we were planning a raid."

The captain waved his hand and a new image appeared. "This is from the last photo mission of Son Tay, taken thirty-one days before the raid. In it you can see Americans in the compound." At a signal, the lieutenant commander turned off the projector.

"I want to close by telling you what has happened in the ten days since the raid. One, we have gotten more inquiries from the Red Cross for mail. Two, our sources tell us that more POWs have been moved to Ho Loa. Three, we know that the treatment of the POWs has improved markedly. In addition, despite the North Vietnamese's efforts to hide news of the raid, we have reliable intelligence that the POWs know about it, and this has improved their morale. That, ladies, concludes my brief. I'll be happy to take questions, but be warned, I can't say much more."

What Charbonneau did not know was a closely guarded, well above Top Secret operation led by the CIA that communicated with prisoners. With the help of Sybil Stockdale, the wife of the most senior POW, James Stockdale, and co-founder of the National League of Families of American Prisoners Missing in Southeast Asia, POWs were regularly sending sensitive information about their condition in letters with secret writing and code words.

After a spate of questions, Charbonneau politely ended the Q&A. He received a standing ovation, and the room exploded in conversations. Janet wondered if Randy had been at Son Tay, and if his squadron mates had known they were part of a raid that might have freed him.

Helen waited until people started leaving, then slid a business card with the logo of the Hanford School District across the table. After her name were the letters RN. "How about we have lunch one day next week? My home number is on the back."

Janet was finding to hard to think, let alone speak.

"Okay," she managed.

Chapter 2
MYSTERIOUS VISITORS

Thursday, December 3, 1970, 1036 local time, Honolulu

The bones in Raul's hip and left leg had healed enough for the cast that went from his waist down to his foot to be removed. He watched intently as the technician prepared a small circular saw with a blade about the size of a fifty-cent piece. The motor looked like the clipper a barber uses, but each time the technician triggered the saw, it made a high-pitched wail. The technician assured Raul that he had never cut a patient, despite its scary appearance.

Well, there is always a first time!

Raul tried not to flinch when he saw the spinning blade start about two inches from the top of his inner thigh. One slip and he'd lose a good chunk of his private parts. With no guide other than the heel of his hand, the technician went down the inside of Raul's leg before he cut the outside. Bits of plaster flew everywhere. The top half of the heavy cast came off with an audible pop.

The technician held up the cast. "Do you want to keep this as a souvenir?"

Raul eyed the curve of angled plaster. "No. Should I?"

"Some people like to keep them. Thought I'd ask. If you don't want it, it gets burned."

Raul stared at the livid scars and stitch marks on his calf and thigh, where the doctors had screwed stainless steel plates to hold his bones together. Before the surgery, they had explained what they were going to do. "No, dump it. I've got all the reminders of the crash I need."

When he was wheeled into his first physical therapy session, Raul thought he knew what pain was. That was before he met the sadist masquerading as his therapist!

Flexing his foot and trying to bend his knee brought eye-watering pain. The therapist said this was just getting the nerves to function and reminded him that pain was normal. Eventually, the ever-cheerful man said, the pain would go away. After each session during the first week, Raul was so exhausted that the aide who wheeled him to his room had to help him into bed. Again, he was told this was normal.

Four weeks into therapy, Raul could tell he was making progress. He didn't need a nap after each therapy session and, except for the scars, the color of his skin was back to normal. He'd begun using crutches, walking for the first time since the crash. This morning, after going back and forth between the parallel bars for thirty minutes, Raul was sure that soon he would not need them.

Despite the progress, he knew he would walk with a limp for the rest of his life. The doctors had said he might need to wear a steel brace and use a cane.

So, yes, he was making progress on the health front. But what was he going to do for the rest of his life? Raul knew he'd flown his last flight as a pilot.

He would continue to receive medical care at the Naval Hospital in Pearl Harbor until he was well enough to go back to the U.S. mainland. His salary and other bonus money from flying for Air America would continue to be paid until the end of the month he left the hospital. The agency would pay for his ticket home, but once he walked off the airplane he would be "retired" and receive a disability pension that was fifty percent of his salary. Between what he had in investments and the pension, he had enough to live modestly, but not enough to live well.

Raul had no idea what he would do.

Friday, December 4, 1970, 0843 local time, North Vietnam

Randy was almost finished with his morning inventory of Camp Insanity when the compound's doors opened. He saw Heckle and Jeckle waiting in the center of the compound. A large truck with no canvas top stopped in front of the barracks and soldiers jumped off. A second vehicle, its canvas top on, stopped in front of his cage.

Maybe another unfortunate bastard got shot down and is going to be my cage mate.

Heckle and Jeckle dropped the tailgate. Colonel Duong peered inside, then stepped back. Heckle and Jeckle reached in and dragged forth an American wearing an olive drab Nomex flight suit. He was handcuffed, and a chain connected his hands to the shackles around his bare ankles. The man had close-cropped blond hair, his face was dirty, and his flight suit was torn.

A soldier in the back of the truck tossed down two bags that Duong unzipped. He said something in rapid-fire Vietnamese to Jeckle, who nodded and took the bags to the interrogation building.

Duong came over to Randy's cage. "I have good news for you. You will have a comrade to keep you company, and in a few days, both of you will be transferred to the Ho Loa prison near our glorious capital of Hanoi. I have been directed to allow you to shower every other day and to provide you with two sets of clothes. You will be fed exactly what our soldiers eat, so I hope you like Vietnamese food. It can be a little spicy for American tastes. This is good news, no?"

"I'll be happy to share my thoughts in the next issue of *The Washington Post*."

"Always the funny man." Duong turned and motioned to

Heckle, who gave the man in shackles a shove forward. "Lieutenant Pulaski, it gives me great pleasure to introduce you to Lieutenant Jeffrey Anderson, also of your Navy. Showers will be in thirty minutes, then Lieutenant Anderson and I will have a little chat."

Anderson's flight suit hung on him as if it were several sizes too large. Randy wondered if this was because he'd lost weight from being in captivity, or if he liked them big.

He waited until Anderson was locked in the other cage and Heckle and Jeckle were out of sight to introduce himself.

"Randy Pulaski, Blue Tail Sluff driver from the Toasted O." Translation: "Blue Tail" was a shortened version of the official squadron name for VA-153, and Sluff stood for "short little ugly fat fucker," the slang name given to the A-7 Corsair. It was short and stubby compared to the long and lean F-8 Crusader. "Toasted O" was the *U.S.S. Oriskany.*

The newcomer took Randy's extended hand.

"Jeffrey Anderson. I'm a Redcock who flew Scooters off the Bonnie Dick." Redcock meant he was from VA-22 that used the call sign Beefeater. A Scooter was an A-4 Skyhawk, and Bonnie Dick was slang for the *U.S.S. Bonne Homme Richard.* "So, Randy, when did you get bagged?"

"October 22. You?"

"A week ago. November 27, the day after Thanksgiving. What got you?" Anderson asked.

"A SAM. Couldn't make it out over the water. You?"

"Triple A. I got hit by either a 37mm or 57mm round just aft of the cockpit, right after I dropped a load on a bunch of trucks south of Mu Gia Pass. It started a fire and the engine quit." Anderson looked around. "You hear about Son Tay?"

"No, what's that?"

"On November 20, the Air Force landed a team of Green Berets at a POW camp about thirty miles west of Hanoi. We thought it held fifty-five of our guys, but it was empty. That night, we flew alpha strikes and Iron Hand missions against targets around Hanoi and Haiphong to distract the North Vietnamese. Nobody knew about the rescue attempt until the next day." Alfa strikes in Naval Aviator speak was a launch of about half the planes on the carrier deck. Iron Hand was the Air Force and Navy's name for surface-to-air missile suppression missions.

"That's encouraging. Maybe they'll do it again."

"One can hope."

"So do you go by Jeff or Jeffrey?"

"Jeff."

"Jeff, be aware of Duong. He likes rubber and canvas hoses, to say nothing of ropes and bamboo poles. Duong has a Russian friend who likes to use his fists."

"You mean like what they did to us in SERE school?"

"Yeah. Did they beat you up when you got caught?"

"Yeah, Mostly with rifle butts. I came down in some small trees and evaded for about four hours before some North Vietnamese soldiers and I stumbled on each other. I had no choice but to surrender."

Neither man spoke for a few minutes, then Randy said, "Duong said we're to get a shower every other day from now on and eat what is served to his soldiers, whatever that is. He also said we're to be transferred to another prison."

"Do you speak Vietnamese?"

"No. Colonel Duong speaks excellent English. Claims he grew up in DC and implies his father is a high mucky muck in their foreign ministry."

"That's interesting. What's he doing in this shit hole?"

"Great question. I don't suggest you ask him."

Saturday, December 5, 1970, 1224 local time, Hanford

Janet and Helen had taken to meeting for long, leisurely meals on Saturdays, when and where they could spend as much time together as they wanted. One of their favorite outings was to drive to Sequoia National Park and hike along one of the trails. Today was a beautiful day for a road trip, and Janet was enjoying the drive, even as she looked forward to lunch with Helen.

Janet drove Randy's 1966 GT350 instead of her Volvo. Each time she'd called it a Mustang, Randy had politely pointed out that it was a Shelby GT350, not a Ford Mustang. The car had started out as a K-Code Mustang, but when it left the Shelby factory it had been substantially modified. Randy's car, one of 1,373 Shelby GT 350s built in 1966, was Wimbledon White with twin Guardsman Blue stripes.

Randy had bought it right after he got his wings. The prior owner had liked to rev the engine, pop the clutch, and disappear down the road in a cloud of tire smoke. Despite this abuse, the engine was still healthy, and the car had never been wrecked.

When Janet had ridden in the Shelby for the first time, she'd thought it was a noisy beast of a car. The third time she complained, Randy pulled into a gas station. She thought he was going to toss her out, but instead he said, "You say you can drive a manual transmission. Show me."

Once she was buckled in, Randy explained that the clutch was heavy and it helped to pause a half second in neutral as you went between the gears. A twist of the key and the 289-cubic-inch, 306-horsepower Ford small block engine rumbled to life, sucking air through the four-barrel Holley carburetor.

Janet grinned at Randy, then almost stalled it as they pulled out of the gas station. Her second shift was smoother, then she accelerated and eased it into third gear. Randy was surprised when Janet double-clutched a downshift into second, entering the ramp of I 5 just outside Fresno. As the turn opened up, Janet mashed the accelerator and the rear end of the GT350 started to swing out. She eased in a correction and kept her foot down on the pedal. As the speedometer passed the ninety mph line, she lifted her foot off the throttle and mouthed the word "WOW!"

She was sure that was when Randy had known he'd found his woman.

"How did you learn to drive like that?" He'd demanded, yelling over the wind of their speed.

"My father. He used to take me to a shopping center parking lot on snowy mornings. He taught me how to put a car into a skid and then control it. Twenty miles an hour, nothing to hit for hundreds of yards; it was a benign environment. At first I was terrified of losing control. Gradually, I learned how to induce and control a skid, or spin the car 180 degrees and keep it on the road."

The Shelby was Randy's prize possession. He'd told Janet to drive it while he was deployed. So every week Janet headed to the windy-twisty roads of the Sierra Nevada Mountains east of Lemoore and drove as fast as she dared. Refreshed, she enjoyed the exhaust rumble as she looked for a spot in the parking lot.

Inside the Imperial Dynasty, a restaurant that had opened in 1883 to serve Hanford's tiny Chinese community, Helen waved from a table in the back. She already had a glass of soda sitting in front of her.

Most of the lunch was spent filling in the blanks that hadn't been covered in their prior conversations. Janet was curious about Helen's life before she'd become a "war widow".

She'd had grown up in Mobile, Alabama where for generations, members of her family had attended Auburn University. Going to the University of Alabama put one at risk of being disowned. In keeping with family tradition, Janet had gone to Auburn—where she'd met Bob Starkey. They started dating during their junior year. She followed him from primary flight training in Pensacola to basic jet at the Naval Air Station in Meridian, Mississippi, and on to Kingsville, Texas, for advanced. After he got his wings, they went home to Mobile to get married before driving cross-country so Bob could report to the A-4 replacement training squadron, VA-125 at Lemoore.

Their honeymoon was spent in a series of motels between Mobile and Lemoore, interrupted by three days in Santa Fe, New Mexico. That, Helen explained, was the "official" honeymoon. Janet laughed when Helen described their hike up Sandia Peak. They found a private grassy area where they spread a blanket, only to have their lovemaking interrupted by a family of hikers.

Janet was guarded about her past. When she hesitated, Helen changed the subject. "So tell me, what do you do about sex? Are you as horny as I am?"

Janet started laughing. "That's a great question, but this is not the place to have that discussion."

"How about some ice cream? There's a place called Superior Dairy that makes fresh ice cream daily. It's by a park that has some tables that are much more private. We can take my car."

After they paid the bill, Helen lead the way to a metallic blue Pontiac GTO convertible. Janet smiled. Naval aviators were notorious for having fast cars. Randy referred to Corvettes as the preferred "ensign mobile" and derided them as "plastic pigs."

It was almost two, and the after-lunch ice cream crowd had thinned out. Helen ordered raspberry, and Janet chose vanilla. After commenting on the delicious creaminess of the ice cream, Janet made a show of using her tongue to take a long lick. "So, where were we?"

Helen giggled. "We were talking about how horny we were. You didn't answer my question."

"Oh God, I'm so horny I can't stand it." Janet wasn't ready to tell Helen was that Randy had been the first man who could satisfy her.

"So what are you doing about it?"

Janet held up her index finger as she slurped more ice cream. "It isn't the real deal, but I don't want to get involved with another man. Too many risks."

"Agreed. As POW's wives, we are supposed to be paragons of virtue. Most of the leaders of the POW/MIA organizations take a dim view of infidelity. They won't say anything, but if you're caught having an affair you are ostracized. Some wives have been without husbands since 1965. That's five years."

"That's a long time without sex. Of course, I doubt it's any easier for the men." Janet's put her lips around the diminishing ball and gently sucked. "So what do you do about it?"

Fascinated, Helen watched Janet turn licking ice cream into a sexual act. It had never occurred to Helen to relate eating ice cream with sex.

The Southern belle's eyes lit up. "About two weeks before Bob left, he hands me this gift wrapped box. He said my mission was to learn how to use them while he was gone. 'When I get back,' he said, 'you can show me how they work.'"

Janet grinned. "What was in the box?"

Helen took a big bite out of her cone, then sucked down the last of the raspberry ice cream. Ever the lady, she used the napkin to pat her lips. "Inside was a collection of different sized dildos, butt plugs, and vibrators!"

"You're kidding me!"

"No, I'm not. Then he kissed me and said, 'These are not a replacement for my dick, merely stand-ins.'"

Janet broke out laughing again. "That's so cool!"

"Want to see them?"

"I do. More than that, I want to try them out!"

Helen stood up. "Then let's go. But I must warn you about Southern women."

"What do you mean?"

"We're brought up to be to be chefs in the kitchen, ladies in the living room—and harlots in the bedroom!"

Sunday, December 6, 1970, 1800 local time, North Vietnam
Randy rapped on the bamboo of Jeff's cage.

"Something's up. Two trucks arrived last night. They looked like leftovers from World War II. My guess is they're getting ready to move us, and we'll be loaded up just after dark."

"Damn, that means I'll miss my evening beating."

"Count your blessings. So far, we've haven't had our hands or legs bound so tight that we'd lose circulation. Or been hung up by piano wire. Or had our fingernails pulled out. Duong doesn't want to hurt us so badly that we're injured. He may be afraid of losing face if he delivers damaged goods."

"I hope you're right. What scares the shit out of me is that on the road we become the target of an AC-130 gunship, or our squadron mates."

"Jeff, look."

Jeff turned around and watched two more trucks enter. One with its canvas top installed stopped in front of their cages. The other stopped a few feet away. Vietnamese soldiers jumped out and formed a circle around the caged Americans.

Randy and Jeff were handcuffed, shackled, and locked to a chain wrapped around their waists. Colonel Duong inspected their restraints, then pointed to the covered truck. Heckle pulled down a small set of steps that let them get into the darkened interior. A soldier used his AK-47 to point to a bench. As soon as Randy and Jeff sat down, another soldier used a bicycle lock to connect their shackles to a tie-down ring on the floor.

Randy's eyes slowly adjusted to the darkness. Opposite him were four grim-faced prisoners.

Once they got going, it was noisy from the exhaust stack that rose up just behind the truck's cab, yet except for the occasional pothole, the ride was surprisingly smooth on what Randy guessed was the Ho Chi Minh Trail. The two Vietnamese soldiers at the back end of the truck kept their AK-47s between their knees and looked bored. Occasionally, one would lift the flap and Randy could see another truck behind them. The convoy ground slowly along at fifteen to twenty miles an hour.

At the first stop, Colonel Duong appeared at the back of the truck. "Everybody out. Dinner. No talking."

The six American prisoners were led to a cleared area where Heckle motioned them to sit down, surrounded by a dozen guards. Randy looked up, hoping to see stars, but they were under camouflage netting. The smell of strange spices and cooking fires whetted his appetite, even though he suspected all they would get was a bowl of rice or some watery soup.

The man sitting next to him looked down and whispered. "I'm Ashley Smith, Captain, U.S. Army, 5th Special Forces Group and the senior guy in the truck. Next to me is Air Force Captain Greg Christiansen, call sign Misty Zero Four. Next is First Lieutenant Henry Cho, also from the 5th Special Forces Group, and at the end is Air Force First Lieutenant Karl Kramer, call sign Nail 515. Cho is injured."

Randy acted as if he was stretching his neck to tilt his head toward Captain Smith so he could whisper, "Navy Lieutenant Randy Pulaski, call sign Power House 310, and Jeff Anderson, call sign Beefeater 307." Slowly he scratched his head and rubbed his face, covering his mouth as he continued. "I was bagged about forty-five days ago; Jeff was shot down last week. You know about Son Tay?"

Ashley looked at him quizzically. "No."

"The Air Force flew in Army Green Berets who raided the Son Tay POW camp just west of Hanoi. We didn't get any of our guys back, but it made an impression. Jeff can tell you more."

"Good shit!" Ashley stopped talking as Heckle and Jeckle approached and handed a bowl of noodle soup to each prisoner. Randy used his fingers to scoop out some noodles and sucked them down.

With Heckle and Jeckle gone and their guards concentrating on their own more substantial meals, Randy asked softly, "How long have you been POWs?"

Ashley answered around a mouthful of noodles. "Christensen was shot down in March of this year, Kramer bailed out of his OV-10 in June, and I was in a Huey on its way to insert my team in the northwestern corner of South Vietnam when we got shot down in August. I was thrown from the chopper and woke up when a North Vietnamese soldier kicked me to see if I was dead. That's when I found out that all the other guys died in the crash."

"That's no good."

Ashley, raising the bowl to his mouth and sipping broth, continued whispering. "Cho was in a special forces camp that was overrun in September. He was in the command post, and as best as he can remember, one eighty-two millimeter round blew the sandbags off the roof and another exploded a whole side of the room. He only survived because was he was sitting behind a bank of radios."

"Where have you been since you were captured?"

"In a camp we think was just north of the DMZ."

Ashley stopped talking as Colonel Duong approached. He seemed more cheerful than usual.

"Everyone back in the truck. Next stop in three hours."

The six POWs weren't chained to the floor this time, so they could shift positions. Randy let the canvas support his head and dozed.

A loud explosion woke him, followed by a shriek and another explosion. The truck swerved, and before it jerked to a stop, the two Vietnamese guards jumped out and started running.

Ashley Smith shouted, "Everybody out! That's an AC-130!" Karl Kramer was the first out, followed by Greg Christiansen, and both waited for Henry Cho to shuffle to the back of the truck so they could help him down. Once Cho was on the ground, Smith pointed to a clump of large trees. "There! Move!"

The Green Beret waited until Randy and Jeff passed him, then followed. About five feet inside the tree line, they sheltered in a deep trench that ran parallel to the road. Even so, they felt the heat and concussion wave as the blast ripped the truck apart. Shrapnel whined over their heads and smacked into trees.

Randy started to stand to see what was happening, but Ashley used his handcuffed hands to haul him back. "Get down, you idiot."

The shrieks and explosions continued for what Randy guessed was another ten minutes. Then the attack was over, leaving the noise of burning trucks and screams from wounded men.

Smith rubbed some dirt onto his face so it wouldn't reflect light, then slowly raised his head to peer over the lip of the trench. "I count nine trucks burning, another on its side, and one is nose down in a ditch or one of these trenches. Some of the North Vietnamese are running around like madmen, others are just standing, probably shell-shocked. We stay here. If they find us, okay. If not, then we see if we can get rid of these chains and make our way south. Agreed?"

All five others responded in the affirmative. It was their duty to try to escape, and for Randy this was his first real opportunity.

Monday, December 7, 1970, 0649 local time, North Vietnam
Randy awoke with a start and froze. Slowly, he counted heads. There were only four.

Kurt Kramer leaned toward him. "Keep your head down. Ashley and Greg left at first light to look for tools to get the handcuffs off."

In the background, Randy heard the crackling from trucks that still burned and occasional pops of ammunition cooking off. "What hit us last night?"

"E model AC-130. They have two forty-millimeter guns and two twenty-millimeter Gatling guns that shoot out the side and can hit targets with pinpoint accuracy. The gunships fly up and down the trail looking for trucks with their infrared sensors. I loved to find targets for them, because they stay around until they finish the job."

"They could have killed us and no one would have known."

"Yeah. POWs are supposed to be transported in clearly marked vehicles. That is, of course if the North Vietnamese followed the Geneva Conventions. We both know they don't."

In daylight, they could see that rough planks along the sides made their refuge resemble a World War I trench. Only a direct hit would have killed them.

Ashley dropped into the trench, carrying what looked like a heavy-duty branch trimmer and a number of backpacks. "I found this in a workshop a quarter a mile up the road. It's not perfect, but it may work."

Randy put one handle on the ground and slid the link connecting the handcuffs between the blades. When Jeff pushed down on the handle, the steel gave way with a soft clink. "Here, let me get the rest of them." It wasn't long before they were free of the handcuffs.

Randy spun the shackle on his left foot around. "Jeff, try the bolt connecting the two halves together. I think it will be easier than the chains."

Jeff pressed down hard on the wire cutter. Nothing. He pulled it back and looked at the bolt. "Progress." He put it back in place and looked up. "Karl, give me a hand and maybe we can get more pressure."

Both pilots pushed and the head of the bolt shot out. Smiling, Jeff said, "That's one, eleven more to go."

Ashley Smith passed backpacks over to Greg. "Take inventory of these. Gentlemen, we have a decision to make. We can either wait until they recapture us, or we head south to escape. What do you want to do?"

Greg started looking through the first bag. "Get the fuck out of here."

"Our biggest problem is shoes," Ashley pointed out. "We all have big feet that won't fit in North Vietnamese army boots. These flip-flops mean we can't go through the jungle. We'll have to use the road or the trail next to it. It'll be slow going. If we see anyone, we have to go into the trees and wait. And another thing. Do we pick up weapons or go unarmed? I'm asking because there are AKs lying all over the place. There weren't many survivors."

Randy spoke up. "As much as I would like to kill as many soldiers as we can, we're not here to conduct a raid that could get one or more of us hurt. Guns and ammo are more weight to carry. I think we need to quietly sneak away, and being unarmed will force us to be stealthy. And if we use a gun to hunt, the sound would alert everyone around us. Given a choice between carrying food and guns, I'd pick food, because it gives us strength to carry on and escape. So I say no guns."

"Do we all agree, no guns?"

Heads nodded in agreement. Ashley looked at Greg, who had the contents of the packs laid out on the ground. "What do you have that's useful?"

"Four metal bowls, two small knives, three bayonets, eight balls of rice and twelve tins of some kind of fish, four pairs of socks and a first aid kit."

Ashley looked at the others and realized that the dull gray and black striped pajamas they were wearing would make them hard to see in the dim light of the jungle.

The Green Beret captain slowly raised his head over the lip of the trench. "You're not going to believe this, but the survivors are formed up two abreast and heading north. Let's wait and see what happens. We may be able to find more food and other things we can use when they're gone."

"I'll go with you when you look around," Randy volunteered.

"You sure?"

"Two sets of eyes are better than one."

Thirty minutes later, Ashley crawled over and out of the trench, and Randy followed, allowing a distance of twenty feet between them. He mimicked Ashley's noiseless heel down, roll to the toe walking style. Three types of sounds filled the air—calls made by animals and bugs, crackling from burned metal cooling, and the hissing of fires.

The first dead men Randy came across were the guards from the back of their truck. They were face down in the mud, their shredded backs covered with a mix of drying blood and insects feasting on the corpses.

After easing a pack off a body, he forced himself to look for things they could use and ignore the fact he was pulling them from bloody, mutilated bodies. His haul included two bayonets and four machetes, two dozen rice balls, and the same number of tins of canned fish.

Randy went still when he saw a familiar, heavy-set man leaning against a tree. It was Duong, or what was left of him. His bloody hands were covered with the guts he had tried to keep from falling out of his torn abdomen; his face was frozen in a rictus of agony.

Grisly as it felt, he thought Duong's boots might fit. As Randy pulled the boots off, the dead man's hands fell to the ground, revealing the long gash across his middle. The putrid stench made Randy gag.

A few feet away from Colonel Duong, Heckle's lifeless eyes stared at the rising sun. A long sliver of metal stuck out from his sternum. Randy walked over and unbuckled the cloth strap on Heckle's wrist. He rubbed dried blood off his aviator watch's lens and restored it to his own wrist. At least now he could tell time.

Further along he found another soldier with large feet and quickly removed those boots. Satisfied, he looked around for Ashley; he, too, was holding several pairs of boots. The Green Beret pointed to the trench and both men headed toward their fellow POWs with their heavy, unwieldy loads. The food was divided into six packs; the chains and shackles were tossed into the wreckage of one of the burning trucks. None of the boots fit well, but with the socks they'd found they were a great deal better than the sandals. Squinched toes were less hardship than open lacerations. Each man now had a bayonet, a pocketknife, a metal bowl and canteen, and the group had four machetes.

Ashley unfolded the map Randy had taken from Duong's map case. "Everyone, gather around. This doesn't have much detail, but it does show the convoy's route and the stopping points." He tapped some notations on the map. "Let's assume these are rest stops like the one stayed at last night, and these are kilometer markers we'll look for as we move south. As we approach way stations, we need to figure out a way around them. I'll take point. Randy, you're behind me, followed by Henry, Karl, and Greg. Everyone, stay about ten feet apart. Jeff, you're going to be tail end Charlie until the first rest stop. Keep checking our six every few minutes."

Henry Cho spoke up. "Leave me here. I don't want to hold you guys back."

"That's not open to discussion, Henry. We're in this together and I am not leaving anyone behind."

"I'm going to slow you guys down."

"If need be, we'll carry you. We're not leaving you, period, end of discussion."

Randy shouldered a pack and climbed up the steps from the trench. He was excited. For the first time since he'd been shot down he was free, and escape was now an option. Being on the Ho Chi Minh trail deep inside North Vietnam didn't seem to matter. The instructors in SERE school were right. This was more mental than physical.

Thursday, December 10, 1970, 1049 local time, Visalia, CA

When she'd moved to Hanford, Janet had looked around for a post office where she could rent a box. The largest U.S. Post Office was in Visalia, a convenient, fifteen-minute drive from the Hanford house, and it could be accessed twenty-four hours a day. She'd sent the new address form to another box in Gary, Indiana.

Today, Janet opened Box 602 and pulled out the sheaf of paper that had accumulated, most of it junk mail. As she flipped through the flyers, however, she found an envelope with a hand-written address buried in a color ad from a local supermarket. After dumping the flyers in the large trash can by the door, Janet got into her Volvo and stared at the letter on the passenger seat. *Do I open it now or wait until I get home?*

Curiosity won. Janet shook the envelope to move the contents to the far side before carefully slitting the envelope open with her pocketknife. Out came a note printed in block letters.

> Hi,
>
> Hope you are doing well. I want to stay with you in Hanford soon for a few weeks. Hope you still have the stuff I gave you when you headed west.
>
> Call this number to give me yours—(312) 451-0298. When I get close, I'll call you to get your street address.
>
> See you soon.
>
> Bernadette

67

This is a complication I don't need. Janet wondered if she should call the number or just pretend she'd never gotten the letter. After her irritation subsided, she stopped at a gas station to get ten dollars' worth of quarters and headed for a mall and its bank of pay phones.

Saturday, December 12, 1970, 1546 local time, North Vietnam

Darkness came early and fast in the jungle. The Americans spent the day skirting heavily cratered sections of the road. The largest holes were six or seven feet deep and ten to fifteen feet across. Older ones were filled with water and coated with grass.

From a rise that gave them a view of a long stretch of road, the terrain looked like a giant muffin tin. Shredded trees were mixed with pieces of trucks, bent anti-aircraft guns and other destroyed war matériel.

Before his OV-10 had been hit by a 37-millimeter shell that started a fire he and his co-pilot could not put out, this area had been Karl's turf. He'd flown over the Ho Chi Minh Trail day and night, looking for truck convoys and troop concentrations. Once he found them, he called for fighters to send down a rain of bombs. Karl could tell the difference between craters made by five-hundred-pound bombs versus ones made by thousand pounders.

Every time they heard trucks coming, the Americans slipped into the woods and lay down. On one occasion, they stumbled on a cross trail teeming with North Vietnamese soldiers. Ashley, as point man, backed quickly away and signaled for them all to find concealment. Luckily, they had been moving slow and quiet, and none of the solders had been looking in their direction for the brief instant that Ashley had been visible before he faded into the forest cover. Hearts pounding, the six Americans waited for the soldiers to pass. From their days flying missions over the trail, they knew truck and foot traffic would increase in the evening.

Late in the afternoon they came across the rest stop. Randy

recognized it as the place where they'd had dinner the night before. They crossed to the east side of the road and kept moving. Thirty minutes later, they came across a single grass-covered bomb crater inside the tree line that would give them cover. They were, Karl estimated, half a mile south of the rest stop.

During the night, Randy's wristwatch was passed from watch stander to watch stander. Its luminous dial let the wearer know when his two-hour shift was up so he could wake his relief.

Sleep wasn't difficult, even though they could hear explosions in the distance. They were all exhausted. On his night shift, Randy watched tracers from the North Vietnamese gun positions hunt an American airplane. Happily, he didn't see the telltale glow of a plane on fire.

When Randy got up in the early morning, with dawn lightening the sky but the sun still below the horizon, his growling stomach was screaming *Feed me, feed me!* Ashley was using a little bow to spin a small stick of wood back and forth, creating enough friction to get a small fire started. Randy remembered doing the same thing as a Boy Scout.

Seeing Randy move around, Ashley whispered, "Take the machete and find more kindling and small pieces of dry wood so we can keep the fire going. Try not to make any noise."

Just outside the crater, Randy found a dead tree shattered by a bomb blast. The first branch he bent broke with the satisfying crack of dry wood. He brought back an armload.

"What did you use to get it started?"

"Belly button lint and a paper wrapping from a rice ball. See if you can find some water."

Randy looked at Ashley quizzically as if to say, "Where am I going to find water?"

"Remember what they taught you in survival school. Look for things that would naturally collect water. And find us some fruit. There should be some growing around here."

Randy picked up two canteens and two metal bowls and headed out on what he thought would be a fool's errand. But he was wrong. Less than twenty feet from the crater, he found yellow-green, grapefruit-sized pomelos lying on the ground. Just above him, six of the juicy fruit were within reach. Nearby he found ferns with water trapped in their leaves. It wasn't much, but he drained what he could into a bowl.

By the time he got back to the bomb crater, Ashley was stirring a mixture of rice, fish, and the oil from the tins in one of their metal bowls with the tip of a bayonet. The rice was turning brown in the oil and the fragrance made Randy's stomach growl even more. While Ashley scraped portions of the rice and fish mixture into six bowls, Karl cut the pomelos into wedges.

"A healthy breakfast with proteins and carbs is served!"

Five-star cuisine it was not, but it was filling. As Randy had learned in survival school, you'd be surprised what you would eat after a day or two without food. By the time they started walking, the sun was well up.

Two hours later, they stopped for a ten-minute break. They were in an area full of truck parts, and where there were trucks there had to be North Vietnamese soldiers. The Americans huddled in the brush at the bottom of a stand of large trees just off the road.

A droning noise that sounded like a large, angry bee caused them all to look up. Karl whispered, "OV-10." A few seconds later, they saw a distinctively shaped plane. The cockpit was in a pod out in front of the two tail booms connected by the elevator in the back and the wing in the front. The plane had the same general layout as the World War II P-38 fighter, but the OV-10 was designed for forward air controller missions. Where OV-10s were hunting for targets, Air Force, Navy and Marines Corps fighter-bombers were soon to follow.

Tracers reached out from several directions as the airplane banked, then dove down toward a position south of them. The marking rocket's white smoke trail drew a line across the blue sky. Within seconds, two brown and green Air Force F-4s pulled out of their dives, leaving a trail of bombs headed toward the ground. The explosions sounded like a rapid series of thunderclaps.

The buzzing returned and the OV-10 marked a spot closer to where they were hiding. They watched the high drag fins on the eight bombs from the first F-4 pop open. The "tail retarding device" on each bomb caused it to drop straight down towards the target, and also gave the pilot time to get out of the bomb fragmentation zone. Clearly visible were the two-foot-long probes on the front of the bombs to set them off two feet above the ground. Randy put his hands over his ears and turned to Jeff. "Mark 82 Snake Eyes," he mouthed.

The explosions were deafening, and they felt the wave of concussion from each five-hundred-pound bomb. Although not very religious, Randy thought this was a good time to cross himself and say a Hail Mary. *My God, I'm going to die in North Vietnam killed by American bombs! The ultimate in friendly fire!*

Randy resisted the urge to run out onto the road and wave, knowing that the pilots in the OV-10 were too high to recognize POW pajamas. The pilot would only see him as a potential target.

A second F-4 appeared. Its bombs fell even closer. Shrapnel chopped its way through the branches of the trees.

Unlike the first set of bombs, these explosions kept going. This set sounded different, and Randy realized the bombs had set something else off. Then he smelled burning diesel oil.

The OV-10 returned, and to Randy it looked as if it was pointing its blunt nose right at them. The two pylons under the fuselage that stuck out like an inverted V were clearly visible. He could see the cylinders that housed the 2.75-inch rockets the OV-10 crew used to mark targets under each end of the V, along with an external fuel tank in the center. A trail of spiraling smoke signaled another rocket was on its way. The rocket was a little black dot until it passed overhead and exploded in the jungle behind them.

They were very vulnerable. Ashley pointed at a zigzag trench whose camouflage had been blown away by the last bomb blast, and all six piled in. Randy prayed that the bombs dropped by the next two F-4s would hit their targets. If any were short, they would all be dead.

He could see the yellow bands around the olive-drab bomb casings, and all of them heard branches breaking moments before the next bomb exploded with a deafening roar. The ground vibrated as if they were near the epicenter of an earthquake.

Randy knelt in a fetal position to make himself as small as possible. The irony of being on the receiving end of what he'd been dropping was not lost on him. If he'd looked up, Randy would have seen the trees not shattered by the bombs bending from the pulse of air that rushed out from the bomb's explosion.

Chunks of shrapnel whizzed through the air and made distinctive smacks as they hammered into the boles of trees, followed by a rain of moist dirt, bark, and branches.

Randy waited a few seconds after the last dirt clod had landed to uncurl and see if any of the others were hurt. Up and down the line, each man was showing the thumbs-up sign.

Somehow, when they'd jumped into the zig-zag trench, Randy had moved to the point position ahead of Karl, so when Ashley passed the word to move out, Randy stood up and started down the trench to the steps he knew would be at either end.

Coming around the corner in the trench, Randy came upon his worst nightmare—fully armed North Vietnamese soldiers. There was a lot of shouting in Vietnamese. Randy yelled "Gooks!" and started to pull himself out of the trench when a volley from an AK-47 stitched the side of the trench around him. He slid back down and raised his hands in the air.

Shit, piss and corruption!

The six recaptured Americans were led down the road and into the jungle at gunpoint between two rows of North Vietnamese soldiers. Behind them, two soldiers carried their packs. In a clearing, they were forced to kneel with their hands clasped on their heads. Randy was sure that the last sound he was going to hear was an AK-47 or a pistol fired into the back of his head.

Two men walked in front of them. One wore the same style red shoulder boards with two gold bars worn by Colonel Duong, with one less star. He was a *trung ta,* or lieutenant colonel. The second officer wore one gold bar and four stars, which Randy had learned meant the officer was a *dai uy* or captain.

The captain fingered Randy's clothing and spoke first. "You escaped prisoners?"

Ashley spoke for the group. "Yes."

"How you get here?"

"We were in a convoy that got bombed two days ago. Just like you."

Nice answer. It positions us in the same shitty situation. And he's speaking English because he doesn't want them to know that he speaks Vietnamese.

"Where bombed?"

"A few kilometers up the road."

"Where guards?"

"I don't know. Some were dead, some walked north."

Henry Cho keeled over. A guard hit him with a rifle butt and he grunted from the impact but didn't move.

"What is wrong with your traitor friend?"

"He is not a traitor. He is an American soldier, just like me. He is partially paralyzed on left side from a head wound. His left leg and arm don't work well."

"Chinese?" The officer let Randy help Cho back into a kneeling position. Cho looked up at the captain. "No, my parents are Korean."

The captain and the lieutenant colonel exchanged words. When they stopped talking, the lieutenant colonel addressed the prisoners.

"You kill guards."

"No, they left us and went north. The convoy commander, a Colonel Duong, was killed by the bombs."

The lieutenant colonel stepped forward. "If we find you killed People's Army soldiers, you die."

Their elbows were tied tightly behind their backs and they were yanked to their feet. A rope with a noose was placed on each man's neck.

Fuck. This again. Randy, you will survive! You will *survive!*

The same day, 1730 local time, Hanford

Rather than drive the GT350 to Helen Starkey's house, Janet drove her trusty, dark gray, two-door Volvo 123S sedan that her parents had given her as a high school graduation present. It had a heater ideal for Chicago and Wisconsin winters, but it lacked air conditioning. It also had a feature designed for Scandinavian winters: the driver could pull a chain to raise a curtain that blocked airflow to the engine. With it up, the engine provided heat in two or three minutes. The owner's manual noted that the driver could use the blind to prevent snow from forming a wall of ice f in front of the radiator.

In Hanford, the Volvo's cold weather features weren't needed. With winter daytime temperatures in the seventies, Janet drove with the driver's side window rolled down and the vent wing positioned to direct air onto her chest.

As Janet parked her car at the curb, Helen called from the front steps, "Hi, take a seat on the couch an pour yourself some wine."

Helen came over smiling as she watched Janet study a promising array of boxes on the table. "I had a meeting in LA last week, so I went shopping. These new toys are from the same store that produces that catalogue I showed you."

Helen placed celery sticks packed with a dip made from Campbell's onion soup, chives and sour cream on a plate and brought the plate to the display table by the couch. She put it down next to the three oblong boxes. "Before I forget, next weekend I'm going home for the holidays to stay with my parents."

"Are you driving or flying?"

"Flying. Good lord, I don't want to spend five or six days each way in the car by myself! I got a non-stop from LA to Dallas and then on to Mobile."

"Nice. Sounds like fun."

"Are you going to go spend some time with your parents?"

"No, my parents and I don't get along. It's a long story. And I don't know Randy's all that well." It was a white lie. Randy's mother called her every week to talk about Randy and speculate on what he was going through. Janet had declined her invitation to spend a few weeks with them.

Helen didn't want to probe. Her guest had an edge that she liked. Something in Helen wanted to find out more, but another part of her brain warned, "Don't go there."

Janet selected a stalk of celery and examined each of the boxes. She looked up and smiled. She was—as Randy described her preference for not wearing panties—"going commando", and she was hungry for a great deal more than celery. "Which one do you like?"

Helen rested her chin on her fist. "I haven't tried them yet, so I don't know. They all looked interesting."

The first evening they'd spent together, all they'd done was laugh about what a terrible porn movie it would have made because no one would want to watch two half-naked women masturbate with dildos. Janet had spent the week using one of the vibrators Helen had lent her, and wanted more. On a sudden impulse, she leaned forward and gently pressed her lips against Helen's. Helen's soft "Oh!" of surprise made an opening, and Janet's tongue darted in. The kiss turned deeper, and very mutual.

When both needed a breath, Helen pulled back a bit. "You've done this before?"

"Yes."

"When?"

Janet smiled. She let her fingers begin a slow dance down the front of Helen's dress, stroking the breasts beneath. "My first college roommate was a lesbian. One night she asked me if I'd ever been with a woman. I said no, but I was a flower child who

75

believed in free love. I let Gracie—that was her name—seduce me, and we made love several times a week for the rest of the year. She taught me a lot about how to please a woman. She said it would come in handy. She was right. Some of the college parties turned into orgies and… well."

Helen intoned, "Ohhhhhh…." She'd only heard rumors about lesbian relationships amongst her sorority sisters.

Janet wasn't sure if this was a reaction to her fingers or what she'd just said. Helen unbuttoned her dress and carefully undid her bra. Janet bent over and took one breast in her hand and the other into her mouth.

Helen moaned, then gently pushed Janet's head back. "Are you going to teach me?"

"If you want me to."

"I do."

Janet dropped a hand on Helen's thigh. The Southern belle draped one leg over the back of the couch and let the other fall to the floor as she lay back to put her head on the armrest. Janet started gently massaging the soft flesh of Helen's upper thighs. *No*, she thought, *we won't need batteries today*.

Encouraged by Helen's soft moans, Janet began to stroke the soft globe that was Helen's clitoris. "You know this will change how you view sex with men."

"I don't care… Oh my God… I'm sooooo turned on. Don't stop… It feels sooooooo good! Oh my God… It's happening so fast. OH… MY… GOD!"

Sunday, December 13, 1970, 0630 local time, North Vietnam

They walked through the night on a trail that ran parallel to the road on the west side. In the distance, they could hear trucks and an occasional string of bombs explode.

It was, Randy thought, a night of twos. The unit that had captured them marched north towards Hanoi in a column of twos. Passing them and heading south was a steady procession of men marching or pushing bicycles side by side. Each bike had four packs, two hung over the front and two more over the rear wheels. Randy was number two in the string of six Americans. Breaks, according to his watch, were every two hours.

At dawn, they stopped at a way station stocked with food and water. In the growing light he could see a network of trenches and bunkers connecting wooden shelters on platforms two or three feet off the ground. Trees in front of these platforms had been stripped of all their branches up to a height of ten feet. The six Americans were directed to a latrine, then tied to trees in front of the largest building.

As soon as they were secure, one of the Vietnamese officers addressed them.

"I am Lieutenant Colonel Vo Cao, Peoples Army of Vietnam. My captain says your story is correct. We passed a bombed convoy last night. Many dead. Papers destroyed. I have sent message to Hanoi to get instruction on what to do with you. I find out later. Sleep now. Eat later. Walk again tonight. If you try to escape, you will be shot."

The same day, 0926 local time, Hanford

Janet slowly opened her eyes and turned on her side. The distinct, smoky smell of bacon and fresh coffee filled her nostrils. A steaming cup of coffee and a handwritten note under a freshly cut flower graced the end table beside the bed.

> Janet,
>
> Thanks for a wonderful night. I want much more of what you have to teach. When you are ready, breakfast will be too.
>
> Helen

The same day, 1845 local time, Hanford

Janet had just put the last of three brown grocery bags on the kitchen counter when the phone rang. She tossed the cold packages of frozen vegetables into the freezer before she picked up the handset.

"Hello, Julia."

The voice was all too familiar. *Bernadette*. The less said, the better. "Yes."

"Where have you been?" The tone on the other end was demanding, yet friendly.

"Grocery shopping."

"I got your address yesterday from the same helpful Navy personnel who gave me your phone number. I'll be there in less than ten minutes."

That meant she had time to put the food away but not enough time to take a shower. She reeked of sex and sweat. Helen had wanted one lovemaking session after another, and it was the first time Janet had felt sexually satisfied since the night before Randy left. *Oh well.*

Not long after, the doorbell rang and Janet went to answer it.

"Hi, Julia. Nice to see you." Behind the woman on the doorstep, a backpack and a suitcase sat on the porch. In the driveway was a battered, two-tone blue Ford Fairlane.

"Hi, Bernadette. Welcome to Hanford."

The short, thin, dark-haired woman picked up her bag and backpack and crossed the threshold into the house. After a friendly hug, Bernadette looked around. "Nice place."

"It is. Come make yourself comfortable. You can have the second bedroom." Janet *née* Julia hoisted the backpack—it was heavier than she expected—and led the way.

Bernadette lifted her suitcase onto the bed. "Where's the bathroom?"

"Down the hall." Janet sat down on the bed and waited, wondering what was in the suitcase and the backpack. You never knew what Bernadette was carrying.

"What do you use the third bedroom for?"

"It's my private dojo. When I found out that Randy was a

78

prisoner of war, I decided to take up martial arts, as much to work out my anger and frustrations as for the mental discipline and fitness. So I practice katas in there."

"What are you taking?"

"Tae kwon do."

"Oh."

Janet wanted to change the subject. "Are you hungry?"

"Yes. What's the latest on your husband?"

Janet led the way to the kitchen and began gathering ingredients for a fast meal. "I haven't been told anything new."

"Goddamn war. Where were you last night?"

"At a friend's—why?"

"I called and called and no one answered. I spent the night in my car."

"Sorry." *No, I am not!*

"I don't want to risk checking into a motel in a small town like this. You never know if they will ask the police to check out a car with Michigan plates."

"I wouldn't worry about that. With all the Navy people around here, out of state plates are common. But it might be a good idea to move the car. It's a bit conspicuous." Janet busied herself trimming the excess fat off a couple of chicken breasts.

"The Feds damn near caught me a few weeks ago. That's why I sent the note. I'm looking for a place to lay up for a week or so."

"The Feds, as in the FBI?

"The one and only. They don't like it when we fire bomb recruiting centers or toss Molotov cocktails at military base guard shacks or naval air station fuel tanks." Bernadette opened the refrigerator and took out a can of beer. After popping the top, she stood opposite Janet. "You ought to know."

Janet ignored this. She coated the chicken breasts with a marinade of honey, soy sauce and sesame oil. She diced two green onions, then sprinkled the breasts with sesame seeds. "We'll let these sit until the rice is ready, then grill them," she said.

Bernadette took the hint that her host wasn't interested in

talking about her prior activities. The leader and one of the founders of the Students for a Democratic Society leaned over and inhaled. "That smells great."

"Thanks. My mother made it all the time."

"Janet, you're still with the movement, right?"

"I am. I don't like this government or its war any more than you do."

"Then what's the problem?"

"I'm lying low."

"Good. I'm still just one step ahead of the law."

"Bernadette, if you get arrested here the FBI will start digging into my past and my cover will be blown."

"Sorry, I didn't think of it that way. I wanted to stay with someone I could trust in a quiet, out-of-the-way city."

"You're welcome to stay for a week or so, but then I think it's best you move on. I can tell my neighbors you're a school friend who stopped by."

"Good, that should be time enough." Bernadette took a long swig of beer.

After dinner, Janet brought what remained of a bottle of wine out to the small back porch. Six-foot-tall hedges surrounded the back yard, and Janet contracted with a local lawn service firm to keep them trimmed. She refused their offer to mow the lawn because she liked the exercise she got from pushing the reel lawnmower.

"Do you still have the stash we gave you?"

"It's split between safe deposit boxes." Janet didn't elaborate. She'd used three different banks, one in Hanford and two in Fresno.

"Good, I need some of the cash."

"We can get it tomorrow when the banks open."

"How's your cover holding up?"

"So far, so good."

"And the plan?"

"I'm following the plan. This is a small town and everyone

knows I'm a navy wife."

"Any of the wives interested?"

"Approaching any of them is very risky. If they oppose the war, they keep those thoughts to themselves. The POW/MIA wives are vocal because they want to pressure the government to get the North Vietnamese to treat our husbands better and bring them home." *Randy is my husband and I am one of the POW/MIA wives. Before Randy was shot down, I would have said "their" wives.*

"Ending the war will do that."

"You have to understand their mindset. Their husbands are military officers who have a sworn duty to obey lawful orders, and they think the same way their husbands do."

"But the war is illegal!"

"They don't see it that way."

"Do you ever talk to your family?"

"No, I haven't spoken to them since graduation. They made it clear that my political views made me *persona non grata* at home. I might as well be dead. You have to remember, my father fought in the Pacific in the First Marine Division, first on Guadalcanal and then on other islands. I have two brothers who are on active duty. One is a pilot in the Air Force and the other is in the Navy. I think he became a SEAL, but I am not sure. I don't know where they are or if they are still alive. Even my younger sister won't talk to me. She thinks I'm nuts."

"Brainwashed by the right wingers who started this war." Bernadette took a sip of wine. "How'd you wind up in Hanford?"

"Well, the plan was for me to marry a serviceman and get a job someplace in the military, maybe get a job on a base where I could gather intelligence. I couldn't meet anyone likely at home because my family would have outed me, so I applied for jobs near military bases. The Children's Hospital of Fresno hired me. One of my co-workers invited me to a party in Hanford, and I met Randy. He'd just started training in the A-7. We began dating and eventually he proposed. After we were married I quit my job; I hated the commute and it wasn't exactly a hotbed of military gossip. There aren't many jobs on a base available to wives that would give us valuable information." *I am not sure I am still part of "the movement." But I do know Bernadette won't hesitate to turn me over to the police to send a message to others who might be thinking of leaving.*

"Do you love him?"

Janet took a drink, knowing she had to be careful with the answer. She didn't want to confide in Bernadette that Randy was the only man who got her going with a series of orgasms before he even entered her, then had the staying power so they both came at the same time. Every time had left her breathless and with stars in her eyes. "Yes."

"Let me ask the question a different way. *Will you betray his trust in you?*"

Janet looked straight ahead at the hedges. She'd already betrayed Randy by sleeping with Helen. But what Bernadette asked was much more.

"Yes, if and when the time comes."

"Oh, it will. Trust me. The Revolutionary Youth Movement we founded continues to grow. We will turn this country into a bastion of socialism." Bernadette sat up and faced Janet. "Julia—I'm sorry, I should call you Janet. Have you started building additional covers?"

"Yes." Janet's driver's license from the State of Nevada was in a safe deposit box, along with two credit cards and a valid U.S. passport that used the fictitious address. As soon as she'd arrived in California, she'd changed her name to Janet Anne Williams. When she'd married Randy she'd become Janet Williams Pulaski. Julia Amy Lucas no longer existed.

Janet drank some more wine. "So just how close behind you, so to speak, are the Feds?"

"I'm not sure. About three months ago, I was walking toward our safe house when I saw cops show up. They got Bill, so I went to where we had a stash and headed out. His trial starts next month, and there is no bond because he's a flight risk. When I was in New Orleans, the couple who took me in said I was on a wanted poster in the post office."

"Almost nobody looks at those. Besides, the pictures are so small and fuzzy it would be a miracle if anyone recognized you. It's when your mug shot appears on TV that people pay attention."

"Hasn't happened yet."

"Bernadette, where are you going from here?"

"Not sure. The Black Panthers have offered me shelter in two cities. I'm waiting for arrangements to be made."

Chapter 3
PHAM'S CAMP

Monday, December 14, 1970, 1200 local time, North Vietnam

The muggy heat caused the Americans to sweat heavily as they marched. What surprised them was that Colonel Cao's men ignored them, except to give them water and food. There were no beatings, either on marches or during rests. There was no attempt at verbal communication, only pointing to a place to sit when they stopped, or tugging on a rope to tell them to get up.

At the next stop, Randy spotted Lieutenant Colonel Cao speaking in hushed tones to another North Vietnamese Army officer. He nudged Ashley and jerked his head in the direction of the conference. At the end, the stranger handed Lieutenant Colonel Cao a number of wrapped bundles that Cao stuffed into his pack, then they moved off in different directions.

"That looked a lot like a payoff."

"I agree. It looked like a negotiation. Something was bought and sold."

The Americans were brought to their feet and the column moved out. Randy looked at his watch that Cao's men had not confiscated. Having a watch and knowing the time was strangely comforting. It was one of the little things that kept him on an even keel. It was 1236.

The Americans walked single file in the middle of the column, wrists tied, linked together by a rope around their necks. Two riflemen and four two-man teams with machine guns were immediately behind them.

Cao's column came to a halt and the Americans were led to forward. Across the road, Randy could another group of People's Army of Vietnam soldiers standing and sitting, obviously waiting for a new set of orders from their commander. They looked much scruffier than Cao's unit, except for the officer in charge, who looked to be about five-foot-four and weighed maybe a hundred and twenty pounds. He also looked familiar.

Randy poked Ashley in the side and gestured with his head. "That's the same guy we saw earlier today."

Ashley squinted in the noonday glare. "Yep. Same guy."

The two Vietnamese officers met in the center of the road and walked back towards the Americans. Lieutenant Colonel Cao waited while the other colonel looked over the six prisoners. Then he said, "I am turning you over to Colonel Trong Pham of the People's Army of Vietnam. He will take you to a camp until you are sent to a prison in Hanoi. You are no longer my responsibility and my duty to you as prisoners of war is over."

Cao said something in Vietnamese to his men, and they formed up and marched back across the road to join the rest of his unit.

Once they were gone, Pham spoke. "My base is fifteen kilometers from here. It is uphill where it is cooler and more comfortable. If you do not try to escape, no harm will come to you. We have been ordered by our government to treat you well."

With that, Pham yelled a command in Vietnamese. Two men shouldered their weapons, sauntered over and picked up the rope that linked the Americans together.

Twenty minutes later, the column stopped and Pham dropped his pack and moved away from his men. Randy watched Pham pull out what looked like an American PRC90 radio. He pushed the earpiece in his ear and spoke.

"Misty 512, this is Turncoat, over."

"Turncoat, this is Misty 511. 512 has returned to base."

"I have business for you."

"Authenticate, Turncoat."

"Kilo Alpha November. Repeat, Kilo Alpha November."

"Authentication is correct, what kind of business?"

"Special forces unit on the march. At least one hundred men. Coordinates are approximately...." Pham consulted a piece of paper and read off a series of numbers using the U.S military's grid square system.

"Misty 511. Thanks for the trade."

Randy turned to Ashley and Karl. "Did I hear what I thought I heard?"

"Yeah, that guy is either is suckering a couple of American planes into a trap, or he is settling an old score."

They got their answer when two Air Force F-100s screamed overhead. The first one pulled up while the wingman banked sharply and descended. Right after the second plane pulled up from a strafing pass, an F-4 flew by—its J-79s loud, even at a distance—and dropped four silver canisters. A second F-4 did the same. Oily black smoke rose above the jungle.

Lieutenant Colonel Cao heard the approaching F-100. Before he even turned around, a twenty-millimeter round went through his backpack and exploded in his chest. He wasn't alive to see his unit burn to death. The intense heat from the napalm sucked the air out of their lungs before they were incinerated. As Cao went sprawling, 500-piaster notes floated into the air, caught fire, and dropped to the ground as ash.

Pham motioned to his men and they all moved out. None of the Americans said a word.

The same day, 1006 local time, Hanford

Earlier in the week, Janet had gotten a call from Norm Blanchard—Randy's roommate on the *Oriskany*—to tell her that he was arriving on Saturday. He said he was bringing something.

When she tried to press him for specifics he was evasive and would only say that he'd promised Randy he would personally deliver the boxes.

The doorbell rang while Janet was in the bathroom brushing her hair after her dojo workout. When she opened the door, there were two young men she vaguely recognized hauling boxes out of the back of a station wagon. Two tall boxes were already on the porch.

"Hi, Janet," Norm Blanchard called out. "This is Brad Dixon. We both flew with Randy. We brought his stuff home."

"Thanks. Please come in. Would you like some coffee?"

Blanchard said, "Yes, ma'am."

"How do you like it?"

Both men answered, "Black."

By the time the two naval aviators had the boxes in the living room, Janet had three white coffee mugs showing the Blue Tail's logo ready on the kitchen table.

"Guys, thanks for coming. I know you want to be with your wives if you just got back."

Norm answered, "Randy and I had a pact. If either one of us didn't come home, we'd deliver what was in the state room and do what we could for our shipmates' wives. If you need something fixed, or moved, or help with anything, please call me. If I can't do it, I'll get one of the other guys to do it. We're not going back to Vietnam for another eight months." He took a sip of the coffee. "This is really good. Better than the brew we got on board the *Oriskany.* The water, no matter how well they purify it, always smells of chlorine and jet fuel!"

Janet wrinkled her nose. "That sounds awful."

"You get used to it."

Norm put two green boxes on the table. Each had a gold crown logo. "These were in Randy's stateroom safe. I was with him in Hong Kong when he bought them. I didn't put them in the cruise box with his personal effects because there was a chance they would disappear when it was inspected in Hawaii."

"The cruise box came in November. When I opened it, there was an inventory on the top."

"Were any of the pictures broken?"

"No, why?"

"I packed it."

"You did a great job."

"Thanks." Blanchard slid the second box across the table. "Open it."

Janet struggled to get the lid open. Inside was a lady's gold President Rolex. She almost dropped the box as one hand flew to her mouth. "Oh, my God. It's beautiful."

"Randy told me that the case and band are twenty-two carat gold."

"He must have spent a fortune...."

"He bought it with the money he won in poker games. The receipts and the certificates that they are real Rolexes are in the bottom of each box."

Janet took the watch out and tried it on. It fit loosely around her wrist as she admired it. "I'll get a jeweler to adjust it properly. O.K. What's in all those other boxes?"

"A really good stereo system. On our last visit to Subic Bay before Randy got shot down, he bought a top of the line Pioneer amplifier and speakers. There's also a reel-to-reel TEAC tape recorder that is supposed to be the best available."

"What's in the Mikasa boxes?"

"One is a place setting for twelve, one is the tea service, and the other is a set of serving dishes. The pattern is called Mount Holyoke and it's bone china with a black enamel pattern trimmed in 22 carat gold. I brought the picture of a place setting that Randy had stashed in his safe. It is really nice. When I showed it to my wife, she said, 'Wow, why didn't you buy it?'"

Norm handed the picture from the Mikasa catalogue to Janet. "It isn't nice—it's beautiful. I'll start unpacking the china while you set up the stereo. You can put the speakers on either side of the book case at the end of the living room."

Thirty minutes later, Janet heard the Ventures playing "Wipe Out" and headed into the living room. She sat down cross-legged in front of the components and spent a few minutes getting comfortable with the controls. Now, she realized, was the time to ask the question she'd been wanting to ask ever since they'd arrived.

"Norm, Brad, were either of you with Randy when he was shot down?"

"I was." Brad spoke flatly.

"What happened?"

"Commander Hancock gave us very clear guidance on what we could tell you and what we can't."

Janet gave him a look, then gestured with her hand as if to say "Out with it."

"Randy and I were section leaders in the same flight of four A-7s. The gooks launched three SAMs at our flight and targeted Randy's plane. He dodged two, but the third one exploded close by his A-7. I'm pretty sure shrapnel cut his fuel line and the engine shut down, so he started gliding toward the coast. I stayed on his wing. Just before we got to the beach his A-7 was hit by flak and he ejected."

"Did you see him get taken prisoner?

"I did. Just before he was captured he radioed, 'Tell my wife I love her.'"

"Was there an attempt to rescue him?"

"Yes."

"Why wasn't he picked up?"

"Janet, I can't tell you."

"Why?"

"Because I can't."

"*Why?* What happened that is so super secret?"

Brad got up off the floor. "I have to go to the bathroom."

Norm waited until Brad had closed the bathroom door firmly. "Look, Janet, I can get in a lot of trouble for telling you this, but the helo pilot who came to rescue Randy didn't even try to make the pick-up. Commander Hancock wants him court martialed for cowardice. There was a big stink about it with the air wing commander from what I heard. Both men think it will get ugly."

"So my Randy is a POW because some fucking helo driver is a coward, is that it?" She was barely controlling her anger.

"That's about it."

"Do you know the shithead's name?"

"He's a ring knocker, and the Navy doesn't like to admit that Naval Academy graduates are not the best, brightest, and bravest. Look, I'm an academy grad, and it's embarrassing to me."

"So when is this going public?"

"I don't know. It… may never come out. Look, I've already told you more than I should have."

Brad Dixon accidentally on purpose banged the bathroom door as he opened it.

Norm leaned forward and spoke in a hushed tone. "Keep this all to yourself, because if it leaks out they'll know the source."

Janet nodded. "Thanks—for everything. It means a lot."

The same day, 1856 local time, North Vietnam

They walked another fifteen miles, mostly uphill, and based on the sun they were going west before they reached a compound within a compound. Pham pointed to a hooch raised about a yard off the ground and told them to go inside and sit at the table. Behind them, the gate to the inner compound was locked and a soldier stood guard.

The walls were made from dried leaves. Compared to the cage Randy had endured, this was a palace. It had a corrugated metal roof that extended two feet out past the walls, creating shade for much of the day. In the back, four sets of crude bunks were arranged in racks of two. In the center there was a table, and on the far wall, a fireplace made from cemented rocks.

Out back there was the remains of what looked like a very large garden, now filled with weeds, and a small, square building. Someone had carved a half moon on the door similar to the symbol put on outhouses, which told Randy that Americans had been here before. *So where were they?*

Ashley interrupted Randy's inspection. "Here comes Colonel Pham."

The small, wiry man waited until the lock was removed and the bar pulled from the gate. Four men carrying AK-47s followed Pham through the open area. The North Vietnamese Army officer walked with a fast, purposeful stride that men taller than he would have trouble matching.

The six Americans leaned on the wooden plank that was the windowsill and looked down at Pham as he came to a stop a few yards from the steps of the hooch and stood at what the Americans would call parade rest. "Good evening. I am Lieutenant Colonel Trong Pham of the People's Army of North Vietnam. This is my camp and it is where you will be kept until I decide what to do with you. I own you, and I mean that literally."

Pham let that phrase sink in. "You may be wondering where I learned English. I went to a missionary school where they taught us French and English. Then, I became an officer in the South Vietnamese Army and commanded an infantry battalion. The North Vietnamese government made me a better offer and I surrendered the battalion and changed sides."

Ashley exchanged a look with Randy. The others reacted with surprise—or anger. But this hardly explained Pham's unusual behavior on the road. What was going on here, anyway?

"As part of the deal, I get *cart blanche* to operate an opium processing camp. We process raw opium here into a base than can be smoked or refined into heroin, and I deliver the finished product to ships that stop at Vinh. I pay the North Vietnamese government a tax on each shipment, and they let me come and go as I please, as long as the opium is not sold in Vietnam. It is, as they say in America, a very nice set up.

"You are now my factory workers. I am a capitalist, and am not interested in creating a socialist workers' paradise. I do this because I make a lot of money at it."

Pham looked at the Americans, one of at a time. "I know you are probably wondering if there were Americans POWs here before you, and the answer is yes. The last group tried to blow up my factory and got horribly burned in the process. I let them die in agony. It took the last one almost four weeks to die. So, when Colonel Cao reported to the military district commander that he had six American POWs, I saw an opportunity. Can needed money, and I paid him ten million piasters for each of you."

So now I'm a slave, Randy thought bitterly, *and the heroin will probably be sold on the streets of LA.*

Pham continued. "Perhaps you are wondering what happened earlier this morning. A few weeks ago, I bought that radio from a South Vietnamese unit along with the authentication codes that are good until the end of December. I used it to, as you say, tie up a loose end. My men shadowing Cao's unit reported he was killed, along with most all of his men."

Pham shifted his stance and put his hands on his hips. "If you try to escape, you will be shot and left for the vultures. There is a pit next to this building. It is there for two reasons. One, it is a bomb shelter. Two, if you disobey any orders, you will be held there in solitary confinement and given only a small cup of water and a ball of rice each day. Obey my rules and you will be well fed, housed, and clothed. Disobey and you will be punished severely, maybe shot. I won't waste my time torturing you. None of you have any information I need. What I need from you is an honest day's work. Understood?"

The six Americans nodded, some slowly, some with an angry jerk of the head.

"Good. You will work four to six hours a day in my factory, depending on how much needs to be produced. My men will train you when the next shipment arrives. I encourage you to create a garden inside this compound. Tomorrow, I will give you seeds and tools. Every few days we bring rice, fish, and meat from Vinh. A large garden will supplement your diet. What you grow, you get to eat."

Pham eyed them, and they stared back. Ashley, as the most senior, spoke. "What happens when the war ends?"

"Ahhh. That is the same question your predecessors asked. You see, now that Colonel Cao and the paperwork he was carrying have been incinerated, my government has no record of your existence. If they look for Colonel Cao's 176th Special Forces Company, they will only find charred bodies."

Pham smiled. "A few years after the war ends, assuming that you are still alive, I will contact your CIA and offer to tell them, for a large sum of money, where six American POWs can be found. You get to go back to your families, and I get to be richer than I am. It is, as we Capitalists say, a win-win situation."

Wednesday, December 16, 1970, 0848 local time, North Vietnam

Colonel Pham proved as good as his word. After breakfast, his men handed three shovels, three hoes, two rakes and a box of seed packets through the wire. Two of the Burpee seed packets had French labels and *Pour saison 1954* stamped on the bottom. Ashley eyed them dubiously, weighing the packets in the palm of his hand.

Greg, who'd grown up on a farm, piped up, "If they were stored correctly, or at least in a dry place, they'll grow. They won't all germinate, but we'll get some." He added, "I hope."

Ashley looked around the hooch. "Alright, gents. Before we start planting, we need to figure out if we have any special skills that will help us survive. Any objections if I go first?"

"Have at it, Captain," Greg chimed, retrieving the seed packets.

"This'll be short. I have none. I don't know a damn thing about gardening!"

Randy looked up. "Don't you speak Vietnamese?"

"I do. And Laotian. But at this point in time, I don't think I want our captors to know that."

Randy nodded. "Got it." Ashley looked at the man sitting next to him.

93

"I'm Greg Christiansen. I grew up in Minnesota on a wheat and dairy farm that was really a collective run by five families. We had a garden where we grew vegetables in the summer."

Henry Cho was next. "For the record, I speak Mandarin, Korean, and Vietnamese, and I also would prefer that Pham didn't know. My mother ran a restaurant, so I volunteer to be the cook." Hank Cho nodded to the man next to him, who put his large hands on the table.

"I'm Karl Kramer, and I don't know jack shit about gardening or languages. I was a political science major!"

They all laughed. Jeff went next. "I'm Jeff Anderson. My parents had a garden, but I spent my teenage years avoiding being roped into tilling it and pulling weeds. Beyond that, I know nothing about farming." Jeff nodded to Randy.

"Gardens in metro Chicago are hard to keep going. My mother grew herbs in the back yard and that was it." When he finished, Randy looked Ashley, "Did you go to survival school?"

Ashley gave a wry smile. "You mean the one with the simulated POW camp that was not very simulated?"

"Yeah, that one. Were there any aviators in the class?"

"No, why?"

"Because we were taught that our tail number on the day we are shot down is important. So what I'm suggesting is we need to find a way to spell out our call signs on the ground. Mine would be Carrier Air Wing Five's letters: N and F, and the numbers three-one-zero. Jeff's would be his air wing letters N and M and the numbers three-zero-two. Greg and Karl, you should know what yours were. Anyway, in the garden and elsewhere, we need to have at least one, if not two of them spelled out at all times."

"Great idea. Let's figure out how."

Greg looked up. "Maybe we could plant sunflowers in configuration?" He was holding up a packet of sunflower seeds.

Chapter 4
FIRST DAY AT WORK

Christmas Eve was a cold day for San Joaquin Valley. Low, thick clouds hid the sun and added dampness to the chill air. From the porch, Janet watched the trees disappearing into gray mist. Lined up on the front porch were Bernadette's backpack, a new fiberglass Samsonite suitcase, and two duffel bags packed with her new purchases. Two days ago, they'd braved the Christmas crowds on a shopping tour of Fresno stores.

Bernadette stopped on the porch and looked at the clouds. "What a yucky day!"

"Look at it this way. It beats having a foot of snow on the ground and the temperature in the teens, with a wind chill that makes it feel well below zero."

"Amen." Bernadette fished her car keys out of the backpack, tossing them in the air and catching them one-handed, then she looked up. "Julia, why did you kill Susan? She was one of the first recruits of the movement."

Susan had been the driver on the night Julia had tossed the Molotov cocktails into the recruiting center. Janet looked into Bernadette's eyes with a cold, hard stare. "You don't know that I did. Susan is dead. Leave it at that."

95

The .45 she'd used was in the gun safe. The spare barrel she'd used that night had been tossed into the garbage at a gas station in Milwaukee, and the empty cartridge case had gone into another trashcan. Without either, Janet knew there was no way the police could trace Susan's murder to her.

Bernadette swallowed hard. "Julia, keep the faith in the movement. We will eventually bring an end to the war, and the government will be forced to take us seriously."

"I know that. I have faith and trust in Bill and you."

Bernadette hugged Janet. "That's good to know. I'll get out of your hair. You can reach me the usual way."

Janet carried the two duffel bags to the car and waited while Bernadette arranged them in the trunk. Before she drove off, Bernadette waved and said, "It was good seeing you! We'll keep in touch. I'm sure we'll have more work for you."

Friday, December 25, 1971, 1848 local time, North Vietnam

Dinner was smoked fish, noodles and some vegetables that Cho turned into a nourishing, tasty soup. They were about finished when Ashley addressed the group. "Its time for telling our personal histories, i.e. where we come from and how we wound up in the clutches of the North Vietnamese. Don't try telling us *War and Peace;* we may be here for a while, and we'll need something to talk about in the long nights ahead, so just the highlights. We just need to get to know each other. Sound good?"

The others around the table gave nods and other indications of assent.

"O.K., I'll lead by example. I'm Ashley Smith, Captain, U.S. Army. All my grandparents came from Russia in 1906 after a wave of social and political unrest swept the country. They realized it wasn't going to get any better and left for the New World."

"And your name is *Smith*? That's got to be the least Russian name I ever heard!" Greg quipped.

"The immigration officer couldn't spell Tupalovsky. He told

my grandfather that his American name was now Smith. Eventually, my family settled in Brookline, Massachusetts. My father owns hotels and apartments. I graduated from West Point in 1965 with a degree in Russian history and was about halfway through my third tour here in Vietnam when the Huey in which I was riding was shot down. I was the only survivor." Ashley's voice trailed off. He looked down at his clenched hands.

Greg decided to fill in the silence that followed. "I'm Greg Christiansen. I'm fourth generation American and my forefathers came from what is now Denmark. When they left Europe, Sweden controlled the land around the Baltic, so for all I know I may be Swedish! Anyway, I grew up in Minnesota on a seven-thousand acre collective, and no, it's not socialism, it's a multi-family business. I always wanted to fly and not be a farmer, so I applied to all the service academies. The Air Force Academy was the first one to say yes. My degree is in mechanical engineering. I wanted fighters and got F-100s. As soon as I transitioned to the jet, I was sent to Bien Ho, and after the first half of my tour I volunteered for the Misty forward air control mission."

Greg took a deep breath. "I'd been flying FAC missions about three months when my wingman told me to bank hard right and there was a large bang. Lights came on all over the cockpit. I tried to nurse the jet to a safer area, but there were flames aft of the canopy. The controls froze and we ejected. Once I got on the ground, I got clear of my chute and contacted my wingman. He said the airplane had exploded just after we punched out. I don't know what happened to my back-seater. I evaded for about twenty-four hours until I stumbled on a North Vietnamese patrol. So here I am."

Henry Cho was next. "I'm Henry Cho. I'm a brand new Green Beret and first lieutenant, so that makes me the most junior officer. My father was an officer in the Third Korean Infantry Division during the Korean War. My parents were granted refugee status, and for years my dad worked at menial jobs. In 1958 he finished college, and now works for Los Angeles County as a building inspector. My mother started out doing bookkeeping for a man who owns several Chinese restaurants, and then opened her own restaurant that serves Korean and Chinese dishes. Before I went off to college, I helped out in the restaurant, doing everything from food preparation, cooking, waiting on tables and washing dishes. I went to the University of San Diego on an Army ROTC scholarship and got a degree in Asian history. I speak Mandarin, Korean, and Vietnamese. I was with an A team in a South Vietnamese Army camp that was about to be overrun. As the communications officer, I went into the command bunker to destroy the secure radios before we left. That's when the lights went out. I woke up a day or so later when I was pulled out of the debris by a North Vietnamese soldier who thought he was moving a dead body. They propped me up against a pole while they shot all the wounded South Vietnamese soldiers. I don't know why they didn't shoot me. My left arm and leg aren't fully functional, I am almost deaf in one ear, and sometimes I suffer from double vision."

Hank Cho nodded to the man next to him, who put his large hands on the table. "I'm Karl Kramer, and I grew up in the Pittsburgh area, the second oldest of four children. My father worked in the steel mills, and I'm the first Kramer to go to college. I couldn't get an athletic scholarship out of high school; coaches told me that, at five-foot-eleven and a hundred and eighty pounds, I was too small and too slow to play Division I football. They said if I wanted to play football in college, go to a Division III school. So, I got an Air Force ROTC scholarship, and then I was a walk-on at Penn State where I was the starting cornerback for four years, and every year I led the team in interceptions."

Karl knew that if the others followed college football even a little bit, they'd know that being a starter at Penn State was a big deal. Jeff looked impressed. "I flew OV-10s and used the call sign Nail 515. I was on my twentieth mission when we were hit in the left engine. It blew the prop and part of the engine off and we couldn't control the airplane, so we ejected. I landed right in the middle of the goddamn trail and was picked right up. The next day, I heard many helicopters and saw a bunch of A-1s, so I'm hoping my back-seater got rescued."

Jeff took the nod from Karl like a handoff. "I'm Jeff Anderson. I was with VA-22 on the carrier *Bonne Homme Richard*, which we fondly call the Bonnie Dick. When I was shot down, I was in an A-4 with the call sign Beefeater 307. This was my second combat cruise. I was bagged by triple A on a road reconnaissance mission. There was a hellacious bang and the airplane slowed like it had gone into a pile of sand. My wingman told me the plane was on fire from the middle of the fuselage back to the tail. I was too busy trying to fly it and hadn't bothered to look in the mirrors. When I saw the rudder sticking out of the flames a little birdie in my brain said, *This airplane is not going to make it back to the boat!* and I ejected. I was on the ground for about two hours when I was captured. Anyway, I grew up in Birmingham, Alabama, went to the University of Alabama and I got my commission by going through Officer Candidate School in Pensacola, Florida. And, just to let you know, my great, great, great—I think that's enough greats—grandfather fought proudly for the South during the Civil War. He finished the war as a brigadier general, so please, all you Yankees, don't hold it against me!"

It was Randy's turn. "My father emigrated to the U.S. after World War II. He was born and raised in Poland and fought with the Free Polish Army. Me, I always wanted to fly. Driving fast cars was a poor substitute. I went to Purdue University, where I got a degree in chemical engineering. The Navy recruiters showed up and dangled this neat program in front of me. Assuming I qualified, I would do the first half of officer candidate school between my sophomore and junior year and the second half the next summer. When I graduated, I'd be commissioned as an ensign and go to flight training. The cool part is that I got longevity for the years after I signed up. It took me five years to get a degree, but I entered flight training with three years longevity." That translated to about three thousand a year more in pay than the Academy and ROTC graduates got. "On the day I was bagged, I was in a Blue Tail 310."

The bios started the bonding Ashley wanted. He suspected they would be in this camp for a very long time.

The Same Day, 1346 local time, Hanford

This was Janet's first Christmas alone. She'd been married six months and she'd been a POW/MIA wife for two. Christmas Day was a big deal at the Lucas household, and Janet wondered what her family was doing. Randy's parents had called, and the sadness she sensed from them made her feel even sadder.

Janet decided she needed a long workout. She went through kata after kata, focused on getting each move right. She was drenched in sweat when the doorbell rang. On her porch, Wendy Hancock held a bouquet of flowers, a box of homemade cookies, and a large thermos. "I heard you were staying here over the holidays, so I thought I would stop by and say hello."

"This is a surprise! Pardon my appearance. I'm working out." After admiring the flowers, Janet picked up one of the cookies. She giggled at the sweet taste and the hint of ginger. "God, I haven't had one of these in years. They're sooooo good. Thanks for bringing them."

Wendy held up the thermos. "This isn't coffee; it's eggnog with more than its share of bourbon. I think both of us need a stiff drink."

Janet led Wendy to the kitchen, where she got two glasses out of the cupboard and put them on the counter. The CO's wife filled the sixteen-ounce glasses nearly to the rims.

"To Randy's health and safe return."

Janet responded as they clinked glasses, "The safe return of all our POWs."

An hour later, the two women had finished the eggnog and Janet was lightheaded. She held up her empty glass. "Thank you for coming over and bringing me this wonderful drink... and for all your calls. They mean a lot to me."

"My pleasure. I don't want you to feel left out. I know you are uncomfortable coming to squadron wives' events, and some of the women are uncomfortable being around you. Each of them knows her man could be the next POW, and you're a reminder. However, they all ask about you and how you're doing."

"I'm doing O.K. I start nursing school at Fresno State in January. Hopefully, Randy will be home before I finish."

"Good." Wendy stood up and wobbled on her feet. "Wow, the eggnog went to my head!"

"Do you need me to call a cab? I'm in no condition to drive you."

"No, that's not needed. I have the perfect situation. It's called teenage drivers. As part of being allowed to drive, our kids run errands or give us rides. My two oldest are sitting out in the car."

Janet laughed, because that's what her older brothers had done to earn driving privileges. The two women hugged. Janet spoke first. "Wendy, again, thanks for coming. I really appreciate it."

"My pleasure. Don't be such a stranger. You're part of the VA-153 family and always will be."

Tuesday, January 5, 1971, 0846 local time, North Vietnam

They didn't have a calendar, so each day they put another small notch on one of the bamboo posts near the fireplace to count the days. Today's notch indicated they'd been at what Randy dubbed "Pham's Phucking Pharm" for twenty-two days.

Their routine was boring. Get up, boil rice or noodles along with whatever meat Pham provided. Work in the garden for two or three hours. Take a break around noon. Have lunch, and back to the garden for a few more hours.

The "Pharm" was forty-five 30-inch military paces long by seventeen wide. That made it roughly a hundred and fifty feet long and sixty wide. Or, as Karl noted, half a football field in size. Their hooch had bamboo and wood studs placed roughly six inches apart, so even though there were gaps in the walls that acted as windows, it still looked like a jail. The enclosed outhouse was nothing more than a board with a hole above a small pit. Everything stopped at nine p.m. when Pham shut down the generator. Candles were not allowed.

This morning, Karl, who was studying the comings and goings of Pham's men, called out, "Here comes Pham, along with two guards and a newcomer!"

Pham stood at the bottom of the steps, looking up at the six faces staring down at him through bamboo bars. "Gentlemen, this is Major Nguyen Phong of the People's Army of Vietnam. He will be instructing and supervising you as you process the opium. He speaks English."

All the Americans kept straight faces, but it took an effort. Pham was the only North Vietnamese in the camp who attempted to look like a soldier. The others wore the uniform of the Vietnamese People's Army, but they were not soldiers. They were in the drug business, and clearly Phong was the same. His "uniform" hung on him like a loose sack. Either they'd just pulled it out of storage and it was the smallest one they had, or the North Vietnamese Army went with the one-size-fits-all philosophy and let individual wearers tailor them. But Army or not, he was in charge, and his manner was aggressive.

"In the factory, you will all wear manacles. Your hands will not be tied. When called to work, you will go one at a time to the gate. The manacles will be put on you and you will wait in line until all of you are so equipped. When you are finished with the day's work, we will reverse the process. Any attempt at either sabotage or escape will result in the individual's immediate execution. All right then, we will proceed. Who will be first?"

Randy raised his hand. "I will."

Both Pham and Phong executed an about face. They went through the open gate, leaving the two guards to escort Randy to the spot where other soldiers had laid out six pairs of manacles. The process to get all six manacled took, according to Randy's watch, fifteen minutes. Once in the factory, Phong arranged in them in a row in front of three long tables topped with sheets of plywood painted a light gray. Between the tables, fifty-five gallon drums sat on a ring of cinderblocks.

Phong pointed to Henry Cho's left arm that dangled by his side. "What is wrong with your arm?"

"It is partially paralyzed. So is my left leg."

"You will be useless here. Go." Phong spat out a series of instructions in rapid Vietnamese.

The two soldiers who'd escorted them grabbed Cho's arm and led him away. Randy started to reach for Hank, fearing that he was about to be shot. But Ashley, who was standing next to Randy, grabbed his arm.

"O.K.," said Phong, "that means you five will have to work harder and longer."

Phong picked up a long, thin rod of bamboo and rapped a pile of material on a sheet of what looked like wax paper. The mass was dark brown, almost black in color. A sticky sweet, flowery smell wafted up from it.

Phong had a high-pitched, reedy voice that matched his short, slight frame. "Opium and morphine base have very distinctive smells. Raw opium smells sweet, like flowers. Morphine has an oily, pungent smell. You will learn the difference. This is the raw gum that is scraped from the opium plant. A farmer uses a sharp, curved knife to make a series of vertical cuts around the pod. After a few days, this gum oozes out. At first, it is cream colored. As it dries and hardens, it turns this color. Farmers in Laos and Cambodia collect the gum and form it into bricks or balls that are wrapped in plastic or leaves. We prefer bricks like this one that weigh approximately one kilogram, so we give them tins to fill."

Twice the bamboo thwacked the table. It occurred to Randy that if Duong had used bamboo instead of hoses, his beatings would have been worse. "Each shipment will be approximately one hundred kilograms. I expect one every ten days."

Randy did the math. If one kilogram equaled two point two oh four five pounds, they were about to process just over two hundred and twenty pounds. If that wasn't a large shipment, what was?

If anyone had told Randy, when he swore to "defend the Constitution and the United States against all enemies, foreign and domestic," that he would be standing as a POW listening to a Vietnamese drug-dealer describe how to convert raw opium into morphine base, he would have laughed.

Phong pointed to the black painted drums. "In each of these drums we will boil water. My men will turn the burners on and off. You are not to touch them, ever. When the water is at a full boil, you will mix in the lime we will measure for you. Based on the weight of the raw opium, we know the amount needed."

He reached between two of the drums and pulled out what looked like a cut-down boat oar. "With this paddle, you will stir the mixture of lime and raw opium until a white film begins to form on the top of the water."

Phong pulled out a second piece of carved wood from between the drums. It looked like a pizza peel with a shallow depression. "With this, you will scoop up the white film, which is morphine, and empty it into buckets that we will provide. When they are three quarters full, you will carry the bucket to the drying table."

Randy raised his hand. "Excuse me, Major, I have a question."

"Yes, you may ask your question."

"Major Phong, how long does it take for the morphine film to form?"

"It depends on how many bricks you put in. We normally add ten bricks and it takes about twenty to thirty minutes, depending on how many impurities are in the opium base."

"Major, how often do we have to clean the drums?"

"That is two questions. What is your name?"

"I am Lieutenant Pulaski."

"Ahhh… You are inquisitive, no?"

"I just wanted to know if we had to clean the drums between each batch."

"No, you do not. The impurities drop to the bottom. At the end of each day we let the water cool, and then we drain out the impurities. The water turns from dark brown or black to gray, then gets almost clear. That's when you will close the valve and add more fresh water. Clear?"

Randy nodded and raised his hand. Phong nodded.

"Where does the water come from?"

"We pipe it from a small river nearby. We are not worried about impurities in the water."

Again Randy nodded.

"Good. Let us move on to the next step." Phong marched to two long tables with tops made from galvanized metal. With the five Americans again in a row, he began. "The buckets with the morphine film are dumped into these vats. Before the buckets are filled again, you will rinse them with fresh water. There is a hose by the first drum. In this second vat is a mixture of ammonia and water. We boil the mixture that you will stir. Yes, it stinks. You will get used to it. When my men are satisfied the mixture is the right consistency, you will open the valve at the bottom and drain the liquid into another bucket. The liquid is poured through this cloth filter into this third drum, leaving a brown paste. You will then scoop out the paste and put it into forms that we will give you. Each form is stacked at the end of the table until it cools. It should take you two to three days to turn one hundred kilograms of raw opium into morphine base. Drying takes two or three days. Then, you will wrap each brick of morphine in three layers of plastic. That takes a day. When all the paste is wrapped, your work is done until the next shipment arrives."

The little Vietnamese man's face hardened. " My men and I will watch you very closely. We know this process. Do not attempt to collect samples. We know, based on the amount of raw opium we begin with, how much morphine base should be produced to within a few grams. If I think you are not working hard, I will encourage you with this piece of bamboo. If you try to steal the opium or try to sabotage the process, you will be shot."

Chapter 5
NEW BEGINNINGS

Friday, January 8, 1971, 1635 local time, Hanford

Despite her ski jacket, Janet shivered as she walked from her car into the house. Thick fog shrouded the valley, and driving back from the dojo had felt surreal. Her normal routine was ten minutes of stretching, followed by practicing katas for at least an hour, then sparring. Today, before the supervised sparring sessions, Janet had spent a good fifteen minutes pounding her frustrations away on the punching bag.

She was drinking a glass of the filtered water she kept in the refrigerator when the phone rang.

"Hi, Janet, it's Helen."

Janet was pleasantly surprised. Helen wasn't due home until Sunday. "Hi, where are you?"

"Home. I left three days early because I couldn't take being around my relatives any more. They were treating me like I was a fragile Christmas ornament. Where have you been? I called the house a couple of times and no answer."

"At the dojo. I walked in thirty seconds before you called."

"So you're all hot and sweaty..."

"And smelly."

"Hmmm, sounds delicious."

"I need a shower."

"I need you. I like you when you are hot, sweaty, and smelly."

Janet could feel her juices begin to flow, knowing what the next few hours would bring. She was glad Helen was back.

Monday, January 18, 1971, 0938 local time, Union City, NJ

The view from his eighth floor apartment gave Raul Moya a clear view of Donnelly Park, the Hudson River and the skyline of mid-town Manhattan. *If I can't fly, at least I can have the eagle's view.* At night, the apartment and office buildings on the other side of the river were stacks of little yellow blocks of light broken by bands of black where the lights were out.

Six months after retiring from the CIA, Raul had bought the eight-story building as an investment in a neighborhood called "Havana on the Hudson" that had seen better days. Many of his tenants and neighbors were Cuban exiles. Raul had paid a fraction of what the building would have cost ten years before, and nothing near what it would be worth in a few years more. It was, he could tell, a prime location.

Rent from the tenants more than offset the mortgage, and he used the extra money to fund updating the elevators and renovating the entire top floor that he kept for himself. And, as renters moved out, the apartments were renovated. The word had gotten out that he had a clean, well-maintained building, and his agent had a waiting list.

To help him get on with his life, the CIA had set up a series of job interviews. The flight operations manager job with the Port Authority of New York and New Jersey interested him the most because it would keep him in aviation. So far, however, no firm had offered him a job.

Raul was watching the wind create whitecaps on the gray-blue Hudson River when the phone rang. He was expecting a call from the Port Authority's HR department, so he went inside. The cold, damp weather made his leg ache and he kept the top of the cane close to his hip as he made his way across the living room. He no longer noticed the weight of the steel brace that went from just below his hip to a plastic plate under his foot.

"Buenos días, compadre. This is Ken."

"Ken?" Raul wasn't sure who was on the line. He knew several Kens.

"Ken, from your former employer. The one in logistics."

"Ahhhh, that Ken." Raul switched to Spanish because Ken from logistics was a fellow Cuban. Ken had run Air America's supply organization. If it was needed, Ken found it. "What can I do for you?"

The reply was also in Spanish. "It is not what you can do for me, but what I think you can do for the agency."

The word agency was odd. Raul had thought he was done with the CIA.

"What do you mean?"

"Meet me for lunch and I'll tell you. All I can say over the phone is that it will be very lucrative."

"O.K. Where and when?"

Raul copied down an address. He'd take a cab to the PATH Station at Exchange Place in Jersey City and then walk from the station to the restaurant. Estimated transit time—about forty-five minutes. Flight planning habits died hard. He'd leave at eleven to make sure he got there by noon.

The restaurant was near the station that had been known as Radio City Row until it was acquired through eminent domain by the City of New York. The Port Authority had also bought the name and right of way from the Hudson and Manhattan Railroad. The renamed line was called the Port Authority Trans Hudson line or PATH. By 1971, the city's announced plan to build the World Trade Center on this land was well underway.

Raul was fifteen minutes early, and the maître d' escorted him to a booth in the back that encircled a round table which could easily seat six. Red napkins were folded in a tent between two settings of polished silverware on the white, starched tablecloth.

The plates had the restaurant's name discreetly inscribed in the brick-red rings that bordered the plates. The leather backing of the booth rose all the way to the ceiling, creating a semi-enclosed space, almost a separate dining room. Other booths were arranged so they opened at different angles to the aisle. Raul concluded that this restaurant catered to those who wanted to have very private discussions.

Raul ordered a cup of coffee, then went back to reading John Fowles' *The French Lieutenant's Woman*. The Ken from logistics he knew was habitually late. But people do change; right on the dot of noon, the waiter ushered a tall man to the booth.

His hair was gray, but his body was showing no signs of being fifty. Ken leaned over the table and held out his hand. "Raul, don't get up! It's good to see you."

"Likewise." Raul put the bookmark back into the novel and laid it on the booth seat.

The two men waited until the waiter left with their drink orders and another server put a plate of crusty rolls and butter on the center of the table.

"How's the leg?"

"It's there. Any time a cold front comes through or we have a significant change in humidity, it tells me about it." Those moments also reminded Raul how lucky he was to have survived the crash. The memory of "The Swede" dying in his arms never faded.

"What do you hear from the Port Authority?"

Raul suspected Ken already knew the answer. He wouldn't be surprised if the CIA had a role in slowing down the hiring process, if they wanted him for something else. "I've been interviewed several times. They like my qualifications and I'm one of the finalists."

"Are you interested in doing freelance work for the agency?"

"It depends. What does the agency want?"

"We're looking for an independent contractor who provides transportation services. We'll set you up in business, but then you are on your own. The agency or one of our clients will tell you where they want something picked up and delivered, and it is up to you to make it happen. You can add your own clients as you wish. The only thing we ask is that the agency gets priority—and deniability."

"Sounds interesting. I don't have any formal training in this type of work. How do I learn?"

"It's just what you did in Africa. Instead of flying the planes, you'll contract with the owners and tell the pilots where to go and when. All you have to do is deliver. We'll start off small and slow and let you gain experience and build your business."

Both men stopped speaking while their main courses were delivered. The break gave Raul time to think.

"What kind of money are we talking about?"

Ken was taking a bite of his N.Y. strip steak. He liked his steaks well done, which meant the chunks needed lots of chewing. "Some transactions will be in the millions, others in the thousands or hundreds of thousands. We negotiate a fee with you to move it. On some occasions, we'll tell you where the cargo is, and then you buy and move it. Other times, you'll be told by the owner of the material."

"And the agency is not involved."

"Correct. Once we set you up, we'll work through cutouts. If anything goes bad, the agency isn't involved."

"When do you want to have me set up and operational?"

"June of this year."

"I'd need to find a place to work from. That will take time."

"No, you don't. The floor you reserved for yourself will work as your office. All you need are a few phone lines. You don't want the overhead, or the visibility, of a big facility."

Raul rubbed his chin. "How long do I have to decide?"

Ken put his fork down. "Today. You are either in or out. If you are in, then tomorrow you come to my office and sign a few papers to set up the bank accounts. With the paperwork done, we'll finalize a plan to get you up and running by June, and communication protocols. Everything from that day on is through cutouts."

Ken had one more item in his pitch. He knew the way to hook Raul was by making the proposition mysterious and exciting. The money was icing on the cake. "Trust me, this will make you more money in a month than working for the Port Authority in a year. But that's the least of it. You get to be your own boss, and you get to travel."

Ken is right. This is a lot more interesting than planning and monitoring a daily flight schedule. When he'd gotten out of the hospital he'd updated his Rolodex, so he already knew many of the people he could call. Raul buttered a crusty roll and bit off a large chunk. It gave him time to think and let Ken stew a bit.

"I'm in. What time tomorrow and where?"

Ken slid a card across the table. "Good. One warning. We don't care who your non-agency customers are, just don't do something that you know would put this country or the agency at risk. We frown on traitors."

Monday, March 22, 1971, 2045 local time, Hanford

On the anniversary of Helen husband's shoot down, many POW wives came by. This tradition began after American aviators started becoming POWs and was one of the many ways the wives supported each other. Shoot-down anniversaries were poignant reminders of how long the individual had either been missing or known to be a POW. They were endured, not celebrated. It was still not known if Bob Starkey was a POW or dead.

Women from the local chapter of the National League of Families of American Prisoners and Missing in Southeast Asia started arriving right after Helen got home from work. Many had been without their husbands since 1965—six long years. Janet felt sorry for their children because they had fathers in name only. This void made having a normal childhood, whatever that was, impossible.

Janet had been with Helen all weekend and busied herself

111

playing hostess. Endless cups of coffee were filled, and the never-ending stream of food was put on plates and served. She stayed in the background and avoided getting into conversations with the other women. For one thing, Janet didn't want to give away their growing relationship. For another, she didn't want to risk revealing her radical political views. She was adamantly opposed to the war. Helen knew about her opposition, just not how strongly she felt. Actually, both women avoided news about the war unless it was about POWs. This was a defense mechanism, since it was an awkward truth that if the U.S. had not been at war, they would each be home in their beds with their husbands, not with each other.

And then there had been the call on Thursday from Bernadette, telling her to check her post office box. A letter with instructions on what the movement wanted her to do was coming.

Exasperated and worn down by the subtle but constant pressure from Bernadette, Janet had told the movement's leader to suggest something that she would be good at. Janet was about to find out what that was.

Between now and then, there was tonight with Helen. It would be like the last two: holding Helen as she cried, followed by bouts of intense sex.

Thursday, March 25, 1971, 1426 local time, North Vietnam

After processing the first batch of opium, Randy concluded there was little they could do to sabotage the refining process. It was too simple, and the output too predictable. X number of kilos of raw opium in, Y number of kilos of morphine base out.

When Pham came to inspect their work, Ashley asked, "Why us? Why don't you use your own men?"

Pham's answer was as calculated as it was cold. "Because I you are an asset I own and control without any interference from any one, family or friends or government. And later I can sell you for a handsome profit. I could not do that with my men."

Cooperation earned rewards. The first was a set of black

baggy clothes as an alternative to the striped pajamas Duong had made them wear; the second was a shower shed. Pham provided materials and they built it. The sun heated the water in two black drums on the roof of the shed, so they got to have warm water showers in the late afternoon. Better food was the third reward. From Vinh, Pham's men brought back ice chests filled with fresh fish, chicken, and pork, along with bags of rice and packaged noodles to go along with vegetables from the farm.

Then, as they got better at the tasks, the pace picked up. At first, hundred-kilo batches of raw opium showed up every two weeks. Then, according to the notches on the pole, they started coming every ten days, and then once a week.

The increased production caused Pham and Phong to smile, but didn't change the fact that no matter what they did or what Pham provided, they were still kidnapped prisoners of war working as slaves. The distant crump of bombs and the occasional sighting of a jet gave them hope and kept up their morale. When that stopped, they would know the war was over. The "Then what?" conundrum was depressing.

After four months together they had settled into their roles. Cho was the cook and housekeeper, letting the others tend the garden and work in the factory. They were all talked out, so not much was said at the dinner table. Randy decided to say what he was sure was on all their minds.

"Guys, listen up. Remember what Pham told us the first day we got here?"

Jeff Anderson answered. "He said no one knows that we exist."

Randy replied, "Exactly. So the question is, how do we change that?"

Ashley was fixated on getting ahold of Pham's PRC-90 radio. "With our aviator's authentication answers, we could convince someone that we exist. But I haven't seen it since our first day. What else is there?"

"Escape," Jeff said. "We get out of here and head east. If we get to the coast, we can steal a boat. Or we get caught by the real North Vietnamese Army. We may get tortured or shot, but there's a chance we'll wind up at the Hanoi Hilton, not imprisoned by a bunch of drug runners playing soldier."

"Randy, you're the chemical engineer. Is there anything we can do to blow up the factory and kill our captors?"

Randy shook his head. "Not really. Any kind of big boom puts us all at risk."

"Not if we know when it's going to go off and we get into the hole ahead of time," Ashley countered. "The blast would pass over us, and the only risk would be if something fell on us. That would be a 'shit happens.'"

One side of Randy's mouth curled up and he rubbed his chin.

Jeff looked at his fellow Naval Aviator and A-7 pilot. "Randy, I've seen that look before. What are you thinking?"

"We'd need a fertilizer high in ammonium nitrate, diesel fuel, a large container, and some sort of detonator. We have the ammonia that Pham gave us to use as a cleaner. So Karl, what plants will do better with lots of nitrogen?"

"All of them."

Randy's mind began to race. "Good. Ashley, ask Pham for the highest nitrogen content you think he can get. Hank, I want you to dry some ammonia to see how much salt we can get out of it. Then we'll take some charcoal from the fireplace and try to make gunpowder."

"Where are you going with this?"

"I want to see if we can make a bomb using old-fashioned gunpowder. Young bamboo, like the stalks they gave us for stakes in the garden, might make an ideal pipe bomb if we pack the ends with mud and let it dry. Black powder is made from saltpeter, sulfur, and charcoal. We have charcoal. Saltpeter is really potassium nitrate. Any fertilizer with high nitrate content will do. What we need is a source of sulfur. I'm going to look at the liquid that comes out of the first stage of the opium refining process and see what we get when it dries. Ashley, ask Pham for a bucket that we can fill with the sediment from the first barrel. Tell him we want to try it as fertilizer."

"O.K. I'll do it."

"Here's the next step: Hank tests the mixtures each time he uses a match to light the fireplace. Black powder is a low-power explosive, but I think if we can put it in bamboo, it will act as a bomb. I agree with Jeff. We need to figure out how to get out of here and into the clutches of the regular North Vietnamese Army."

Ashley propped his elbows on the table and rested his mouth on his fingers. "Creating a bomb is risky. If Pham finds out what we're doing, it will go badly for us. So, we're either all in or we keep the status quo. It's either-or."

The dim light from a single sixty-watt bulb added to the atmosphere of conspiracy. Ashley turned to his fellow Green Beret. "Hank?"

"I'm in. I'll work on the fusing and the mixture. I started out as a combat engineer."

"Karl?"

"In."

"Greg?"

"In."

"Jeff?"

"Absolutely in."

"O.K. Randy, you're the bomb designer and project engineer. Hank, since you're left alone in the garden and the hooch most of the day, you're the builder. We start tomorrow."

Friday, April 2, 1971, 1546 local time, Hanford
The sight of the letter in the P.O. box triggered a mixture of fear, anticipation, and excitement. Janet had no idea what was in it, or how she would react once she read its contents. It sat unopened on the passenger's seat as she drove home.

In her kitchen, she stared at the letter as she sipped a glass of Chivas Regal. The three fingers of amber liquid meant no trip to the dojo that afternoon. Any hint of alcohol and the sensei sent you away. Show up a second time with alcohol on your breath and you were told never to return as you were ushered out the door.

Finally, she slid her pocketknife under the flap. Inside was a note with familiar handwriting and a half of a torn photograph.

Janet,

Be in Mexico City on the first Monday, May 17th. It is after finals. Book a room at the Hotel Geneve de Ciudad in the central business district. Plan on being gone until the middle of September.

Your contact will have the other half of the picture.

Bernadette

The torn photo fell face down on the coffee table. When Janet turned it over, she saw it was one Bernadette had asked a passerby to take of the two of them on a park bench in Hanford. Janet's half showed Bernadette.

Four months? It must be some type of training program. Summer school and registering for the fall semester were now out the window. As for Helen....

It can't last. We agreed to split once our hubbies were home. The longer we're lovers, the harder it will be to split up. Why doesn't this fucking war end? Then we can find out if our husbands are alive or dead.

Friday, April 30, 1971, 1423 local time, North Vietnam

Rivulets of blood ran down the American pilot's shins and thighs where slivers of bamboo had been inserted. The man's dark face was a mess of bruises from earlier beatings and partially healed cuts. Bloody saliva dripped from the unconscious man's mouth to pool on the floor of the interrogation room in the Cu Loc POW camp in a southwest suburb of Hanoi.

Enrique Payá was the most senior of four Cuban interrogators. All were from the Girón Brigade, sent to Vietnam supposedly to help repair battle damage. Their real purpose was to interrogate

American POWs.

Lieutenant Colonel Payá was from Cuban Intelligence Directorate or *Dirección de Inteligencia*, also known as G2. He examined his handiwork. The next round would consist of yanking out the bamboo slivers, leaving tiny splinters under the skin that would cause infections. If the new round of torture didn't wake the prisoner, Payá would douse him with ice-cold water. If that didn't work, they would return him to his fellow prisoners and see if they could awaken him. If not, he would die. *No es gran cosa. Hay otros para interrogar.* No big deal, there were others to interrogate.

"*Teniente coronel* Payá." The voice came from one of the Vietnamese officers who ran the prison. He was known as "The Lump" because he had a large fatty tumor on his forehead. The Cuban turned around. "Yes, Colonel Dang."

"The papers you were waiting for have arrived."

"Good, how many?"

"Seventeen were authorized. Along with the paperwork documenting the transfer to G2, you will get a file I prepared with the information we gathered on each pilot.

"Excellent."

"May I ask where you are planning to take them?"

"Los Maristas in Havana. It is where we hold all our counter-revolutionary prisoners."

"Will the Americans find out that you have them?"

"I doubt it. Anyway, what can they do? Invade us? They tried that once using Cuban traitors and it didn't work."

Friday, June 4, 1971, 1032 local time, Jersey City, NJ

At the suggestion of the CIA, ownership of Raul's building was shifted to a new corporation, International Property Management, to separate it from the operating company, International Logistics Services or ILS. His lawyer reported that the changes went through the government and financial institutional bureaucracies like shit through a goose. Raul was sure the CIA had paved the way.

While the eighth floor was being gutted, the CIA found Raul a temporary place to live. Tenants on the seventh floor had their leases bought out and found new apartments that were as nice or nicer. Their moving expenses, security deposits and first six months' rent were paid by International Property Management through the agent Raul had hired to manage the building.

It didn't take the remaining tenants long to realize that the new phone lines, revamped steel fire escapes, new boilers that provided more hot water and heat, and new elevators—which incidentally restricted access to the seventh and eighth floors— were major improvements.

When his tenants saw Raul in the hall, they thanked him, but expressed fear that the changes, which must be costly, no? would affect the rents. He assured them that he was not about to raise the rents to rates they couldn't afford.

Licenses from New Jersey and New York to purchase and carry firearms, and the Type 11 Federal Firearms License, arrived in the mail. This gave Raul and his firm the authority to import, purchase and sell ammunition (including armor piercing), firearms, and a long list of explosive devices. The package included record keeping requirements and instructions for paying appropriate taxes.

All the construction work was done and the final walkthrough was on June 1. Raul moved back in the next day. On June 4th he was still settling in. During a break from unpacking, through a pair of binoculars Raul watched a couple unfurl their boat's sails as it exited the marina on the west side of Manhattan. A Port Authority helicopter flew through his field of view. Raul was musing about what working for the Port Authority might be like when the phone rang. *Why does it always ring when I'm on the other side of the office?*

"Allo, International Logistics Services." He didn't feel the business had gotten to the point where he could just use its initials.

"Good morning. My name is Max. A mutual friend gave me your name. We need some cargo moved in about two weeks."

"From where to where, and what's the weight."

"From a place in the Middle East to Angola. Pickup and delivery date is flexible by a day or two. Twenty-five thousand pounds already crated and on pallets."

"What will the manifest say?"

"Farm equipment."

He knew better than to ask for details. When he'd been a contract pilot for the CIA, he couldn't count the number of times the cargo manifest had said "Farm equipment," "Medical supplies," or "Factory machinery" when he knew damn well that he was carrying weapons and ammunition. If a customs inspector got curious, he always had a bag full of greenbacks to make him turn his head.

"What type of airport are we taking off and landing at?" Raul knew better than to ask the name of the departure airport and destination until an agreement was reached.

"Departure airport's shortest runway is nine thousand feet. Destination is twenty-five hundred miles away and has five thousand feet of smooth dirt and gravel, not asphalt. Both are near sea level."

That meant no jets. "Who does the loading and unloading?"

"My people load, customer unloads. You provide the plane and crew. Plane should be on the ground for only an hour or two. We may have up to ten passengers and their baggage for the trip back. No special needs."

"Is gas available at the destination?"

"No."

Raul knew that "no special needs" meant that no special medical equipment was needed for passengers, and that hazardous material would be in the baggage. "How soon do you need an answer?"

"How soon can you have one?"

"Twenty-four hours." Raul knew two owners with four-engine

Douglas DC-6Bs parked in the Middle East. These airplanes had been built in the 1960s for the U.S. Navy as C-118Bs and had reinforced floors. Twenty-five thousand pounds was well within their payload. They could make the outbound leg non-stop but would need to stop for gas for the return trip home.

"Give me a phone number and I'll call you tomorrow about the same time with a price."

International Logistics Services was open for business.

Chapter 6
NEW SKILLS

Monday, May 17, 1971, 1413 local time, Mexico City

The days before Janet left were filled with decisions. It was more than what to wear. What identity should she travel under? Julia Amy Lucas? She'd had a passport since she was sixteen. It was two years from expiring. Or as Janet Anne Williams? That passport was one only a year old. Or as Janet Williams Pulaski? Randy had insisted she get one with her married name, and it was brand new. Or as Jamie Elizabeth Symonds? This passport showed her as a resident of Nevada and had arrived a month ago.

For this trip, she decided, she would be Julia Amy Lucas. It was the name Bernadette knew. Janet planned to play dumb broad if she was asked why she hadn't changed her passport to match her married name and new address.

Then there was money for travel expenses. That solution was simple. She pulled five thousand dollars out of the movement's safe deposit box, and at a local bank moved the cash into two blue billfolds, each filled with twenty-five 100-dollar American Express Traveler's Checks. Janet didn't want to park the Volvo in a parking lot for four months, so she called Brad, who came over and disconnected the battery of both cars and put them on stand jacks. He gave her the name of a friend who was an instructor in the A-7 RAG who would reconnect them for her when she got back.

Monthly bills were easy. She met with an accountant and gave him signed checks covering her recurring bills, along with a check for one thousand dollars to cover the water and utility bills, which would be minimal. He would mail them on the assigned dates.

Helen insisted on driving Janet to LA. Her lover questioned her cover story about bumming around Mexico, Central and South America for several months, but eventually, at least on the surface, Helen accepted it.

Except for a few hours on the nearby beach, they spent their last night together riding their favorite double dildo. It vibrated and pulsed as they sat face-to-face, kissing and stroking each other until they collapsed or the batteries wore out. No worries, Helen had brought a bag of spares!

During dinner at a nearby restaurant, a short walk from their hotel in Venice, Helen got a glazed look on her face and shuddered. She put her hand to her mouth to muffle the moans, and her Alabama drawl thickened as she spoke. "When I got dressed, I put a small vibrator called a butterfly on my clit.... I've always wanted to have an orgasm in public, and now I just did."

Janet laughed.

As the airplane approached the Mexican capital on Sunday afternoon, Janet could see a gray-blue layer of pollution hanging over the city. Looking at the haze from an airplane was different from living in it. Outside the terminal, the acidic mix of wood and charcoal smoke, ozone, and car exhaust tasted and smelled awful. It made LA on a bad day seem like breathing pure air.

The second thing that hammered her was the altitude. Mexico City was at seven-thousand, three-hundred feet, and Janet had never been that far above sea level other than one trip to the Rockies to go skiing. The walk to a restaurant in the Zona Rosa's pedestrian mall forcibly brought home to her that the air had much less oxygen, and the pollution made her want to take a shower.

Then there was the poverty. This was the first time Janet had been outside the U.S., other than a trip to Europe. From the Boeing 727 she'd seen shantytowns on the hillsides surrounding the city. From the taxi, she saw the vibrant mix of rich and poor neighborhoods. Every block was a reminder that she was in a Third World country.

When she walked into the lobby of the Hotel Geneve de Ciudad after dinner, the front desk clerk waved at her. *"Señora Lucas, I have an envelope for you."*

Janet took the light gray envelope; it had her name written on the front. *"Gracias, Señor Lopes."* In her best college Spanish, she asked the clerk when it had been delivered and was told it had arrived less than thirty minutes before.

In her room, she slit open the envelope, using the razor-sharp, four-inch blade on the bone-handled switchblade her oldest brother had given her as a birthday present. She always kept it in her purse. Inside was a typewritten note.

Go to the Angel of Independence Monument. It is only a few blocks from your hotel. Sit on the bench next to the large blocks of stone. Be there at 10 a.m. tomorrow. I will present my credentials.

José

Using a map, the concierge showed Janet how to get from the hotel to the *Plaza Angel de la Independencia.* It was, he said in Spanish, a pleasant fifteen-minute walk. "But," he warned, "be careful crossing the street because many of the drivers are crazy."

Back in her room, Janet opened her suitcase. In it was a present Helen had given her the night before, with an admonishment that she was not to open it unless she was horny or bored, or both. Now was a good time.

Underneath the wrapping paper was a note on top of a golden box with brown lettering. Inside were a dozen chocolate truffles, slightly melted from the heat.

Janet,

Think of me as you are eating these. They are as delicious as you are. Come back soon and in one piece.

Helen

The note made her smile. She popped a truffle into her mouth. The smooth chocolate coated her tongue with delicious creaminess as the liqueur released its flavor. It did make her think of Helen.

Tuesday, May 18 1971, 0942 local time, Mexico City

It only took Janet eight minutes to get to the monument. Being early gave her time to walk around the statue before sitting to watch the green VW Beetle cabs race around the plaza. From her chosen spot Janet could see up and down the tree-lined *Paseo de la Reforma*. Other than pigeons and people crossing the plaza as a short cut to another part of the central business district, there was hardly anyone nearby.

Janet waited. She'd brought a paperback, intending to read, but instead, she watched those who approached… and passed on. She held the switchblade in her right hand. It felt warm and comforting. She spotted a man wearing a white shirt and slacks who paused for a second, then headed in her direction. He sat down on the bench next to her.

"*Buenos días, señora.* I am José." He held out the torn half of a picture. Janet had her half stuck in the paperback. She showed him that they fit together.

"*Buenos días.* I am Julia."

"I understand you speak some Spanish?"

"Very little."

"You will learn." José looked at the woman sitting on the bench. A pair of dark green eyes stared coldly back at him from beneath sandy, almost brown hair. She looked fit, and he sensed this woman had an inner strength. If she was afraid, it didn't show. *She will do very well.* "Did you bring the extra passport photos with you?"

"I did." She handed him a folder with photos she'd had taken right after getting her hair cut. Helen had liked her shorter, more mannish "do"; it matched her aggressiveness in bed.

"This evening a package will be delivered to you. In it will be your ticket to Havana on a Mexicana Airlines flight tomorrow morning, and a Canadian passport under the name of Jennifer Rachel Bertrand with a visitor's visa for Cuba. There will be information on your Canadian background. Memorize it, then flush everything but passport and travel documents down the toilet. When you get to Havana, you will be met where you collect your luggage."

Janet nodded, and José walked away.

Wednesday, May 19, 1971, 1056 local time, Cuba

As the Mexicana Airlines Boeing 727 approached landing, Janet saw the bright blue waters of the Gulf of Mexico and a harbor with just a few large ships. The two Spanish-built stone forts on either side of the harbor mouth stood out from the rest of the city, which looked like a maze of apartment buildings and large houses.

Walking down the stairway to the concrete ramp, the brightness of the sun sent Janet scrambling to find her sunglasses. By the time she got them on, her skin was already moist from sweat. The flight attendant had announced the temperature in Havana was 91 degrees Fahrenheit and the humidity 80 per cent.

A few steps outside immigration, a man holding up a sign with the name "Jennifer" printed on it in large letters approached and told her in heavily accented English that he was her driver. He loaded her bag into a 1955 Chevy that had seen better days, and drove her to a large, three-story house. Janet guessed it had once belonged to a wealthy Cuban who was now either in the U.S., in a jail in Cuba, or dead.

After leading her to a large sitting room, the driver pointed to a small threadbare couch. She sat down and he left, carrying her bag to who knew where. She checked her watch, not the wonderful Rolex Randy had bought for her, but a cheap Timex she'd bought for this trip. Thinking of Randy, she felt a stab of anger and grief.

She'd been there five minutes when a man entered, carrying a file of papers. He dressed as if he'd come out of a clothing store in LA.

He extended his hand. "Welcome to Havana, Jennifer. I'm Enrique Payá. I hope you had a pleasant flight." He rolled the R in his first name in the classical Castilian Spanish pronunciation, even though he was speaking in English.

Janet shook his hand. "Thank you, I did. I am interested in hearing what you have planned for me."

"You don't know?"

"No." Her voice was flat and unemotional.

Either this woman has cojones the size of watermelons or she is naïve as hell. I will bet, based on what I read in her dossier, on watermelons. "Well, let me tell you." Payá flipped open the file, which proved to be a dossier on her; it contained her training plan, background notes, and itinerary.

"Your movement has asked us to train you as an assassin." Enrique let this astonishing pronouncement hang in the air.

"Interesting." *That explains the grilling I got from Bernadette about how much hunting I'd done with my brothers and father, and what I knew about guns.* "So where and when do we start?"

"Do you want to know about the course and what you will be doing for the next few months?"

"I do." *I wonder where Enrique learned English.*

"Good. Before I begin, I must give you some ground rules. From this point on, you will have a Cuban identity card and internal passport. For the purpose of this course, your name is Luna. During the course, you will meet others undergoing different types of training, and everyone goes by only their first names. If any instructor asks you, tell him your last name is Serrano. It is a common Mexican last name. Understood?"

"Yes." *Serrano is also a chili pepper hotter than a jalapeño. An interesting choice of name.*

"The course will be difficult and challenging. If at any time you cannot continue, we will have to decide what to do with you. There are, as you can imagine, only a few options."

Yeah, kill me, imprison me, force me to stay on this island for the rest of my life, or send me back to the U.S. knowing they can blackmail me for the rest of my life.

"Most of your training will be in Spanish. I understand you speak some. Is that true?"

"I do, but I don't speak very well." Enrique switched to Spanish. "By the end of the course, you will." He held out his hand. "May I have your Canadian passport? You will get it back when you leave, and it will be yours to use as you see fit. As part of this course, you will learn more about the Canadian legend we crafted for you."

"Legend?" Janet asked.

"That is another word for a cover."

Janet handed him the blue passport.

"Do you have your American passport with you?"

"No."

"Where is it?"

"In a safe place." It was in a bank vault in Mexico City.

Enrique studied the young woman in front of him. *She is not sweating and doesn't appear to be nervous. This tells me that she can control her emotions. She does not act like an amateur and has already made a smart move by stashing her U.S. passport.* "Well, then, let's start your training."

Enrique led Janet to a room where the contents of her suitcase were laid out on a table. Next to the suitcase was a brown paper bag. On the other side of the rom, two women in green fatigues and red berets stood at parade rest. Enrique turned to Janet. "Are these all your things?"

She flipped over a few items of clothing, then looked in all the pockets of her suitcase. There was nothing missing. *"Sí."*

"Please empty your purse." Janet complied. Enrique picked up the switchblade. He opened and closed the blade several times. "Very nice."

"It was a present from my brother."

"The knife will be returned to you when you leave, along with the money. How much is here?"

"Four-thousand, five-hundred dollars in traveler's checks, and about fifty dollars' worth of Mexican pesos in my wallet."

Enrique spoke slowly in Spanish. "Here is your uniform. More clothing will be waiting for you at the training camp." The brown bag contained a shirt, pants, white athletic socks, boots, and a red beret. Enrique pointed to a bathroom. After changing, Janet looked in the mirror and saw a different person looking back. Her name was Luna Serrano—the name sewn over the breast pocket said so.

The next step was a visit with a nurse, who asked in English about her vaccinations. Janet tried to explain she had a shot record that showed she didn't need any shots. The nurse shook her head and gave Janet injections in each arm. She pointed to Janet's right arm and said, "Yellow fever." Then she pointed to her left bicep. "Diphtheria. Next week you will get shots for typhoid and bubonic plague."

After a simple meal, Janet boarded a small twin-engine turboprop airplane with a sparse interior. She smiled, thinking that if Randy were with her, he could tell her what the airplane was, who manufactured it, and something about it. She translated the logo *Fuerza Aérea Revolucionaria* as Revolutionary Air Force.

Enrique was the last of eight passengers—four men and four women—to board. All were dressed the same: black boots, tan fatigues, and a red beret. Janet was, as Randy would say, the only *gringo* on the plane.

There was no terminal where the plane landed an hour and ten minutes later, no vehicles that would suggest it was an airport, other than a fuel truck parked at the far end of an empty ramp, and a small bus. For a second, Janet wondered why the windows on the gray bus were open. *Oh, right. No air conditioning.* When the driver passed a faded, battered road sign, Janet saw it was for the *Aeropuerto Trinidad.*

A strange, pungent smell poured into the bus through the open windows a as they drove through a town, a mix of the uncollected garbage that lay everywhere, manure left by farm animals roaming the streets, smoke from coal fires, and exhaust from cars with tired engines. To one used to the relatively clean air of the San Joaquin Valley, it was an unpleasant odor.

The bus emerged from the city limits, and as they passed fields the smell changed from acrid pollution to the almost pleasant smell of freshly spread manure. Janet could see the road ahead disappear into the hills. They were about to climb into the Escambray Mountains north-northwest of Trinidad.

The driver pulled off the paved road onto one of packed red dirt, stopped, and four armed guards came out of a small shed to inspect the bus. Enrique, who sat next to the driver, gave the officer a sheaf of papers.

The officer waved to the guards, who opened the gate. Gears ground as the driver forced the shift lever into first, and the bus lurched forward on a road that was only a single vehicle's width.

An unsmiling woman strode up to Janet after she got off the bus. *"Soy Sargento Mayor Gómez. Sígueme, te llevaré a tus aposentos.* I am Sergeant Major Gomez. Follow me. I will lead you to your quarters."

Janet's quarters were a small building built on pilings so the floor was three feet off the ground. Sergeant Major Gomez pointed to the top bunk on one of the two racks in the room and turned to face Janet. Speaking slowly in Spanish, she said, "You have a meeting in the main classroom building in thirty minutes. I will come get you."

Janet nodded and said, *"Bueno."* She was pleased that she

understood Gomez.

Alone, Janet looked around the building. Besides the two racks of bunk beds, in the center of the room was a wooden table and four chairs. Against the wall opposite the door was a row of large metal lockers. On one was printed the name "Luna." From the porch, Janet could see the building the Sergeant Major had said contained the bathrooms and showers. The words "*Spartan*" and "*communal*" popped into her mind.

On her bunk, Janet found six more blouses similar to the one she was wearing, three pairs of the same long pants, four pairs of shorts, white athletic socks, and two pairs of boots, all neatly arranged in a row. Each uniform top had the name "Luna" embroidered over the right breast pocket. Six sets of pale gray panties and bras were at the end of the bed. Janet held up the bra and chuckled, wishing she could fill it out.

During the orientation they were told to expect to get up at 0630, have breakfast, and start training. Some of the classes would be physical conditioning, the rest would be specialized, based on what each of them was there to learn. Lights were to be turned off at 2130. This meeting was followed by dinner. The new arrivals ate separately and were herded back to the meeting room. Then there was another lecture. From the slides and what she could understand, it was about the history of the Cuban revolution.

When Janet got back to her quarters, the clump of boots on the steps announced the arrival of her roommates. Two—Zuilaika and Bedri—were Angolan. They smiled and said "Hi," then they giggled and spoke to each other in their native Umbundu and went back outside.

The third woman, a tall blonde, looked at Janet and said in English, "American, no?"

"*Si, soy americana.*" Janet replied.

"It's O.K. I would like to practice my English. I am Monika and I am from West Germany. When we are here in the cottage, the instructors don't care what we speak. Outside, we have to speak Spanish."

"I'm Luna."

The wooden chair scraped loudly as Monika pulled it out before she sat down. "And what city are you from?"

Let's see, on Sunday, I was an American. When I boarded the plane in Mexico City, I was a Canadian. Enrique didn't tell me what I should be here, so who am I? Janet's guard went up. Was Monika an informer, a student, or both? Was keeping your mouth shut part of the training and the constant testing?

Janet decided to play it straight. "I live in a small city in central California called Hanford."

Clearly it didn't register with Monika.

"I grew up in Heidelberg. It is known for its university and its castle." Monika uncrossed her legs. She appeared comfortable and relaxed. She had long legs and her breasts pushed out the pockets on her shirt. Janet had instant breast envy.

Monika sighed. "I have been here a month and it's train, train, train. Only day off is Sunday. The best thing is the rum and fruit juice they give us every night. Or you can have two bottles of local beer. As a German, I can tell you the beer is not bad."

"When do they bring the drinks?"

Monika smiled. "You missed them. They come at 2000 hours. You were in orientation."

"Oh," was all Janet could say. A little rum and fruit juice every night would be good.

The blonde looked at her watch. "It is 2115, so I am going to bed." Monika loosened her boots and pulled her shorts and top off. Janet tried not to be obvious as she admired the German woman's body. Undressing in front of three other women was something she was going to have to get used to.

Thursday May 20, 1971, 1926 local time, North Vietnam

When there were no drugs to process, the six Americans were free to tend their garden. Other than occasionally entering the compound for a cursory inspection, Pham left them alone.

131

It was dinner time, and Randy asked a question that had been on his mind. He had been wondering what, if he could have known was in store for him, might he have had done differently to avoid ending up in this dismal limbo. And what about the others? "So, Ashley how'd you decide on West Point?"

Ashley finished chewing before he answered. "It's strange. I'd always wanted to be a soldier. Getting in wasn't the problem. I had the grades, and my Congressman rarely used his appointments. That part was easy. But my family was horrified."

"What do you mean?"

"My parents, good liberals that they are, wanted me to go to an Ivy League school. Both of them had worked their way through college. The G.I. Bill helped pay for my dad's electrical engineering degree from Worchester Polytech. My mom got a degree in art from Boston University."

Ashley walked his chopsticks across the table, then made them dance. "The thing was, I was accepted into almost all the Ivy League schools they urged me to apply for. My procrastination in accepting any of them infuriated my parents. One afternoon, an officer from West Point called to tell me I was accepted and the official letter would arrive in a few days. I told him that I would definitely be coming."

The Green Beret shook his head as he thought about what had happened next. "I didn't tell my parents. I got home from school a few days later to find my mother waiting, holding a letter for me. I knew it was my acceptance letter, she didn't."

Ashley's faced worked oddly in the dim light as memories flooded over him. "That was a Friday, and at dinner I told my parents I was going to go to West Point. There was this utter silence while no one said a word. Then my older sister, who was a junior at Radcliffe, let fly an anti-war, anti-military diatribe. My younger brother, who was fourteen, didn't say anything. He knew a storm was coming. Finally, my father said, 'That's an interesting choice, Ashley. Tell me why." Not 'us,' as in 'your parents,' but 'me'. Then my mother said, 'I might as well start saying Kaddish for you.' Kaddish, if you don't know, is the Jewish prayer for the dead."

Randy interrupted. "I didn't know you were Jewish."

"Surprise, surprise!"

Everyone around the table laughed. "So what happened next?"

"It took a while before my father accepted it. My mother never did. A few weeks later, it was the first Passover Seder. In my family, that is a big deal. After the service, my grandmother asks me where I was going to go to school. Apparently, neither my mother nor father had told her. Maybe they didn't want to upset her. Maybe they hoped I'd somehow change my mind. So I say, in a loud clear voice, 'West Point.' And the conversation at the dinner table stops as all twenty-odd relatives stare at me."

Ashley leaned back. "My grandmother looks at me and says, 'Jews don't go into the Army.'" His voice took on a sing-song quality, and a distinct accent that was absent from his usual speaking voice. "'They become doctors, lawyers, dentists, accountants, businessmen, writers, artists, and actors. They even run hotels. But they don't go into the Army.' I told her that it was my choice, not hers, not my parents', but mine alone. It was what I wanted to do. You have to understand, my father's mother saw herself as the family matriarch, so this open challenge was not well received. She looked at me and said, 'You'll get killed, and for what?' My mother ran sobbing into the kitchen. After that night, my mother and grandmother tried at least a dozen times to talk me out of it, but in the end my parents drove me to West Point, showed up at every parents' weekend, and my grandmother came to my graduation!"

Ashley took a deep breath. "My being here is my mother and grandmother's worst nightmare. I need to get back to the U.S. alive to prove they were wrong."

Friday, May 21, 1971, 0926 local time, Cuba

The first session every morning after breakfast was political indoctrination. Each day, the message and subject was different but the purpose was clear—to make sure they were dedicated socialist/communist revolutionaries. *Entrenamiento de armas de fuego* ran from 0830 to 1230. This was followed by an hour for lunch, two hours of tradecraft, *habilidades tácticas,* and then *mano a mano, entrenamiento de combate.* Translation: a morning of firearms training followed by tactical tradecraft skills, ending with two hours of hand-to-hand combat.

When Janet arrived at the gun range for the first time, she was surprised to find there was only one other person, an instructor whose name tag said "Juan". He was standing in front of a row of pistols on a table.

"Have you ever fired any of these?"

Janet pointed to the Colt Model 1911. "Only that one."

Juan handed her the pistol, butt first, and a magazine, then pointed toward a target Janet estimated at five meters down range. "*Bueno.* Show me."

From the time she'd asked if she could shoot her older brother's .22 caliber rifle, her father and brothers had taught her to treat every gun as loaded until you knew otherwise. Janet pulled the slide back far enough to see that the firing chamber was empty, then rapped the magazine on the table to make sure all the rounds were properly seated. With practiced expertise, she slid the magazine into the pistol, racked the slide, and flicked the safety off. She spread her feet a little wider than her shoulders, her left foot slightly forward, and folded her left hand under and around her right. After taking a deep breath and exhaling, she squeezed off all seven rounds and ejected the magazine. The bottom of a Coke can could have easily covered the seven holes in the center of the target.

Juan nodded and held up his hand. *"Preste atención."*

He picked up the wooden target stand and moved it to ten meters away. Then he took pieces of tape and covered the holes made by the bullets from the first magazine. Janet reloaded. Using her thumb, she released the catch holding the slide open, letting it slam forward and shove a round into the ring chamber.

Using the same stance, she shot all seven rounds. This time the group was about an inch and a half in diameter.

"Bien, muy bien." Juan took the .45 and picked up a small pistol and a spare magazine. "This is a Makarov. It is smaller, lighter, and it is what we prefer to use for close-in work. Try it at five meters."

Janet aimed and dry fired it several times before she loaded the first magazine. The Makarov had much less recoil than the .45 or the Smith and Wesson .357 revolver her father had let her shoot. At five meters, all eight rounds were in the center, ten ring.

After shooting a magazine at ten and another at fifteen meters, Juan had Janet do move-and-shoot drills with the targets at different distances. He had her do each sequence three times. Each time, the bullet holes were in a tight circle that punched out the center of the bulls-eye.

The Cuban was smiling. His report would note that Luna was a natural shooter. He'd never had a student this good.

Then he had her shoot left-handed, thinking he would get a different result. The first magazine was all over the target. All the rounds from the second magazine were in the eight, nine and ten rings. The bullets from the third one were all in the ten ring. This, he reflected, was truly rare; she was indeed a natural.

Janet liked the small Soviet-designed pistol. It was easy to handle and had very little recoil. When Juan called the session to a halt, Janet estimated she'd fired over two hundred rounds.

"Tomorrow, *Luna,* we will start with drawing and shooting from behind cover. And I will see how good you are with a rifle. After that, I will design a course just for you. Whoever taught you to shoot knew what he was doing."

Janet nodded. *"Gracias."* She turned away so Juan would not see how the reference to her father and brothers made her eyes water.

Saturday, May 22, 1971, 1045 local time, Cuba
Photos of people on the targets added an element of realism to

the drills, and simulating the power of life and death made practice exciting. At first Juan started by having Janet fire a double tap standing still; then while she moved forward, diagonally, backward, and to the side. To change things up, Juan put dummy rounds into some of the magazines so that Janet could practice clearing jams and misfires as well as reloading.

After about three hundred rounds, Juan changed the drill to two rounds into the chest and one to the head. Then he had Janet practice single shots to the head from different positions and distances.

When Juan called for a break, the clock on the wall told her they'd been shooting for two-and-a-half hours. Sweat stains discolored her uniform shirt under the armpits, around her waist, and behind her neck. As she drank from a glass of water, Juan's assistant laid four bolt action rifles on the table.

Janet recognized one: the U.S.-made Model 1903 Springfield. It was the weapon her father had carried as a Marine sniper in World War II and Korea. The other three, she learned, were the German-made Mauser Karabiner 98K, the British Lee Enfield, and the Russian-made Mosin-Nagant. In slow Spanish, Juan explained that all four had been designed before World War I and were very accurate.

Asked which one she'd like to shoot, Janet pointed at the Springfield.

Lying on her stomach, Janet lined up the sights on a bull's eye at one hundred meters and squeezed off the first round. It was in the eight point ring. The next four were all in the small, three-inch circle of the ten ring.

Juan had his assistant move the target to 250 yards. The group of five holes was larger, but all were tens. He handed her another five-round stripper clip and she added five more holes near the center.

Lying on the mat, waiting for another one of Juan's assistants to put tape over the holes in the target, Janet realized she was enjoying the training. The more physical and the tougher it was, the more she liked it. And shooting turned her on.

Tuesday, July 20, 1971, 1726 local time, North Vietnam

After dinner, Hank put two bowls on the table next to each other. In his right hand, he held a piece of thin rope, glowing red hot at one end. "Everyone take a seat. It's time for show and tell."

The others grinned, and Ashley said, "By all means, show us."

"Well, we're a long way from a nitrogen-based explosive or even basic gunpowder. What we have is a fast-burning powder. To make it explosive, so to speak, we need something that can accelerate the rate of burn."

Cho touched the first bowl in the row. "I've been playing with mixtures and ground them with our new mortar and pestle provided by Pham, so the grains are more uniform. This is the first attempt."

When he touched the power with the red tip of the cord, the flame flashed hot and red.

Hank Cho blew on the glowing cord and held it over the second bowl. "This one has roughly 20% more dried ammonia chloride. Watch." He touched the grains in the bottom of the wooden bowl. *Whoosh.*

The men around the table felt the heat. "Not an explosion, but a much faster burn rate and much hotter. We still need something to accelerate and sustain the burn rate to increase pressure in a closed container and give us an explosion. That's what sulfur does in black powder, but we don't have enough match heads to get enough sulfur to make a bomb, so we need a replacement."

Randy knew they were on the right path. The container only had to be strong enough to hold the pressure for a few milliseconds before rupturing to release the explosion. "Any ideas on what we could use?"

"I do, but the question is, can we get it?"

The Same Day, 1623 local time, Cuba

Every few days, she was asked to come to the administrative

office. She was handed two or three postcards from places in South America and asked to write a note to a friend. It was, Enrique explained, a way they are building a cover for her time in Cuba. Some went to Helen, others to Bernadette, although she was sure that someone in Cuban intelligence was already keeping Bernadette informed of her progress through the course.

Thursday, July 22, 1971, 08260 local time, Hanoi

Every day had been much the same for Commander Richard O'Reilly since he'd arrived at the Hanoi Hilton over eight months ago, and each day had been a huge improvement over his time in Duong's prison camp. For hours at a time he sat in front of a table of Soviet and North Vietnamese officers who peppered him with questions. Tape recorders captured every word, to be transcribed and reviewed for the next day's session. His cell was spare, but fairly clean, and the mattress almost comfortable. He was fed the same horrible food the gooks ate, but at least it was fresh. The worst part of evenings was the boredom. The best part was that he was not tortured.

One morning, O'Reilly was taken to the camp for POWs referred to as "the Plantation." There the POW camp commander briefed him on the BACK U.S. guidelines for POW conduct in Vietnam, over and above the official Code of Conduct for POWs. The acronym stood for:

B—bow, i.e. don't bow in public

A—air, i.e. don't broadcast anything over the air

C—crime i.e. don't admit to any crimes

K—kiss, i.e. don't kiss, hug, shake hands with the North Vietnamese or make any other gesture that suggests you like your captors.

U.S.—unity over self, i.e. unity of the POWs as a group over what is best for an individual if it violates any of the B.A.C.K. principles.

O'Reilly told his fellow POWs that he'd been interrogated by both North Vietnamese and the Soviets. When asked by his fellow

POWs if he'd shared any secrets, O'Reilly said no, he'd given them nothing of significance, even though the North Vietnamese kept him alone in a cell and tortured him.

What O'Reilly didn't know was that the POWs were clandestinely communicating with the CIA and DIA about their treatment and the kind of information their captors were after. By the time O'Reilly had arrived at the Plantation, the POWs were in five prisons—Ho Loa, a.k.a. the Hanoi Hilton, the Plantation, Camp Faith, the Zoo, and the Dogpatch. This consolidation allowed the POWs to strengthen their organization and share their knowledge of how they were being treated by the North Vietnamese.

What made his fellow POWs suspicious was that, despite saying he'd been beaten and tortured, he didn't show any of the telltale signs—bruises, broken bones, dislocated joints, or missing fingernails. O'Reilly showed up looking well nourished, not significantly underweight like the other POWs.

Then, in a letter to the POW leadership, the CIA described a five-minute videotape, aired by the North Vietnamese, of O'Reilly admitting to deliberately bombing hospitals and schools.

No one at the Plantation told O'Reilly that they knew about the tape. Instead, the word was quietly passed that other POWs should be careful what they said around O'Reilly. He was tagged as a traitor and a collaborator. His assigned roommate, an Air Force F-105 pilot who had been a POW for five years, was asked to befriend O'Reilly and learn what he could so that after the war, he could be tried as a collaborator and maybe even for treason.

Saturday, July 24, 1971, 1754 local time, Cuba

On Saturday afternoons, the instructors organized matches between the students so they could test their hand-to-hand combat skills. Each match was a series of three 3-minute rounds. Since Janet had won the tournament the previous Saturday, she had the honor of picking her first opponent today. Standing in the center of the ten-meter-diameter ring marked on the padded floor, she pointed at the GRU instructor who taught interrogation techniques and hand-to-hand combat.

"Major Uglov, I want you." Talking in the stands ended abruptly. The referee looked at Janet and whispered, "*¿Estás segura?*" Are you sure?

"*Sí, estoy segura.*"

The referee motioned Major Uglov out to the mat and checked the padded sparring gloves he pulled on. Neither combatant wore protective headgear.

The rules were simple. The winner was the one who scored the most hits to the body or take downs. Hits to the head were frowned upon. If the referee decided a blow was a deliberate attempt to injure the opponent, he had three choices:

1. Disqualify the attacker and end the fight in favor of the victim;

2. Award points to the victim; or

3. Take away points from the aggressor.

Stepping out of the ring to evade an opponent's attack cost you a point, and the referee momentarily stopped the fight and restarted it from the center of the ring. If one was pushed beyond the line, the ref stopped the match until both participants were back in the center and no penalty was awarded.

At five-foot-five, Janet was—as Randy would say—a one hundred-and-twenty-pound lean, mean, fighting machine. Uglov was at least five inches taller and fifty to sixty pounds heavier, and he was known for hammering his opponents. Janet thought he liked hurting people, because he bragged about torturing prisoners all over the world.

Uglov leaned forward. "*Usted sabe que esto va a doler.*" You know this is going to hurt.

Janet looked him in the eyes. "*Lo sé. La pregunta es, ¿a quién le va a doler más, tú o yo?*" The question is, who is going to be hurt more, you or me?

Uglov spoke in English. "Americans are cowards. I beat many American pilots in Vietnam. They squealed like pigs."

Janet didn't take the bait but wanted to stir Uglov's emotions. She'd heard this before and wondered if Randy had been one of his victims. She spoke in Spanish, rather than give him the satisfaction of getting her to speak in her native tongue. *"Veremos quién está chillando al final de esta pelea!"* "We'll see who is squealing at the end of this fight."

As soon as the referee blew his shrill, screeching whistle, Uglov charged at Janet, just as she expected him to do. She circled left, away from the Russian's dominant right hand. His first jab missed and she easily parried the second.

Janet moved. Uglov stalked. For three minutes it was a chess match, with Uglov punching and Janet ducking or dodging punches from the man who had six more inches of arm length. By the end of the first round, neither fighter had a point. Janet used the thirty seconds between rounds to catch her breath. It felt like her pounding heart wanted to jump out of her chest.

As they moved to touch gloves at the beginning of the second round, Janet knew Uglov was not going to let her get away. His ego was involved. None of his opponents had ever made it to the second round un-hit. Those students who survived the first round did so on raw courage and an ability to withstand his powerful blows.

Their gloves had barely separated when out jabbed his left fist. That was a surprise, and it hammered Janet's chest right between her breasts. She had been anticipating a right. Nevertheless, she had leaned back to soften the expected blow. Even so, it hurt, and it was a point in his favor and the first point of the match.

Janet saw the right hand coming and ducked under and inside to avoid the blow and drive both fists into Uglov's solar plexus as hard as she could. Uglov staggered back and his arms dropped, letting Janet hammer a one-two punch into the GRU officer's gut. Two more points! Uglov took an involuntary step back and bent over at the waist, wheezing.

She glanced at the referee, who signaled the points; it was

now three-to-one in her favor, and the referee had not stepped between them so there was no pause in the fight.

Janet sprang forward and kicked. She missed her target area—his lower rib cage—and, instead, her locked instep smashed into the Russian's groin. Uglov's eyes bulged as he sucked in air through his mouth.

The Russian staggered away, avoiding Janet for a few seconds, then lunged and swung at Janet's head with right and left fists. When the punches missed, Uglov tried to grapple. Janet ducked under the wildly swinging arms, side-stepped Uglov's lunge and, without hesitating, slammed both fists into his chest and then her right into the side of his head, just as she had been trained.

Uglov gasped, struggling to breathe as his eyes rolled back into his head and he keeled over in a heap. The Soviet GRU officer's body twitched two times, then was still.

The referee motioned Janet to the far side of the ring and called for a medic. Two medical attendants rolled Uglov onto a stretcher and carried him to an ambulance that drove off in a blare of sirens and flashing lights.

No one came near Janet when she sat down at the end of the bottom row of bleachers and wrapped her arms around her knees so no one could see how much she was shaking. Sweat dripped off her face and her uniform was soaked. She wondered if Uglov was dead.

That night, Janet ate alone. She wasn't sure if it was by her choice or if others were afraid of her because she'd felled Uglov.

Saturday, July 31, 1971, 2036 local time, Cuba

Janet sat on the railing with her back to a thick corner post. The sun was a bright orange ball sitting on the top of the ridge on the west side of the valley. She closed her eyes and let it warm her face.

An empty bottle of Hatuey beer sat on the railing like a lonely soldier beside her drawn-up knees. A half-full one was in her hand. Her liquid supper. She agreed with Ernest Hemingway, who'd written in his Pulitzer Prize-winning novel, *The Old Man and the Sea,* that the beer had a distinctive, hoppy taste.

Earlier that afternoon, the Soviet instructors had glared at her as it was announced to the trainees that Uglov was dead. Sometimes, the speaker intoned, students and instructors die in training accidents and this is the price they pay to fight imperialism, fascism and colonialism. Today's sessions were cancelled, but tomorrow they would begin again.

Her perch gave her time to think about her time in Cuba. Janet had believed she was physically and mentally tough when she'd arrived, but now she was much tougher. How that would play out when she got back home, only time would tell.

"Hi, Luna. The canteen just delivered your favorite punch— rum with orange juice, lots of pulp and slices of orange."

Janet turned to see Monika walking toward her with two glasses, so she knocked back the beer. If she drank the punch, she'd have a buzz the like of which she had avoided since she'd arrived in June.

Monika was the only person in the camp with whom she had more than a cursory relationship. The Angolans had left with their comrades, so Monika and she had the cottage to themselves now, but Janet had been keeping to herself.

"Luna, you showed courage when you fought Uglov." Since no one was around, Monika spoke English.

"I was just doing what I had to do."

Monika sat down next to her. She wrapped her hand around Janet's ankle and began to caress it. "What was that?"

"Uglov was a bully. I wanted to take him down a peg."

Monika looked at Janet, puzzled by the idiom. Her hand went up and down Janet's calf, gently massaging the relaxed muscle.

Janet took a long drink of the rum and orange juice mix. She was enjoying the buzz and Monika's touch. "Uglov needed to be taught a lesson to make him less arrogant and more humble. Looking back, I think he liked to hurt people, physically and mentally. Do you know what a sadist is?"

Monika thought for a moment. "Yes, I do."

"I think Uglov was a sadist."

"I didn't like him, either. He beat up many students."

Monika's wandering hand caressed the area behind Janet's knee. It was one of the most sensitive parts of her body.

"Ummmmmm."

"Do you like my touch?"

"I do. I like it a lot."

"Luna, do you like men or women better?"

"I go both ways, but I like women better."

Monika's hand moved to the inside of Janet's thigh, just under the edge of her shorts. Janet's involuntary gasp was encouraging; the German trailed her fingers up Janet's thigh until they were close to her crotch. Janet was sure that Monika could sense the heat, if not touch her wetness.

"I know that."

"How?"

"Because I see the way you look at me."

"It is that obvious?"

Monika's face was now scant inches from Janet's. "Yes, at least to me. I only like women."

"Hmmmm...."

"We can reserve one of the private couples rooms for two hours tomorrow."

Janet shuddered again. It had been a long time since Helen had taken her to the pleasure places she craved. And yet.... She gently pushed Monika's hand away.

Shaking her head as she tried to catch her breath, Janet looked in Monika's eyes and spoke softly. "Monika, as much as I would like to make love to you, the answer is no. I came to Cuba to learn skills I did not have. You can tell by my reaction that I like your touch, but having a sexual relationship with a beautiful woman like you is a complication that neither of us need. I fear the Cubans and the Russians would use it against us."

Monika leaned away and took a long drink of her rum and orange juice. "It is a shame, but I understand. I was hoping we could satisfy each other."

Janet had often heard Monika's stifled moans as she worked herself over after the lights went out. Janet kissed her forefinger and placed it on Monika's lips. "I would like very much to make love to you, but this is not the time nor the place."

Wednesday, August 25, 1971, 1127 local time, Havana

Enrique was waiting for her as she entered the mess hall for lunch. "Luna, you are leaving today. We have one more training exercise that we will complete in Havana. A bag is on your bunk for you to pack your uniforms. I'll meet you here in thirty minutes."

As Janet climbed into the car, she hoped no one would search their bunk room. If they did, they would find the note she'd left under Monika's pillow.

It's my time to leave. Some other time and some other place, we can be together. Good-bye and good luck.

The route back to Havana was the reverse of the trip into the Escambray Mountains. Enrique was silent most of the way, but when they got to the José Martí Airport outside Havana he said, "Do not worry about this last exercise. It will only take a few minutes and we are all confident that you will pass. Then you can go home and wait for your first assignment."

"I'd like to leave on Thursday or Friday morning. Can you make me a reservation at the Hotel Meridor in Mexico City?" She assumed that the Cubans would follow her and she'd need to lose a tail in Mexico City so she could get to the Banamex branch where her passport was in their vault. Maybe she was being paranoid, but she was about to leave Cuba as a trained assassin, and they might want to watch her for a few weeks to see if she went to the CIA.

"If you pass, consider a flight on Thursday done."

"Enrique, whatever happened to Major Uglov? It was not my intent to kill him."

Enrique looked out the window for a long while, then turned to Janet. "The official story is that he died of a heart attack, which is, to some degree, true. He would have died from a heart attack if your blow to the side of his head hadn't fractured his skull."

Enrique touched her thigh gently with his forefinger. "Luna, I will tell you two things that you will not repeat. One, your willingness to fight Major Uglov was an act of courage. I believe you wanted to give him a taste of his own medicine. Two, we had already requested that the GRU transfer him back to Moscow, but they didn't want him back. You solved our problem."

Now it was Janet's turn to gaze out the window. There was a building with a sign on the front that said *Dirección General de Inteligencia*, which Janet translated as "General Directorate of Intelligence."

"So, Enrique, what is this place?"

"Villa Marista. Some call it Los Maristas. It used to be a boys' school run by Marist Brothers. Do you know who they are?"

"Aren't they Catholic monks?"

"Yes, they run schools around the world, usually in poor nations like Cuba. They are French monks who want to educate people and make Jesus beloved around the world. In Cuba, they had a school in Havana and another one in Cienfuegos. Castro didn't like their view on socialists and communists, so the schools were closed. The monks went to other schools outside Cuba. Our directorate of intelligence has offices in the building and uses the monks' quarters as cells for political prisoners who have committed crimes against the state."

At the entrance, a guard saluted after Enrique showed his identity card. Despite the heat and humidity, Janet was wearing long pants. As they passed through another guard post she observed the guards watching her, suspecting they were wondering what kind of figure she had, where she came from, and could they get her in bed.

Enrique opened the door to a room with a conference table and chairs. A guard brought him a bulging Manila envelope. Spread out on the table was her suitcase and the clothes she'd brought from California.

"Make sure that everything you brought with you is here. There are also some rolls of film that you can have developed. The photos will be from the places you visited while you were on your vacation."

As she went through the clothes, she was more worried about whether they would fit than if they were all there. Four months of physical training had made her much more muscular, and the blouses might be tight at the shoulders. Then she smiled, thinking that a tight blouse on a good-looking woman might not be a bad thing.

"Thank you. They're all here." Enrique handed her the envelope. Janet flipped through her wallet.

The credit cards were still there, along with the Canadian passport and driver's license. A quick fan of the traveler's checks and a check of the register told her that none had been taken. She made a mental note to call each credit card company and ask for new ones; she was sure that the Cubans had recorded the numbers. "Everything is here."

"Good. Follow me." Six doors down the hall, Enrique opened another door. The room was a hallway to the door of a small cell. On a table, there was a Makarov pistol with a suppressor and a single round.

Enrique pointed to the door. "In there is a prisoner who has been sentenced to death. He had a choice, be shot or hanged. He refused to make a choice. Take this pistol and execute him. As soon as you do, your training is complete and you will have a seat on a plane to Mexico City tomorrow."

Janet peered through the thick, reinforced glass. A blindfolded man sat in a chair with his hands handcuffed behind his back and his ankles secured to the floor.

She came back to the table and picked up the Makarov. After locking the slide in the open position, she pressed the small button on the butt of the pistol and dropped the magazine into her hand. It, along with the firing chamber, was empty.

"Enrique, have a guard take the blindfold and manacles off and stand him up against the wall. He has a right to see his executioner."

"As you wish." Enrique stuck his head into the hallway and gave orders. Three armed men came through the little hallway and entered the cell. The prisoner struggled, trying to get away from the guards, whom he probably assumed would take him to a room where he would be tortured.

"Order them to leave the cell."

"Why?"

"Enrique, I don't need their help. What is the man's name?"

"Does it matter?"

"Yes, Enrique, it does."

"José Ramírez."

"What was his crime?"

"He shot a Cuban army general in cold blood."

Janet peered into the room. "Who is he?"

"He was a lieutenant colonel in our intelligence directorate."

"Do you know why he killed the general?"

"Yes, before he shot him, he called the general an incompetent butcher because his tactics got many of Ramírez' fellow Cubans killed in Angola. Ramírez was right; the general was incompetent and was brought home."

"Thank you, Enrique." Janet pulled off her beret and the bobby pins that kept her hair pinned up. With a couple shakes of her head, her sandy brown hair cascaded down past her ears. After running her fingers through her hair to make it half presentable, she slipped the 9 X 18-millimeter round into the magazine and shoved it into the pistol.

The Makarov cartridge is different from the 9mm x 19 round, known in the West as the nine millimeter Luger, after the pistol for which it was originally designed. The Makarov's ninety-five grain bullet was 20 grains smaller than the Luger's and left the barrel 100 feet per second slower.

Janet knew that at this range, the slower, smaller Makarov round would be good enough. She tapped on the bottom of the butt to make sure the clip was seated and pulled the slide back and released it, seating the round in the chamber.

Hiding the pistol behind her back, Janet entered the room and stood with her back to the door. "Lieutenant Colonel José Ramírez, you have been convicted of murder and sentenced to die. Is that true?"

Ramírez looked at Janet and smiled. "Yes, señorita, it is. I killed General Gómez so he would not get any more Cuban soldiers killed because of his mistakes. If my death prevents more Cuban soldiers from being butchered unnecessarily, then it is worth it."

Janet pulled out the pistol and aimed at the head of Ramírez, who came to attention. "Any last words?"

"It is wonderful that the last thing I will see in this world is a beautiful woman. Long live Cuba."

Janet squeezed the trigger, noting that the hole was almost a quarter inch to the left from her point of aim. The sights were off. Janet walked past the guards hurrying into the room with a black plastic body bag and handed Enrique the empty Makarov. "Satisfied?"

"Completely. I like your style."

Friday, August 27, 1971, 1736 local time, Los Angeles
Helen stared at the contents of her refrigerator, trying to decide if she was going to go out for dinner, eat leftovers, or make herself a nice dinner. Undecided, she closed the door and headed for the bedroom, thinking what she really needed was great sex.

She was unbuttoning her blouse when the phone rang. She made a halfhearted attempt to keep the annoyance out of her voice when she picked up the phone. "Hello."

"Hi." The familiar voice jolted her. Janet! "I'm using a pay phone and don't have much change. I'm arriving tomorrow on a Western Airlines flight that gets in just before 11. Sorry for the short notice, but can you pick me up? If not, I'll rent a car and drive home."

"Janet! Oh my God! Of course I'll be there!"

"Great. It's been a long time and I can't wait to see you."

"Me too." Then there was a dial tone.

Helen put down the phone and twirled in a circle, her arms outstretched.

The airport in LA was a good four hours away. Did she want to leave in the morning and risk getting stuck in Los Angeles' unpredictable traffic? God, no. A late night arrival at a hotel near the airport would allow her to sleep in on Saturday morning and be fresh for Janet's return.

The next morning, Helen stood in the throng outside customs and immigration, wondering how much Janet might have changed. In the push and shove of people meeting and embracing all around her, it was difficult to see who was clearing customs. And then, suddenly, a gentle caress on the back of Helen's neck was sending a shiver throughout her body. She whirled around and threw her arms around a smiling Janet. After a tight hug, she pushed Janet back. "You look ... different."

"How so?"

"Besides your longer hair, I don't know. You look thinner, maybe leaner. Did you lose a bunch of weight?"

"Not really. It's the same me. I walked and ran a lot whenever I could. And yes, I need to go to a real beauty salon. I want something much shorter."

"How about more mannish!"

"That works."

"Janet, I got your postcards. I could tell you were having fun."

"I was. I'm glad you got them. You know the post offices in these third world countries. They could have gotten lost or taken

150

weeks to get to you."

Neither said much in the crowded parking lot. Once they were in the car, Helen spoke up.

"I hope you are not in too much of a hurry to get back to Hanford. I extended my hotel reservation here, thinking it would be nice to have each other all to ourselves, without worrying about neighbors coming to call. Or phones ringing," she added ruefully.

"It's a great idea, especially if the hotel has a salon."

"Good. I've learned a few things while you were gone. I can't wait to try them on you."

"Wonderful!" Janet already felt herself heating with anticipation. She needed the intense sexual release that Helen could give her.

Chapter 7
NEVER NEVER LAND

Friday, October 22, 1971, 2136 local time, Hanford

On the first anniversary of Randy's shoot down, Janet didn't want the other wives to come over, but she relented because she was a part of a unique sisterhood and together they were stronger than if they suffered in silence. For several hours she welcomed visitors, accepted consolations with as much grace as she could muster, and let the buzz of conversations wash over her.

After the last POW/MIA wife left, Janet headed for the kitchen, expecting to spend a dismal hour cleaning up stacks of cups, saucers, and dishes. She was stunned by what she saw instead. What wasn't already put away was drying on the dish rack. Leftover food was wrapped and neatly stacked in the refrigerator, which someone had taken the time to clean out.

"What did you expect?"

Janet turned around to see Helen standing in the doorway of the kitchen. One hand was on her shapely hip, the other on the doorjamb. She was wearing absolutely nothing.

"I... need to write them all thank-you notes."

"We don't leave messes for each other to clean up. If you remember, you all did as much for me."

"I'd forgotten."

Helen put her arms around Janet's shoulders and kissed her, running her fingers through her lover's hair. "I love this new haircut. It is so you."

Janet leaned into the embrace. "It's much easier to take care of." Helen undid Janet's skirt and it dropped to the floor in a puddle.

"Good, that way you'll need less time in the morning. You're mine tonight, and if anybody asks, I just stayed to help you vacuum and make sure you were all right."

"Oh, you can do all the... vacuuming you want," Janet managed, before word became completely unnecessary.

Monday, December 13, 1971, 0026 local time, North Vietnam

The shriek of a bomb followed by a nearby explosion woke everyone in the compound. The first blast was followed by a second, then a third and a fourth. All six prisoners made for the door to look outside to see what was happening.

By moonlight they could see Colonel Pham shouting orders. Men were lining up with open packs, into each of which went fifteen bricks of the dried morphine the Americans had just finished wrapping that afternoon. In front of the shed, another group of men were opening boxes full of loaded magazines for their AK-47s.

Hank Cho turned to his fellow POWs, translating the shouted orders. "Those men are going into the jungle with the dope. The others will take apart and hide the factory equipment. Apparently they have a prepared hiding place."

"What about us? What are they saying about us?" Another shriek, followed by a blast. This time, they could see the flash from the explosion.

Ashley yelled at Pham, who looked in their direction and then went into his office. He came out with a pack, an AK-47, and a pair of binoculars hanging around his neck. Streaks of light came down from the sky. They heard a series of rapid-fire booms, then saw tracers, followed by a series of explosions.

Greg yelled over the noise, "That's a C-130 gunship. They must have a hot target out in the open."

Pham came jogging up, holding his binoculars in his left hand to keep them from bouncing around. "You stay in the compound. Get in the hole if you think it is safer. We'll be back in a few days. If the People's Army comes, surrender to them."

The six Americans piled into the hole and pulled the galvanized metal cover over their heads. The theory, Greg Christiansen explained, was to eliminate their heat signature, which the gunner on the C-130 could see. One or two forty-millimeter rounds in the hole and they would all be mincemeat.

It was quiet for about five minutes, then the rapid-fire booms started again. A steady stream of wham, ping, ping, thump, thump. Wham, bang, bang, ping, thump, ping, thump. Clods of dirt thumped on the hole's metal cover as they huddled together with their hands over their ears.

And then silence. Using Randy's watch, they waited thirty cautious minutes before they slid the cover back, then Ashley stuck his head out. "Holy shit," he murmured.

The building where Pham and his men lived was burning. One truck was on its side and the other was a ball of fire. In the flickering light, they could see the factory shed was a mass of twisted metal. Ashley and Randy did a quick check of the perimeter fence. Parts of it were completely destroyed. The inner fence appeared to be intact. The fires provided enough light to survey the damage to their hooch.

Ashley counted six holes where shells had ripped through the roof. The shrapnel had chewed up the floor. Two shells had exploded in the sleeping area, shredding their straw mattresses. Another had turned the table into a pile of matchsticks.

"Sleep inside or outside?"

"I like what's left of my bed," Randy said. "It's better than being eaten by bugs on the ground."

"Agreed. At first light we'll decide what to do. Right now I think it would be foolish to try to break out."

FORGOTTEN

Dawn broke slowly. Low clouds and drizzle hid the sun and added a humid chill to the air. Randy shivered as he padded over to one of the windows of the hooch that overlooked the garden. Fires that had been burning bright last night still flickered.

Three rows of four holes about two feet wide and a foot deep chewed up the gardens. One of Pham's buildings was completely flattened. Another was still burning, and only the walls were left. The third had holes in the roof and the walls looked like Swiss cheese.

Carefully, Randy walked around the garden. The damage looked worse than it was. He estimated it would take them a day to reset the plants, if they decided to stay.

Jeff Anderson had the cover of the hole on its end and pointed at the holes in the thin metal. "Hey, guys, look at this!"

Karl had jumped into the hole and pulled five chunks of Made-in-the-U.S. shrapnel out of the soft earth. He held up the largest chunk of jagged metal. "If we'd been standing up, some of us would be dead."

Randy, who'd been walking around the inner compound, went behind the hooch. "Ashley, I found a way out!"

The Green Beret worked his way into a three-foot space between the hooch and the fence where a shell had cut the pole in two. Randy pulled it back and opened a hole a man could walk through.

Ashley looked at Randy; both knew what this meant. "Out-fucking-standing! I'll go back into the hooch and get everybody ready. You and Greg go look through the buildings and see what we can salvage. If you need help, holler."

In one corner of the collapsed building Pham used as a warehouse, Randy found a stack of ammunition crates with containers of loose AK-47 rounds. He couldn't read the Russian markings, but the number 500 told him how many cartridges were in each sealed metal tin.

He dumped a canvas bag of grenades on the floor. Looking around, he found a row of similar bags and dumped five more in a pile.

Rooting around the debris, he collected eight metal canteens, six metal bowls, three machetes, and four bayonets. Under a sheet of corrugated metal that had fallen down, he found tins of canned fish, chicken, and pork, which he stuffed into the six packs.

Scattered on the floor were cartons of cigarettes. Each carton was wrapped in cellophane and had four paper packs of matches at the end. Randy used a bayonet to rip open as many as he could as fast as he could to get the matches. Time was of the essence; Pham and his men could return any moment.

When he came out with the second load of three packs, the other five POWs were waiting for him. Their conical straw hats were pulled down low to hide their faces. Randy distributed packs and gear as he reported his findings.

"Ashley, the building that's still standing has what remains of the armory. There's a pile of grenades we should set off on our way out."

"Good idea. Do you think you can do it?"

"Sure. I pull the pins on a bunch of grenades and then wedge them so the spoons can't fly off. Then I pull the pin on the last one and roll it in. What's so hard?"

"You should have been a Green Beret."

Back inside the building, Randy pulled the pins on six grenades and carefully wedged them between crates so that when the crates moved, the handles would fly off and, seconds later, the grenades would explode. Not seeing any of the telltale plumes of smoke that suggested a grenade was armed, he pulled the pins on two grenades and rolled them into the pile. One moved a box and he heard the ping as the handle flew off. He took off running.

Outside, Randy yelled for everyone to get down. The group that was assembled at the end of the access road. From there, it was about five hundred yards to the main road.

The first detonation was muffled by the concrete walls of the building. Ashley got every one up and started walking as fast as they could down the access road.

Each successive grenade went off at shorter and shorter intervals. Finally, there was a loud explosion, and when they turned around the roof of the building was flying through the air under a column of rising smoke. By the time they got to the main road, they could no longer hear the firecracker sound of exploding ammunition. Only the plume of smoke told them that the ammunition and cigarettes were still burning.

Greg found what looked like a road map in the remains of Pham's office. He didn't read Vietnamese, but he could tell from the symbology that it showed mountains, roads, and rivers and, most importantly, it showed the shore of the Gulf of Tonkin. What he couldn't tell by the map was the location of Pham's camp.

The road outside was oriented roughly east/west. Their plan was simple.

Step 1—walk to the coast.

Step 2—steal a boat.

Step 3—sail south until they either ran into a friendly ship or made it to South Vietnam.

As they came around a bend two hours into their trek, Randy, who was on point, held up his hand with his fist balled. There were half a dozen large holes in the ground. Bodies and parts of bodies littered the area. He motioned for the others to move into the jungle.

Ashley came up and asked quietly, "What's here?"

"Last night's target. Based on the wreckage, there are at least a dozen trucks blown to hell. Lord knows how many bodies. What makes me suspicious is that no one's around, so they're either in the trees hiding, or dead, or have left. What do you want to do?"

"Let's wait ten minutes."

"How about if we creep forward about a hundred feet to get a better look?"

"Good idea." Ashley turned around and whispered to the others, "Wait here."

Beyond the second crater, Randy crawled behind a large tree

and stood up a few inches at a time. All the tricks that his father had taught him to avoid spooking whatever they were hunting ran through his mind. *Damn, the remains of the truck are in the way.*

"Ashley, stay here. I'm going around the chassis."

Randy slowly crawled forward ten feet and stopped. Then another ten feet and stopped.

As he inched closer to the end of the chassis, he smelled human feces. Then he found the source. Randy stared at the body; everything from the hips down was gone. He tried not to gag. His father had taught him how to butcher and dress an animal in the field. This was different, very different. He'd never seen the insides of a human being before up close and personal.

Ants and other bugs were already feasting on the carcass. Randy felt a few ants starting to climb over him as if he were a bump in the road on their way to a buffet.

Using the engine compartment as cover, Randy studied the road intersection. He could see more trucks and human forms, some blackened by fire, others lying where they'd fallen or been blown. It looked like a scene from Sam Peckinpah's movie *The Wild Bunch* that had been making the rounds of the ready rooms on the *Oriskany* just before he'd been shot down.

The intersection looked familiar. *Shit, this is where we were sold into slavery! There's where we emerged from the trail on the west side and headed up this very road. I wonder where Colonel Pham is now. Did he create this carnage? Does he know we're gone? If he does, will he come after us or just let us go?*

Randy heard a moan. And another. Slowly he moved his head toward the sound. He saw one soldier trying to drag himself towards another. As he moved, he left a trail of blood. Around one leg that was black with blood he'd already tied a tourniquet. *Where is he going?*

Two men carrying a stretcher emerged from the woods to his right. They collected the wounded man and disappeared back into the jungle. A half a dozen more came out and started checking the bodies. The dead were left where they lay. Others that showed some sign of life were loaded onto stretchers and carried back into the woods.

Time to go.

When he got back to the group, he told them that they had to find a way around. Ashley looked at the map and pointed north.

A few hundred feet later they came to a large crater surrounded by shattered trees. Ashley motioned everyone to stop and started picking up small branches with leaves. "Here, stick the branches through the straps. It will break up our shapes and make us harder to see." When this was done they resumed their spread out line formation, Randy on point.

Randy turned around. Before they'd added the leaves, he'd been able to easily see Jeff Anderson, the last man in the line. Now, Karl and Jeff were almost impossible to find in the jungle foliage. Only by knowing what they were wearing could he discern the arms and legs and so make out their shapes.

He used the technique taught to him by his father. Put one foot down slowly. When you are sure that nothing will make noise, put your weight on it and repeat the process with your other foot. Every few steps, Randy paused and listened. It made for slow but silent going.

The briefed plan was for Randy to take three steps forward and then one laterally. This would move them at a diagonal past the North Vietnamese soldiers. Once they thought they were clear, they would cross the road and head to the road that led east and down out of the mountains toward Vinh.

Voices! They all squatted down and froze. All could hear commands in Vietnamese that faded away. The group waited ten minutes, they continued moving cautiously. Randy stopped when he smelled burning diesel fuel. It was mixed with a putrid smell he could not identify.

Randy turned around and a put his thumb and forefinger to his nose, then motioned with his right hand to the left of where they were heading. Ashley nodded and Randy slowly stood up and started moving.

A hundred yards later he stopped. He could see a clearing ahead of him through the foliage. He pulled a branch back to get a better view. Fifty feet in front of him was a long trench filled with the charred remains of human beings.

Two soldiers pushed wheelbarrows loaded with four large paper sacks toward the trench. The men lifted one sack and let the heavy bag hit the ground with a dull thud. While one held it upright, the other slit open the top and dumped the contents on the ground. The other seven sacks were emptied along the edge of the grave. The soldiers started shoveling white powder over the charred bodies. The scent was unmistakable—lime.

This is right out of the fucking Russians' playbook. Burn the bodies and cover them with lime in a mass grave so no one will ever be able to tell who was buried here. Just like the Katyn Forest!

Ashley interrupted Randy's train of thought with a tap on the shoulder. Randy pointed at the mass graves and then pointed to the left.

It was late afternoon before they decided they could safely cross the road. At thirty-second intervals they ran across and headed north. About an hour before dark, the six made camp a hundred yards off the road.

Based on the map, the consensus was that beyond the ridge ahead they would come to the eastbound road. From there, they estimated they were twenty-five kilometers from the Gulf of Tonkin and freedom.

Tuesday, December 14, 1971, 1426 local time, Hanford

It had been four months since she'd come back from Cuba, and so far nothing. Janet was waiting for the shoe to drop in the form of a member of the FBI knocking on her front door.

When the renewal for Randy's membership at the Visalia Sportsman's Association arrived, she hand-delivered the check and walked around the grounds. The outdoor facility, she realized, was a perfect place to practice her marksmanship. Shooting is like riding a bike in that, once you know how, you never forgot. However, for an assassin, it was a perishable skill that should be practiced weekly, if not daily. To do that, she needed firearms and ammunition.

Janet drove the six hours to Reno to buy guns of her own. She still had the .45 she'd brought with her to California, but she wanted more weapons, particularly rifles. She took the Mustang and enjoyed blasting through the mountains of the Sierra Nevada on the turns and twists of California Highway 88. It was between snows and the road was dry.

The Yellow Pages gave her the names and addresses of gun shops. She picked one at random, based on an ad that attracted her, and found it easily. The man behind the counter wore a name tag that said his name was Harold, and he made a point of saying it was Harold, not Harry. It was a preference Janet understood. Her parents had named her Julia, and she hated "Julie."

She told him she wanted a semi-automatic pistol, and Harold laid out a row of semi-automatics on the counter. Janet examined each one before evaluating the fit and balance in her hand. With the muzzle pointing at the floor, she'd look around and then aim the weapon at imaginary targets in the store.

She went through the same drill with each pistol. Those she rejected went back into the case. Janet settled on the Browning Hi-Power semi-automatic and a Walther PPK/S. "I want to shoot them before I buy them."

"No problem." Harold pointed at the Browning. "Do you know the history of that pistol? While not as significant as the Model 1911, it broke new ground in pistol design."

Janet tapped the pistol with her finger as if to say, "Tell me."

"The Hi-Power was the pistol John Browning was working on when he died in 1926. A Belgian engineer who assisted him finished the design. Production started in 1935, and it is the first mass-produced pistol with a double stack magazine. The Hi-Power carries fourteen rounds, one in the chamber and thirteen in the magazine."

"Interesting." She'd fired the Browning in Cuba and liked it. Juan did not. "I like being able to shoot fourteen rounds without reloading." *As much as I love the .45, the 1911's magazine holds only seven. And I'm more interested in accuracy than the size of the bullet.*

The Walther PPK/S fired the smaller .380 round that the Germans dubbed the *nine-millimeter kurz* for short cartridge. It had the same size bullet that the Makarov shot, 95 grains, but it had a much higher muzzle velocity and therefore more stopping power. She liked the feel of the pistol in her hand. It was small and very concealable.

Harold led the way to the pistol range and put both pistols and a box of ammo for each on the table. He clipped a target to the hanger and worked the pulley so that the target was five yards away.

"Too close, Harold. Move it out to ten yards. I'll fire one magazine at ten and then another at fifteen. If I want more, I'll fire at fifteen."

His eyebrows went up, but Harold, a retired police officer who'd served a tour in Korea as an infantryman, did as asked. Most people liked the closer range because their resulting groups were tighter. He loaded a magazine for the Hi-Power and stepped back so he was just off to her right side.

Janet stood with her right foot slightly ahead of the left and shoulder-width apart. As she leaned forward, she brought the weapon up and checked her grip with her trigger finger on the trigger guard. Janet repeated the process three times before she squeezed the trigger. She let the trigger come slightly forward to the reset position and squeezed it again and again. The bullets left the gun at roughly a quarter of a second apart.

Without looking, she ejected the magazine and started reloading it. "Harold, would you run it out to fifteen yards, please?"

After firing the first two rounds at the new distance, Janet squeezed off the remaining twelve rounds in six double taps. With the slide locked back, she put the Hi-Power down on the table and turned to the salesman. "I love it."

Harold saw the results before he finished reeling in the target. None of the holes in the paper were outside the ten-ring.

With the PPK/S Janet repeated the process. At ten yards, she emptied the first seven-round magazine and then the second. She loaded a third and fired it at fifteen yards. With the pistol empty, she turned around.

"Even with the short three-inch barrel, it's pretty accurate. Now I know why James Bond uses this pistol."

Her comment got a smile out of Harold.

After hefting several rifles and using the same process, Janet picked a Model 1903 with matching serial numbers, made by the Springfield Armory. Her inspection of the bolt and the barrel told her it had not been fired often, if at all. It was why she didn't mind paying a premium for the old Army rifle.

Janet would have preferred a lever-action rifle, but Harold explained that they were not available in 30-06 because the tubular magazine required round-nosed bullets, not the pointed 174-grain ones used in 30-06 rounds.

Because the Winchesters ejected the spent 30-30 cartridge upwards, mounting a scope was difficult but not impossible. He showed her a Savage 99 and the side ejection port, but, again, Janet wanted the higher velocity 30-06.

All that was left was to pick a scope. That took about half an hour. As she laid out the cash for the weapons and ammunition, Harold asked, "Janet, where did you learn to shoot?"

"My daddy taught me. He was a sniper in the Marine Corps."

The gunsmith said the scope mounting would take about an hour. Janet said she'd come back after lunch. Besides having lunch at a diner, she stopped at another gun store and bought a thousand rounds of .380 and nine-millimeter, and five hundred of 30-06. At a third store she bought four spare magazines to go with the two that each pistol came with, along with a dozen empty stripper clips for the .03 Springfield. Now she had what she needed to practice at the gun club.

Back home, Janet laid a towel out on the kitchen table and put the six magazines in a row, along with the dozen stripper clips. Carefully, Janet loaded the stripper clips first. Then came the ones for the Walther. She was halfway through the second Hi-Power magazine when the phone rang. Janet held the magazine in one hand as she picked up the phone.

"Hello."

"Luna?" The voice was clearly Hispanic.

"I'm sorry, there is no one by that name who lives here."

"*Mis disculpas.*" My apologies. Click.

Janet knew what to do next. She put the weapons back in the gun safe, except for the Walther. It went into a holster in the small of her back clipped to the belt on her jeans. The five loaded spare magazines went into her purse. Then she drove the Volvo to a pay phone at a gas station two miles away.

She dropped a dime in the slot and dialed a number. The operator asked for another dollar seventy-five. Janet dropped in seven quarters.

The phone rang once. "Allo."

"*Esto es Luna.*"

The man rattled off a series of instructions that Janet repeated back to show she understood.

Thursday, December 16, 1971, 2226 local time, Miami

It had been a long day after a short night. Janet had driven down to LA so she could get some sleep at a hotel near Los Angeles International Airport before getting up at 0500 to catch a non-stop flight to Miami that left at 0730.

She had boarded the flight as Janet Williams Pulaski, but as she gazed out the small window at the banks of sunlight clouds she decided that she would never travel using that name again. It stood out, and it was too easily traceable back to her. In the future she would book tickets under a false identity. Lesson one for the day. And cross-country air travel, unless it was first class, was not

164

very glamorous. She winced as she tried find a more comfortable arrangement for her hips and feet. The smell of cigarette smoke was thick in the circulated air.

Walking out of the air-conditioned terminal into Miami's humidity was an instant reminder of Havana. Condensation on her sunglasses blocked her vision and her clothes immediately clung to her.

She drove to the small, unbranded hotel in Coral Gables where she'd been told a package would be waiting for her and she was to stay. Lesson two: book hotels under an identity different from one used on the airline ticket, and make her own hotel reservations. Before she pulled into the parking lot, she spent ten minutes looking for surveillance. Even though she saw nothing suspicious, she was nervous when she entered the hotel lobby.

The desk clerk gave her a big smile after she gave her name, found the folder with her reservation and handed her a key. *"Que tengas un dia maravilloso.. Feliz navidad."* Have a wonderful day. Merry Christmas.

When she turned on the light, lying on the middle of the bed was a brown 9x12 envelope. *So much for sleep.*

The six-inch blade popped out of the handle of her knife with a comforting thunk as she plopped down next to the envelope. *That was dumb. Lesson three for the day: I should have checked the bed for a bomb. That's what I get for being tired. It won't happen again. They left out all these lessons during the tradecraft course in Cuba. What else did they not tell me? There's much I have to learn and the question is, will I learn it before I get killed or arrested?*

She pulled on a pair of thin latex gloves and put her nose close to the envelope. No oily odor of plastic explosive. Janet ran her fingers gently over the top to see if she could feel a wire before she turned it over slowly to check the bottom.

Satisfied, she slit the envelope and dumped out its contents— four pictures of a man and a sheet of paper with a name and an address. In the black and white photos the target's facial features were clearly discernible.

After sliding the photos back into the envelope, Janet pulled out the bottom drawers in the small dresser. She was greeted by the pungent smell of gun cleaning solvent emanating from a cigar box. She checked the box found no untoward surprises, so she slowly lifted off the top.

Inside, she found a Makarov pistol with a threaded barrel, four magazines, a box of fifty rounds and a suppressor wrapped in a rag. Janet spread a towel on the desk and field stripped the pistol to make sure nothing was amiss. *Other than the lessons learned, so far this is following the script taught to us in Cuba.* But Janet didn't intend to let her guard down—ever—when she was dealing with these people. At any point they could decide she was a liability. That was inevitable, unless she made herself invaluable.

Holding the barrel, she dropped each round into the chamber to make sure it fit perfectly. Two were marginal and were set aside. Once the pistol was re-assembled, she dry fired it several times to get a feel for the trigger and reset position. The added weight of the suppressor made it harder to point and aim, but if the six-inch long silencer did its job, the sound of the Makarov would be lost in the ambient noise.

With all four magazines loaded, Janet racked the slide to put a round in the chamber, then dropped out the magazine to add a round so it was full. The loaded pistol, without the suppressor, went under her pillow. And so to sleep.

Sun streaming through the blinds woke Janet. She looked at the clock and saw it was 0612.

A quick shower, then she dressed in comfortable, casual clothes, placed the Makarov in her purse and went out the door. Next step was finding a pay phone not near the motel. She drove to a gas station with an outside phone booth, parked, and placed her call. She wondered if she would wake the person she was calling.

"Allo."

"*Soy Luna.*" This is Luna.

"Bienvenida a Miami. Recibió mis paquetes?" Welcome to Miami. Did you get my packages?

"Sí."

"¿Usted sabe que su misión?" You know your mission?

"Sí. ¿Qué tan pronto tiene que ser completado?" Yes, how soon does it have to be completed?

"Dentro de una semana." Within a week.

Janet thought she could tell the difference between Mexican and Cuban Spanish. This man was definitely Cuban.

"Y el dinero?" And the money? *First things first! I'm not doing this out of the goodness of my heart. I didn't believe a word of the revolutionary bullshit your employer tried to pass off as history while I was in Cuba.*

"La mitad se ha depositado. Usted recibirá la otra mitad cuando esté muerto." Half has been deposited and you get the other half when he is dead.

"Bueno."

Thirty-seven thousand, five hundred U.S. dollars had been deposited in a numbered bank account in the Bahamas. The Cubans had set it up for her, and supposedly she was the only one who had the codes to withdraw funds or check the balance.

The word *"bueno"* was followed by a dial tone. Janet smiled as she hung up the phone. Then she went into the gas station and bought her first purchase of the day—a better street map of Miami than the one from the rental car company, along with a cup of coffee and four donuts.

Munching on donuts, Janet drove to the street where her target lived, in an area known as Little Havana. It was 0758.

A whitewashed, six-foot cinderblock wall surrounded the house's front and back yards. She'd just parked a hundred feet from the driveway when the gate opened and a white Ford Town Car pulled out. Janet got a quick look at a well-manicured lawn, shrubs, and palm trees as she drove by.

She dropped way back to avoid being noticeable. If they didn't end up at the man's office, she could find where he worked another day.

Ten minutes later, the Ford pulled into a reserved spot in front of a four-story office building. *I'm in luck. There's a six-story parking garage across the street.* She found an open spot on the corner of the fifth floor, facing her target's office building. After locking the car, she went down the stairs and crossed the street, considering possible lines of fire from the parking lot.

The law firm of Flores, Foca and Mendez occupied Suite 301. The only other address on the floor was *Libre Cuba* in Suite 302. *I found you, Javier Flores!*

She rode the elevator to the third floor and walked it end to end, checking for surveillance cameras and evaluating potential escape routes before taking the stairs back to the lobby.

On her way to her car, Janet passed a stack of orange cones in a corner of the garage, the kind traffic departments used to block off lanes. She snagged three. After backing out the car, she used the cones to block off her corner spot. Hopefully, this would keep someone from using the spot that gave her a perfect view of the entrance to Flores' building.

A nearby sporting goods store had exactly what she wanted, a pair of eight-by-fifty binoculars made by Bushnell. The clerk was apologetic; he only had the one pair left, and it had range marks specifically made for hunters to help determine how far away a target was. He knew bird watchers objected to these, and surely the lovely young lady was a bird watcher? But binoculars were a popular gift this Christmas, and it was uncertain they would get more in before the holiday. Janet contained her excitement and pretended to be disappointed as she counted out two fifty- and four twenty-dollar bills to cover the cost and sales tax.

Janet went to a phone bank, dropped a dime into the slot and dialed the number she'd memorized from the phone book in her hotel room.

"Good morning, Flores, Foca and Mendez." The voice was female and had no trace of a Spanish accent. Janet decided to respond in English. "Yes, I was wondering if your firm does tax work. I have a problem that needs a creative solution."

"Yes, we do. Any of the partners can help you with that. Do you need a CPA, too?"

"Maybe. Are you open during the holidays?"

"Oh, yes! Our firm has many clients who need legal work completed by the end of the calendar year, so we will all be here. May I make an appointment with one of the partners?"

"I will call you back. I am out running errands and don't have my date book with me."

Janet waited until she heard an "O.K." from the receptionist before she hung up. She'd gotten what she wanted; no vacation for Javier Flores. Next step was getting the right weapon. Even with a silencer to suppress noise, doing the job in the man's office would be messy. This had to be a long range hit, and for that she needed a rifle.

Friday, December 17, 1971, 1611 local time, North Vietnam
None of the Americans wanted to admit they were tired when they'd accomplished their first goal—getting out of the mountains. Every hour and every step took them closer to the sea and freedom. But the going was grueling, and the truth was they were all exhausted.

Every two hours, they would stop for twenty minutes. Getting up and going again from their last break was tough; they were all dog tired, hungry and dehydrated. It would be dark in an hour and they needed to make camp for the night.

All of them had bug bites all over their bodies from sleeping on the ground. Beds of leaves kept them out of the mud, but didn't keep away the creepy crawlies that feasted on their flesh.

Now, well off the Ho Chi Minh Trail, they'd seen very few soldiers or even civilians. They'd left the road to follow a stream that emptied into a larger river called the Sông Lam, a.k.a. the Sông Ca, which flowed into the Gulf of Tonkin. How they would skirt Vinh and steal a boat was still an open question.

During the last stop, Randy had studied the map and said, "I think we're about here. If we go directly east, through this area, we can cut off a couple of miles. There are a couple of small roads we have to cross, but there are trees to give us cover. Going directly east will make our navigation easier. In the morning the sun will be in our face and in the afternoon, at our backs."

Ashley studied the map for a few seconds. "It can't be any more difficult terrain than we've covered so far. "

"It is pretty flat from where we are to the coast. Both Jeff and I have flown over it. The trouble is, the coastal plain is where most of the North Vietnamese live, so as we get closer to the coast, the risk of being spotted goes up. The only other choice is moving at night, but that too is a risk because there is a curfew. No one is supposed to be out after 2200."

Ashley looked around at the men. Greg was the first to speak. "I'm all for anything that gets us to the coast faster."

Jeff nodded. Karl said, "Me, too."

Hank was the last one. "I'll make it. Count me in."

"Good, let's eat and fill our canteens tonight and move out tomorrow as soon as we get up."

Using the bayonets and machetes, Greg and Karl dug a small pit for a fire. They didn't want a flame that was visible. Smoke was another problem. Hank positioned himself by one the trees on the edge of the woods as a lookout until the fire was ready.

Cooking was simple. Edible leaves and tinned meat were dumped into a metal bowl with water from the stream. The mixture was boiled until it was ready to eat.

To purify drinking water, they boiled it in the steel bowls they used for cooking and carefully poured it into empty canteens, leaving any sediment in the bowl. Due to the small size of the metal bowls, they had to go through this process eight times to fill their canteens. If any sediment got into the canteen, they joked that it was sterilized dirt and was therefore O.K.

The empty tins and other waste were put in the bottom of the fire pit and buried with the dirt they'd shoveled out. In the morning this was tamped down and brushed with a branch to disguise its presence.

Sunday, December 19, 1971, 0523 local time, North Vietnam

Lightning flashed followed by the rippling, rolling sound of thunder. Rain was coming. Randy crept close to the edge of the woods to get a better view of the sky.

Shit, we're going to get pissed on big time, and we have no shelter.

Randy reported back and asked, "Ashley, do we want to keep moving or stay here in the woods?"

"The Vietnamese farmers generally don't go out in this type of weather unless it's absolutely necessary. That's both good and bad. It's good because no one will be outside to see us. But it is bad if someone looks out a window and does."

"I say we move as far as we can toward the coast and stay out of sight."

"Randy, moving through the jungle in heavy pouring rain is more difficult and dangerous than you think. Everything is slippery and the going is slow. If someone gets hurt, we have to carry him. I don't think it is worth the risk. I say we spend the time before the rain starts building a shelter, and make sure the matches will stay dry. No one will hear us hacking away at tree branches with this thunder."

They all agreed. Partially dry was better than soaking wet.

The same day, 1246 local time, Miami

Janet had nothing to do on Sunday. Sitting outside Flores' house would be a waste of time. On her way to returning the Hertz Ford rental car she'd driven by the house; then, in an Avis Chevy Bel Air, she scouted it again. Each time, there were two cars and three bodyguards outside the gate. Trying to kill him at home would violate one of the rules she had been formulating— avoid shoot-outs. They take too long, attract the wrong kind of attention, and the results are unpredictable.

A long run helped relieve Janet's frustration. After showering, she headed to a bank of pay phones near the hotel she'd moved to, about two miles away from the one where the Cubans had made the reservation.

"*Hola.*" It was the same voice as before.

"This is Luna."

"*¿Así que ha olvidado su español?*" So, have you forgotten your Spanish?

Janet noted the sarcasm in the man's voice. "*No. Quería para ver si hablas inglés.*" No, I thought I would try English. *I wanted to test you and see if you spoke English.*

"*Lo que sea. Hablemos ingles.*" Whatever. Let us speak English.

"What do you have for me?"

"I will give you the address of a Cuban restaurant where the food is very good. Go there for dinner. When you pay the bill, ask if Amtrak is still planning to move its trains from the Allapatah Station. They will tell you, 'Yes, but not until 1977.' Pay in cash and they will give you a dinner receipt in a folder that will also contain a key to a locker at the train station. In it is not what you wanted, but it is good enough."

Dial tone.

The restaurant and the locker were easy to find. The black duffel bag went unopened into the trunk of the Bel Air and then to her hotel room.

Janet covered the desk with a beach towel. Wearing latex gloves so she wouldn't leave fingerprints, Janet unzipped the duffel bag and pulled out a rifle and a long, cylindrical object wrapped in a rag that was held in place with four rubber bands. Unrolling the rag revealed the bolt, a suppressor and a six-power Leupold scope. Last out was a small, heavy box wrapped in several layers of packing tape. In it, Janet found seventy-five rounds of Yugoslavian-made 7.92 X 57-millimeter ammunition for a Mauser 98K rifle and five stripper clips held together by rubber bands.

Under the desk light, Janet looked at the stampings on the

barrel. The German markings were still there, but the numbers didn't match and she didn't know enough about the proof marks to know where or when the rifle had been originally made. She knew enough about Mausers to know a stamped "X" over the Wehrmacht markings indicated that the gun was put together from parts captured by the Soviets during World War II. Whoever was on the phone was right. It was a good rifle for the job.

In Cuba she'd consistently hit the center of mass at five hundred meters with a scope. At a hundred meters, she hit targets of photos of men between the eyes without a scope. From the top of the parking garage to the front of the building where Flores worked was between three-hundred-and-fifty to four-hundred yards.

She mounted the scope and screwed on the silencer. Then she turned out the lights in the room and opened the curtain. Sitting on the floor with her elbows on her knees, Janet tracked targets on the road and practiced squeezing the trigger.

So far, so good! Now she had to find a place to test the rifle and make sure it was zeroed in.

Monday, December 21, 1971, 1538 local time, North Vietnam
When rain finally stopped in the early afternoon, the six Americans started walking, slightly bent over to disguise their height. All of them were wet, from humidity, sweat, and the rain that had penetrated their makeshift shelter or been blown in by the wind, but they weren't soaked, and they were rested.

They had debated whether they should stop moving by day and walk only at night. They were out of the jungle and all around them were rice paddies, dikes and huts. If they walked during the day, they could hide in plain sight, hoping their dirty gray clothes and straw hats would let them blend in.

At night, they would be harder to spot, but it would be harder to navigate, and if they were spotted they'd be conspicuous. After dark, few North Vietnamese civilians were outside their houses.

With the clouds overhead, the light was fading. They hoped to

173

be able to make it to the river by dark and find a place to hide.

Their chosen path along the edge of the woods skirted a row of rice paddies and a recently planted field. As they came around a bend, Karl spotted two farmers guiding a plow behind a water buffalo less than fifty yards away. One yelled and pointed in his direction Two more farmers came running, and a third ran toward the village beyond the paddies.

Ashley said, loud enough for all to hear, but not enough for it to carry, "Let's go back into the woods and get away as fast as possible."

The stand of trees was about a hundred meters wide and the same long. Enough to hide them for a few minutes but not large enough to offer cover if searched thoroughly.

Randy turned to the others. "According to the map, there's a road about a half of a mile in front of us that follows the river. We need to get across it so we can hide in the marshes."

Just as they got in position to move out, three trucks full of Vietnamese soldiers came to a halt less than fifty yards from where they were hiding. One man stood on the back of the truck with a loud speaker. "Americans, we know you are hiding in the woods. If you do not come out with your hands up, we will hunt you like animals and shoot you on sight. You have thirty seconds to surrender."

Tuesday, December 21, 1971, 1206 local time, Miami

When Janet pulled into the parking garage, she was pleasantly surprised to see that the pylons were still there blocking the space. She stopped, looked around, and before she got out of the car, pulled on a pair of latex gloves. She stacked the pylons near the stair well. With that done, she parked the Bel Air in the spot.

The Mauser lay on her lap as she watched who came and went from the building where Flores had his office. To help pass the time, she was trying to read an English translation of Monique Wittig's *Les Guérillères*.

She'd bought the novel in a used bookstore when Helen and

she were in Venice, California. *Les Guérillères'* heroes were lesbians fighting bloody battles as they tried to overthrow a patriarchal, male-dominated world and create their own country. Wittig's odd combination of prose and poetry made a hard read; she closed the book and put it in her purse.

For the umpteenth time, she checked the rifle in her lap. With the driver's window down, all she had to do was lift the rifle into position on the doorsill, aim, and squeeze the trigger. By placing gauze over the scope's front lens, held in place with two thick rubber bands, she eliminated any chance that someone would see a reflection.

If all went well and Flores came out, she could make the shot and make a four-thirty flight to Dallas out of Ft. Lauderdale with a connection to LA. Plan B was buying a ticket for an evening flight to either D.C. or New York and spending the night there before flying to LA. Plan C was spending the night here and leaving on the first flight to Dallas that had a decent connection to LA.

As Janet sat there, she sipped on a bottle of water. The empty bottle she tossed onto the back seat. Suddenly, a series of loud, hammering noises startled her. She hopped out of the car and peered over the concrete wall. Two men were attacking the pavement with jackhammers. *Perfect!*

She'd figured that, as a Cuban, Flores probably wouldn't head for lunch until after twelve. Sure enough, Flores exited the office building just after 1230. When he stopped to light a cigarette, she forced the air out of her lungs and squeezed the trigger. The cigarette and the lighter went flying as the bullet tore Flores' chest open.

The rifle went on the floor and Janet drove out of the garage at a normal speed, paid for her parking, and headed north to Fort Lauderdale. At each stoplight, Janet completed another step in field stripping the Mauser. She stopped at a gas station to get something to drink and dropped the duffel bag with the barrel into a large dumpster.

A mile or so later, Janet pulled into a McDonalds, bought a hamburger, then dumped the suppressor and the remains of the food into the trash. By the time she neared the rental car facility, both the Makarov and the Mauser were in bits and pieces in various trashcans and dumpsters along the highway.

Eleven hours after Janet ended Javier Flores' life, she walked into the Los Angeles Airport Marriott Hotel. On the first flight, she had been nervous and kept her nose buried in *Les Guérillères*. On the trip from Dallas Love Field to LA, she was more relaxed and managed to doze.

In the quiet of her hotel room, Janet paced, aroused and frustrated. She wondered where Helen was.

In a moment of clarity, Janet realized two things.

One, she really liked killing people.

Two, she was more lesbian than bi. The thought of having sex with a man was unappealing. She liked the way women smelled, and tasted. She liked the softness; she liked breasts. And she really liked being the strong one. She wondered if she could make love even with Randy, when he came home. Shaking her head, she didn't know if her mind was saying no or that she didn't want to think about it.

Wednesday, December 22, 1971, 1122 local time, North Vietnam

The set-up was drearily familiar, Randy thought. A concrete walled room, armed goons, himself tied to a chair with a three-inch-diameter bamboo pole run under his armpits. Jeff had been the first to be dragged from their cell for isolated interrogation. Now it was his turn.

His slim and trim interrogator must have studied Western military manuals. Every move he made was done with practiced precision, as if he were a student at one of the U.S. military academies. Randy mentally dubbed him Captain Ringknocker.

Captain Ringknocker ordered the guards to lift and twist the bamboo pole. This sent lightning bolts of pain through Randy's upper torso and he screamed in pain. He thought they were going to break his back before he passed out. A bucket of cold water brought him back.

As his vision cleared from the eye-watering pain, Captain Ringknocker was in his face.

Question—"How did you escape?" *Answer*—We found a hole in the fence after the camp was bombed and walked out. Lieutenant Colonel Pham's men had left.

Question—"Where is Lieutenant Colonel Pham's camp?" *Answer*—I don't know. All we have is a guess based on the map we used.

Question—"Who was Lieutenant Colonel Cao?" *Answer*—I don't know, other than he sold us to Lieutenant Colonel Pham.

Question—"What happened to Colonel Duong and his men?" *Answer*—They were killed by American bombs when the convoy was on the road north.

Question—"How many Vietnamese soldiers did you kill?" *Answer*—None.

Question—"How do you know he was making morphine base?" *Answer*—Because he told us that was what we were making.

Question—"How much were you making?" *Answer* —"Roughly every week, we processed enough opium to make approximately one hundred one kilo bricks I don't know what happened after we finished wrapping them for shipment."

Question—"Are you telling me that a lieutenant colonel in the People's Army is a drug dealer?" *Answer*—Yes.

That "yes" got him two blows from rifle butts. The questions were repeated, and each time he gave the same answers. Then more questions, and more rifle blows.

If Captain Ringknocker didn't like the answer, you got a rifle butt slammed into your body. Randy let the pain take over. There was nothing he could do to stop it, so he just endured.

Suddenly, the two guards untied Randy from the chair and lifted him by the bamboo pole. His battered legs couldn't bear his weight, so they dragged him back to the cell. The good news was he wasn't leaving a trail of blood.

When the guards shoved him into the cell, he pitched forward. Painfully, he pulled himself into a sitting position next to Jeff Anderson. His fellow Naval aviator's eyes were swollen shut.

Anderson touched Randy's shoulder. "When we're all back together, we can debrief."

Randy shifted, trying to find a comfortable position. There was none. "Yeah. Good idea."

Their eight-by-ten-foot cell had only one bench that was supposed to be a bed. If four of them scrunched their shoulders, they might be able to sit on it side by side. At one end, a steel door with a grating allowed the guard to watch them. In the corner of the concrete room was a small porcelain toilet without a seat, and in the center of the floor was a grating covering a drain.

The cell had two sources of light: a single incandescent bulb attached to the fixture in the center of the ceiling that was never turned off, and a ten-inch-tall window that ran almost the entire width of the cell on the wall opposite the door. It had no glass, just steel bars every six inches.

The smell of the sea came through the window and mixed with the scent of dirty, unwashed bodies. Each guard who brought what might be called a meal wrinkled his nose at the ripe, pungent smell, a miasma of body odor, urine, feces, and mud from farmer's fields fertilized with manure.

Smelling the sea was a depressing reminder of how close they'd come. The trucks that had carried them to their current prison had covered what would have been the last few miles of their hike. As they passed through the center of Vinh, Randy had seen the Gulf of Tonkin. *Close, but no cigar!*

For fifteen days—despite the lack of food, the constant fear of being recaptured, and the physical effort of walking—they'd been free men. They'd had a goal—get to the coast, find a boat, and escape. The pain of not making it to the gulf was worse than the torture. What they needed was a ray of hope that might ensure their survival. Randy knew their bodies would give out before their minds gave in.

One by one, the men were brought back into the cell. Hank Cho was dumped on top of Greg Christiansen. Karl Kramer came back looking like he had been the loser in a boxing match. Ashley was shoved into the cell with such force that he slammed into the back wall and collapsed in a heap.

Randy took a deep breath. He waited for the resulting pain in his ribs to subside, then said, "Captain Smith, as the executive officer of *Pham's Phucking POWs*, I can report that we are all present and accounted for. Our material condition is battered, but not broken. We *will* survive."

He looked around the room and saw a smile or two. Ashley groaned as he lifted himself onto one elbow. "Lieutenant, every day we are alive, it is a moral victory over these bastards."

One by one, they began to move their battered bodies, and Jeff Anderson spoke up. "Gentlemen, have no fear; we will survive. It is in the cards."

Randy looked at Jeff. One of his eyes was swollen shut and there was blood below his nose. "How come you are so sure?"

"Because I am the third Anderson to be a POW. My great, whatever number of greats it is, graduated from West Point in 1855 and was a major in the First Regiment, Alabama Volunteer Cavalry. He was wounded at the Battle of Chickamauga in Tennessee and captured. He was taken to a Yankee POW camp on Johnson's Island in Sandusky Bay on the southern shore of Lake Erie. After the war, he made it back to his home in Alabama."

Anderson pushed himself into a sitting position and wiped the blood off his face with his right sleeve.

"Then there was my father. On his tenth mission, my dad's B-17 took a flak burst, then an ME-109 pumped it full of twenty-millimeter cannon shells. When the left wing caught on fire, my dad ordered everyone to bail out. His unit, the 100th Bomb Group, lost nine B-17s—that's 90 men—on the first mission to bomb the Messerschmitt factory in Regensburg, Germany. Anyway, nine of the ten men got out before the plane exploded. My dad spent the rest of the war in Stalag V-A outside Ludwigsburg."

Randy eased himself down on the floor. "Does your wife know all this?"

"Yeah."

"And she still married you?"

Jeff choked on a laugh. His nose was still seeping blood. "Yes, she did. Jessica was due last month, so I am assuming I am a father by now. When I get back, I will have to introduce myself to a child who doesn't know me. That's what keeps me going. I want to see my kid."

They heard voices outside and Hank Cho, who was closest, whispered a translation. "We're to be brought before some bigwig." When the door was opened, two soldiers, each with an AK-47 held ready, came in and stood against the wall on either side of the door. Another soldier came in, holding his arms out and his hands together, the signal for them to do the same and be handcuffed. Once the steel bracelets were in place, a rope with a slipknot was looped around each man's neck and tightened so that the wearer could feel the pressure on his throat.

A rifle butt in Ashley's back propelled him out the door. Neither Randy, who was second in line, nor the others needed any encouragement, yet each was hit as they left the jail cell, the blows adding more bruises to the ones they already had.

In a large room they were pushed into a line against a wall. Four soldiers and their AK-47s took positions, two behind the table in front of them and one on either side.

The four North Vietnamese soldiers' heels came together but their rifles remained pointed at the Americans when the door opened. An older man entered, wearing a clean uniform with red-bordered shoulder boards with four gold stars in a row and two gold bars crossways on the insignia. Behind him, Captain Ringknocker marched in, carrying a folder in his left hand that he pressed against his mid-section in a precise, military manner.

Randy had learned enough from Ashley about North Vietnamese army ranks to know the stocky—some might say "pudgy", others might say "well fed"—officer was wearing the insignia of a senior colonel. He was the equivalent of a U.S. rear admiral or brigadier general. In contrast, Captain Ringknocker looked like most of the Vietnamese he'd seen—thin, wiry, and about five-foot-four.

Captain Ringknocker placed the folder on the table and stepped back in a precise military manner so that he was just behind the senior officer's right shoulder. He came to attention with the stomping of both feet in what Randy thought was a attempt to mimic a Nazi storm trooper.

The captain spoke in a reedy and high-pitched voice. "Americans, come to attention. Show respect for a senior officer." Ashley spoke in his best parade ground voice. "Americans, *attention.*" He waited a few seconds. "Dress right... Dress." Each officer ignored the pain from their latest beating and put his left hand on his left hip with his elbow bent precisely at ninety degrees. At the same time, each POW turned his head so his chin was aligned with his right shoulder.

The Green Beret captain and West Point graduate waited until they were perfectly aligned, each man's left elbow touching the right elbow of the man next to him, then commanded, "Ready... Front."

All six heads snapped around to face front and their hands dropped in unison so their thumbs were aligned with where the seam of their trousers would be. All six were now standing at attention in a line that would make any U.S. Marine drill instructor proud. Randy forced himself not to smile. *Good move, Ashley. Fuck you, Captain Ringknocker!*

The senior colonel crossed his arms and spoke in rapid Vietnamese. Captain Ringknocker listened, then addressed the Americans. "Senior Colonel Đàm Quang Trung of the Vietnam People's Army thinks you are saboteurs, not prisoners of war, because you are not wearing the uniform of the American Army. Therefore, you are war criminals and will be tried as such. In the Democratic People's Republic of Vietnam, the punishment is death."

Ashley spoke. "We are prisoners of war. We were being held in a camp and were supposedly being transferred to a prison in Hanoi. The camp where we were being kept got bombed and the guards left, so we took the opportunity to escape, as is our duty."

After his words were translated, the colonel opened the folder and flipped through the pages before laying them out. He then rearranged them. Randy guessed he was putting them in the same order in which they were standing.

The chubby colonel turned to the captain and spoke. Captain Ringknocker nodded every few seconds, then translated. "Senior Colonel Trung has checked with Hanoi. They do not have any record of any one of you being captured. That is why he thinks you are commandos who failed in your mission. He thinks you were sent here to rescue prisoners of war. Where are your insignia, your identity tags?"

"They were taken from us when we were captured." The senior colonel did not wait for a translation. Instead, he spoke to Captain Ringknocker, who bowed slightly before clicking his heels and turning to the Americans. "Senior Colonel Trung says each of you tells the same story from the point where you were all being transported to Hanoi. You use different words, but all say the same thing. Either you have rehearsed this, or it may be true. Senior Colonel Trung has checked with Hanoi and yes, a Colonel Duong was killed in an attack on a convoy. Lieutenant Colonel Cao's unit was reported wiped out while headed to a new assignment. That part of your story is true. Senior Colonel Trung wants to know where Lieutenant Colonel Pham's camp is located."

Ashley responded. "Give me our map, and I can show you. It will be an educated guess."

Captain Ringknocker translated and the senior colonel nodded and said something to a guard, who ran into the hall. The Americans could hear shouting in the corridor. Nothing was said until a soldier came in, carrying the map they had used on their trek, and spread it out on the table.

Pointing first at Ashley and then at the map, the captain spoke. "You. Show me the camp."

Ashley over the map and looked at it intently. What he was really doing was looking at the row of papers in front of the senior colonel. "Here, this is where we were held."

The senior colonel looked down and spoke one word. Ashley knew what he said. "Impossible."

Captain Ringknocker looked Ashley in the eye and raised his fist. "You are lying. There are no People's Army camps up there."

Before he could strike, the Senior Colonel shouted a command and Captain Ringknocker lowered his fist.

"Yes there are. We spent several months there." Ashley tapped the map again. "Near this road intersection. The Americans bombed it and killed many of your men. We walked past it. It is probably fifteen or twenty kilometers west from the intersection."

Captain Ringknocker translated. When he finished, the senior colonel sat back in his chair.

There was another exchange in Vietnamese while Ashley stood at attention in front of the table. The senior colonel waved his hand to tell Ashley to go back to the other Americans. The West Point graduate did a precise about face, marched back, and completed another about face to resume his place in line.

Colonel Trung spoke softly to Captain Ringknocker with his back to the Americans. Then he stood up. The other Vietnamese soldiers came to attention as the senior colonel exited.

Captain Ringknocker stomped his feet as he came to attention in front of the Americans. "Senior Colonel Trung is the commander of the Fourth Military District and has ordered me to ensure that you are given a shower and razors to clean up. Your clothes are to be washed and you will be moved to a cell that has beds. When you are clean, you will be fed. This is following the policy outlined in the November 29, 1969 Politburo Resolution No. 194 of the Democratic People's Republic of Vietnam in how we treat our prisoners of war. Senior Colonel Trung has told me to warn you that any attempt to escape will be dealt with very harshly."

Captain Ringknocker, pivoted to the right, slammed his boot into the concrete floor as he finished his turn and barked a command at the soldier at the door.

Chapter 8
CATCH 44

Monday, January 3, 1972, 1453 local time, North Vietnam

In the days after their capture, or as Hank Cho said, their second re-capture as a group and third capture over all, they were moved to a large cell where they were kept in what they called "decent" conditions. The room had a sink with running water, toilet, and three double bunks.

Each morning after breakfast, they took two laps around the compound surrounded by ten armed guards. In his best imitation of a Marine drill instructor, Randy called a cadence as the six men marched in formation. Out of the corner of their eyes, they could see the North Vietnamese soldiers eyeing them. Some laughed and pointed at them, other ignored the six Americans.

Access to a shower came next. Each man was given a razor with which to shave. When he was done, the guard collected it.

A lunch of noodles and vegetables in a watery broth followed; then in the afternoon, if it was not raining, they were again allowed to march around the compound. Ashley, if for nothing else than to amuse himself, counted the paces and concluded that they marched about a mile each day.

Dinner followed. It was different from lunch in that it came with a ball of rice and a piece of meat in the broth. No lights were allowed after dark, so they talked until they drifted off to sleep.

On the second day of their 'new treatment,' Captain Ringknocker was lording over them during their meal. He sneered at Ashley. "Captain, you Americans are not very smart."

Ashely looked at the North Vietnamese Army officer, thinking that he had something on his mind and wanted to say it. So, he kept quiet.

"Do you know how my countryman knew you were not North Vietnamese civilians?"

Ashley shook his head. Out of the corner of his eye, could see the other five had stopped eating.

"It was your backpacks. No North Vietnamese farmer has one. They carry everything in baskets. As soon as he saw you, he knew you were not a civilian. No uniform, no baskets equals enemy."

One afternoon, right after they finished their afternoon walk, the air raid sirens sounded. The bolt on their door slammed open and Captain Ringknocker stuck his head in. "Out. To the bomb shelter," he snapped.

The six Americans walked as fast as they could down the corridor, flanked by armed soldiers. Out in the courtyard, an A-6 shriek overhead, chased by three streams of tracers. Randy could see the helmets of the two crew members as the pilot rolled into a sixty-degree left bank away from the compound, exposing the belly of the airplane. The grease smudges on the external tank and the yellow stripes on the noses of the five-hundred-pound Mark 82s were clearly visible. The Fourth Military District headquarters was obviously not its target, or they'd all be incinerated.

The Americans and their guards ran into the bunker, where they were shoved into the corner while the guards blocked the door. The bunker dulled the noise but not the effect; the ground shook violently and chunks of concrete fell from the ceiling. Dust particles looked like light snow as they slowly fell to the floor.

Randy mouthed "SAM sites" to Jeff Anderson, who mouthed back "Not this close to the port. Probably PEEE OHHH LLLL..."

Randy knew the letters stood for "petroleum, oil and lubricants," which the Navy was fond of targeting. Destroy enough of the sites and soon the trucks along the trail stop running. Both Randy and Ashley put their arms on the shoulders of a shaking Hank Cho, who had his head down and his arms wrapped around his knees. The Americans knew that ever since he'd been pulled out of the collapsed bunker, he was scared of closed-in spaces.

"Imagine yourself someplace else, or think about something different."

Cho laughed nervously as the ground shook. "I am, and I don't want to lose face in front of the enemy." He nodded in the direction of the North Vietnamese soldiers. "They're just as scared as we are."

"Yeah. I don't like being bombed, and I don't want to be entombed in a North Vietnamese Army bunker."

"I'm how when I was going to school, my mother noticed there were a lot of Asian students at U. C. San Diego, so she went to her boss and talked him into opening a restaurant near the campus. It served a mix of Korean, Japanese, and Chinese food. I was told to make sure every Asian kid knew it existed, so I went around the campus handing out menus! If it didn't succeed she would have lost face, and I couldn't let that happen."

"Hank, the air strike will end soon, and we'll get out of here."

"Yeah, they're not like artillery barrages that go on for hours. I'll be O.K." He sat up straighter and took a deep breath.

"I keep thinking, I need to get back home and find a nice Korean girl. If anyone will have me, the way I am now. I might have to ask my mom to help." He shook his head. "Before I was commissioned, I persuaded my mother that arranged marriages were un-American, and that I could find an acceptable wife without her help. She is very traditional, but she understood that assimilation into American society was just as important as maintaining our Korean culture. Some traditions could be modified. My equating an arranged marriage with being un-American convinced her. When my dad didn't object, she gave me her blessing. That's how I was allowed to start dating when I was in college. It was a new and wonderful experience. Before, I had only met eligible women under very controlled circumstances." He looked around. "What I wouldn't give to be on a date now, even an arranged one."

The bunker vibrated from another bomb explosion, and Hank hunched over spasmodically.

Randy could see fear in the faces of the North Vietnamese soldiers. They were just as afraid of dying as the Americans were, and everyone in the bunker had the same aspiration: get out alive.

Gently, Randy lifted Hank's chin off his knees. "Well, if we do get blown up, you'll be in good company. But I don't think this compound has any military value. As long as the bombers learned to aim and hit their designated targets, we should be all right."

As suddenly as it began, the bombardment ceased. All of them waited, unsure if the silence was simply a lull in the bombing or the actual end. The guards did not seem at all anxious to leave the bunker to find out. It wasn't until Captain Ringknocker came to investigate that the Americans were lead out and taken back to their cell.

Right after breakfast the next morning, Captain Ringknocker informed the Americans that they were being transferred to Hanoi. The guards brought them to the same room where they'd met Colonel Trung. On the table were six backpacks that contained rations for the two-day trip to Hanoi, a spare set of clothes, soap, toothpaste, and toothbrushes.

Once they each had a backpack, they were handcuffed and led to a military truck that looked as if it had been taken directly from World War II U.S. Army stock. Most likely, it had been left by the French. Once they were seated, manacles were secured around feet and then linked to their wrists. To a man, they were excited. Soon they would be with their fellow service members, albeit in the Hanoi Hilton. It was, they all agreed, a step on the road to going home.

FORGOTTEN

Captain Ringknocker lifted the canvas and looked inside. Two soldiers climbed into the truck and sat at the back end of the benches that lined the side of the truck. Randy's aviator watch showed that it was 0730. He wondered if there would be newer POWs at Hanoi who could tell them how the war was going, what the news was back stateside. He wanted to go home! He wanted to drive his Shelby and take Janet to their favorite restaurant for a steak dinner, and to make love with her in their own bed. And he definitely wanted to vote in the next election.

The truck came to a sudden halt. One guard peered out, spasmed, and fell backwards with a bloody hole in his forehead. The flap opened from outside, and even as the second soldier raised his AK-47 two suppressed gunshots sent him slumping to the floor with an expanding dark stain on his chest.

The flaps were pulled fully open and a familiar face appeared. Randy's heart sank.

"Ahhh, my slaves. I have come to take you back to my camp. It is being rebuilt. You didn't think you were going to get away from me, did you? I have plans for you, now and after the war. You are more valuable to me alive than dead. Plus, I need more trucks."

Colonel Pham laughed. He stepped aside to let his men toss a dozen bodies into the center of the truck. "You, of course, won't mind sharing the space with some extra cargo." The last one to be loaded was Captain Ringknocker. He had a single hole in the center of his forehead.

Back in their hooch, Hank Cho looked at the glum faces of his fellow POWs. "Ironic, isn't it? We're POWs, but not POWs. We're rescued from being POWs by a psychotic capitalist who kills his own countrymen because we're more valuable as slaves than as POWs. Go find the logic in that."

That got a smile from the other five.

"It's like that book, *Catch 22,*" continued Cho, "only worse. In that war, World War Two, it was easy to get out of the army. All you had to do was ask—and be crazy. If you were crazy, they didn't want you. But only a sane person would want to get out of the army, so if you asked… you weren't crazy, so the law didn't apply to you. See? Now take the situation we're in, and let me give you a lesson in numerology. Asians, particularly Chinese, are big into the symbology of numbers. Some are considered to be lucky, others are bad.

"Where are you going with this?" a depressed Randy Pulaski inquired.

"We're not going to be repatriated with the rest of our fellow POWs because Pham wants to ransom us at a time and place of his choosing, right? Chinese like the numbers six, eight and nine, because the words for these numbers are similar to words that have good meanings. Eight is related to making money. Nine is close to the word meaning 'perfect.' Six is close to the word that means 'going well.' Sixty-six means it is going really well. How many of us are there? Six. So that is a good thing."

"For Pham," snorted Jeff.

"So?" Randy was still skeptical.

"Hang on, mister impatient one, and learn something about Asian cultures. So, my Korean mind began to think about numerology, and there are three bad numbers: three, four and seven. Three is associated with the words 'spread out.' Seven is associated with being upset. One could say that we're upset. Then there is the number four. In Chinese, the word for that number is similar to the word for death. Well, I think our situation can be described as Catch 44. It is worse than death. We're in never-never land. We're alive, yet no one in the North Vietnamese government, much less our own, knows we're alive. We're MIA, presumed—you pick the word—dead, captured, fate unknown."

Hank held up his hand. "We ought to refer to anything we can't fix, or that's illogical, or bad, as Catch 44. The world assumes we're dead, so let's defy them by living. I know it doesn't make much sense, but to my Korean mind, it works."

Ashley laughed. "It's so illogical, I love it!"

Chapter 9
TRANSITION

Friday, January 21, 1972, 1646 local time, Hanford

Janet tossed her car keys onto the kitchen counter. The bag containing her pads and the practice weapons for the dojo she dropped on the floor. She took a pitcher of filtered water out of the refrigerator, filled a sixteen-ounce glass and gulped it down. The dryness in the San Joaquin Valley always made hydration an issue. Like most of her friends, Janet drank filtered water because the local water, while safe, had a chemical, alkaline taste.

She was about to take a second drink when the phone rang.

"Hello."

"A package has been mailed to you. Call when you get it." Dial tone. The voice was Hispanic. It meant more work.

Janet was thinking, *This is good,* when the phone rang a second time. Again, she answered with a non-committal "Hello."

"Hi. Did you just get home?" Helen's southern accent sounded more pronounced than usual.

"I just got home from the dojo. What's up?"

"Can I come over? I need someone to talk to."

"Sure."

"I'll be right over. And if you're all hot and sweaty, don't shower. I like you hot and sweaty. I want to try something new.

191

I'll tell you when I get there."

It was Janet's turn to host what Helen referred to as their "weekend therapy sessions." But a quaver in Helen's voice warned Janet that something was amiss, and their plans for going clubbing might go by the wayside.

When Helen arrived, it was obvious that she had been crying. Once inside, Helen threw her arms around Janet and rested her head on her shoulder. "Just hold me tight for a while."

Janet ran her hands down Helen's back in a soft caressing motion that she hoped would soothe her. "Let's sit down on the couch and I'll hold you. Then you can tell me what's wrong." The "O.K." that came out sounded like it came from a little girl.

Janet sat down first with her back against the armrest. She spread her legs so Helen could lean back against her breasts. Janet entwined her fingers with Helen's, who pressed their hands into her lap. Janet used her legs to pull her friend close.

"Now, what's going on?"

"My... my mother has cancer. She had surgery last week. The doctors will start chemotherapy and radiation, but they are not hopeful. They say she has maybe six months to live. A year if she is lucky."

"Oh my God! I'm so sorry." Janet kissed Helen gently on the shoulder. It was meant to be comforting, not sexual. "What about your father, your brother and sister, do they all know?"

"Yes. My dad wants me to come home for my mother's last few months. He's acting like she is already dead. So is my little sister."

"Can you take a leave of absence?"

"If I go for more than thirty days, I have to take an unpaid leave of absence. After sixty days the district can fill my position. So, if I go to be with her for... for the next few months, they want me to resign."

"Can you afford to do this?"

"Yes," Helen sighed. "Daddy has money. That's not the problem."

"Then what is?"

"Oh Janet! I don't want to watch my mother to die. Not this way. I adore her, and I will miss her terribly. We talk all the time, and then over the past two weeks, she was never home when I called. Now I know why. She didn't want to tell me the bad news. But that's only half of it."

"What's the other?"

Helen twisted around and put her hand on the side of Janet's face. "You. I don't want to leave you. I know we agreed never to use this word to describe our wonderful relationship, but I love you. It is not just the sex. I love everything about you. When you walk into a room, I don't just get turned on, I flood. You touch me and I get weak-kneed. That's how you make me feel. I *love* you!" Helen's eyes searched Janet's.

"What about when Bob comes home?" *I have to play this very carefully. We have to end this relationship and go our separate ways. This is the perfect way to do it. You need to go take care of your mother. By the time she passes away, I'll be long gone.* "Helen, you're not planning to hit him with divorce papers as soon as he arrives in the States, are you? Or worse, divorce him while he is a POW, like some of the other wives have done?"

"Oh, heavens no. I would never do that to Bob. I'll talk to him and take care of him until he gets adjusted to being back home. Maybe he will be okay, sharing me with you, as long as we keep it discreet. We Southerners, we're all about keeping it discrete, aren't we? And you never know, things may change, and why deal with a problem that may resolve itself?"

"Helen, do you mean Bob may not come home alive?"

"Yes."

Janet was silent for a while. "I agree that's a possibility. No one knows if Randy or Bob are alive except the North Vietnamese, and they're not talking. At least Bob is on a list of POWs." Janet switched subjects. "So what's this new thing you want to try?"

Helen twisted around and put her forearms on her lover's

shoulders. It let her look straight into Janet's eyes. "You know I like to explore and try new things. I want to try bondage and discipline. If I like it, and I think I will, I want to go deeper into that world."

Janet didn't say anything. Her mind was racing and she began to caress Helen's inner thigh.

Helen took a deep breath and then kissed Janet, deep and slow, and Janet returned the favor. Helen put one leg on either side of Janet so that her calves were on the armrest. It opened up the way for Janet's fingers to get to her swollen clitoris. Her touch made Helen gasp with pleasure.

"Janet," Helen purred, "make me feel better."

"I will take you to places you've never been before..."

"I'd like that very much."

Monday, January 24, 1972, 1639 local time, North Vietnam

Just after sunrise, a convoy of three trucks rolled into the camp. The first truck was loaded with lumber and bamboo poles of varying lengths. The second carried a similar load, but its trailer also loaded with spools of barbed wire, chicken wire, and four bundles of steel rebar.

The third truck, the only one that had its canvas cover erected, contained sheets of plywood and bags of cement. It towed a generator. An hour later, a fourth truck showed up with a mixed load of plywood and lumber. Its trailer was a tank on wheels.

The American's were ordered to unload the fourth truck first. Immediately behind the tailgate they found out why. Lashed to the stakes along the side of the truck were shovels, picks, four disassembled wheelbarrows, and other farm tools.

When they were done, Lieutenant Colonel Pham came over.

"I have a bargain for you. I am sure that one or two of you are engineers by training. You help us build our new buildings, and I will give you a field to farm that is bigger than the one you had before. I will get you wire, and you can make posts from the trees you cut down. However, whenever you are in the woods, you will be guarded. In return, you share the produce with us."

Ashley, as the leader, spoke for all the Americans. "Before we agree, we want better meat than what you gave us before, more cooking utensils, and spices. Plus, we get to improve our hooch."

"Agreed. It is in my interest to keep you well fed."

Karl spoke up. "I've built barns before with less. This should be a snap."

Ashley stepped forward and stuck out his hand. "We agree to help. Better food, better building, less confinement." It was an agreement with the devil, but better food would make them stronger and improve their ability to survive.

Pham shook Ashley's hand. "Captain Smith, I remind you that anyone who attempts to escape while working on the farm or the factory will be hunted down and shot."

That night, as they sat around a small fire and Hank prepared a Chinese noodle dish in a steel pot, Randy turned to Ashley. "You know, when you made the bargain with Pham, you did the same thing Colonel Nicholson did during the movie *The Bridge Over the River Kwai*."

"You're right, but there's a big difference. He did it to get better treatment and change the focus of his men from being in captivity to doing something productive, even if it helped the Japanese war effort. He knew that the Brit POWs who survived would go home at the war's end. We are not helping their war effort, and we'll have to wait to be ransomed, if that even happens. We need to think about our long-term survival. If we get another chance to escape, we need to be healthy enough to rescue ourselves, because no one else is going to."

Thursday, January 27, 1972, 1220 local time, Los Angeles
The Mexican restaurant designated in her instructions was not far from the beach in Playa del Ray and the western ends of the runways at Los Angeles Airport. Boeing 707s and Douglas DC-8s passed barely two hundred feet overhead, and Janet stuck her fingers in her ears to deaden the high-pitched shriek.

After an hour spent strolling the beach like any tourist, Janet hadn't seen any signs of surveillance. Just in case she'd missed any, she went to one of the beach restrooms and replaced her Bermuda shorts and golf shirt with a wig, jeans, floppy hat, and oversize sunglasses. Then she went to the restaurant and asked for the Julio Mendoza reservation, table for two, and placed an order for cheese enchiladas.

Getting to the table early gave her a chance to take the Walther from her purse and put it between her legs. The press of its cold steel against her inner thighs gave her goose bumps.

As far as Mexican food went, the place was average—tasty, but not spectacular. She'd just cut a chunk from the second enchilada when a man entered, carrying a gift-wrapped box. The waitress pointed to Janet's table. The man waved, and she waved back. In Spanish, the man told the waitress that he was bringing a present for his favorite niece. When the waitress had taken his order for a drink and gone, he leaned over the table and spoke. "Senorita, everything you need is in the box." His English was heavily accented.

Janet untied the bow and opened the wrapping paper slowly. Underneath a pink blouse, Janet saw a Manila envelope. Beneath that were a Makarov, loaded magazines, and a suppressor.

"Thank you, Uncle Julio. I love it."

"Antonio Valencia will not be in Los Angeles for more than a few days. Then, poof! he may disappear again. We were lucky to get a copy of his itinerary."

The waitress approached with his drink.

"It is so good to see you, Uncle Julio," Janet said loudly, in Spanish. "I am sorry you can't stay for lunch."

The man downed his drink, got up and pecked her on the cheek. "I am told that you do very good work." With that, he left.

Friday, January 28, 1972, 2135 local time, Los Angeles
Janet pretended to read a book while she watched Valencia nurse a drink in the bar of the Los Angeles Hilton's lobby. Janet

196

had been surprised that he was easy to find, easy to track, and had no discernible security.

Her brief said he was known for taking boats to Cuba and returning to Florida with high-ranking Cubans who wanted to leave Castro's socialist paradise. She didn't care why. Before she'd met her "Uncle Julio," half of the $75,000 fee plus $10,000 in expenses had been deposited in her offshore account.

She was about to walk up to the bar and initiate a scenario in which she would play a lonely business woman who wanted a good fucking. The thought of a man just about to have an orgasm while she blew his brains out made her smile. Her plan abruptly changed when a woman walked up to Valencia.

There was a short conversation, and Valencia put several bills on the table. The two walked out of the bar. Janet followed them into the same elevator and waited until he pushed a button. She gave a big smile and said, "Oh, thank you."

Valencia ignored Janet. His eyes were fixed on the other woman's large boobs. Assuming they were real, Janet thought she might want to bury her face in them herself.

After getting off the elevator, Janet followed them down the hallway, checking for security cameras and seeing none. This was an older Hilton, and they had not upgraded it with modern security systems. *Good.* She stopped, facing a door a few rooms down the hallway, and fumbled around in her purse as if she were searching for her key. Once she heard their door close, Janet ran to the door and heard a discussion about money. Hooker!

Janet went to her own hotel and tossed some clothes into a small bag. At the front desk of Valencia's hotel, Janet apologized for not having a reservation. The clerk said they had plenty of rooms available. She paid cash for a room and signed the registration form as "Jessica Lund." The clerk told her that the bar and restaurant were closed and room service ended in a few minutes, at eleven. Her room was two floors above Valencia's, on fourteen.

After searching the room, she set the alarm for two a.m. and tested it twice. To quell the butterflies churning in her stomach, Janet field stripped the Makarov and reassembled it as she thought about her new plan. Then, still wearing latex gloves, she practiced picking the lock to her door from the inside. Her skills were was rusty; it took several tries before she could do it easily.

Janet stepped into the hall and closed the door. Her first attempt at picking the lock took twenty seconds. Her next two took between ten and eleven seconds.

At two a.m. Janet took the elevator to the twelfth floor, wearing a blond wig and a floppy hat that hid her face. No light was leaking out from under Valencia's door when she pressed her ear to the door. No voices. Out came the picks. Once the lock gave up its security, Janet slowly twisted the handle.

With a long set of forceps, she felt for the safety chain. It was not connected. Janet eased the door open just wide enough to slip inside, hoping light from the hallway wouldn't wake Valencia. The door closed with a barely audible click. Janet pressed her back against the wall as she eased toward the bed with its two sleeping forms. *Shit, he paid her enough to spend the night.*

In the ambient light, she could see Valencia sleeping on his back. The woman was on her side with her boobs pressed against him and one arm draped across Valencia's chest.

Something in Valencia's mind must have sensed danger, or else he was not asleep. His eyes opened. "What the...?" The last sound he heard was the *pffittt* of the suppressed Makarov. The bullet went through the bridge of Valencia's nose and into his brain. The woman stirred, and Janet couldn't take a chance. Training took over and she put a bullet through the hooker's head before she woke. *What a waste.* Janet picked up both casings and slipped them in her pocket.

With her index finger, she checked each form for a pulse. Nothing.

Janet cracked the door and saw that no one was in the hallway. She took the elevator down to the third floor and got off. She waited for another elevator and took it to the tenth before taking the stairs to the fourteenth floor.

Inside her room, she mussed up the bed to make it look like she'd slept in it. Fully clothed, Janet sat on the bed and looked at the clock. It was 0216. She now had to force herself to wait until 0600 when she could walk through a lobby full of travelers heading out to catch early flights.

Despite being calm on the outside, Janet's heart was pounding. She couldn't concentrate on a book, and watching TV was boring. Masturbate? No, she had to keep focused.

At 0430 she heard the people in the room next door start to move around. One, then the other, took a shower. *Great idea!* Janet spent the next thirty minutes showering and drying off before she put on the clothes she'd brought. She'd come in as a blonde but was leaving as a brunette.

By the time she finished packing, it was 0530. Time to go. As she'd expected, when the elevator door opened it was full of people heading out to catch early flights. She blended in. In the lobby she was relieved to see no police. They probably wouldn't be called until housekeeping found the bodies, or somebody couldn't reach Valencia.

In her mental replay, she'd taken two risks—staying in the same hotel as her victim, and meeting someone who gave her the target and the Makarov. If the clerk remembered her, the police would find a dead end when they tried to track down the mythical Jessica Lund and would quickly realize that their chances of catching the professional hit man were between slim and none.

Along Manchester Avenue, she made her first drop. The barrel and handle went into a paper bag, then into the trashcan at a 24-hour gas station. After a few miles on I-5, Janet pulled into a Tote'Em convenience store, where she bought a bottle of apple juice and two donuts. In the bathroom, she changed clothes again. Into the bag that went into the trash went the suppressor, along with the blouse she had been wearing. She washed her hands, using lots of soap from the dispenser and bleach from a small bottle in her purse, to neutralize any gunshot residue.

Janet forced herself to remain cool as she drove along I-5 at a steady sixty-five. At the junction of State Highway 99 just south of Bakersfield, she bought gas, a bag of potato chips, a can of Coca Cola, and an Almond Joy. Into the trash went the Makarov's slide and her jeans, as well as the spare magazines.

Back on the highway and with the evidence gone, Janet had two hours to drive before she got to Hanford. Adrenalin was still pumping through her veins when she pulled into her driveway a little after ten-thirty in the morning.

She went into the living room and poured herself four fingers of scotch. She enjoyed the taste and the burning sensation as the liquid worked its way down to her stomach. She realized that she was not only horny, but hungry as well.

Bacon and eggs went down, along with a second glass of scotch. The food settled her stomach, but didn't take care of her sexual needs, and Helen was away. In bed with one hand on her favorite vibrating dildo, moving it in and out, the other caressing her clitoris, the orgasms started slow and kept coming in stronger waves as her fingers and the vibrating dildo worked their magic.

When she had had enough, Janet looked at the clock. It was 1235. She was sexually satisfied and eighty-five thousand dollars richer.

With the money from this hit, and the one in Miami, and the remaining money that she'd kept from SDS, she now had $400,000 in the bank. *The plan is to get to $5,000,000 and disappear. I may be masquerading as a revolutionary, but I am a mercenary and a capitalist at heart.*

Saturday, February 13, 1972, 1207 local time, North Vietnam
The beatings at the hands of Senior Colonel Trung's interrogators and the trek during the attempted escape had taken a physical and mental toll, and the six Americans knew it. Joking about their lack of strength and stamina didn't make the problem go away. What it did was force the engineer in Randy and Karl to remember how buildings were built before gasoline engines.

200

Levers, wedges, and pulleys, along with gravity, became their friends.

During a break, Greg Christiansen looked at Pham's new, half-built office building. "You know, if I didn't know better, I'd say this is like a barn raising. When I was a kid, whenever someone needed to build a new house or barn, we'd all go help."

Ashley tossed a hammer so it landed at Greg's feet. "Well, farmer boy, when we get this built, you, sir, are going to be the chief farmer."

"You are, of course, assuming that I know what to do."

"I am. So you'd better have a green thumb. It's the only way we can have a decent diet."

"Yeah, but all we grew was soybeans, corn, and wheat. Remember, I joined the Air Force to get *away* from farming."

"Too bad, so sad. You know more about it than any of us."

Greg used the back of his hand to wipe the sweat off his face, wishing he had spent more time doing farm work than avoiding it.

His ancestors had come to America to take advantage of the Homestead Act of 1862 that gave them free land if they agreed to work it for five years. The first generation acquired the 160 acres allowed by the law. More relatives came and got their own free land. Christiansen Brothers and Sons prospered, and generations expanded by acquiring land near or adjacent to the original farm.

By the time Greg was born, there were three complexes. The smallest one was six thousand acres, and the largest, just over ten. The family business included a large dry goods store, and John Deere and Chevrolet dealerships in nearby Mankato.

On December 8, 1941, his father had volunteered to join the U.S. Army. When asked his occupation, he gave the recruiting officer a five-minute description of the family businesses. As a result, to his chagrin, he spent the entire war as a supply officer, ordering and inspecting shipments of grain, and never left the U.S.

From the time he was a little boy, Greg was given daily chores that increased in complexity and importance as he got older. He often referred to the family homestead as a working farm because no one ever stopped working. Learning how to fix things was a necessity. Greg knew that when he graduated from college he would be "farmed" out, which meant a job in one of the family businesses.

It was a life he didn't want. Greg wanted to fly, so he applied for an Air Force ROTC scholarship and the Air Force Academy.

There were only congratulations from family members when he was accepted by the Air Force Academy in 1964. His father was especially proud. Four years later, Second Lieutenant Greg Christiansen entered flight training, and fifteen months later he flew his first combat mission in an F-100. Six months later, he was a POW.

Monday, February 14, 1972, 1207 local time, Toronto

Toronto's damp cold and biting wind burned one's cheeks and reminded Janet of a Chicago winter. Even the remnants of the snow were the same—black and white piles of crusty ice piled along the sidewalks, covered in gritty dirt.

The flue effect created by the buildings of Toronto's central business district accelerated the Arctic air, pushing the wind chill down to the equivalent of minus fifteen Fahrenheit, according to the news. Janet didn't care what the number was; it was fucking *cold*.

Janet knew she needed new clothes as soon as she stepped out of the cab at the Royal York Hotel on Front Street. It was the same hotel where Queen Elizabeth and the royal family stayed when they came to Toronto.

The clothes she'd bought in California simply were not warm enough. Her shopping list included boots with thick soles that would keep out the cold, gloves that would keep her hands warm, and a heavy woolen coat. The concierge told her the Hudson Bay Company flagship store on Bay Street could provide everything she needed.

When she checked in, the clerk handed her a note that

instructed her to call a number to discuss her needs. *Needs, hell! I need a good fucking and a warm coat. Then we'll talk. Unfortunately, getting laid will have to wait.*

Once she was back in her room with her new purchases, Janet dialed the number.

"*Hola.*"

Janet was surprised to hear a woman's voice.

"Luna here."

The woman asked for the name of her favorite roommate at camp.

"Monika."

"There have been some changes. We should meet."

"Where? Someplace warm—and inside."

They agreed on three o'clock that afternoon at a location the voice suggested.

Another lesson. Learn the local terrain ahead of time so that I can choose a meeting place. And stop using the name Luna. It ties back to Julia Amy Lucas, a.k.a. Janet Williams Pulaski.

Toronto was building a subway system designed so that once residents entered they could go almost anywhere in the city center. Shops, restaurants, office buildings, even hotels would all be accessible without ever having to put on a coat. The network of tunnels had come about when building owners realized they could create a new source of revenue in their "basements" by developing an underground shopping mall. They pushed the provincial and city governments to invest in the idea as a benefit to residents: a more convenient way to get around, especially during the long, cold winters, as well as a source of tax revenue.

Janet found the PATH system easy to navigate. Signs and maps were everywhere. It was as advertised—a mall where one could buy anything, from groceries to lingerie to clothing to booze, and walk from point A to point B without going out in the frigid cold.

To make sure she wasn't being tailed on her way to the food court under the headquarters of the Canadian Imperial Bank of

Commerce, Janet stopped in front of store windows so she could identify the people behind her by the clothes they were wearing. As one last check, Janet ducked into a bookstore to see if anyone came in looking for her.

At the food court, Janet bought a soda at a Tim Horton's and sat at a table on the opposite side from where the feminine voice wanted to meet. She was fifteen minutes early and had time to check for surveillance. Five minutes before the appointed time, Janet moved to the restaurant, picking a chair at a table so her back was to a wide pillar and she could see almost the entire food court seating area.

Janet waved when she saw a woman wearing a dark brown overcoat and matching fur hat with an orange scarf—the agreed upon signal. She was carrying a shopping bag with a Hudson Bay logo. Janet stood and hugged the woman as if they were old friends. The stranger sat down, confident that the individual sitting across the table matched the description she'd been given, and the passport photo she'd been shown.

"I brought you a present. It's what you like." *Translation—I brought you a Makarov with a suppressor.*

The woman had a slight accent that Janet found hard to place. She wondered if the woman worked at an embassy or was a contractor or a deep cover agent. Her dark complexion didn't go with her platinum blonde hair color. She either dyed her hair or it was a wig.

Janet didn't like this face-to-face style of meeting, with its risks and demands on her time. That was going to end with this project. But first she had to get through the next two assignments. "Thanks. I will call you when I know what else I need."

She leaned forward and asked in a soft voice, "So, what has changed?"

"We have information that one of your targets—Ramon Rojas —is planning to go to Miami next week. We don't want him to leave Toronto."

"O.K., that makes him number one."

"The other man—Benedicto Figueroa—is a womanizer."

"What does that mean?"

"He spends a lot of nights in bars looking for women he can seduce."

"That sounds normal."

"Yes, it is. But he likes rough sex and sometimes beats up women. His benefactors pay his victims to keep quiet."

"Interesting. Do you know what bars he goes to?"

"I can get a list."

"Good, please do. Drop it off at my hotel in an envelope. Meanwhile, I need to get to work."

The sun was already going down when Janet got back to her hotel room. She'd forgotten how early it got dark in the winter this far north. By four-thirty in the afternoon the sun was gone, and the temperature dropped faster than the sun.

The gift-wrapped box had a Makarov and suppressor wrapped in cloth, five magazines, and a box of ammunition taped closed, along with more photos of the targets and a typewritten profile with details on their lives.

Target one—Rojas—was married and in his late forties. He lived in the center of a three-building complex bordered on the north by Alexander Street and on the south by Wood Street.

Janet looked at the map and memorized the route—north on Yonge and turn left onto Wood to get to the park between the buildings—then set out. Right after Shuter Street, the stores on Yonge changed from known retail brands to shops selling sex toys, used books and clothing. Three blocks or so later, it changed again. Restaurants appeared, along with a drug store and higher-end retail shops.

At Wood, Janet turned left. Half a block on she stood in the circle that was in the park between the center and the western building. Each apartment had a balcony. Many had barbecue grills, skis, and other belongings that could be stored out in the cold propped up against either the railing or the side of the building.

Janet walked into the elevator in the westernmost building and pushed seven, the top floor. At the end of the hallway, she found the stairway that led to the roof access door. It was locked, but since there was no warning saying the door was tied into an alarm system, Janet picked it in a few seconds. Cautiously, she opened the door and left the deadbolt extended so she would not be trapped on the roof.

Walkways laid out like a flat ladder flat let her get to the edge of the roof that sloped gently down toward a small, foot-high wall. Janet crouched down as she made her way to the edge. Every few feet there were openings in the wall, through which she could see the other building. Assuming the information about Rojas was accurate, this was a perfect spot.

The same day, 1750 local time, Newark

A gray, cloudy sky and waving tree branches in the park across the street were typical of a Northeast winter—drab, cold, windy, and damp. It would get worse later in the day when the rain started and then turned to snow.

The annoying sound of a buzzer interrupted Raul's musings about the weather. Someone was at the front door. Raul pushed the intercom.

"Raul, it is Hector. Hector Juarez. Do you remember me from our days in *Fuerza Aérea de Liberación?*"

Raul remembered the intelligence officer who'd briefed him during the Bay of Pigs invasion. He'd seen him at reunions off and on during the years. The last time had been four years ago, just before he'd gone to Southeast Asia. But it paid to be careful, so… "Tell me something to convince me that you know me."

"You've had two crashes in a B-26. Both times, the other pilot died. One was in Laos and one Nicaragua."

"What was the name of the pilot in Laos and where did he die?"

"His nickname was "The Swede." The crash was at Lima 36."

Raul pressed the intercom. "When you press eight on the

elevator, I will authorize it to come up to the eighth floor. It will be good to see you."

As Hector stepped out of the elevator, he heard a door unlatch and there, standing in front of him, leaning on his cane, was Raul Moya.

"Please come in."

The two men shook hands warmly.

"May I offer you a drink, Hector?"

"How about a beer?"

"Sure. Give me a minute."

Before he returned to the living room, Raul watched Hector look around, then sprawl on one of the two couches that formed an alley. His ski jacket, gloves and wool ski hat he piled on the center cushion. After handing Hector a bottle of Pabst Blue Ribbon, Raul sat on the opposite sofa.

"*Salud, compadre.*" Raul tipped the bottle toward his former comrade in arms.

"*Salud.*" Hector took a long swig from the bottle. "This is quite a set-up. I'm glad to see you're doing well. How's the leg?"

"It is still attached. And, yes, business has been good. What brings you out of the warmth of Miami?"

"God, it's cold up here. I don't know how you stand this weather."

"The natives say you get used to it. I dress warmly and stay inside as much as possible. The summers are really nice."

"All three months of it."

"Actually, from May to October it is fine." Raul took another swallow and again tipped his bottle toward Hector as if to ask the question, "What brings you here?"

Hector put his bottle down and met Raul's eye. "Are you interested in expanding the type of services you provide?"

Raul didn't say a word. After a moment, Hector elaborated. "Are you interested in brokering wet work?"

"As in assassinations?"

"Body snatches, break-ins, that kind of work."

"Where do I get the people and customers?"

"We provide the customers and can recommend people to do the work. Or, you can find your own."

"How do I get paid?"

"You set that up with the buyer. You will need accounts in countries where they have strict bank secrecy laws."

I already have those. "Who sets the prices?"

"You do. Whatever profit you make, you keep. If the buyer doesn't like your price, he can go with someone else."

"Are you here on behalf of the agency?"

Hector picked up his bottle of beer and drained it. "They're one of the firms who asked me to see if you were interested."

"Who are others?"

"Let's just say they are organizations who want to eliminate loose ends and would prefer not to do it themselves. Some are willing to pay more than others. What earns a premium is no blowback."

"Mafia?"

"They like to do their own dirty work, but yes, sometimes they use outsiders."

Raul, who had been sipping beer while Hector spoke, put the empty bottle down on a coaster. "What if I don't like it?"

"You stop taking contracts. However, I will tell you that the margins are better. There are no written contracts, no receipts, and no customs paperwork unless it is needed."

That makes me *a loose end.* "Are the customers willing to work through a cut out so they don't know who I am?"

"That would be preferred. You never have to meet, so neither of you, quote, know each other, unquote. How you communicate is up to you."

"What about tools of the trade, like weapons?"

"Ahhhh, that's where I come in," Hector said. "I have a sideline business and can get you anything, well, almost anything, that your contractors need. All it takes is a little time. And money."

"So let me summarize. Buyers come to me, we negotiate a price that includes my fee. I find the people to do the work. If the contractors need guns and explosives, you're my primary supplier and we agree on a price for your stuff. That's the expenses part."

"That's it, in the proverbial nutshell."

"When do I need to let you know?"

"Now. If you say yes, we have some details to work out. If you say no, then, thanks for the beer and I'll see you at the next reunion."

Raul sat back on the couch. *Running cargo is lucrative. I've made almost a half million dollars after expenses since June. This could make me rich. Or it could kill me. I like rich and can manage the risks.* "I'm in."

Wednesday, February 16, 1972, 0626 local time, Toronto

Finally! There was light on the horizon. Dawn was coming, even if sunrise was still hours away. Janet had been lying on the wood decking that acted as raised walkways since 0430. Her long underwear, wool overcoat and socks helped, but she felt like a corpse—cold and stiff.

The Dragunov rifle sat next to her on its bi-pod. It was pulled back so that the barrel and the suppressor could not be seen unless one looked down at the building. Behind her was the viola case that had foam cutouts for the barrel, stock, scope, and three ten-round magazines. If she needed more ammunition, or more than one magazine, she had problems.

The light came on in the target's apartment. If the intelligence she'd been given was right, Rojas came out on his balcony every morning to look at the weather and sip his coffee. If true, this ritual would save her the messy task of breaking into his apartment and killing everyone so there would be no witnesses.

Janet did small exercises to wake up her stiff joints. They were thankful for the movement. The bipod squeaked as she slid it forward so the suppressor was just inside the gap in the wall.

Light coming through the curtains let her focus on the door

handle with the Soviet-made SVD-type scope. Using the graph and chart in the reticle, Janet estimated the range at five hundred yards and well within the eight-hundred-yard effective range of the 7.62 X 54-millimeter cartridge.

Bullet drop, according to her ballistics chart, would be about three inches, even though the bullet would be traveling from the eighth floor to the fourth. For a chest hit she would aim at his chin, and the 151-grain bullet should pulverize his heart beyond any hope of revival at a hospital.

There were higher buildings around Janet, and the longer she lay on the roof, the greater the chance she would be seen. But at 0630 she was still under the cover of darkness, and her dark clothing blended with the shadows.

The door on Rojas' apartment slid open a few inches, then a hand pushed it fully open. Rojas appeared in the doorway, turned around and went back inside.

One part of Janet's mind said, *Oh shit, he's not coming out.* Another part willed her body not to shiver and controlled her breathing. The sliding door stayed open. Then it widened and Rojas stepped not his balcony, coffee mug in hand.

Through the scope, she could see the steam coming off the coffee. If there had been better light, she could probably have seen if he liked his coffee light or dark. Janet exhaled. Squeeze. The Dragunov shoved back into her shoulder with a tinny bang that wasn't noticeable above the street noise.

She saw Rojas jerk from the impact of the bullet. The scope's field of view let her see the mug fly out of his hand, spraying coffee all over the wall before it shattered on the balcony's concrete floor. As his body slid down, his head dangled loosely and left a bloody trail on the wall.

I must have hit him at the bottom of the throat, and the bullet blew out his spine. Not what I aimed at. Shit. Janet disassembled the rifle, stowed the parts and closed the viola case. At the door to the roof, she removed the masking tape that kept the latch from engaging and stood in front of the elevator, willing it to arrive.

Her worst fear was that someone from an apartment would come out and wonder who she was, but no one did. Rather than go back down Yonge Street to Union Station, Janet walked a block west to Bay and headed toward the lake. Her fast pace got the stiffness out of her joints and her circulation going. Underneath her warm clothes, she began to perspire.

At Union Station, Janet found an unused locker large enough to contain the viola case. Freed of her burden, Janet found a stand that sold hot chocolate. With her coat slung over her arm, Janet took a sip of the sweet, hot liquid and headed back to the Royal York via the underground.

Friday, February 18, 1972, 1700 local time, North Vietnam

Large raindrops hammered the hooch's corrugated metal roof. The rain pouring off the edges of the roof formed a translucent sheet between Randy and the outside world. He looked at his watch and shouted, "Hey guys, I know this is depressing, but it's five p.m. and my beer low level light is burning brighter than ever. It's time for happy hour. I could use a drink of anything alcoholic. Ashley, do you think Pham would provide us with a six pack or, better, a bottle of scotch?"

The Army Green Beret came over to where Randy was staring out the window. "I doubt it. Where would he get it?"

"Vinh. He goes there all the time."

"Are you serious?"

"As a heart attack. Ask, all he could say is no."

Ashley nodded his head. "Why not? It should be good for a laugh. Maybe he'll want to improve our morale."

The same day, 2100 local time, Toronto

Janet walked up the steps and under a flickering sign of the Red Lion. The bar was on Cumberland Street in Yorkville, a trendy, wealthy neighborhood north of the central business district, and it was supposed to be one of Figueroa's favorite hang outs.

The cover charge was ten dollars, After shoving her hat and gloves into a sleeve, Janet handed her coat to an elderly Asian lady at the coat check window, who gave her a numbered token. Her oversize purse with the Makarov Janet kept slung diagonally across her chest. The strap emphasized what little cleavage she had under her tight beige turtleneck sweater.

Just past the coat checkroom, one sign announced, "Lots of dancing and small bar" and pointed upstairs. Another placard, pointing down the hall, offered "Not much dancing and big bar."

Seeing the downstairs bar was packed, Janet went up the wide stairs and settled into one of a dozen empty bar stools. Behind her, a band taking up the opposite corner played soft music.

The bartender plopped a napkin in front of her that immediately was soaked. He bent down and pulled out a towel, dried the surface, and dropped another napkin in front of her. This one stayed dry.

"Laphroaig. Three fingers, neat." The scotch would give her something to sip while she waited.

The bartender smiled. "Not what I would have guessed. I'll have to charge you for a double."

"That's O.K. What would you have guessed?" Janet put a twenty-dollar bill on the counter to pay for the drink.

"I pegged you for wine, a merlot or a burgundy."

"Sorry to disappoint you." Janet turned away to look at the half dozen couples on the dance floor and the tables where a group of men sat.

Several men tried to "chat her up." After she'd turned down a third potential suitor, the bartender came over.

"Are you waiting for someone, or looking?"

Janet smiled. "A little of both."

"Is he a regular here?"

"I think so." She put another twenty-dollar bill on the bar and slid it forward. "His name is Benedicto Figueroa."

"You a cop?"

"Heavens, no!"

212

"Does he owe you money?"

"No."

"Are you a jilted girlfriend, ex-wife, mother of his bastard?"

Janet giggled. "None of the above! I heard he is a good fuck."

The bartender's jaw dropped noticeably at this response. "Yeah, I know him. Usually gets here about now. Good-looking guy, longish black hair, well built, and takes care of himself. I think he's Cuban."

"That's him. I want to find out if the rumor is true."

The bartender smiled. "Hang on a second, let me check downstairs." He dialed a number and talked for a few seconds before dialing another number and talked longer.

"He's here and standing in line for a drink. I told the bartender downstairs to tell him that there's a good-looking woman up here who wants to fuck his brains out. If he's interested, he'll come on up." The twenty-dollar bill disappeared into the bartender's pocket.

Janet put another twenty on the bar. "Thanks."

This bill followed the last one. "Name's John. I get off at one. If he doesn't show up, I'll be happy to show you what I can do."

Janet looked at him and guessed they were about the same age. He was in good shape, and probably as horny as she was. She wondered if a man was better than no woman. "I may take you up on that." *Would I really?*

She slid the glass toward John. "A refill, just one shot." Another ten dollars went on the bar.

Janet saw Benedicto before he saw her, in the mirror behind the bar. There was enough light so she could watch Benedicto's head move—a hunter searching for his prey. He started taking inventory, beginning in the closest corner and then moving up the wall in a practiced pattern that Janet recognized. *He, too, has been trained in the intelligence world.* She kept her glass raised to her lips, to conceal her eyes in case he also checked the mirror. She saw when he spotted her. His movements became concentrated, focused. *Target acquired.*

213

Benedicto turned the chair next to Janet so the back was facing her, then slung his leg over the seat.

"So you want to meet me?"

"I do." She toyed with her drink and tilted her head.

"Do you have a name?"

"Jennifer Bertrand."

"You live around here?"

"Not far."

"How do you know my name?"

"A friend told me about you." Janet gave him a deliberately appraising look that lingered on his chest and groin.

"Does that girlfriend have a name?"

"She does." Janet smiled her prettiest smile, showing her perfect white teeth. "But girls don't broadcast their secrets. My friend told me that you were the only man who could satisfy her." *Yes, play to his ego.*

"How do you like it?"

"Any way you want. Just as long as you can stay hard long enough so I get off—several times a night."

Benedicto made a face. "I fuck many girls. Some don't like me, others keep coming back for more."

Janet wanted to close the sale. "Look, if you don't want to fuck me tonight, I can find someone else. I don't mind if it gets a bit rough, but I don't do bondage. Your call."

She turned around to start to lift her purse.

"Stand up."

Janet knew what was coming next. She stood up, feeling her tight jeans hug her curves. Facing him again, she leaned forward and whispered. "I shave my pussy."

Benedicto gave her a big smile. "Let's go. Do I need to take care of your bar bill?"

"No, John's been taken care of." She gave the bartender a parting smile. His answering smile was a bit rueful as he got a good look at what he'd be missing.

When they got to his Chevrolet Impala, Benedicto turned to

her and spoke.

Janet just looked at him as she slid into the passenger seat. "What did you say? I don't speak Spanish."

"I said you are beautiful. We are going to have fun together."

What he'd really said was, "You're going to give me a blowjob, and I am going to screw you in your cunt and then in your ass."

By car, Benedicto's house was ten minutes away. Not much was said, other than he asked her what she did for a living as she stroked his upper thigh and felt his dick straining against the front of his pants. Janet told him she sold women's costume jewelry to retail chains and small jewelry stores in Ontario and Manitoba.

He pulled into the driveway of a small, two-story house. Inside, it was clean and neat.

"Drink?"

"No, I'm good. All liquored up." Janet peeled off her coat and placed it over a couch. She didn't want to touch anything in the house. She came over to Benedicto and kissed him, sliding her tongue into his mouth.

"I am very horny." One hand helped him unbutton his shirt while the other stroked his erection. Once she got his shirt unbuttoned, she pulled off her sweater and unhooked her bra, letting it drop to the floor. Then she slowly pulled out his belt and dropped his trousers to the floor.

He grabbed a handful of Janet's hair and forced her head toward his fully erect penis. "Get me off!"

Janet got down on her knees and took his penis in her right hand with her thumb at the base of his scrotum. Her left hand cupped his balls. Before his penis could enter her mouth, she squeezed as hard as she could with her left hand and twisted with her right.

Benedicto let go of her hair as he staggered back, clutching his private parts. "OWWWWWWW!"

Janet sprung to her feet and her right hand lashed out. Rigid fingers drove into his throat just above his breastbone, then the palm of her left hand crushed his nose. Benedicto's head snapped back and blood streamed from his broken nose. He tried to speak, but only hissing came out as he struggled to get air through his crushed esophagus.

Quickly, Janet unzipped her purse and pulled out the Makarov. Rather than risk him recovering and coming for her while she took the time to screw on the silencer, she wrapped a loose cushion around the muzzle and squeezed the trigger. Foam blew out in all directions, and a dark blotch of blood started to form in the center of Benedicto's chest, spreading as he fell to his knees.

Now that she had time, Janet screwed on the suppressor and aimed it at his chest. She said in Spanish, "No one likes a bully. Especially one who beats up women."

A second round spat out of the Makarov, striking Figueroa's chest about half an inch to the left of the other one. He gasped. Blood was filling his lungs and his heart was barely functioning. As much as Janet wanted to watch him die, she squeezed off a third round that went into his left eye.

Once the empty brass casings were in her pocket, Janet dressed and pulled on her gloves before opening the door and stepping into the cold. As she walked east toward Yonge, she deposited pieces of the Makarov in trashcans along the way. Once that was done, she flagged a cab that brought her back to the Royal York.

She was tempted to go back and see John the bartender, but that would necessitate an explanation. As it was, if he ever found out that Benedicto was murdered, or if the police retraced his steps, John could describe her, but not her name. She'd paid cash, and he had been at the other end of the bar when she'd spoken to Figueroa.

Janet stayed up late that night, thinking about how she was going to change the way she was contacted. The current system was much too direct and made her nervous. The Cubans knew where she lived. If they wanted to turn her over to the FBI or any other agency, she would never know it until it was too late.

216

Moving was her first order of business. It would create space and give her time to change the process of how she would work with her customers.

The second problem was finding a way to have sex without getting into a relationship. Killing a certified creep had been deeply arousing, and Janet knew that masturbating just wouldn't be enough to satisfy her.

Technically she was still married to Randy, but she'd long since rationalized her way through being unfaithful when she and Helen began sleeping with each other. In her heart she hoped he was still alive and would make it home, but every indicator said that she was a widow, even though it wasn't yet official.

On Sunday, snow delayed her flight out of Toronto to Chicago by three hours and she missed her connection to Fresno. In Chicago, American Airlines offered her a flight to LA that left in two hours. The delay gave her time to book a room at a hotel near LAX and a rental car. She planned to drive to Fresno on Monday morning, turn in the rental car at the airport, pick up her Volvo, and be home by afternoon.

It was well past eight on Monday morning when Janet rolled out of her hotel bed. While she was looking for her credit card to pay for breakfast, a card for the After Supper Club fell out of her wallet. It was one of the places that Helen had wanted to go with her.

Thinking no one would answer the phone at ten on a Monday morning. Janet dialed the number, planning to leave a message. She studied the card. It was very businesslike in its appearance, i.e. black raised type, name, title, business name, address and phone number. She was surprised when a woman answered, but she managed to speak smoothly.

She decided to use her real name. "Hi, Maureen, my name is Janet. A friend gave me your card. Do you have time to answer some questions?"

The answers were interesting. The club was near the

217

Hollywood-Burbank Airport, about 45 minutes from Janet's hotel, assuming she didn't get lost. She gathered her belongings, checked out, and set forth.

A massive, stained wood gate with the address number in black on a brass plaque blocked the driveway. She pressed the intercom button and Maureen's voice was clear as a bell. "You found us! Park next to my Porsche."

The door in the twelve-foot-high wall swung open, revealing a bright red 911S coupé and an electric blue Chevy Malibu SS 396 convertible, their paint glistening in the sunlight.

The door to the house opened and a woman stood in the doorway. Maureen was about five-foot-nine, slim, with a shock of natural red hair to go with her very fair skin. "Come in, come in. I'm Maureen Winston." She pointed to another woman. "And this is my business partner, Brittney Waldon. Mondays are really slow, so we come in and spend a couple of quiet hours and then go home. When you called, we'd just gotten here."

Brittney was very tall. Janet guessed she was six-three, maybe taller, and that was without heels. She wore gray pants and a pink golf shirt. She had closely cropped blonde hair, in a style similar to Janet's. Brittney laughed as she and Janet shook hands. "We must go to the same hairdresser!"

"I guess so." Janet was surprised at how comfortable the two women made her feel.

"Let's get the important part out of the way. We were going to order in some Chinese food for lunch; why don't you join us?"

"Sure." *I might as well have lunch before I head north.* Maureen pointed to a couch in her office, which was the size of a large master bedroom, and handed Janet a menu. "Good. Let's order. It will be nice to have someone to talk to besides Brittney."

Janet studied the menu and gave Maureen her choice. Brittney sat down at the other end of the couch and twisted so she could face her guest. Her long legs were crossed at the knees and she rested one arm on the top of the sofa. Maureen took the single chair. The top two buttons on her blouse were undone and Janet saw that the redhead was wearing a black leather bra. "Coffee?" she asked.

"Black, please, and a bit of sugar."

Maureen poured the dark liquid into a cup with delicate pink and light blue flowers around the rim. If Janet had looked at the symbol on the bottom of the cup, she would have seen the Rosenthal logo.

When she finished pouring three cups, Maureen passed one to Janet. "Let's talk some more, and then either Brittney or I can give you a tour. If you're interested, you can join. If not, we've had a chat and a good lunch."

"Sounds great." Despite how guarded she was about her life, Janet felt relaxed, as if she had known both women for years.

"So, let's continue our conversation. Are you married?"

Janet paused for a second before she answered. The word that came out answered the question her subconscious asked as well as Maureen's. "No."

"Do you prefer men or women, or both at the same time?"

"Hmmmm, good question. Occasionally I might like a man, but I prefer women. In the right setting, I might try group sex."

Brittney reached out and let the back of her fingers brush against Janet's arm that was resting on the top of the cushion. Maureen asked her next question. "Do you like the harder stuff, bondage and discipline?"

"I tried light bondage once, and I could take it or leave it."

"Well, if you want to explore any bondage fantasies, I run another facility called La Maison. It is just for those who like rough trade."

Janet nodded. "That's good to know." She didn't know what else to say.

Maureen pursed her lips. "Janis, I have to ask this. Are you addicted to any drugs like heroin or cocaine? If you are and we find out later, we kick you out, literally. If we find out that you have a sexually transmitted disease, we also kick you out. Legally, we can't do more. Turning the member over to the authorities

219

opens a real can of worms around the individual's intent, because it is not a crime unless the person deliberately goes around infecting people."

"I don't do drugs or, for that matter, drink very much. And I don't have any diseases."

"My kind of girl!" Brittney's hand caressed her forearm and Janet could feel her groin responding. The back of her brain wondered what it would be like to have those long legs wrapped around her. She wondered how Brittney tasted.

"Questions?"

"Could you go over the operation again?" The stirrings in her crotch made it hard to concentrate.

"Sure. This is a place where people come to have sex with no strings attached. We're open six days a week. Members start arriving around eight or eight thirty. You never know who is going to be here on any night, although we do have ladies-only and guys-only nights. They're on the calendar we mail out at the end of the month. Our members are mostly between twenty and I'd say forty-five, but there are some men and women who are in their fifties. If you want to meet someone, we have an answering service that sets up dates. You can spend the night, but have to be out by ten the next morning, and the cost for overnighting is $25. We don't have a liquor license. We provide glasses and mixes, but it is strictly bring your own booze."

Maureen drank coffee, then put her cup down. "We operate like a country club. There is an initiation fee of $2,500 and monthly dues of $75. Each time you come, there's a cover charge of $10 to cover the four-star hors d'oeuvres prepared here in our kitchen. We take cash, check, or credit cards. Once you are a member, we send you a bill every month. If you go 30 days past due, you can't come in until you are current. Go beyond sixty days past due and, unless there are special circumstances, you are out and we keep your initiation fee. If on the other hand, you want to leave and are current, we give you your $2,500 back."

The redhead tilted her head. "Brittney, what did I leave out?"

"Nothing I can think of, other than a bit about the building. I can tell Janis about our facilities if she wants to take a tour." Her hand caressed Janet's forearm again.

Janet looked at Brittney. "I'd like to see the place."

The phone on Maureen's desk rang and she mouthed, "I'll order lunch." Brittney pointed to the door and Janet took the lead. As they headed out, Brittney ran her hand gently up and down the small of Janet's back as she guided her down the hall. Janet felt an impulse to purr.

"Soooo, this used to be a two-hundred-and-ten room Holiday Inn. When Maureen and I bought it, it was run down and the owners were bankrupt. We remodeled it to meet our needs."

Brittany opened the door to a reception room tastefully furnished with comfortable chairs and coffee tables so that it looked like a large living room.

Brittney's hand on Janet's back moved up and down, and she nodded toward a door on the far side. "That door leads to a couple of smaller rooms." Brittney's hand guided Janet from the small of her back, then slowly slid lower over the curve of her backside.

"Mmmmmmm..." came out Janet's mouth before she could cut if off.

The taller woman looked down and smiled. "This place will do that to you. Come, let me show you some more." Brittney took Janet's hand. "The third and fourth floors are all rooms that people rent for group sex. We added insulation throughout the hotel, so you can't hear what's going on in the next room."

"So if I were to come here for an evening, it'll cost me ten dollars to get in and twenty-five for the night."

"That's it. For that, you get all the sex you can handle."

Janet let her fingers entwine with Brittney's and squeezed gently. "I like that part."

"Me too." Brittney led Janet to one of the group sex rooms. Cushions and pillows were stacked neatly in two corners. A padded table shaped like a Christian cross was in the center. "This is one of our play rooms. They're an extra twenty-five dollars.

You can do anything imaginable in this room, and every week people do. We have several members who like to be strapped down on the table, have a cock in each hand, one in the mouth, and one fore and aft at the same time."

Brittney let that sink in as she let Janet look over the room. "We have ten of these, but you need to reserve them in advance if you want to bring a group. Don't wait until the day before. They are very popular."

The tall woman led Janet to the elevator and the fifth floor. With a master key, she unlocked a room. "We bolted the outside sliding doors shut because we don't want people having intercourse on the porch where they can be seen by our neighbors. Or worse, fall off. No one likes hospital bills. Or lawsuits." She pulled the sheer curtains apart to give Janet a view of the hills to the north and east of where they were. Then she stood behind Janet, gently massaging her shoulders and the back of her neck. Her fingertips slid forward and down to the top of her breasts.

Janet enjoyed the movement of Brittney's strong fingers and turned her head. "Are you always this aggressive with new members?"

Brittney blushed. "Good lord, no! But you excite me, and you seemed to respond to me. I love women with bodies like yours. You must work out a lot. What do you do?"

Rather than answer, Janet looked up, willing Brittney to take the initiative. She wasn't disappointed.

Fifteen hours later, the newest member of the After Supper Club walked into her house. She'd spent the night with Brittney, who'd taken her to places Helen never had. For the first hour on the drive home, she had a hard time concentrating on driving. When she thought about Brittney, she'd lift her hand to her nose to smell Brittney's musk. Each time, it brought a smile to her face. She was simultaneously sexually satisfied and still turned on.

She'd just changed into her gi when the phone rang. The realtor she'd hired wanted to tell that she was about to get an offer on the house. *Wonderful! Now I need to find another place to live and start packing.*

Thursday, March 23, 1972, 1526 local time, North Vietnam

Twenty thousand feet above Pham's Phucking Pharm, the leader of a section of two Air Force F-105s violently jinked to get a 2,000-pound bomb hanging on the aft lug of the bomb rack to come off. The bomb hadn't released during his attack on a bridge west of Hanoi, nor had it come off as he pulled five g's on the pull out from his dive bombing run.

The Air Force's standard procedure was to head to a "safe" area and try to get rid of the bomb. The pilot had already gone through his "jettison stores" checklist and the bomb was still there and he could sense the drag and weight of the weapon. His wingman—about fifty feet in trail and twenty feet below—reported the arming wire had come free and the little propeller on the nose was spinning, which meant after twelve hundred revolutions, the weapon was armed. *Shit!*

With his left foot, the pilot pushed the left rudder, causing the airplane to yaw sharply. As soon as the nose started to move laterally, he shoved the right rudder pedal to the stop and used the stick to keep the nose of the F-105 pointed in the direction he wanted to fly. The bomb started to oscillate drunkenly. At last it came off, the jet lurched suddenly free of the bomb that plunged towards the jungle below. The pilot never saw the clearing he'd just overflown. Or where it hit. Once the bomb came off, both he and his wingman headed for their home base in Thailand.

Inside the chicken wire that now surrounded the farm, the POWs had built a small bench as a place to rest and eat. Ashley, who was sitting at the end of the bench, looked over at Randy. "Next week, we change from NF 302 to NM 310. How long do you think it will take?"

"A day or two. I was thinking about using some of the scrap lumber we have back at the camp to outline the letters and numbers, then put the pots with the herbs in the middle. I think it will make them much more noticeable from the air. We need—"

Both heard the shriek of a bomb a fraction of a second before they heard the explosion and felt the concussion. They saw black smoke boil up and debris fly through the air. The guards came running, gesturing and shouting to get the POWs headed toward the compound.

Randy dashed into their hooch. Hank Cho was staring at ragged holes in the side of the building, torn by chunks of shrapnel. Above, there were jagged holes where chunks of the bomb casing had ripped through the corrugated metal.

A smoking, forty-foot diameter, thirty-foot deep hole in the ground had replaced the factory. The shed, 55 gallon drums, and drying tables were either in little pieces or simply gone. The large tank of diesel fuel was burning furiously, and the generator was twenty feet from its base.

Pham stood on the edge of the crater, watching his men pick through the wreckage. Ashley said what Randy was thinking. "Oh, shit, Pham is going to blame us for this."

"Don't go paranoid." Karl Kramer made his way over to the window to stand alongside the Green Beret. "Tell Pham that if this was a planned attack, the Air Force or Navy would have dropped more than one bomb and we wouldn't be standing here. It had to be someone dumping hung ordnance."

Ashley turned to his fellow POWs with a grin on his face. "I think it is time we negotiate building an improved bomb shelter for his prize workforce. We may even get to build one for him as well, which may, accidentally on purpose, have some fatal defects."

Friday, June 30, 1972, 1526 local time, Tehachapi, CA

Janet checked her Visalia mailbox for the last time before getting in line to turn in her two keys. She had to decide which forwarding address to leave—the one in Bakersfield under the name of Janet Williams Pulaski, the one in Palmdale rented by Jamie Elizabeth Symonds, the box at a post office in Burbank near the After Supper Club leased by Jennifer Rachel Bertrand, or the one in Tehachapi where mail for Janis Amy Goodrich was sent.

Janet carefully sifted through the pile. There was a bill from the After Supper Club and an envelope with the club's July calendar, and a letter from Helen forwarded from the house in Hanford. There was also an envelope with a return address she didn't recognize. The rest was junk mail that went into the trashcan just inside the post office's entrance.

The letters from Helen were getting shorter and farther apart. She could tell from the tone of the note that watching her mother waste away from cancer was breaking Helen's heart. But this letter had two items of good news. Helen had enrolled in Emory University's law school and would start in the fall. And she had found another lover, one who was into bondage and discipline. So Helen wouldn't be coming west any time soon. It was time to stop responding, as a signal she understood their relationship was over.

To put a wall between the Cubans and herself, Janet had given her contact the number of an answering service in LA to use if they wanted to reach her. Janet had hired the service over the phone and paid an initial deposit by mail. From now on, Janet would only respond using pay phones. Packages from the Cubans would go to her post office box in Burbank.

There was still one issue left to resolve—getting weapons. Janet didn't like meeting another human being to take delivery. Yet she wanted to test the weapon to make sure it was properly zeroed. If that wasn't possible, she wanted a supplier who would provide rifles with the "dope" on the gun and its scope.

Buying her own meant that there would be a record and a salesman who could identify her. For work outside the U.S., it also meant that she had to smuggle the weapon into the country and then dispose of it. Bringing the gun home was not an option. There had to be a better way to get "clean" weapons. It was something she had to figure out for her own safety.

The drive down Highway 101 from Hanford to Highway 58 in

Bakersfield took about two hours. It was another fifty minutes to her new ranch in Stallion Springs, California.

On a whim, two months earlier she'd walked into a realtor's office in Tehachapi, California, and told the realtor that she wanted some place off the beaten path with some land.

After a few minutes asking Janet questions, the woman had said she had a property Janet would love. Sheltered in a notch full of oaks and pine trees a half a mile from the road, the thirty-three hundred square foot California ranch house was perfect. The back door was three hundred yards from rocks that almost went straight up. According to the survey, the house was five hundred feet below the ridge top.

Most of the front was floor-to-ceiling windows that gave her a view of the entire valley that contained the town of Stallion Springs. Redwood paneling and trim gave it a rustic, ranch look, and the house came with five hundred acres of fenced grazing land. At four thousand feet above sea level, the house would be cool in the summer and reasonable, she hoped, in the winter.

Janet rationalized that once she took control of scheduling her own contracts she would never have to hurry to catch a plane; so, depending on traffic, the time to the airports in LA—two and a half hours to Burbank or Ontario, three to LAX and another forty minutes to Orange County—didn't matter. If she was tired, she could hole up in a local hotel near the airport or spend the night at the After Supper Club. What could be bad about that!

She bought the home under the name of Nevada resident Jamie Elizabeth Symonds. Rather than take out a mortgage she paid cash. In a few years, she would pay to change the name on the owner documents to another one of her other fictitious identities.

Janet had used the change in communications methods to demand three things from the Cubans. One was a fee increase to $125,000 per target. Demand two was that there would no longer be any personal contact. And, three, the Cubans provided clean, zeroed weapons. She would tell them what she needed on each hit and set up a delivery protocol. She'd more than proven her worth.

The letter with an unfamiliar return address containing a hand written note that caused Janet to drive to Mojave, California. If anyone decided to trace the call, it wouldn't lead to where she was now living.

The envelope was addressed to "Occupant." The note, a three-by-five index card, simply said in block letters.

I have lots of work for you because you come highly recommended by a family member. If you are interested, call 800 458-1756 at any time and we can work out the details.

No name, no signature. There were only a few people in Cuban intelligence who knew how to contact her. Was there a leak, or did they want to share her skills with others? If not, did they care if she was a freelancer? *Paranoia in my line of work keeps me alive and out of jail.*

She stopped at an outside bank of phones well away from the gas pumps at the a stop. Janet waited in her car until the only person using a phone finished. Her drawstring purse with rolls of quarters, dimes, and nickels went on the polished steel shelf beneath the phone. The toll-free number required a dime to dial.

"Allo." The voice answering the phone was clearly Hispanic.

"You sent me a note asking me to call."

"I send lots of notes. Where was yours sent?"

"California."

"Where in California? It is a big state."

"Hanford."

There was a pause. "Ahhh, yes, the lady in Hanford. It has been a while since I sent that one. I thought you had decided not to talk to me, or that the address was bad."

I'm not going to tell him I moved. If this goes any farther, then I will give him one of my post office boxes. "Well, here I am on the phone. How did you get my address?"

"From a cousin."

By family? Or by intelligence agency? He may know my real name or the name I used in Cuba. "What kind of relative?"

"Good question. Blood. It is thicker than politics. He is the son of my mother's sister."

The speaker shifted slightly in his chair and put a cold beer down on a coaster. It was almost six-thirty in the evening in New Jersey, and he'd thought he was finished for the day when the phone rang.

So, is he Cuban, too? I wonder if he is with the Cuban Dirección de Inteligencia? "Were you given a name?"

"No, only an address."

"A description of me?"

"No. My cousin said you were an attractive woman who was utterly ruthless. And there's no blowback and you don't leave a mess behind for the buyer to clean up."

"What kind of work do you have for me?"

"What you were trained to do in the mountains of an island with a government that likes to sponsor revolutions. I have many customers who can take advantage of your skills. They pay much better than your current employer, who is a cheapskate."

He's appealing to my instincts as a capitalist. Yes, I am a greedy bitch. "Go on."

"Are you interested?"

"Yes. But I am not cheap."

"I assumed that. Can you give me an idea of what you charge?"

Janet had been thinking off and on about this. She didn't like the fixed fee arrangement she had with the Cubans.

"It depends on the assignment—the greater the risk, the higher my fee. $250,000 is the minimum. After we discuss the project, we negotiate the fee. Terms are half within twenty-four hours or the next business day, deposited in my account after I accept the contract, the remainder within forty-eight hours of completion."

Janet paused and the voice said, "Go on, I am listening."

Next demand. "You provide the weapons and any other equipment I need to my specifications, and you can pass on the expense to the buyer. For each assignment, we can work out delivery."

"Two hundred and fifty 'K' is expensive."

"But worth it. You contacted me."

There was silence. Janet wondered if she'd asked for too much, but since she didn't hear a dial tone, she didn't say anything. It was, as they say in chess and checkers, the other player's move.

"How do I contact you?" *Shit, that was easy. Maybe I should have set the base higher.*

Janet gave him the phone number of the answering service and the address of the post office box in Palmdale. The answering service personnel had never seen or met her; she called twice a day for messages. They didn't call her. She said to leave the message for Friendly Housecleaning Services. The name got a chuckle.

"Do you work outside the United States?"

"I can. There are some places I won't go. I'm not interested in assassinations of country presidents or high government officials or elected leaders. Too much potential heat."

"I don't take those projects either."

The speaker in New Jersey took a long pull on his bottle of beer. "Do you need help with documents?"

"It depends. I am always looking for reliable sources who keep their mouths shut."

"No problem. I have people I trust who can help you, if you need them, and who pride themselves on not revealing who their customers are. Either you pay them or I take it out of your fee."

I already have three U.S. passports, besides the ones in my married name and my maiden name, and one that's Canadian. How many more do I need? And I have credit cards that are valid for each identity. But why should I waste my resources if I can get fresh ones for each assignment? "Good, we'll cross that bridge when we come to it. How do I reach you?"

"This number works best. I have some jobs coming that you will like. Allow me to suggest a way we can work together. I call the number you gave me. You call me back and we discuss the project and negotiate the fee, which I will get approved by my customer. Once we agree, I send you a package of additional information. When you get it, you confirm that you received the package and accept the assignment. At that time, I will consider you under contract and will deposit half the money. If you haven't already, you'll tell me what type of equipment you need. Agreed?"

"Yes, that will work. How do you know that our calls will be secure?"

"When I want to be discrete, I use pay phones, just like you do. This number is only used by a few trusted colleagues and customers. Conversations about assignments are handled via pay phones."

Janet laughed. Before she could answer, the Hispanic voice said, "I will be in touch soon."

"What do I call you?"

"The Broker."

Before Janet could say another word, she heard a dial tone.

Tuesday, July 18, 1972, 0953 local time, North Vietnam
Karl Kramer stopped pulling on the hoe and bent down to pick up a weed. As he tossed it into the basket, the sight of dark clouds building in the west told him two things. One, the incessant rains of the summer monsoon were coming; and two, combat missions over the trail would cease.

During the monsoon, the cloud base dropped to several hundred feet above the ground and hid the mountains on both sides of the narrow valleys. Any mistake in navigation would mean, in aviator parlance, "hitting a cloud with a very hard center."

FORGOTTEN

Karl studied the guard leaning against a tree twenty feet away. The man's AK-47 was slung over his shoulder as he focused on rolling a cigarette. Karl leaned on the handle of the hoe and turned to Randy. "You know, I could tackle that bastard and his ribs would shatter when my shoulder slammed him into the tree. We could then walk into the jungle and be out of here."

"Yeah, but then where would we go? We don't have anything with us that you need to survive."

"True, and I'm not sure if all of us could get away before the rest of the guards reacted. It was just a thought. But you know, Randy, in many ways this camp is just like where I grew up."

"What do you mean by that?"

"Steel mill towns like Braddock, Pennsylvania, are like prisons without walls. The company owns you. They pay you but you are not free to move. There are only a couple of places in the country where they make steel, and every factory is unionized. Move from one to the other and you have to start at the bottom because you have no seniority. It doesn't matter how good or knowledgeable you are."

Karl looked at the sky again. "My dad was in the Army in World War II. He joined in 1942 when he was eighteen. When he came back, he had to make a living because he couldn't afford a car to drive back and forth to the nearest college, so he couldn't take advantage of his GI Bill. So, he went to work in a steel mill. Twenty-five years later, he's a foreman making O.K. money, but there still isn't enough left over to send his kids to college. My older sister got married to, guess what, another steel worker. Same story. My ROTC scholarship was my ticket out of town. My younger sister is working her way through nursing school in Pittsburgh. My little brother is still in high school. He's an above average student, but no genius and not a jock. So he's stuck unless he joins the military. If he doesn't, my dad will get him a job in a steel mill, he'll get married, join the union, and when we're all old and gray, he'll be living in Braddock making steel, assuming the mill hasn't closed."

"Ouch."

"It is not as bad as I make it sound, but it is pretty dreary. Last time I was home, the price of steel was dropping like a rock and production was cut back. Everyone was afraid they'd shut down the mill. What happens if they shut down the steel mill? People head somewhere, hoping to live off their life savings until they find work. Homes full of furniture will be abandoned. Some people will turn to drugs. My dad said the company—U.S. Steel —was saying that the price of steel will come back and they will modernize the plant. But when? The workers see the union can't protect them and has priced its members out of their jobs. The company has choices—stay in Braddock and invest in the plant and pay the workers more, or move. I'm betting they'll move."

"That's pretty ugly."

"Yeah. I think about it all the time. I wonder if my dad still has a job. He's almost old enough to retire, but will he still have a pension? My mom is a secretary for the school district. The plan was that my mom and dad would have enough between Social Security and their pensions to live on in their old age. If the pensions and the medical benefits go away, they're fucked. What really bugs me is that I am stuck in this godforsaken place and I can't do anything about it."

"You've got to accept that you can't help. If you don't, it will eat at your insides and you'll die here. Then what? You'll never be able to help them. We're all going to get out of here, trust me. I don't know if it will be six months, a year, or ten years, but we will get home alive."

"I keep telling myself that, but it's hard to be optimistic. I keep thinking and worrying about my parents."

"Welcome to the club. We all have something to worry about. Be glad you don't have a wife or fiancée like Jeff, Greg, and me."

Friday, July 21, 1972, 0826 local time, Bakersfield, CA
Ever since she'd moved to California, locals had told Janet that the heat in the Central Valley wasn't too bad because it was a

"dry" heat. To someone who'd grown up in the upper Midwest, a hundred was hot, no matter whether it was dry or humid. The only good news about the "dry" heat was that her perspiration evaporated quickly!

The wind through the rolled-down windows of her un-air-conditioned Volvo kept the temperature in the car pleasant as Janet drove out of the mountains toward Bakersfield, hoping to finish her shopping before noon when it reached ninety. At a red light she looked through her mail. Buried in the pile she'd pulled out of the post office box was a rumpled letter. The hand-addressed note from Wendy Hancock had been sent to her home in Hanford and forwarded to her Bakersfield post office box.

Her first reaction was, *Oh shit, what does she want?* With some trepidation, Janet tore off the end and shook out the note.

> *Janet,*
> *No one has seen hide nor hair of you for quite awhile. You haven't been to any of the POW/MIA functions. The other day, I went by your house only to find out it had been sold. I was wondering if you are O.K. I wanted to see if you would to come to our house for a family picnic. It is not a squadron event, just my husband and me, and the wife of another pilot who was lost in this last deployment and her children. I thought you two might want to talk because, like you, she's having a rough time.*
> *Please call. The number is 559-486-3146. Looking forward to hearing from you.*
> *Wendy*

She balled up the letter and tossed it into the foot well of the passenger side, thinking, *Goddamn war! It won't leave me alone!*

Janet liked Wendy, even though they were a generation apart. She was a very traditional wife, but also a very strong woman. In a different set of circumstances, they probably would have become good friends. With her new line of work, that chance was gone.

The POW/MIA wives told her not to give up hope, yet one part of Janet's brain said Randy was dead and his body rotting in some godforsaken rice paddy in North Vietnam. Another part of her mind was convinced that his irrepressible spirit—the part of him that had attracted her—would see him through and he would come back.

She didn't know what to believe. If Randy came back, what would she do? The Randy part of her life was stuffed in a compartment in the back of her brain. Opening it would be like opening Pandora's box, and Janet didn't want to go there.

Shit, shit, shit. Janet drove back into the post office and bought a postcard. She thought for a few seconds, and then began writing in the space allotted.

> *Wendy,*
>
> *It's the end of July and I just got your note. Yes, I have moved because there is nothing left for me in Hanford. I will be there for Randy if and when he comes back. Thank you for your kind thoughts, but I have to move on.*
>
> *Janet*

She hoped that sent a clear enough message. *I am not interested in meeting other wives in the same boat, and if Randy comes back, I don't intend to shit can him.* For a second she hesitated, holding the card in the slot. Rationalizing that she would deal with Randy's return if and when it happened, she let go of the postcard.

Monday, September 11, 1972, 1129 local time, Tehachapi
When Janet first explored the cave behind her house, she found it went deep into the mountain. A hundred feet in, there was a dogleg to the right; then, after another hundred feet, the cave

ended. Her powerful flashlight showed the current residents were snakes, birds and small mammals.

Janet didn't like snakes, particularly poisonous ones. It took a few days, but starting at the mouth and working her way in, she used a shotgun to kill twelve rattlesnakes, ranging from two feet long to almost six. The carcasses she dumped in the field in front of her house so predators and vultures could have a feast.

With the snakes gone, Janet wanted to turn the cave into a shooting range. After a few attempts, however, the echo and concussion reverberating from her .45 made it a painful place to shoot.

When she asked a gun store owner in Tehachapi where the nearest range was, he gave her a map to a place along a ridge in the desert just north of the junction of Highway 58 and Highway 14. He said it would take about thirty minutes to get there from his store. There, he said, she could shoot to her heart's content and no one cared about the noise. His only caution was that if it had rained recently, you needed four-wheel drive. As a way of thanking him, Janet bought five fifty-round boxes of nine-millimeter .45 and .380 ammunition, along with a hundred rounds for her .03 Springfield.

There were no signs to remark the range, but two things told her she was in the right spot. One was the ravine that rose hundreds of feet above the valley floor, as described by the gun store owner. Then there were all the empty brass cartridges littering the ground.

Two hours later, she'd fired all the .380 and nine-millimeter ammo in the drills she'd learned in Cuba, and was just starting with the .45 when the sound of a diesel engine laboring through the sand made her stop. Rather than keep shooting, Janet made sure all six magazines for the .45 were loaded by the time the truck parked about ten yards from her Volvo.

Out climbed two men, who looked as if they were in their early thirties. The passenger wore a baseball cap with a San Francisco Giants logo on the front. The driver was pulling on a bush hat. He came toward Janet, waving. "Hi there! Do you mind if we do a little shooting, too?"

Janet, who was holding the .45 behind her back, shook her head. "Nope, I'm almost done. I've got two more magazines to fire and then I'm out of ammo, so it'll be time to go back." The reality was that she had six.

"Cool, we'll wait."

"Suit yourself."

Janet watched as the men set up a collapsible table and laid out two bolt-action rifles and an AK-47. Deciding they were not a threat, Janet went back to chasing cans with the Colt.

She was in the midst of a reload when one of the men came up to her. "That's pretty good shooting."

"You mean, that's pretty good shooting for a woman."

The man tipped his floppy hat. "No ma'am, that's dammed good shooting for anyone. I haven't seen that kind of skill since I left the Marine Corps."

Janet gave him a beauty queen smile. "Thank you. I apologize, but some guys don't think women can shoot."

"Not me. I left the Marines because a female Viet Cong sniper who went by the name of 'the Apache' put a round in my chest. I lost half a lung, so I had to leave the Corps. A Marine friend by the name of Carlos Hathcock tracked the bitch down and killed her. She deserved it. Besides sniping, the Apache liked to catch individual soldiers and torture them."

"Yeah, war makes people do strange things."

"Name's Bill, Bill Willard, and that's Jerry Barnes." Jerry put a hand to the brim of his baseball hat.

Janet held out her hand. "Janet Pulaski." After they finished shaking hands, Bill made a gesture with his hand as if to say "Go on, keep shooting." Janet turned and quickly went through the .45 magazine.

"Really good. You ought to teach shooting."

"Thanks, but no thanks."

"Who taught you?"

"My dad. He was a Marine sniper in World War II and liked to hunt. I'm not a hunter, but I do like to shoot."

"Well, we're up here to zero in our rifles. We're going hunting in Colorado this fall and see if we can get an elk or two. I just bought this new Remington 700 and had it modified to make it just like the rifle I carried in Vietnam. It's time to zero it in and see if it was worth the money."

As if on cue, Jerry brought the new rifle over to Bill, who handed it to Janet. She looked into the magazine and saw the bolt hadn't been inserted. She pointed it up the mountain and picked out a rock. The scope had a military dot-style reticle to allow for bullet drop and drift. She liked it better than the Soviet style SVD scopes. Handing back the rifle and its Leupold ten-power scope to Bill she said, "Very, very nice rifle."

"Thank you. If you want to stick around, I'll let you fire it after I make sure the bullets are going where they are aimed."

Janet hesitated. Bill wasn't wearing a wedding ring, and she hadn't had a man inside her in a long time. Then her brain took over. "Thanks, but no thanks. I have to get back to work. I'm leaving on a business trip tomorrow."

Bill knew no when he heard it. "See you around. Maybe next time."

Saturday, December 23, 1972, 1423 local time, Kauai

This was Janet's first trip to Hawaii and her second assignment from The Broker. Her first had required a two-week stay in Boston. Locating Niall Branagan, a stocky man with a shock of red hair, hadn't been difficult, but getting to him had. He lived in a flat with three other men, so the at-home seduction angle was went right out the door. Sitting at a bar table next to Branagan and his friends one night, and listening to them talk while she started at the TV, Janet learned he was going skiing that coming weekend.

She'd followed him Friday night to a bar in a lodge near the base of Waterville Valley Ski area. When he took an empty seat at the bar, Janet took the one next to him and started the conversation. After a second glass of wine and accepting an offer for dinner, Janet had caressed his thigh and suggested they go to his room rather than the restaurant.

In the hotel room Janet got aggressive and they peeled off their clothes. Once her mark was naked, she pushed Niall Branagan on his back. A few fondles later, his member was fully erect and Janet straddled him so she could lower herself on his penis. She felt the warmth inside and let Niall buck his hips. It was, as Janet had experienced many times before with men— wham, bam, thank you, ma'am.

Janet leaned over and kissed him before she sat back up and headed to the bathroom. Niall had his eyes closed as he enjoyed his sexual satisfaction. He opened them to see the business end of a suppressed Makarov she pulled from her purse. Janet wondered if he even saw the flash before the bullet ended his life.

On the drive back to Boston that night, Janet let the evening's events run through her mind. Getting her target into bed had been the only way she could get him alone. Sex, she rationalized, was a weapon, just like the pistol. But having sex with the target made her uncomfortable and vulnerable, and Janet didn't like being vulnerable.

What surprised her was that she hadn't feel the pleasurable sensation of a warm penis entering her vagina. It felt like an intruder in her body. Janet wanted to believe that it was her focus on completing the contract, not a lack of interest that took away any pleasure. Yet the more she thought about it, the more she realized that men simply didn't turn her on any more.

The job in Kauai was supposed to be simple. Kill a moneyman who'd pissed off a Chicago mob family. For reasons unknown, and of no concern to her, they wanted to use an outsider to settle the matter.

He was hiding in a house on Pe'e Road east of Poipu on the south side of Kauai. On her jogs back and forth past the long driveway, she saw the same burly man sitting on the front porch.

Since the temperature was in the eighties and it was not about to rain, his partially zipped windbreaker screamed bodyguard.

Reconnaissance left her with three questions. *One, how do I get past the guard and into the house? Two, how many more guards are in there, and where are they? Three, once I'm done, how do I get off the island before the search for his killer begins?*

Her options to quickly get off the island were limited. She could either take one of the three daily flights to LA, or one of the dozen or so to Honolulu and then a flight to the mainland. In the end, Janet decided on a morning flight to Honolulu and then an afternoon flight to LAX. That way, she'd be off Kauai as soon as possible, hopefully before the bodies were discovered.

To get a look at the house from the ocean side, Janet rented a small kayak and paddled down the beach just outside the surf line. The effort was exhausting.

As her kayak drifted a hundred yards from the house, it was clear her only option was to work her way along the rocks until she got to the house. Moving along the slippery, volcanic rocks in the dark was going to be difficult, but it was the only way other than storming in through the front door. That could lead to a firefight that would bring the police and her getting hurt.

Before she left the hotel, she strapped her two throwing knives onto her forearms and packed a small pack with a pair of Makarovs, her lock picking tools, duct tape, a fifty-foot coil of rope, and a change of clothes, everything triple bagged to keep dry. A backup set of clothes sat on the back seat of her rental car.

Down the road from the house, Janet slipped off the path into the trees between two buildings of a nearby condominium complex. From there, it was a few hundred feet down to the water, and the three-quarter moon gave her enough light to navigate. Before she pulled on a pair of reinforced rubber diving gloves and started picking her way through the rocks, Janet looked at the cheap diver's watch. It was eleven p.m.

Twice she fell on the slippery, abrasive volcanic rocks. The second fall ripped open her wet suit and gashed her shin. She wrapped duct tape around the wetsuit and kept going, knowing the wound would need to be cleaned and bandaged when she got back to her hotel room.

As she peered over the edge of the rock wall twenty feet above the surf, she could see one bodyguard sitting on a lawn chair with a shotgun in his lap. Staying in the shadows, Janet crawled to the trees that separated the target house from its neighbor. The sentry's head bobbed twice, telling her he was struggling to stay awake.

Janet rolled on her side so she could take off her pack and screw the suppressors on each Makarov. As she got to ten yards away from him, the sentry stirred and looked around. Training took over and the Makarov in her right hand came up. Pffftttttt. His head jerked and then slumped over as the 95-grain bullet destroyed his brain. One down. She was sure there was at least one more.

Gently, Janet tried to open the sliding glass door on the lanai. It was locked. *Shit!* There was no lock to pick, just a dead bolt that could only be opened from the inside. A flapping sound caught Janet's attention. Down the wall, she saw curtains fluttering out of an open window. She hobbled over. She had one knee on the sill when she heard the deadbolt click open.

"Johnny!"

The familiar Chicago accent was unmistakable. A light came on and a head peeked out the door. "Goddammit, Johnny, the boss will fucking fire us if he finds out any of us are sleeping…."

When the inert form didn't react, the man pulled back into the house and turned off the light. Slowly, he emerged carrying a short-barreled, semi-automatic shotgun. Janet pressed her back against the wall and slid back into the shadows.

The man peered to his right. It gave Janet a clear shot at the back of his head where most of the motor nerves were located. Pfffftttt Pfffftttttt. Two rounds spat out of the Makarov. The man banged against the sliding glass door as he collapsed in a heap.

Janet slipped inside and searched the ground floor. Nothing. In the master bedroom on the second floor there were two forms on the bed. Each was dispatched with a single round to the head. Five rounds. *Reload!*

It was time to leave and change clothes. Standing in the foyer, she looked down. Blood, her blood, was leaving a trail on the tile floor. The duct tape had gotten stretched by her exertions and blood was seeping out and down her leg.

"Who the fuck are you?" Janet's head whipped around just before a man's shoulder slammed her into the wall. The Makarov went clattering across the tile floor. Her assailant stepped back and tried to hit Janet, who managed to parry the first blow. As she ducked, the second blow glanced off the side of her head. The man grabbed Janet around the throat and lifted her off the floor as he pinned her against the wall. There was no way she was going to pry his hands off her throat and she couldn't get enough leverage to kick him in the balls.

Knowing she only had seconds before he crushed her throat, Janet stopped trying to peel back his fingers and attempted to stick two fingers into the man's eyes. He turned his head enough to dodge her attack. His movement allowed her to pull one of the throwing knives out of its sheath on her wrist. Out of the corner of his eyes, the man saw the danger, but it was too late. First, she drove the knife hard into the bone of the forearm of the hand on her throat. The man screamed and let go, blood streaming from his arm. Rather than ignore the wound and attack Janet again, he stepped back.

Janet flipped the blade in her hand and flung it as hard as she could. The knife went in up to the hilt between two ribs. He looked surprised as Janet flung the second knife, which embedded itself in his belly. He backed up until he was leaning against the far wall, holding his flabby stomach. His retreat gave Janet time to dive for the Makarov, grab it and fire. The shot opened a hole in his chest. Propped up on an elbow, she fired a second bullet into the man's forehead.

With her chest heaving, Janet looked around. There was blood

—hers and his—all over the place. As she changed clothes, she wished she'd brought long pants. In the downstairs bathroom, she wiped as much blood from her shin as possible and stuffed the bloody towels into her backpack.

Outside the house, there were no sounds of alarm. As normally as she could, Janet walked to her car in the condo complex's parking lot a few hundred yards from the driveway. Every few steps, she turned around to make sure that she wasn't leaving a trail of blood.

Thankfully, there was a space near her hotel room. Once inside, she pulled out her first aid kit and rummaged around until she found the bottle of hydrogen peroxide. She carefully cleaned the gash with soap and water, then gritted her teeth as the hydrogen peroxide bubbled and burned, cauterizing the wound. After her tears cleared, she patted the wound dry before emptying a tube of Neosporin on a folded-over length of gauze. From strips of one-inch-wide adhesive tape, Janet made butterflies that went over the gauze. With those in place, she used more tape to secure a bigger gauze bandage in place.

She wasn't done. The bloody towels, one from the hotel and two from the house, went into the tub filled with four inches of hot water and a bar of hotel soap and shampoo.

Within seconds, the water had a pinkish hue. That was her sign to change the water, which she did three times.

In between rinses, she pulled on a pair of pants and went down to the ice machine. Using a plastic bag, she made an ice pack that covered most of her shin to keep the swelling down. Her biggest fear was the wound would become infected because she hadn't gotten all the particles of volcanic rock out of the gash.

The do-not-disturb sign went on the door and her alarm clock was set for seven. Janet's escape plan now included a stop at a local drug store, getting to the airport two hours before the flight, and redressing the wound at the airport. Her only worry was that the police would be called to the house before she boarded the plane. She thought that, with all the bodies and guns lying about, police would be inclined to assume the killer was among the dead, and by the time they figured out there was an extra type of blood, if they ever did, she would be long gone.

She figured that the wound, if it didn't become infected, would take a month to heal and would leave a jagged, four-inch scar on her right shin. If it became infected, maybe the Broker knew a doctor who would treat her and not ask too many questions.

Monday, January 8, 1973, 1209 local time, Stallion Springs
Janet tossed her keys into a tray on the kitchen counter along with the bags of groceries that needed to go into the refrigerator or freezer. With that done, she sat down on one of the bar stools at the counter and dialed the answering service number from memory. There was a message from Brittney, who'd missed seeing her at the club over the holidays and wanted to see her.

A second message was from a man who said it was urgent that she call on Monday. It was one of the numbers The Broker's used to set up time for a call to a pay phone.

Message number three was from a woman who identified herself as a member of the Department of Defense on the POW/MIA task force. She asked that Janet call her and left both a toll-free and a regular number.

Chapter 10
BAD NEWS RELEASE

Tuesday, January 9, 1973, 0913 local time, Stallion Springs

Janet paced back and forth, sipping her morning cup of Kona coffee. While in Kauai, she had had her first cup made from the bean grown on the island of Hawaii and had brought back three bags.

The cause of her pacing was the last of the three messages she'd gotten from her answering service the day before, the one she hadn't returned yet.

The Broker had told her a package was on the way and the project would require some negotiation. Brittney had wanted to make a date for Thursday night.

With some hesitation, Janet dialed the number in DC and took a deep breath. Maybe they would be at lunch. "Good afternoon, this is the POW/MIA office in the Department of Defense. Deborah Kane speaking. This is not a secure line."

"Good afternoon, Deborah, my name is Janet Pulaski. Amy Hazlet left a message with my answering service asking me to call her." Janet sat down on a stool in the kitchen.

"Yes, Mrs. Pulaski, thank you for calling us back..." There was a pause, and Janet thought she heard pages being flipped. "Mrs. Pulaski, please wait while I transfer the call."

Janet drummed her fingers on the tile countertop during the second or so of silence before the phone buzzed twice and was picked up.

"Hi Janet, my name is Amy Hazlet. Thank you for calling. I'm sorry we had to call an answering service, but we didn't have a direct line to call."

"No problem. I set it up this way. This way I don't get calls from people wanting to sell me stuff or anti-war activists. You wouldn't believe the people who want to take advantage of you because your husband is a POW."

There was a chuckle on the line, then a pause. Amy's voice became softer, the kind of voice that was used by grief counselors and funeral home employees. "Janet, as the wife of a Naval Aviator who is missing in action and presumed to be a POW, I am sorry to say I have to give you some bad news. A list of the men being held by the North Vietnamese, Cambodians, Viet Cong, and Laotians has just been released. Your husband's name is not on it."

Janet's eyes began to water. It was time to be strong. Despite her infidelity, she still loved Randy. "Does the department know if he is dead?"

"No, we don't. All I know is that he was known to be taken prisoner, but is not among the men who are about to come home."

"How many men are coming home?"

"Five hundred and ninety one."

"I am assuming that Randy is not the only one who we know was captured but not coming home. What's..." Janet struggled for a word as she wiped the tears from her eyes. Drops were already on her cheeks. "... next?"

"Here's what I can tell you. Lieutenant Pulaski's status is going to be changed from MIA presumed to be a POW, to MIA, status unknown. This will enable the government to continue his pay and let you retain commissary and exchange privileges as well as medical care. Then, as part of the peace agreement, there is a provision that will enable the U.S., with the help of the North

Vietnamese, to continue to search and recover either the remains or those who might be alive."

"So there is hope he may still be alive?"

"Yes, Mrs. Pulaski. It is a very slim one, but, yes, there is hope."

"Do you know when the government would declare MIAs dead?"

"No, I do not."

Janet didn't say anything. She was dealing with several emotions. One was genuine grief. Another was relief that she would not have to explain to Randy what she did for a living.

Amy interrupted her thoughts. "Mrs. Pulaski?"

"Yes."

"I want you to know how sorry I am for your loss. These men died for their country and there is no greater honor."

"Amy, I know it must be terrible to have to make these calls."*If we weren't in this goddamn war, none of them would have died and you wouldn't have to make the calls.*

"It is. It's tough, very tough." There was a pause. "Would you rather notify Lieutenant Pulaski's parents, or should I?"

"I'll do it. I need to call them anyway. Just so you know, my head tells me he may be dead, but my gut tells me he is still alive." The last time Janet had called Randy's parents was just before she left for Kauai, to wish them a Merry Christmas. *Now I have to tell them that their oldest boy is MIA and more than likely dead.*

Tuesday, January 23, 1973, 1641 local time, North Vietnam

For the first time in a week, the sky was clear. No overcast, no puffy cumulus clouds building into thunderstorms and—most importantly—no rain, just clear blue sky. That was the good news. The better news was the rain had filled the fifty-five-gallon barrels on top of their shower hut, and after a couple of hours of sunshine they could take warm showers.

Pham's Phucking Pharm was now, according to Greg's

estimate, just over three acres and large enough to lay out two call signs at a time. By the end of the day, Karl Kramer's tail number, NL 502, was added to NM 310. Each letter and number was four military paces—or roughly 120 inches—long and made using a raised pile of dirt between two "railings."

As Randy wiped his hands in a futile attempt to wipe off the sticky black mud, he looked up at the sky. No contrails in the sky that indicated the U.S. was still flying over North Vietnam and the war was going on. It could be, he thought, another bombing halt. Or better yet, the war was over and soon Pham would ransom them to the CIA.

None of the Americans knew the U.S. had ceased air operations over North Vietnam on January 15 and accelerated its evacuation of South Vietnam. Their allies in the south would soon be on their own. Later that day, Secretary of State Henry Kissinger would sign the Paris Accords. As part of the Accords the North Vietnamese agreed to release the POWs and ensure their allies in South Vietnam, Cambodia, and Laos released the men they held. There was no expectation on either side that they would find any more men who were missing, not alive.

Thursday, January 25, 1973, 1436 local time, Chicago

The outside air temperature was, for Chicago, a relatively mild 15 degrees Fahrenheit. It was the damp, icy wind that went right through her as she stood on cold concrete and waited for the rental car bus. Each shiver reminded Janet why she would never live in Chicago again.

As Janet drove to her hotel, the snow started coming down at nearly forty-five degrees from the vertical. The elder Pulaskis had invited her to stay at their home in Logan Park, one of the Polish neighborhoods in Chicago, but she had politely declined. She had come for a memorial service for Randy. His father insisted Randy was dead based on what the Russians did to the Poles during World War II. Officers were tortured and shot. Enlisted men were sent to special camps where they were starved and worked to death. Few Polish POWs survived the war.

Before the memorial service, Janet gave Randy's parents his Rolex, along with his class ring and other jewelry that his squadron mates had brought back from the ship. Janet kept all Randy's gifts, her engagement and wedding rings, their wedding album, and several pictures taken of them together before he went to Vietnam, along with the GT350.

That night, she stayed until midnight talking with them. His parents reminded Janet of her mother and father—caring, wanting their children to be happy and successful, and in love with the United States of America, warts and all. Randy's brothers and she agreed that if she ever decided to sell the Shelby, they had the right of first refusal. The agreement was documented in a letter they all signed that had the car's model and serial number.

Before she left, they agreed to stay in touch with each other and with the POW/MIA office in the Pentagon, as well as the Association of POW and MIA Wives. If his body was ever found, they all wanted his remains repatriated so he could be buried with full military honors in the U.S.

Janet had planned the trip so she could have all day Thursday to herself in Chicago before flying back to Los Angeles. When she woke up, the flurries had changed into a full-fledged snowstorm. Looking out the window, she guessed there was at least six inches of snow on the top of her rental car.

The forecast for another six to ten inches drove her to the phone. She called American Airlines and had her flight changed to one scheduled to leave just after two. The reservation agent warned her that it would take her longer to get to the airport, but didn't tell her that the flights were delayed or cancelled.

With her bag packed, she plunked down on the bed and stared at the TV set, wondering if she should drive by her parent's house in Evanston. So close, yet so far.... Janet waffled back and forth, then looked at her Rolex. It was almost ten, and there was no way she could make it there and back and still catch her flight.

FORGOTTEN

Monday January 29, 1973, 1426 local time, Vinh

The sergeant in charge of the guard detail at the entrance of the Fourth Military Region's headquarters compound looked at the photo in Lieutenant Colonel Pham's identity booklet and compared it to his face. Then he told Pham to wait while he made sure Pham was on his list of authorized visitors before he handed the booklet back.

"Senior Colonel Trung is expecting you. Do you know where his office is?"

"I do. Thank you, Sergeant." The guard took one step backward and saluted.

Once inside, Pham was directed to a row of four wooden chairs opposite where Trung's adjutant had his desk. Overhead, a fan turned lazily. There was nothing in the office other than a West German-made copier on a small table, a row of file cabinets under the obligatory portrait of Ho Chi Minh, and the chairs. He found the lack of motion or even commotion in the office curious. Experience told Pham it was either a mark of Trung's organization and leadership skills, or there was a crisis someplace.

The senior colonel came through the door and Pham stood up and came to attention.

"Ahhh, Lieutenant Colonel Pham, it is good of you to come."

Pham bowed slightly from the waist as a form of salute. Trung acknowledged the gesture with a wave of his hand and turned to his adjutant. "Captain Ti, Colonel Pham and I are going to take a short walk. When we get back, can you have something for us to drink?"

The captain bowed his head and said, "Yes, sir. I will have tea and mineral water waiting."

Trung gestured to the open door. Neither man spoke until they were outside. Pham, being the junior officer, waited for Trung to start the conversation.

"I have news. The Americans have signed a peace agreement and agreed to leave the rebellious country to our south by the end of the year. We will use the time to build up our forces and, once the Americans are gone, we will crush the South Vietnamese."

"That is very good news." *Now I don't have to worry about stray bombs destroying my factory again. It cost me hundreds of thousands when I could not make deliveries for several weeks.*

"Well, it also presents a problem for both of us."

"And that is?"

"The agreement calls for our government to provide a list of all the men that we and our allies are holding. We are required by the treaty to release them. Some would say that would include the six men you are holding."

Pham didn't respond for a few seconds. "Technically, sir, the Socialist Republic of Vietnam is not holding them. My organization is not part of any government."

Trung turned to the younger man. "Pham, that is a clever answer which may not be acceptable to our leaders in Hanoi. Remember, you are a lieutenant colonel in the People's Army of the Socialist Republic of Vietnam, and your base is provisioned by the republic. That makes you part of the government. There is going to be a time when their presence will be discovered. And then what?"

"Again, sir, officers in Hanoi will be blameless. They did not know, and, again, they were not keeping them prisoners. My organization is not part of the government. Now that the war is over, I can resign my commission." Long ago, Pham had decided to stick to this story.

"Then the government will consider you a criminal." Trung took several strides before he spoke again. "What is there for you to gain by keeping them prisoner?"

"Money. A lot of money. Now as slave labor, and later as hostages. I am confident that in a few years we can get a million U.S. dollars or more for each one of them. You will, of course, get your usual fifteen percent in your Swiss bank account."

Statements from the private Swiss bank of Banque Hottinger & Cie SA were smuggled into Vinh on ships that shuttled back and forth to Hong Kong. To open an account in the Zurich-based bank founded in 1786, one had to deposit either seventy-five thousand U.S. dollars or one quarter of a million Swiss Francs. It was an amount that Trung had no problem making. However, it was illegal for him to have such an account. "And you are confident that the Americans will pay?"

"Sir, the plan is already in place. Either through an intermediary or directly, I will contact the CIA. I believe that the U.S. government will want them back, and I will be happy to take their money. They will protest, of course, but Hanoi doesn't have to be involved."

"The leaders in Hanoi will lose face."

"No they won't. They can say the prisoners weren't held by their government or any of their allies."

Trung walked for ten meters while he considered Pham's answer. He decided to change the subject. "I am on the promotion list for major general and won't be here much longer. From what I have been told, I will be either the number two person in the Border Defense Force or in the logistical department on the general staff. The decision won't be made until they decide who will be sent south to lead the next offensive." It was a typical Vietnamese conversation. There was the topic being discussed, and the real one, which was not. Pham knew Trung was telling him four things.

One, once Trung goes to Hanoi, his ability to protect me is limited.

Two, he is moving up higher in the government and, therefore, the risk of the true nature of our relationship becoming public increases. He could have me killed, but he knows my family's contacts in Hanoi would expose him in retaliation.

Three, any embarrassment I cause Hanoi must be minimized and must not affect Trung.

And four, he wants his share of the money I get from ransoming the Americans.

"Sir, congratulations on your promotion." Pham took a few steps. "When we contact the CIA, we will make it clear that

Hanoi had no knowledge of the six Americans. I can always claim they were held in Laos. My camp is just a few kilometers from the border. Any records of their existence have been destroyed, by American bombers, no less, so how could anyone in Hanoi have known? No one will discover the source of your money."

We both know that if the People's Public Security Force knew about your Swiss bank accounts you would be stood up against a wall and shot. You'll never be able to spend your money in the Socialist Republic. So, Trung, what are you planning to do? Defect to a country where you can enjoy your millions? Maybe that is the real conversation we should have, because both of us know I can smuggle you out of Vietnam.

Trung nodded and headed back to the office. "Do you need any more material to rebuild the factory?"

"Yes. The requisition I dropped off today is for supplies so we can expand operations."

"Good, I will make sure the materials are ready for pick-up tomorrow."

"Thank you, Colonel. We have a five-hundred-kilo shipment that will dry in four or five days. You will be notified when we are ready to put it on a ship. Our customers are demanding, it and while they understand what happened, they still want their heroin. They, too, have customers."

"Yes, it is very capitalistic."

Friday, February 2, 1973, 0823 local time, Stallion Springs

Every morning she was home and it was not snowing, Janet ran her ranch's half-mile access road to Banducci Road, then headed east, past a vegetable farm. At the intersection of Banducci and Pellisier she made a U-turn and headed back. As she passed the gate to her ranch, Janet sprinted up the gravel driveway that rose one hundred feet in elevation. According to the odometer on her Volvo, her route was 5.3 miles long.

Despite the forty-degree temperature, Janet was sweating. She gulped down a large glass of water. A glance at her Rolex told her that it was 1123 in Washington, DC. She had a call to make.

"This is Amy Hazlet."

"Amy, good morning, this is Janet Pulaski. Do you remember me?"

"I do, I do. How are you, Janet?"

"I'm fine. I was holding onto hope that Randy would come home, but it was no surprise that he was on the list of the missing." It was a lie. Her heart and gut, despite what her brain told her, were convinced Randy was still alive. "Do you have a minute?"

"Sure, what's up?" Amy was a psychiatrist hired specifically to help wives and family members whose loved ones were POWs or declared missing in action.

"What's my legal status? I am married to a man who is missing in action. The chances of him coming home are slim, at best."

"That's a fair question. In the eyes of the Department of Defense, you are still married and entitled to all the benefits of a dependent of a service member on active duty, as long as you do not file for divorce or remarry. As long as he is MIA, he is not legally dead."

"Well, it is hard to have a social life wearing a wedding ring." Janet instantly regretted saying that.

Amy was about to head to the West Coast to help the wives and their returned husbands adapt to being back in the U.S. For those who had been in captivity for ten or twelve years the adjustment would be difficult, and many marriages would end in divorce. Some POWs were learning their wives had moved on. Some of the returning POWs were finding out that coming home was a new definition of hell.

As the wife of a Naval Officer who'd served in Vietnam on a Swift boat, Amy understood the emotional trauma of being at home while her husband and the father of their children was at war. As a psychiatrist, intellectually and professionally, it was an interesting assignment.

"Janet, you're in a difficult situation. I can't tell you what you should do about a social life. That's for you to decide. I think that if your husband came back to you and if you were truthful with him, he would try to understand. The only thing the legal beagles have told us is that once you divorce Randy you lose all your benefits."

"It's not even an issue at this time, really. But I did want some clarity."

"Hold on, Janet. What else is going on? Do you need money?"

"No, I'm O.K." She didn't want to tell anyone how O.K. she was.

"The department is supposed to announce how long they will hold the MIAs in that status. History says it will wait five years before declaring them dead. I know that puts wives of MIAs in limbo, but that's what I know. I can call you when I know more."

"Thanks." Janet knew there wasn't more that Amy could tell her. After a few more polite exchanges, she hung up.

A little over two hours later, she was in a hotel room in Lancaster, California, registered under a phony name and home address. For the call she was expecting, a pay phone would not do. Data sheets and photos of targets were spread on the bed around her. At precisely 1230 Pacific Time, the hotel phone rang. Janet picked up the receiver.

"Hello."

"Do you have the materials on the project I sent you?"

"I do." She chose her words carefully. "If I read this right, your customer wants three people in three different locations serviced in LA in a single day. Is that right?"

"Yes."

"One is in Santa Monica, another in Long Beach, and the third in Pomona. Does your customer know about LA traffic? Just driving around could take six to seven hours, and that's if one doesn't get stuck in traffic."

"That's the job. You can either take it or turn it down."

"Will they consider one day being twenty-four hours? Can servicing them over a twenty-four-hour period spread out over two calendar days?"

"I think they will accept that. I'll check."

"Good. One more thing. I am assuming that the contacts may know each other. I can't prevent them from communicating. What happens if one disappears?"

"The contract is for all three. If you only get two, then you have not fulfilled the contract. The buyer will expect you to finish the contract whenever and wherever he resurfaces."

"That's a problem. There are some places I will not go."

"I understand. Are you going to take the contract or not?"

"Let me make a dry run and I'll call you on Tuesday. In the meantime, tell them my fee for all three is one point two million, and ask about the timeline."

"O.K." *Click.*

Janet spent an hour studying the photographs and a street map of Greater Los Angeles. Satisfied she had the beginnings of a plan, she changed into her gi and drove to the dojo she visited four days a week. The fight in Kauai had alerted her she needed to be better prepared if a man grabbed her. She was now working toward a black belt in Aikido to go with her third-degree belts in karate and its offshoot, tae kwon do. From the dojo, it was on to the After Supper Club.

Chapter 11
ACCIDENTS HAPPEN

Tuesday, February 13, 1973, 0146 local time, Los Angeles

The house was on the corner of a block in a quiet neighborhood in Pomona, and backed onto an alley. It wasn't anything special—single story, about 1,800 square feet. To get to the garage, one had to go through or over a six-foot-high chain link fence along the property line between the driveway and the alley. A wooden six-foot-tall privacy fence separated the driveway from the back yard.

Unlike the front of the house, which was bathed in streetlight, the back had useable shadows. A casual observer might think the fencing was there to keep dogs and pets in and provide a safe, protective place for children to play, but her reconnaissance told her that her target lived alone.

Why someone wanted the three hits within 24 hours was still a mystery to Janet. When she'd asked for an extra hundred grand for each, the Broker hadn't hesitated in agreeing. So what was she missing? Ever since she'd accepted, the question bothered her.

Janet's black jogging suit was pulled over a pair of black hot pants and panty hose. Under the jacket, she had on a grey cotton turtleneck. Her hair was bunched up under a ski hat that was pulled well down on her face.

256

As soon as she got back to her car, she planned to take off the jogging suit, undo the bobby pins, shake out her hair, replace her sneakers with a pair of two-inch heels, and look like a woman out on the town. If a police officer stopped her before she changed clothes, the torso harness with pistol, spare magazines and tools she needed to break into a house would be hard to explain.

Climbing the fence would be noisy, but the lock on the gate was a cheap brand available at any hardware store. It took longer to insert the two picks into the keyhole than to get the tumblers to release. The rubber wheels supporting the gate moved silently across the concrete when she pushed the gate open slowly just enough to slip in.

The owner used the same brand lock on the gate to the back yard. With the lock removed, the latch clacked when Janet opened it. She headed to the shadows in the back yard. Seeing the telephone box, she looked for the wires that would connect it to one of the new burglar alarm systems she'd read about. Not seeing any, she moved to the back door where the dead bolt and lock gave up their protection in fifteen seconds.

With the suppressed Makarov in her right hand, Janet used her left to slowly twist the knob and open the door, half expecting an alarm to start blaring. The only sound was her breathing.

Now came the hard part—finding her target in a strange house. From where Janet crouched at one end of the kitchen she could see the living room and a hall that that headed to her right.

Movement was now the biggest danger. Janet was afraid of creaks in the floor that would alert her target. The last thing she wanted was a gunfight or more hand-to-hand combat.

Janet had been very lucky in Kauai and knew it. Her assailant had been arrogant enough to think he could overpower her and stupid enough not to use a weapon. Every time Janet replayed that fight in her mind, she vowed she would not make such mistakes again.

That hit was on her mind as she slowly made her way down the hall, wondering why this man didn't have any security. Did he not know he was a target?

Janet checked the first room, an office. In the dim light, it looked like any other room. Next was a bedroom with a bed, a chest, and an empty closet. It, too, was empty. Then came the bathroom. It had two doors—the one she was standing in and one she suspected led to the master bedroom.

Her first peek around that doorframe revealed a shape in the bed. Janet's second look was long enough to watch the form breathe. She froze three steps into the room when the man stirred and rolled on his back. The face in the dim light from the streetlights matched the photos she'd studied.

One round from the Makarov created a pool of blood on the pillow. Janet touched the man's throat to make sure there was no pulse. The brass from the spent cartridge glinted in the ambient light; she pocketed it and left the house the same way she'd entered.

She walked to the rented Chevy Malibu, parked two blocks away, and drove away. Inside her hotel's parking garage, Janet tore up the fake temporary license plates and tossed them in the trashcan, replacing then with a fresh set. Her Rolex told her that it was 0255.

One down, two to go.

The hotel alarm clock rang at 0930. Janet lay on her back, surprised at how tired she felt. Maybe it was the stress of this triple assignment. She had checked in using her Jamie Symonds I.D.; she had to remember to use that name, and respond to it, when she ordered room service. Breakfast, she hoped, would make her feel better.

Janet tossed a fiberglass suitcase on the bed and opened it. Inside, wedged into the foam compartments, was a rifle in six pieces that The Broker said he wanted back. The longest piece was the twenty-four-inch barrel with a built-in suppressor that screwed into piece two—the receiver section with the trigger, bolt, and a well for the ten-round magazine.

Piece three was the ten-power Mil-dot scope that had set screws to secure it to the receiver.

Piece four was an adjustable steel tube with a large foam pad on the butt plate and a moveable cheek pad to help maintain an optimum firing position.

Piece five was a device that clamped onto a notch at the end of the barrel and could be used either as a bipod or a unipod.

Piece six was a ten-round magazine.

Two cardboard boxes with military markings contained forty-four 30-06 M2 armor-piercing rounds. The black-tipped 163-grain bullets had a tungsten steel penetrator designed to punch through half an inch of steel.

When Janet had tested the rifle out in the desert, the bullets had easily penetrated the three-quarter-inch-thick piece of scrap steel she'd gotten from a machine shop. At roughly five hundred meters, she'd fired an entire magazine of conventional rounds as fast as she could, timing herself at 10.87 seconds. All hit the target in a group less than three inches in diameter.

Janet took her Rolex off and laid it on the bed. At the moment the second hand struck twelve, she popped open the case and with practiced motions, assembled the rifle. It took almost ninety seconds. She took a deep breath and, when the hand passed twelve, broke down the rifle and put each piece into the case before latching it. Disassembly took less than a minute.

Based on her dry runs, when Janet left the hotel she had a six-hour window to kill her next victim. For LA, it was typical winter weather. Cool, but not cold, overcast in the morning that broke up in the afternoon.

Several months ago, watching a female giant egret stand motionless in the pond in front of her house, she had been surprised by how the bird's mix of matte gray and white feathers helped it blend into the background, even though the reeds were green and shades of brown. Then and there, a mix of grays became her clothes colors of choice. Now she donned a set of medium-grey jogging pants and matching jacket over a darker grey turtleneck. While a jacket wasn't a necessity for the weather, it hid the torso harness with the Makarov.

Janet pulled on a pair of latex gloves in preparation for picking the lock on the door to the roof to the ten story building, then stopped abruptly. She remembered latching the deadbolt after her last scouting run, but now it was open. Whoever had come up on the roof of the ten-story building since then was either careless or had left it open for some reason. *Or was someone waiting for her?*

Janet placed a soda can half full of rocks so that, if the door were opened, the can would fall over noisily to tell her she had unwanted company. A careful reconnaissance of the roof found nothing out of order, and no other visitors. Janet wrote off the unlocked door to a careless security guard or worker or someone who liked to come on the roof and sunbathe.

Satisfied, Janet crawled to the edge of the roof and lay next to a covered vent that provided concealment. Across the street and five stories below she could see her target. The front of his office desk paralleled a floor-to-ceiling green-tinted window. A credenza with a six-button phone was behind him and against the window. She could go for a back of the head shot, but preferred to wait for… yes.

He spun around to pick up the phone, his face filling the scope and confirming his identity. Distance wasn't the problem. How the tunnel effect of wind moving between the buildings of downtown Long Beach would affect the flight of the bullet was problem one.

The bigger unknown was problem two—the path the bullet would take after it passed through the glass at a downward angle. The distance the bullet traveled through the thick glass was slightly greater than if she had been shooting perpendicular to the target. It was impossible to estimate how the glass would change the bullet's trajectory. She hoped the armor piercing rounds would go straight through the glass. Or worst case, shatter it so the second would penetrate. Janet planned on two, possibly three, shots. Each additional shot exponentially increased the risk of her being spotted and captured. This second kill was the riskiest of the three.

Janet's finger tightened on the trigger and the rifle shoved back against her shoulder. The man looked down at the growing stain of blood on his upper body, then looked up for the source of pain. She ignored his startled expression as she worked the bolt to feed the second round into the ring chamber. Janet was sure he was looking directly at her when she squeezed the trigger a second time. Her target jerked again as the bullet hit his breastbone. Experience said it was a kill shot. Janet rolled onto her side and her practice of disassembling the rifle took over.

Within five minutes of pulling the trigger Janet was driving to the parking lot off Ocean Avenue in Long Beach, a new fake temporary tag on the rental. In a bathroom stall she shrugged off her torso harness and clothes. On went a pair of Bermuda shorts and a pale blue golf shirt.

Back at the car Janet headed toward Union Station to find a baggage locker for the rifle. With that done, her grumbling stomach encouraged a stop at an In-and-Out Burger on the way to her hotel for a shower.

Two down. One to go. The key to the baggage locker was swabbed down with alcohol and then washed and dried before she dropped it into a padded envelope already addressed to a P.O. box The Broker had given her.

Janet had saved the easiest hit for last. When she'd begun her surveillance, she'd worried that she might have to kill the target, his wife, and children based on her rule number one—leave no witnesses. But while she was following the target's chauffeur-driven black Ford Victoria from the office where he worked, he'd stopped at an apartment complex in Santa Monica. Janet had watched a young woman throw her arms around the target's neck and kiss him passionately before they went inside.

She'd taken a seat on a bench near the complex's swimming pool where she could see the apartment door. Just after dark, the man had emerged, kissed his mistress good-bye, and headed for his car. *Gotcha,* Janet had thought. *If I have to apply rule number one, at least it won't be your wife and kids.*

Now she was sitting on the same bench. The sun was at her back, casting her face in shadow. The Makarov in her backpack was ready to go. At 4:36 her target arrived, right on schedule.

Janet turned to the page she had folded down the corner as a bookmark and began reading Frederick Forsyth's *The Odessa File.* She'd found the author's earlier book, *Day of the Jackal,* fascinating, so she'd bought this one.

At 5:45 Janet moved into the shadows of the stairwell. Twenty minutes later, the door opened. Her mark kissed the woman, who had one hand on his crotch and the other around his neck.

The door closed. As he wiped his lips with a handkerchief, Janet fired a single shot into the man's forehead. He collapsed in a heap against the wall of his lover's apartment. Janet retrieved the empty brass cartridge and slid the Makarov into her backpack.

As she drove away, the chauffeur/bodyguard was still standing by the side of his car, assuming that his "protectee" was spending a few extra minutes with his mistress.

At the first stoplight, Janet field-stripped the Makarov and put the frame and barrel in one plastic bag. The slide and magazines went into another. The plastic bags went into paper bags, and at the first gas station she came to, Janet dropped one bag into the trashcan outside the door. At another, she filled up the rental car with gas and the second bag went into the dumpster out back. From the lone pay phone she left a message on The Broker's answering machine saying the job was done. All that remained was returning the rental car at the Avis facility at Los Angeles Airport and finding her Volvo in the long-term lot.

The traffic heading towards Burbank was a bitch, just as Janet had figured it would be. It had been a long twenty-four hours, but now she was a million, two-hundred thousand dollars richer. It was time to change identity and blow off some steam at the After Supper Club, riding the high of her last kill.

She checked in and went to the room she'd reserved for the night. Janet tossed her bag on the bed and turned on the hot water for a quick shower. Out of her suitcase came a revealing blouse, two-inch heels, panty hose, and a leather micro mini-skirt that left nothing to the imagination and gave her the "I want to be fucked" look, which was exactly the message she wanted to deliver.

It was ladies night. A sign on an easel indicated one room was for couples looking to meet other couples or single women, and another was for single women looking for a partner for the night.

Her growling stomach encouraged Janet to fill a plate with spring rolls, satays and fried dumplings. She parked herself at the end of the bar of the single's room and downed a Coke.

A gliding stroke started on the back of her neck and went down her spine, giving her goose bumps. Janet turned to find Brittney swinging one of her long legs over the next bar stool.

The After Supper Club's owner put her glass of scotch down on the bar. The glass never seemed to be empty and never seemed to be filled. It was, as Brittney told her one night, her way of appearing to be drinking while she was working.

"Janis, you look like shit. What happened?"

"I had a hectic two or three days."

Brittney pressed her leg against Janet's. It was, Janet knew, a violation of Brittany's rule not to sleep or play with members when the club was full of guests.

"You need to be fucked, don't you?"

"I do."

"I can't tonight. Wrong time of the month, plus I'm in bitch mode. I have to send some people home, never to return." Brittney didn't enjoy her role as the club's enforcer. They had a male bouncer at the club to help her take care of rowdy guests.

"That doesn't sound like fun."

"Believe me, it isn't. Hopefully, I won't need your martial arts skills!"

"I'm too whipped to fight."

"I can see that." Brittney spun around so that her back was to the bar and she could scan the darkened room. "Ever tried a threesome with two other women?"

"Are you recommending one?"

"Stay here and eat. It will help rejuvenate you, and I have just what the doctor ordered."

Brittney slid off the chair and disappeared into the crowd. The bartender, seeing that Janet's glass was empty, refilled it with ice and cola.

In the mirror that ran along the back of the bar, Janet saw Brittney return, holding hands with two other women. She slid off the bar stool to greet them. "Janis, meet Ava and Sandra."

Janet guessed the two women bracketed her age. Sandra was an attractive, slim brunette who was probably in her forties, conservatively dressed in a blouse with a tie and pants suit. On the left side her hair was short, and on the right side it hung down over her ear. Janet thought it was femininely mannish, just like her clothes. Sandra smiled and held out her right hand. It was warm, soft, and smooth, which told Janet that she took care of her skin. On her wrist, she wore a diamond bracelet that glinted and sparkled in the muted light of the room. The stones, if they were real, were worth a small fortune.

Ava was Asian, and if she was of legal age, it wasn't by much. Long, jet-black hair cascaded over her shoulders and framed a nice face and bright almond eyes. She wore a sleeveless dress that came down to her mid thighs and revealed the top of surprisingly large breasts.

Introductions done, Brittney stepped back and caught Janet's eye. A wink and a nod was followed by the mouthed words "Go, girl," as she disappeared back into the thinning crowd.

Bright sunlight woke Janet up the next morning. At first, she just lay there enjoying the musk of the two other women.

Slowly, she pulled herself up and looked around. The only clothes in the empty room were hers and they were neatly draped over the chair. Janet didn't remember doing that the night before.

What she did remember was shedding her clothes as fast as she could as two women kissed and caressed her. And then, the orgasms started. It wasn't her first daisy chain, but it had been one of the best.

Janet pulled the sheet up around her waist. The movement sent another pulse of female scents to her nostrils. The clock radio on the end table showed 0938. She flopped back on the pillow, feeling relaxed and satiated.

By the phone, there was note in very neat, flowery and precise handwriting.

Janet,

We thought you were wonderful and hope you enjoyed last night as much as we did. We want to meet you again for another private party, maybe one that could last for a whole weekend.

Brittney knows how to reach us.

Sandra and Ava

Janet stood under the shower for a good ten minutes, letting the hot water stream all over her body. Before she left the club, she stopped by the office and penned a thank you note to Brittney. She underlined the words "It was wonderful" three times and signed her name.

As she drove out of the gate, Janet reminded herself to call her answering service. By now there would be a message with a twenty-digit number, a Pictet & Cie deposit confirmation code for the final payment of six hundred thousand, which pushed her nest egg to over 5 million. That thought made her smile. Janet had picked the Geneva-headquartered bank because it had offices all over the world, which she thought could be useful when she retired. It was also not a bank the Cubans had recommended. When she'd given The Broker the transfer instructions, he'd

265

simply said, "Good choice."

She also planned to stop at the dojo for a long workout. Pummeling and kicking the heavy punching bag for ten or fifteen minutes was good practice, great conditioning, and wonderful therapy. In the classes, she would do kata and drills for as long as she could, which was often several hours.

When the light turned green, Janet pressed down on the accelerator and started to shift into second gear as she crossed San Fernando Valley Road on Sunland Boulevard. A screech of tortured rubber was followed by a loud crunching sound, accompanied by steel screaming as it was torn into shapes that bore no resemblance to how it had been stamped and welded. Janet's hands were ripped off the steering wheel and her head banged into the door pillar. The mangled Volvo came to an abrupt stop bent around a utility pole.

Friday, February 16, 1973, 1346 local time, North Vietnam

Seeds from every plant in the jungle blown in by the wind loved the fertile, turned soil. Weeds were identified with the Mark 1 eyeball and pulled one at time by the Mark 1 hand to be dumped by the bucketful in the compost pile.

The common term for the organic fertilizer they spread on the field was night soil. In reality, it was a mix of vegetables and fruit trimmings, weeds, ash from their fireplace, lime, and human waste from their latrine. The ash and lime kept flies and parasites from laying eggs in the human waste.

Every week, one of the Americans made the "shit run." The unlucky man got to shovel the gloppy mess at the bottom of their latrine into a wheelbarrow and take it to their compost pile. On his return, the person making the "shit run" got to take a bonus shower.

Over time, the mound of rotting vegetation and human waste grew, even as the material in it decayed. Mixed with bags of dried manure provided by Pham, the compost gave them a potent, natural fertilizer.

"Shit runs" were made rain or shine. When Ashley had started the unpleasant task that morning, the night rain had turned to a light drizzle. When he finished his shower, there were patches of blue sky. The he stepped out of the shower area, Lieutenant Colonel Pham waved him over.

"Captain, you and your men need to stay in your building and lower the rain shields. Do not look out, or you will be shot. Four of my men will be assigned to watch you inside your quarters."

Ashley made a face. "Why?"

"It is none of your business. You will go immediately." Pham's voice was harsh and threatening.

The guards directed the Americans to sit at their table, three on each side. On one side, Randy, Ashley, and Greg rested their chins on their hands and pretended to look at their comrades.

Through the two-inch slits between the bottom of the plywood and the waist-high walls they could see an American jeep and a small truck park in front of Pham's headquarters. Senior Colonel Trung got out of the truck and shook hands with Pham.

Randy forced himself not to react as his brain connected the dots. This explained how Pham had been able to ambush Captain Ringknocker. Trung must have given Pham the route and timing.

Trung probably provided documentation saying the heroin shipments were something they were not, or bribed the customs police. Or both. Just as clearly, Trung must be Pham's source of supplies. A military district commander could arrange to get whatever he wanted, and get it sent anywhere.

An hour later, as soon as the trucks left, there was a shout outside their hooch. The guards, who were as bored as the Americans, turned the blocks and left, leaving the Americans to raise the sheets of plywood and tie them up.

There was a hurried discussion to come up with questions for Ashley to ask that would not give away how much they knew or guessed. Then Ashley headed out the door and waved to Pham, who walked over.

"So, Colonel Pham, is the war over?" Ashley's hand rested on the fence wire.

"Captain Smith, why would you think that?"

"Simple. No American planes have flown over the compound for at least a month. We used to see their contrails. Or we would hear them. That's more than any bombing halt. So, is the war over?"

"No it is not. The war will not be over until the People's Army is victorious in the south."

"Then why have my countrymen stopped flying over North Vietnam?"

"How would I know? I am not in their headquarters. Maybe they have other targets."

Ashley yanked the wire in anger. "That's a bullshit answer and you know it. The war is over, isn't it? The other American POWs have been released, haven't they?"

Pham's face hardened as he stepped closer to the wire. "For you and your comrades, the war was over when the People's Army captured you. You will go home when I—Trong Pham—say you can go home. Not a moment sooner. For now you are my prisoners, and you will continue to serve me. If not, you will never see America again."

The drug dealer turned away and started issuing orders to his men. Ashley muttered, "You bastard, you fucking bastard," under his breath. *If I ever get out of this shit hole, I will hunt you down and kill you just as I would a rabid dog or a rat, because that is what you are.*

Wednesday, February 21, 1973, 1156 local time, Los Angeles

Janet's eyes fluttered as she stirred, blinking at the image of Randy's face close enough to touch. She tried to reach out, but stabbing pains caused her to gasp and stop.

Now fully awake, she opened her eyes and quickly shut them; the light hurt. Slowly, she opened them and squinted at a plain white ceiling. The room had a sterile, clinical smell, and she could hear a soft beeping sound.

Janet looked left and saw her bandaged arm in an elevated sling. She tried to flex her fingers but the effort generated sharp jolts of pain.

Looking down, she could see her left leg was held off the bed by a sling. It, too, was swathed in bandages. Janet started to lift her right hand and it was very, very heavy. She got it high enough to see her forearm taped to a board with an intravenous tube taped to the back of her hand. Farther up, the tubes started in two bottles up by her head.

I'm in a hospital, but which one? How'd I get here?

With the next breath, she recognized the cool, clean, almost pure odor as oxygen. She'd first smelled it when Randy had helped her into an A-7 cockpit and let her breathe 100% oxygen through his mask. He'd told her it was great for curing hangovers.

Janet's dry tongue felt like sandpaper. She needed a drink of water.

"Good morning! I'm glad to see that you are now with us." The voice came from a woman wearing a nurse's uniform. "I'm Elaine McAllen and I'm the head nurse for this floor."

Janet's voice croaked as she spoke. "Where am I?"

"Would you like some water?"

Janet nodded.

Elaine held out a cup with a straw and gently helped Janet bend forward at the neck. She took two sips. The effort was exhausting. The nurse eased her head back onto the pillow.

"More."

Another nod and the process was repeated.

"Where am I?"

"Providence St. Joseph's Hospital in Burbank. You were brought here after you were in a very bad automobile accident. You had to be cut out of the car and are lucky to be alive. After surgery, you spent a few days in the intensive care unit before they brought you to my floor to wait for you to wake up."

"What happened?"

"I was told you were broadsided by a guy who'd had way too

269

much to drink. He hit the passenger side of your car so hard that it rolled three hundred and sixty degrees before it slammed into a telephone pole. More I don't know."

Janet forced her brain to think and not drift off. "How badly am I hurt?"

Elaine stood by the bed and held Janet's hand. "Now that you are awake, we can talk to you. Try not to doze off."

"What do you mean by that?"

"It is now Wednesday, the twenty-first. You've been in a coma since the accident last Thursday. That's almost six days. For the past few days, you were showing signs of coming out, but you never know with head injuries."

Janet let her eyelids close. They felt as if they were held down by weights. She felt her right hand being shaken gently. "Stay with me. Stay awake, Janet."

She opened her eyes. This time, instead of Elaine, there was a man standing next to her.

"Hi, Janet. I'm Dr. Sam Goodman. I was the surgeon in the emergency room when they brought you in. I'm glad to see that you are out of the coma."

"Me, too." Janet's words got a chuckle from the two of them.

"I am going to give you a drug that will keep you awake for a few hours. During this time, we want you to try eating some soup. Do you think you can do that?"

She nodded her head and tried to lift her right hand. It came up a few inches. "I'm going to need some help."

"Nurse McAllen will help you. I'll come back and we can discuss your injuries and prognosis so you know what it will take to get you back on your feet."

"Great." Janet thought her voice sounded like hoarse croaking. Elaine held out the water and Janet sipped.

"Good. I am going to raise the back of your bed slowly so you are sitting up. Let me know if it causes you any pain. Then I'll order some chicken soup." Janet nodded. She heard a soft whirring sound and her chest ached as she was moved to a position about forty-five degrees from the horizontal. She felt herself breathing in short breaths and decided to take a deep breath. As soon as she tried to fill her lungs, eye-watering pain shot into her brain. "Aaaahhhh," came out of her mouth.

"Careful! You have several broken ribs. Deep breaths are going to be painful for the next few weeks."

After Nurse McAllen left, Janet lay there, examining the room. The training to observe and remember one's surroundings was hard to turn off. There was a single, pale green padded chair off to the side. Nightstands were on either side of the bed and in the corner was a door to what she assumed was a bathroom. On the other side, there was a drawn back curtain that revealed an empty bed between hers and the door to the room.

Six days. I've been here for six days! Jesus fucking Christ.

It was hard to concentrate. Janet forced herself back to reality and stared at the ceiling. *Let's take one thing at a time.*

When Dr. Goodman came back, followed by Nurse McAllen, he examined her arm and then her leg, then switched his attention to the bandage around her head. Up until this time, Janet hadn't known she had one there. But then, again, she couldn't see what she looked like.

"Hi." She forced out the word.

"Janet, are you ready to talk?"

"Just try to stop me." It was still an effort to speak.

The surgeon chuckled at her attempt at humor. "Good. Let's start with your injuries. When you were brought here, you had a cracked skull and a severe concussion. That was the most serious injury because that is what knocked you out and almost killed you. On top of that, you have three broken ribs and two cracked ones, along with a punctured lung. Your left shoulder was partially dislocated and the humerus, which is the bone between your shoulder and elbow, was broken cleanly in two, as if one had snapped a twig. The radius and ulna bones in your forearm were broken as well. We think your shoulder and hip took the brunt of the impact when the force of the collision slammed you into the door. Your left hip was also dislocated and the femur broken. Both the tibia and fibula in your lower left leg also had small fractures." Dr. Goodman paused for a few seconds. "Got all that?"

Janet took a breath. "I think so. All the major bones in my left arm and left leg are broken, along with three ribs, and I have a cracked skull. Oh, and my left shoulder and hip were dislocated. In short, I'm pretty fucked up and lucky to be alive."

The doctor laughed. "I like your spirit. And, yes, you summed it up pretty neatly."

"So what's the good news?"

"There's lots of that. You're not paralyzed, nor did we have to amputate any of your limbs. Based on our examination of you as we prepped you for surgery, you are healthy as a horse. I don't know what you do to keep fit, but for a woman in her late twenties, you are well muscled and have a strong heart and lungs. Since the broken bones fitted back together easily, we decided against plates. I think all they need is time to heal. Eventually, you will recover, but it will take time and lots of rehab."

"When does rehab start?"

"Today. After we get some food in you and know that you can keep it down, we'll unhook the IVs. Then the rehab specialist will be up to see you. There are things you can do in the bed that will help speed your recovery. We want you to move to minimize muscle atrophy. We'll need you to stay ahead of what we call the pain curve, and Nurse McAllen will tell you more about that later. Questions?"

"What's the bad news?"

"You may never regain full motion in your arm or leg. How much you'll lose is hard to tell at this point. If you sit around and don't push yourself, the loss will be significant. If you push yourself, then you'll regain close to one hundred percent. You are still in your twenties and that improves your chances of regaining full movement. You need to ask yourself, how hard do I want to push yourself? If I were a betting man, I'd think you will take on whatever we toss at you."

FORGOTTEN

The same day, 0823 local time, North Vietnam

Porters had arrived in the middle of the night carrying packs filled with balls of raw opium. For most of the night, they'd heard thunder and saw lightning, but no rain. Then, to use one of Minnesota farm boy Greg Christiansen's favorite expressions, "It rained like a cow pissing on a rock." Working on the farm was out of the question.

While they waited for Pham to unlock the gate so they could go to work, Ashley looked at the glum faces sitting at the table. "O.K., guys, we've all had a tough week. I know it's eating at all of you, just as it's eating at me. Chances of rescue are somewhere between slim and none, and slim left town when Pham killed Captain Ringknocker. That's point one. Point two, if we try to break out, some of us will get killed, and then what? We'll be hunted by Pham, who will be highly motivated to find us before the People's Army does. So, we have two choices. Do our level best to survive, or we can feel sorry for ourselves, and sure as shit it will kill us. And, gentlemen, I don't plan on dying in the People's Republic of Vietnam." He looked at each one of them as if to say, "Let's get it out on the table."

Randy was the first one to speak. "I agree. We're eating well enough to prevent malnutrition, and unless we come down with some weird disease, we should be O.K. That leaves what's in our heads. We either let it eat us up inside until it destroys us, or we continue to play mind games with Pham, win a few mental victories, and do what we can to keep our spirits up. We control what we can control. As long as we do that, we survive. Call me the eternal optimist, but I think time is on our side. I just don't know if it's measured in days, months, or years."

Karl Kramer, the least talkative of the group, tapped the table with his right forefinger. "The way I look at it, Pham could kill us at any time. Or he could work us to death. He's chosen neither, which to my mind means he has some kind of plan for us. What it is, I don't know, but I do know one thing. When you get down to it, it is all about money for Pham. He sees us as either a source of money or his ticket out of North Vietnam, or both."

Hank Cho, who often kidded the others about their lack of understanding of the Asian mind, lifted his left hand so it rested on the table. It wasn't getting better. He just hoped it wouldn't get worse. "He's an Asian. Pham thinks in terms of years, maybe decades. He will take small steps over time, and unless you have the map that is in his head, you won't know where he is until he's there, so to speak. With Pham, it is all about when and how he can get the most for us. Like Karl and Randy said, it's all about money. We just don't know the time-table."

Jeff tossed the chopsticks he'd been fiddling with on the table. "I don't know about you guys, but I am not a quitter. We never give in and we never lose faith in the fact that one day, we will return to the U.S. of A."

"Hear, hear!" sounded around the table. They all looked at each other. Despite any inner doubts, each was determined not to let their fellow POWs down.

Friday, February 23, 1973, 0956 local time, Los Angeles
Janet worked the ball in the palm of her hand. The therapist said that every hour she needed to squeeze it as hard as she could ten times. She was determined to do it every thirty minutes and squeeze fifteen times. He also wanted Janet to "fire" the nerves in her leg by flexing her toes ten times, as far as she could in both directions. She did twenty every thirty minutes.

The first few times she moved her toes the pain brought tears to her eyes, but she forced herself to keep going. Soon, the pain didn't show up until the fourth or fifth flex, and then was only a dull ache that faded after a few seconds.

Janet lay back on her pillow and stared at the ceiling. She wondered why it was Randy's face that had brought her out of the coma. He was smiling and looking down at her with wide open, questioning eyes in his "Ready Randy, I want to fuck" look. He loved to wake her by stroking her clit. Randy told her that it was always a race between whether she would have her first orgasm of the day or wake up. Getting a good fuck in the morning and then right after he came home and then again before they went to sleep was one of the things she really missed about him.

A teenage candy striper fed her a breakfast of apple juice and oatmeal, then the ever-cheerful Elaine came in with a little tray. "I see you doing your hand exercises a lot. Next time I come up, I'll bring you your watch. It's in the hospital's safe."

Janet flexed her hand and it felt good. "Thanks. Any chance I can have a phone to use? I need to make some calls."

"I figured you might. I'll have one brought up. And someone from the administration office will stop by to fill out paperwork to complete the admitting process. Are you right or left-handed?"

"Right."

"Good, you can sign the forms. Also, the officer who wrote up the accident wants to visit you. He'll bring the police report. And I think someone from the city district attorney's office wants to get a statement from you."

"I'll be happy to talk to them. Better I see the police officer first, though." *I want to know what happened before I talk to DA.* Janet looked around. There was a cabinet that had a hanging closet. "Where are my purse and clothes from the car? I had a bag with clothes in the trunk."

"Your purse is in the night table. I'll get that. The clothes you were wearing were full of blood and were cut off in the operating room. I don't know where they are. The police went through your bag and brought it here after the accident. It is in the closet. If you wish, I can have the clothes cleaned and brought back here."

The police officer arrived next. He'd actually witnessed the accident, as the intersection was part of his beat. He'd seen the other driver plow into Janet's car, and when the driver had staggered from his car and vomited all over the pavement, the officer had tested his blood alcohol level. The officer didn't tell Janet that the man had reeked of booze and had 2 bottles of Michter's 20 year old Single Barrel Bourbon Whiskey in his car, one empty, the other half full. Not did he tell her that this was the man's 3rd DUI. He did give her a copy of the report, which she read through.

About a half an hour later, a woman dressed in the light gray working habit of a nun entered the room, pushing a small table. "Good morning. I am Sister Melanie from the admitting office. How are you doing?"

"I'm happy to be alive and, I hope, getting better."

"Dr. Goodman is one of our best surgeons. He spent two years in Vietnam in a field hospital. He was in the Emergency Room when you were brought in and went right to work."

Janet didn't say anything, but thought that at least something good came out of the Vietnam War. *Compared to a wounded man, I must have been child's play.*

"I have to complete our admitting records. I'll fill them out and you can sign them. One thing we do not know is what kind of health care insurance you have. If you don't have any, it won't change how we treat you, but if we need to contact an insurance company, we will take care of that."

"I am a military dependent. My husband is MIA, but I have been told by the POW/MIA office in the Pentagon that my benefits will continue until he is declared dead." *Good thing I sent all my Jamie Symonds documents to my Palmdale address right after I landed in L.A. Explaining two sets of ID to a cop is not something I'd want to try.*

"I am so sorry to hear that. It must be very hard."

Janet decided to play on the nun's desire to show empathy and sympathy. "It is. My husband was seen being captured, but he was not one of the ones released by the North Vietnamese. So he is still MIA."

"Oh...." Sister Melanie didn't know what to say. "Do you have your dependent's ID card? If not, we have a number to call and verify your status."

"My wallet is in my purse, which is in the cabinet next to you. If you can hand that to me, I will get it."

Janet's old ID picture showed her hair shoulder length, not the short style she now preferred. She made a mental note to get it updated, even though it had not expired. Also in her wallet was a card with Amy Hazlet's phone number. "Here's my ID card, and call this woman, Amy Hazlet. She can verify my status and provide information on how the government is supporting the wives of men missing in action."

"Thank you. I'll make copies and bring them back to you." Sister Melanie re-arranged the forms on her desk and made a few notes. "I'll be back later this afternoon with the forms all filled out so you can sign them. It will take all of five minutes."

After Sister Melanie left, a man came in and plugged a phone into the wall. He said, "You're in room 236, which is also your extension. This card has a number people can call and be connected to your room. To dial a long distance number, dial eight and then the number. For local calls in the LA area, dial nine. The long distance charges will be billed directly to your room."

"Thank you. Can you put it next to me? It is hard for me to reach."

The man did as he was asked. Janet waited until he was gone before dialing the Broker's toll-free number. It was a number they used for general information, not to discuss specifics of tasking or money. She was surprised when he answered the phone.

"Hi, it's Jamie." It was the name she used and it never went with a last name.

"Good work. Your customer is very pleased. He has another assignment for you. I should have the info next week."

"It'll have to wait. I'm in the hospital." Janet paused as she debated how much she was going to tell him. "I was hit by a drunk driver and am pretty badly messed up. It'll be several months before I'll be able to do anything."

"Oh, man. Look, call me to let me know how your rehab is going. I was in a plane crash that messed me up pretty bad. It's not fun, and in my case I never regained full use of my leg. Get fit as soon as you can, because you are one of my best assets.

Everybody likes you." The Broker wanted to, but didn't, tell her that he'd dubbed Janet *la estrella roja de la muerte*—the red star of death.

"I will." There was a dial tone. Janet left a message with Amy Hazlet's secretary to let her know that a hospital might call. From memory, she dialed the After Supper Club's office. "Brittney, it's Janet."

"I got your note. It was sweet. Sandra called and wanted me to give her your phone number. Is that O.K.?"

"Sure."

"You sound off. What's wrong?"

"I'm in the hospital. I was hit by a drunk on the way home from the club."

"Whaaaaattt!!!!"

Janet gave Brittney the *Reader's Digest* version of the accident and her injuries. "The good news is I'll live. Look, I need some help."

"Girl, tell me what you need, and I'll do my best."

"The other driver was drunk. I have his name from the police report. I want to hire a private investigator to find out everything there is to know about the creep."

"Lawyer first. Let him tell you what you need to do. One of the members of the club is a very, very good trial lawyer. He can hire the PI for you."

"Great. If my insurance company doesn't take my condition seriously, I'll use the lawyer to sue the asshole and his insurance company. He was driving a fucking Bentley."

"Then Jack's your man. I'll give him a call. He'll want some kind of retainer. Where can I reach you?"

Janet read off the info on the card.

Wednesday, February 28, 1973, 1306 local time, Alexandria, VA

In the Defense Intelligence Agency headquarters, Petty Officer Glastonbury was studying an array of pictures laid out in pyramid formations on a stainless steel table in the photo interpretation center. The apex of each pyramid was an original photo with a white box inscribed "POW camp." The next row was the first set up of blow-ups with items of interest highlighted in more white boxes. The third row had further enlargements of each item of interest; at this level of magnification the film's grain was beginning to show. A white-outlined box in the lower right-hand corner contained the day, date, time, and photo platform by which the original photo had been taken, along with the classification of the picture. All were marked "Top Secret."

Next to the photo array, a photo interpreter had plotted locations on Tactical Pilotage Chart J-11D, which covered most of North Vietnam. The chart's large, 38 by 58-inch size and scale (one inch on the map equaled 500,000 inches of terrain) allowed map makers to accurately mark elevation changes, the location of small roads and towns, and other geophysical data.

"Attention on deck." Three men—the photo interpreter, a petty officer first class; his shift leader, a chief petty officer; and his section leader, who was a lieutenant; all wearing dress blues, came to attention as the Chief of Naval Operations (CNO) entered the room, followed by the Chief of Naval Intelligence (CNI).

"Good afternoon, gentlemen." The CNO walked to the table and turned to the officer. "Lieutenant Hendricks, what is so interesting that I had to come over to take a look?"

The lieutenant stepped forward. "Admiral, sir. What you are seeing is just a sample of what we found. Each pyramid has photos of the same camp in North Vietnam, taken every month over the past two years. These photos were selected because they clearly show what we think is a location with American POWs who are still alive."

The Admiral's eyes widened. He looked back at the pyramids of photos and turned to Hendricks. "Are you sure?"

"Yes, sir. I am, and so is the whole team. I would bet my life on it."

"Those are pretty strong words, Lieutenant. Prove it."

Glastonbury handed the Chief of Naval Operations a photo

from the second row of the closest pyramid. "Sir, look at the letters. This one was taken about a month ago. It clearly shows the letters N and M and the numbers 310, along with the letters N and F with the numbers 302." The petty officer pointed to the second pyramid. "Then, a month later, the same area had SE 04."

The admiral looked at the photos. "Interesting. Very interesting."

Hendricks spoke up. "Sir, Petty Officer Gastonbury looked up the tail numbers of planes that were shot down. NM is Power House 310 that went down on October 22, 1970. The pilot of the A-7 was Lieutenant Randall Pulaski. SE 04 turned out to be Misty 04. The pilot, First Lieutenant Greg Christiansen, is MIA, but his back-seater—Jim Robbins—was rescued. NM 302 gave us some problems, but it turned out to be Beefeater 302 that was an A-4 flown by Lieutenant Jeffrey Anderson. All these guys landed alive and were known to be taken prisoner. And now they are MIA."

The admiral rested his knuckles on the table and studied the pictures for a few seconds. He turned to the young intelligence officer. "So, Lieutenant Hendricks, you think these guys are still alive and being held by the North Vietnamese."

"Yes, sir, I do. Our pilots are trained to use their modex numbers to signal who they are, but over time the modex numbers changed. We have one more to decipher; that is NF 515. We know it is not an A-6, so we're looking at Air Force records. We're pretty sure it is Nail 515, which went down in 1970. We know there was a rescue attempt, but we're still waiting on the details."

"Lieutenant Hendricks, who else have you shown the material to?"

"No one, sir." The lieutenant nodded to the rear admiral. "The head of the photo interpretation unit took it to our boss, and he brought it to you."

"Lieutenant, get all your facts together and then put together a bullet-proof briefing that supports your analysis. Make sure you can show the history. How long will it take?"

"Sir, I'd like a week."

"Lieutenant, I have a meeting with the Chairman of the Joint Chiefs on Monday afternoon. I need it by then. Can you do it?"

"Yes, sir. It will be on your desk Monday morning."

"No, Lieutenant, I want *you* in my office on Monday morning *with* the briefing, ready to take me through it. Then, *you* get to deliver it to the members of the Joint Chiefs of Staff."

Hendricks squared his shoulders. "Yes, Sir!!! I'll be there." When CNO left, Hendricks felt week in the knees. He'd briefed captains and one star admirals before, but never CNO or the members of the Joint Chiefs. *Fuck this up, Hendricks, and you'll be lucky to be the mess treasurer at some obscure naval base out in the middle of nowhere. Do it right and something good may come of it.*

Thursday, March 8, 1973, 1007 local time, Los Angeles

Janet's physical therapy was exhausting, but she was making progress. Her therapist bragged in her presence to Dr. Goodman that Janet was a "work-out commando." He'd ask her to do an exercise ten times, and she'd do it twenty. Dr. Goodman smiled and told Janet that her next set of X-rays would show if her leg was up to bearing weight yet.

The bandages were off and the stitches removed. Only the Ace bandage wrapped around her chest remained. What was left were vivid red scars—two on her left arm and one down the outside of her thigh—which, she was told, would fade over time.

Progress would get Janet out of the hospital. It would let her enjoy taking a shower instead of sponge baths. Progress would get her back to work, allow her to have sex, and get her a pile of money from the drunken bastard who'd done this to her.

Once she'd gotten the PI's report, she'd had a very direct conversation with her lawyer. The driver who'd hit her was loaded, even when he wasn't tanked. He'd caused her physical damage that would never completely heal, and there was accompanying trauma. The Volvo had been her last link to her MIA husband. (The lawyer had been very sympathetic at that, and

Janet had heard him mentally ratchet up the dollar amount of her claim.) If he wouldn't settle out of court for 7 million dollars, she'd take him to trial, and with the police report and police officer's testimony, she'd win. She was certain the case would never go to court, for along with all that wealth the man in question had a very public persona.

And if the bastard didn't pay, she was going to take him to the desert and kill him very, very slowly before feeding him to the vultures.

When Janet confided these plans—except for that last bit—to Brittany, who visited nearly every day, Brittany smiled.

"I think you'll get it. Just knowing that Jack would be opposing counsel is enough to cause most people to settle out of court. Which means you will wind up being what some people call 'comfortably well off'. By the way, if you need a good CPA, call Sandra. She's the club's accountant and specializes in clients with unusual needs."

"I didn't know that."

"She and Ava would like to spend more time with you, as would I. Why don't you call her?"

"O.K. I will."

Brittney wrote down a number on the back of one of her business cards. "What else can I do for you?"

"Oh God! I'm so horny I can't stand it. The other night, I started to masturbate, and when I took a deep breath it hurt. It was a weird combination of pain and pleasure. The pain became unbearable, so I stopped."

"Hmm. I can't help with that right now, so what else?"

"I need a truck." Janet pointed to the night table right behind her. "There's a brochure in the drawer."

Janet waited until Brittney had the Chevy K5 Blazer brochure in her hand. "I found it in one of the waiting rooms. It's perfect because you can select four-wheel drive when you need it. I want one with a 350 cubic inch V-8 so I can carry shit and haul ass when I want to go fast. Do you know a Chevy dealer who can give me a good deal?"

"We have several members who are car dealers. The only one I know personally is the one who sells Porsches. Let me check it out. Do you want new or used?"

"New. And, I'll pay cash."

"Are you going to buy it sight unseen?"

"No, I'll want to drive it first. But I don't want to drive home in a rental."

"Why do you need a four wheel drive car?"

"You've never seen my driveway. It is gravel and a half-mile uphill to the house. When it rains or snows, getting up or down is a challenge." The Blazer would also be perfect for going out into the desert to shoot and she wouldn't have to worry about ripping off something vital as she navigated the rutted road.

"I've not seen your house, but I'll take your word for it."

"You're invited any time I'm home. The trick is catching me."

"I know how that is." Brittany sighed regretfully. "Work always interferes."

Friday, March 17, 1973 1545 local time,
Clark Air Force Base, The Philippines

The remains of a hamburger, French fries, and a bowl of chocolate ice cream sat on the table, and Richard Aloysius O'Reilly was enjoying the taste of an ice cold Coca Cola, because nothing tasted more like the U.S.A. than Coca Cola after a burger and fries. He was home! His group of POWs had arrived at the Air Force base north of Manila two days before. After a medical exam, the initial debriefing started.

The meal had been delivered to the conference room where O'Reilly spent the morning with his de-briefers, Gary Reeger, a Navy air intelligence officer who'd made four deployments on a carrier to Yankee Station during the Vietnam War, and Norm Blanchard, an A-7 pilot who'd made two combat cruises to the Gulf of Tonkin. Both men volunteered to interview newly released POWs. Blanchard waited for O'Reilly to finish his soda before he turned the tape recorder on and resumed the questioning. "After you were shot down and before you were taken to a prison, did you meet any other American POWs?"

"Yes, one."

"Who?"

"His name was Randy Pulaski. He was a lieutenant and, if I remember correctly, an A-7 driver."

Blanchard forced himself to remain neutral while his mind raced. He'd been VA-153's air intelligence officer, a lieutenant commander, when his roommate Randy Pulaski had been shot down. Randy was listed as MIA, presumed KIA, and this was the first time he'd heard Randy's name in any report by a POW that mentioned his friend was alive after he was captured. Now there was a glimmer of hope that they could find out what happened to his friend. The North Vietnamese response to all requests about POWs the U.S. believed to be taken alive was that their presence was "unknown."

"Tell us everything you know about Lieutenant Pulaski." While Blanchard's tone was matter-of-fact, inside, his heart was racing.

"Sure. He was bagged about eight or nine days before I was shot down. I was brought to a compound that looked like an old French army fort and stuffed in a bamboo cage. We were both beaten up pretty badly by a Vietnamese colonel by the name of Duong. A couple of days later, I was moved to solitary confinement in a prison someplace near Hanoi."

"What kind of shape was he in?"

"He was O.K. No broken bones, just bruises. Duong liked to use hoses."

"Do you know what happened to him?" O'Reilly asked.

"No. He was left there when I was taken to Hanoi. My guess was it was because I was a commander and he was a lieutenant."

"How were you taken to Hanoi?"

"In the back of a truck. It took two days. Most of the time I was wearing a hood so I couldn't see anything."

"Were there any other POWs in the truck?"

"No."

"When you were interrogated, were you questioned by individuals from any other country?"

"No, just the North Vietnamese."

Blanchard knew that was a lie. The CIA and the DIA debriefings of other POWs revealed that Cubans and Soviet GRU officers interrogated them. Several POWs mentioned in their briefings that before O'Reilly arrived, they were asked specific questions about the about the Standard Anti-Radiation Missile. They suspected the Vietnamese were either fishing or cross-checking answers.

"How were you beaten and tortured?"

O'Reilly took a deep breath and sighed, shifting his expression to one of sorrow. He went through the same story he'd told his fellow POWs.

As he made notes, Blanchard became even more convinced that O'Reilly was not telling the whole story of what had happened. Blanchard had seen the publicized written and videotaped confessions, and he knew the details of O'Reilly's career before he was shot down. More significantly, so far eleven POWs had said that they thought O'Reilly was a collaborator and should be court-martialed. The most damning one had come from the POW who'd functioned as the camp "doctor" at the Plantation. He'd said that when O'Reilly arrived at the Plantation, he showed no signs of torture. For a man who'd been in captivity for almost eight months, O'Reilly had not lost very much weight, and that meant he'd been fed better than his fellow POWs. Blanchard kept his face still, and kept writing.

Tuesday, April 17, 1973, 1907 local time, Washington DC

The cherry blossoms were in full bloom as the Chairman of the Joint Chiefs and his wife walked past the Lincoln Memorial. He was, his attractive, middle-aged wife noted, pre-occupied. She knew better than to press; there was much about his work that he could not tell her. What caught her attention were his frequent references to retirement, because until a few weeks ago he'd rarely talked about retirement, despite having been on active duty since 1933. He loved the Navy and would, if he could, have stayed until he died.

She poked gently at his arm. "What's eating at you? You seem so distant. The war, your third major one, is winding down. The boys are coming home. What's wrong?"

The chairman turned to his wife. "I am sure we left men behind in North Vietnam and the North Vietnamese didn't gave us a full accounting. The evidence is convincing." In that one sentence blurted out to his wife, the chairman violated more regulations on classified material than he could list, to say nothing of his oath of office.

His wife stopped and looked right into his eyes, as she had done many times in the past. "Are you sure?"

"Yes. Last Friday, I had to tell—no, order—a lieutenant and his team of photo interpreters and intelligence specialists who had the probable names of the POWs and very good photos of camps where they were being held—to ignore the intelligence and send it to an archive. They were to take no further action nor look for any additional information. And why? Because neither the President nor the Secretary of State were interested in their evidence. They told me that until we have pictures of their faces, not just their call signs, we don't have enough proof. I then I asked them to authorize missions to go look, and if they are there, bring them home. The President said no because it wasn't worth the risk of restarting the war."

"What did the Navy intelligence people say?"

"They were stunned. They had enough to convince me that live American POWs were left behind. What they didn't know was that I only told them the first part of the order I was given."

"What didn't you tell them?"

"I didn't tell them to destroy the evidence. What I did was tell them to stand down, archive what they have. Then I told them to identify as many of the possible POWs as they can. In doing so, I violated a direct order from my commander in chief, the President of the United States."

The admiral's wife held his arm. "How many men are we talking about?"

"They found four, and were convinced they were on track to find maybe another four or five. The president wasn't even willing to approach the Vietnamese with the evidence."

"Oh, my God! It will be a scandal if it ever gets out."

"Yes it will, and that's why it is time for me to retire. The knowledge that we knew we left men behind will eat at me for the rest of my life. Now you share my burden."

Saturday, June 16, 1973, 0733 local time, Tehachapi

Three times during the past week, thunderstorms and heavy rain had pounded the desert, and brown plants had turned green. Those that flowered, did. Despite rain, the ruts in the road through the desert's sand were dry, and the Blazer's ground clearance and suspension smoothed out the ride. Janet spun the light blue truck around so that its back faced the ridge.

First, she set out a stand with a bulls-eye target stapled to the front. Then, on the folded-down tailgate she laid out her Walther PPK/S, Browning Hi-Power, Colt Model 1911 and a dozen loaded magazines for each, in a neat row on a towel. She pulled on her shoulder holster for the Walther and shoved magazines into the empty pouches.

It had been three months since the accident. Janet took in a deep breath and exhaled with a satisfied "Ha!" as she surveyed what she had arranged. It was wonderful to feel her chest expand and contract without pain.

Janet smoothly drew the German-made PPK/S and pointed it at the target. Originally designed in 1931 as the *Polizei Pistole Kurz* or short police pistol, the PPK didn't meet the minimum weight standards stipulated in the U.S. Gun Control Act of 1968 and could no longer be imported. The manufacturer, Carl Walther

Sportwaffen, had combined the heavier slide from the larger PP or *Polizei Pistol* with the PPK's frame and barrel and created a well-balanced, very accurate .380-caliber pistol. The 380's .95-grain slug was not a man-stopper like the .45's 230-grain bullet, but the PPK/S was small and easily concealable, and the .380 still provided enough punch to be deadly.

Janet exhaled and the first round went off; a hole appeared in the black center of the target. The remaining seven followed in short order. When she checked, all were within a two-inch circle.

Not good enough. She applied black masking tape to the holes and reloaded. This time she fired deliberately, with about two seconds between rounds. The holes were all within two inches of each other. Better. She dumped out the empty magazine, reloaded, and fired. Another group of holes touching each other appeared. They could all be covered by a one inch circle.

Janet moved the target back to ten yards and shot three magazines. The tight groups pleased her, so she replaced the target and began to fire double taps. The first round went into the center of the target and the second hole was less than an inch away. In twenty minutes, all twelve magazines were empty and the center of the target was obliterated. The sun was well up and Janet could feel the temperature rising. By noon this part of the desert would be approaching, if not exceeding, one hundred degrees.

As she downed a glass of water poured from a gallon jug, Janet decided she was ready for moving drills with the Walther. First, she stood and fired as she moved sideways. Next she walked toward and backward from the target, each time emptying a magazine, reloading while moving in a different direction.

In each "run" she concentrated on her footwork—heel down, roll to the toe. Don't cross your legs!

Satisfied that her skills were returning, Janet decided to skip the Hi-Power and go right to the .45. After another glass of water, she started the same way she had with the Walther. The Colt Model 1911 was much heavier and harder to control with her small hands. The second rounds on the double taps were often an inch or two away from the first. Not good enough!

Janet was reloading the .45 as she moved diagonally from the target when she heard a voice behind her. "That's great shooting, pretty shooter girl!"

She turned to see the smiling face of Bill Willard. "I haven't seen you out here in a long time. Where have you been?"

Janet pulled off her sound suppressors. "Actually, I was in a serious automobile accident. I spent a couple of months in the hospital and just got home a few days ago." *Why did I say that?*

"I see you haven't lost your touch."

"How long have you been sitting there?"

"About fifteen minutes. I was admiring your technique, to say nothing of you. Don't take this the wrong way, but you are very easy on the eyes."

Shit! He could have killed me. I was so focused I didn't hear him drive up. Yes, Janet, you are out of practice, and your situational awareness sucks. Janet smiled and turned all girl. "Thank you, that's very kind of you."

"Not kind, true. I've been around a lot of Marine and Navy special operators, as well as police SWAT team members, who would do anything to shoot as well as you do."

"So what brings you out here?" Janet wanted to change the subject.

"Same as you. Want to shoot away from the constraints of a public or police range."

"Well, you'll have the place to yourself. I'm almost finished."

"Please go ahead. I'll just sit and watch."

Janet fired off the last six magazines and put the pistol down. "I'm done. I'll grab the target stand and you've got the place all to yourself."

Bill came over and rested his hand on the Blazer. "Not so fast, shooter girl. What are you doing when you leave here?"

"Cleaning my guns! I like to clean guns of all kinds." It was meant to sound phallic. She looked at him as she levered her rear onto the tailgate. Bill had a grin on his face.

"You can clean mine any time!"

"The question is, which one? The ones in your truck or the one between your legs?"

Bill's jaw dropped at the directness of her question.

This was fun, but Janet realized she needed to shut this down, now, fast, and hard. "I thought that would get to you. But the truth is, I'm not really interested in guys."

"So, you're a... a... a..." Bill struggled for the word.

Janet smiled as she looked at him. "The word is lesbian. And I am very, very butch, which means I am the *man* in the relationship."

Chapter 12
INTERLUDE

Wednesday, January 9, 1974, 1655 local time, North Vietnam

It was one of those days. There was no hiding the black mood that hung over all the Americans. Ever since they'd been thrown together, when one got down another would pick him up, but not today.

Their collective depression showed in their furtive "I know what you are thinking" looks and, worse, silence. No one was talking.

It started when Randy found the numbers 1-2-74 on a wad of newspaper he'd been given to start a fire. He took a sharp breath as if he were hurt. Ashley, who had an armful of kindling, looked down. "Are you alright?"

Randy pointed at the piece of paper. They knew the years by the seasons, but the actual date and how long they'd been in captivity was a matter of frequent debates and arguments. The paper was concrete proof, and depressing.

Ashley squatted down and arranged the wood under the drum as he read the text. "It's from the daily newspaper in Vinh."

Randy did the math. He'd been a POW and factory slave worker at least *one thousand six hundred and forty days.* Randy had just turned twenty-five when he was shot down. Now he was approaching thirty.

Randy wasn't sure which was more depressing—being a prisoner for over four years OR that he was approaching thirty OR the prospect that he might rot in Pham's camp for many more years. It made life in the camp hard to face.

The others had different reactions, ranging from laughter to anger. In the end, no matter how they looked at it, knowing that they had been POWs for more than four-and-a-half years and didn't know when they would go home was depressing.

Randy knew that to survive he would have to find a new reservoir of resolve. Giving up mentally meant he would waste away. Committing suicide was not an acceptable option.

He would persevere. He would survive. And, he would help the others do the same.

Monday, June 17, 1974, 2111 local time, Los Angeles

An eight-foot redwood fence around the hot tub behind Brittney's condo gave Janet and Brittney privacy. The fence blocked the line of sight from the taller office buildings around the three-story condominium complex.

The tall blonde purred as she rested her head on a folded towel. "Hmmmm, it feels so nice when you do that."

"Like this…." Janet caressed both thighs.

"Yessssssss."

Janet slid forward and draped Brittney's knees over her shoulders. "Tell me about Maureen. You never talk about her."

"There's not much to talk about. She's my business partner. We met five years ago and thought there was a market for people who wanted to have sex with a variety of partners in a safe environment."

"When I stop by during the day, she's rarely at the club."

Brittney let out a groan of pleasure. "Hmmmmm, keep doing that, I like it."

"I know." Janet used her fingers to press into the soft flesh around Brittney's vagina.

"Ohhhhhh... Where was I?"

"Talking about Maureen."

"Ohhhhh, keep doing that....." Brittney shuddered. "Maureen and I have different tastes in sex. She runs La Maison because she's into bondage and discipline... ohhhhhh..... She turned her hobby of being a domme, you know a dominatrix, into a very profitable business... keep doing that, oh my god, it feels wonderful... I love when you.... Ohhhhhhhhh!"

Brittney lifted her head to look at Janet with wide-open eyes as the waves of pleasure took over.

Janet smiled. "Having trouble talking, are we?"

Brittney held Janet's hand. "Yes." She laughed. "You're not even touching my clit and you are getting me off. That's how turned on I am."

"That's my job..."

"You're very good at it."

"Thanks."

"Anyway, Maureen and I met while we were trying to get a commercial real estate deal closed. We went out to lunch to discuss some of the aspects of the transaction and one thing led to another. At a dinner, we talked about an idea that became the After Supper Club and La Maison. She runs La Maison and I run the After Supper Club. They're two separate businesses under one holding company."

"Were you ever lovers?"

"No. Everybody thinks we were, but we never slept with each other."

"How big is La Maison?"

"It has a thousand or so members. Maureen bought a rundown, seventy-room mansion in Santa Clarita that had a riding stable and a separate house for the servants. It sits on forty acres. When she saw the place come on the market, she had to have it. It took a year of re-modeling to get it ready, but now it's an amazing place. Do you want to see it?"

"Sure."

"Just let me know when you want to go. We can go together or you can go by yourself. It's only about a thirty-minute drive from here."

The timer buzzed and Janet stayed in the water and admired Brittney's glistening, long, slim, wet body as she strode toward the towel rack. Brittney rubbed her hair and wound a towel around her head, then turned toward the spa. "Come on, Janet, let's get dried off so you can finish what you started, and then it is my turn."

Thursday, June 27 1974, 1237 local time, Hong Kong

Besides being the newest and best five-star hotel in Hong Kong, the Mandarin's 26 stories made it the tallest building in the British colony. Designated by *Fortune* magazine in 1967 as one of the eleven best hotels in the world four years after it opened, the Mandarin was the pride of the city.

From the pier on the Kowloon or mainland side of the colony, taxies carried riders along the new Cross Harbor Tunnel that came out on reclaimed land, connecting Kellett Island to the island of Hong Kong. A drive down Gloucester Road turned into Connaught a few blocks from the Mandarin.

The ride through the tunnel gave Pham a chance to marvel at the engineering that allowed thousands of cars to cross under Victoria Harbor for a toll of five Hong Kong dollars, or about one U.S. dollar.

Pham rode the elevator up to small suite on the 18th floor. When the door opened in response to his knock, he bowed respectfully and shook his father's hand, then hugged his mother. "Come in," the senior Pham said. He wore a white shirt and dark slacks. "We can eat and talk. I see the jungle is treating you well."

"It is, Father. We control the jungle rather than letting it control us." The older man smiled. He'd spent years fighting the Japanese as a scout with the French Foreign Legion. When the French pulled out, he'd moved from Hanoi to Saigon because he didn't want to live under the Communists. He'd told his family that living in a free but imperfect country was better than living in a prison masquerading as a socialist democracy.

A discrete knock was followed by the words "Room service."

Pham's mother, a slim, attractive fifty-five-year-old, wearing a soft, yellow, flowing *ao dai* with white lace down the front, went to the door. She directed the waiter to push the cart to the center of the sitting room. After signing for the food, she served her husband first and then her son. A nod from the family's matriarch was the signal to start eating.

By Vietnamese standards, the Phams were extremely wealthy. By American standards, they were on the poor side of very rich. "Father, how much longer are you going to stay in Hong Kong?"

"Maybe another week. Our application to immigrate to the United States has been approved. Your mother and I are debating whether to travel by ship to Los Angeles or fly."

"What about the family business?"

"We're out of it. I turned over the cement and rice exporting to the employees who want it. I left them with enough money to run the business, and if they don't get greedy, they will do quite well."

"What are you going to do in America?"

"I don't know yet. That is one of the reasons I came to Hong Kong. I will probably open an import business."

Pham's father had told him that the legal part of their business made them money to live comfortably, and exporting raw heroin made them rich. He had always been careful to process the opium and export it rather than distribute it within Vietnam. The police were more concerned about drugs that stayed in South Vietnam than those that left.

"Have you seen Colonel Trung recently?"

"I see my brother every month. He has been promoted to major general and will soon be transferred to Hanoi." He sighed.

"If his government learns he is wealthy, it will end badly. When we were at the Sorbonne, he came under the spell of a professor who filled his head with nonsense about the glories of socialism and communism. When the country split and he changed his name and went north, our father disowned him. To his dying day your grandfather regretted his decision, but he was too proud to admit it." The older man paused. "Did your uncle say that he wanted out?"

"No."

"Ask him the next time you see him. If he does, you and I will help him get clear."

"Yes, Father." It was a given that his father would do what he could to help his headstrong brother escape Vietnam.

"And your operation—you have everything you need?"

"Yes, Father. As you know, we are making good money."

"Good. We will need to find a replacement for you next year. Then you can come join us in the U.S."

"But what if the Americans know I defected?"

"Your personnel file in the South Vietnamese army ends with your last assignment. There is nothing else in it. How do I know? I have the original record that says you served honorably in a safe place. That is your ticket to the United States."

"Father, there is a complication."

"Such as?"

Pham spent the next ten minutes telling his parents about the six Americans. When he finished, his father leaned over. "That it is a brilliant way to make money. But you have created a huge problem for Dat, and indirectly for me. The Americans might revoke my visa if they believe I was involved." Before his father could say another word, his mother stood up and faced her husband and her youngest son. "I have lost one son to this goddamn war. My daughter is in a wheel chair for the rest of her life because a Viet Cong bomb blew off her legs. Another son lies in an American hospital in the Philippines. I do not want to lose another son. Do what you have to do to make sure that you come back to us alive."

Pham watched his mother leave the sitting room. What his mother didn't say was just as important as what she had said. *If you have to kill the Americans to save yourself, do it.*

FORGOTTEN

Janet sat on her porch sipping a second cup of coffee. Her muscles had the pleasant ache that came from strenuous exercise. She'd gone on a run that morning, then done katas for over an hour.

As she pointed her feet to flex her calf and thigh muscles, Janet noted that her left foot now flexed almost as much as the right. It was progress. She rolled slightly to the right and looked at the scars: whitish stripes with ladder-like stitch marks. Over time they would fade, but never go entirely away.

Janet closed her eyes and could sense the sun's brightness through her eyelids as her mind reviewed the eight simple rules that kept her from getting caught.

Leave no witnesses.

Never buy or take possession of the weapons I plan to use until I need them.

Always work alone and avoid any face-to-face contact with anyone in the chain that tasked me.

Select only those assignments with manageable risk.

Always allow time for reconnaissance and study. Don't be rushed into a hit.

Political figures are off limits, also certain countries.

Always have a plan B, C, and, if needed, the outline of a plan D, for the hit and the escape.

Always have at least two spare identities with me and rotate the ones I use on assignments.

Each time Janet thought about how she made money, her brain came back to the same point. Everything about being an assassin went against the moral values she'd been taught in Catholic school and by her parents. *Life is sacred. Thou shall not murder.* It was in the Ten Commandments.

After three-plus years, Janet was sure government intelligence agencies paid for most of the hits. *Who else has that kind of money? The Russian Mafiya? The Italian Mafia?* But murder was illegal, no matter who sanctioned the hit.

I don't care as long as I get paid. I wonder, how many freelancers like me are out there? How many did the Soviets and the Cubans train?

Do I quit? I already have enough money to live well for the rest of my life, but could use more. I'm not ready to quit because I like what I do—and the money.

And if I retire, then what? Would someone order a hit on me?

Wednesday, July 25, 1973, 0636 local time, North Vietnam

Sweat from the steamy heat ran down his face and woke Randy. He looked at the dull, galvanized metal roof of the hooch and then closed his eyes again. The sight was a daily reminder that he was a prisoner of war.

Jeff Anderson sat on the edge of his bunk just a few feet away. "What's eating you, shipmate?"

"What do you mean?"

"Don't bullshit me, Randy. You were up half the night tossing and turning, so something is bugging you. What is it?"

"Is this your day to play shrink?" Randy didn't mean it to sound surly and defensive, and he instantly regretted it. "Sorry, Jeff, I didn't mean it the way it came out."

"Yes you did, and it's O.K. as long as you tell me what the fuck is wrong. There are six of us in this shit hole who depend on each other for survival. We're either all gonna make it or we'll die one at a time of broken hearts. I believe I am looking at the guy who said that. So, again, what's going on?"

"I spent the night thinking about my wife and wondering how she's dealing with me being a POW."

"And your conclusion is?"

"I don't have a clue."

"Can you do anything about it?"

"No."

"Then why worry? Look, I keep wondering about my kid. I found out three months into the cruise I was going to be a father. Assuming nothing bad happened, I have a three-year-old rug rat that I've never seen and who doesn't know his father. I think about it every day and there is not a goddamn thing I can do about it. We will deal with it when, not if, we get home. When I get back, I will be the best father in the world. That's my goal."

"Jeff, I worry if she's O.K."

"All that proves is that you are normal. Look, I know you are not the kind of guy to marry a lady who is helpless and so dependent that she cannot function alone nor look out for herself. We have to trust our wives can deal with the shitty hand they were dealt. We got different ends of a shitty stick and family has to be shoved into a little locked compartment in the back of our minds until we set foot in the good ole Ewe Ess of Aaay!"

Randy managed a tired grin. "Yes, Doctor Freud."

Monday, July 8, 1974, 0605 local time, McLean, VA

Gary Savoy checked the number of the address plaque against the card he had been given. They matched. He entered the five digit code into the cipher lock, making sure he felt the button reach the detent before he pushed another number. A loud clunk and the door unlocked.

As the new head of the CIA's POW/MIA desk, arriving early gave him a chance for a little reconnaissance. The space was the usual cube farm, with a separate office and conference room for him. As he walked to the door in the corner, he thought *Perfect!* It looked like a wonderful place to spend the years until he retired.

He stood in the door to his office. Files were spread out on *his* desk in *his* office. Along the wall, there were three stacks, four-high, of the off-white cardboard file boxes.

The conference room was a mess. On the table there were more files, photos, and other documents in neat piles. He picked up a file and began to read, estimating he had about an hour before his staff showed up.

As a kid, Gary Reginald Savoy hadn't been big enough to play football and couldn't hit a curveball, but he could run very fast, and that got him a track scholarship and a ticket out of LA's ghetto.

When he got to USC, he quickly found out that the track coach was more interested in winning track meets than ensuring Gary Savoy graduated. Winning kept the track coach employed, not graduating students. In a meeting with the team's black athletes, the coach said that they should focus on "winning their events, NCAA championships and making the Olympic team. Don't worry about your course selection, classes and grades," he told them, "I'll take care of that."

During the first semester, Gary began a friendship with a long-distance runner on the team who happened to be white, and began to wonder why there were separate meetings for the black and white team members. Comparing notes, he found out the same coach encouraged the white kids to go to class and make the dean's list. If they needed help from a tutor, the coach arranged for one. Unless a black athlete demanded it, academic help wasn't provided.

His track coach was a legal version of the "fixer" he'd known in the ghetto. Instead of fees for fixing something, the coach stayed employed by ensuring his black athletes made the university look good.

Gary Savoy wasn't in college to be a runner. He was determined to be the first member of his family to finish high school and graduate from college. When he tore his right Achilles tendon at a January meet in the middle of his junior year, his coaches discarded him like a burnt-out race car because he could no longer run fast. But the school had no choice but to continue his scholarship, because he had a dean's list GPA.

In the fall of his senior year, a stranger sat down at the table where Gary was studying in the student center. He asked if Gary was interested in doing something for his country.

One question led to another, and right after graduation he

found himself in Virginia, applying to be a CIA field agent. During his formal interviews and testing, he saw black people everywhere. They were accepted for what they did and what they knew. The color of their skin wasn't important.

It was during training that Gary found he had a gift for languages. He added Ashanti, Swahili, and other Niger-Congo dialects to his fluent Mexican Spanish.

In Angola, he learned that having lighter skin was both a help and a hindrance. When dealing with the Portuguese who ruled the country, the color of his skin helped because they knew that someplace in his lineage there was at least one white person. When he met with the rebels, it was a hindrance. He had to prove he had African blood flowing through his veins.

Very quickly, Gary Savoy built a reputation as a man who got results without embarrassing his employer. He learned it wasn't necessary to take out the leader of an organization to change its behavior. Remove one or more key advisors, and suddenly the leader was hearing new voices. With a little planning, he could control or influence the advice they provided. In a year, he became the CIA's "fixer" in central and southern Africa.

After fifteen years, five years in Brazil followed by ten years in Africa, Gary asked to come home to a desk job. He was afraid that the next time he started a car, it might blow up, or that he would die in a hail of bullets.

As the new head of the POW/MIA desk, he was told to build a fact base on what was known and not known about American POWs who might still be alive in Southeast Asia. He was to be ready to answer questions from the Director of the CIA, the Congress, and the President.

The math was simple. At the end of the war, the U.S. had a list of 1,350 men thought to have been shot down and captured alive. Only 591 were returned as a result of the Paris Accords. That left 759 unaccounted for.

Track had taught Gary that luck was the intersection of opportunity, preparation, and smart, hard work. The CIA taught him how to get things done in a way that no one would notice. He'd benefited from those skills by stashing away money from agency expense accounts, where the only receipt needed was mission accomplishment. If a million or two went missing in the process, no big deal! There was always more. Now, all Gary had to do was ride out his time until he could retire with full benefits. He didn't give a good god damn about MIAs.

Wednesday, April 14, 1976, 1140 local time, Palmdale, CA

For this meeting, Janet had recommended a small, family-owned Mexican restaurant. It was quiet, the food was great, and it was only a few blocks from the dojo. The man sitting by himself at a table looked just like the pictures Janet had seen in Helen's living room, only his hair was grayer and he looked a older. As she walked toward the table, the man stood.

"Bob Starkey?"

He held out his hand and then the chair. "That's me. Janet, thanks for coming. I hope it is not an imposition."

"No, not at all. I come to Palmdale all the time." After exchanging pleasantries about the weather and ordering, Janet asked the question that was on her mind. "Bob, why did you call me?"

"Two reasons. One, until I get back into a flying billet, I'm assigned to the Joint Pacific Accounting Command at the Naval Base in Pearl Harbor. Our mission is to find any additional POWs who may still be held. And, when possible, locate, identify, and bring home the remains of American service members. Randy was one of the MIA cases given to me. So, I wanted to assure you that we are doing everything we can to bring Randy home."

She gave him a hard look. "Alive or dead?"

"Janet, that's an interesting question. Do you think he is still alive?"

"Yes, I do. I don't have any proof, but knowing him tells me he is still alive. The Randy I know will do everything he can to resist and not cave in to torture. He will also find a way to survive. So, the conspiracy theorist in me says he is being held by an organization that is not part of the governments of Vietnam, Laos, or Cambodia. And, they want something—probably money —to return him to the U.S."

"Very interesting theory. Just so you know, I've heard it from several people."

"So, I am not crazy?"

"No, you are not. The trouble is, no one has any proof. All we have is circumstantial evidence, and no one has come forward with recent photos of live Americans being held captive."

Bob toyed with his fork as he looked down at the table, then spun his half empty glass of lemonade around a few times. Neither spoke. Janet waited for the question she knew was coming.

"I understand from Helen that the two of you became good friends after Randy and I were shot down."

What does he mean by that? I am not going to volunteer anything.

"Yes, we were."

"Do you and Helen still talk?"

That's a nice way to get me to talk about where we are in the relationship.

"No. She sent me an invitation to her graduation from law school. I called her to tell her that I couldn't make it and haven't talked to her since."

"You know we got a divorce."

He's as uncomfortable on this topic as I am. How much did Helen tell him about us? Or did he put two and two together? I do look dike-ish. "She told me that, yes."

"That's all you are going to say?"

Ouch! He knows more and wants to hear it from me. No way. "Bob, look ... I appreciate you coming out to Palmdale to meet me. When Randy and you got shot down, our lives changed in ways we couldn't imagine. It was very, very tough on Helen and me, on all of us. I know while you were having the shit beat out of you and were rotting in the Hanoi Hilton you believed that you could come home and pick up your lives as if nothing had happened. In some cases, that was true. In others, it wasn't. I wish neither of you had been shot down. I wish didn't have to live in this limbo. But I can't change what happened. Life takes us to places we never imagine, and we have to deal with that or go insane."

Janet knew she sounded harsher than she intended, but it was a cold reality.

Bob Starkey pursed his lips. "I didn't realize you were a philosopher. And I am sorry I touched a raw nerve. Well, I better go. I have to catch a flight back to Honolulu."

He started to reach for the bill, but Janet took his hand in hers. Alarm bells went off in her head. *This man is in a dangerous place in his own head.* "Bob, you didn't do anything wrong. You didn't fail. In fact, you succeeded, because you were one of the lucky ones that made it out. Don't feel guilty about it, about anything that happened. You should be proud you survived, and that now you can help bring others home! And don't beat yourself up about Helen. You didn't lose her; *she* changed while you were a POW. There was nothing you could do. It would have happened sooner or later. Just think what it would have been like if you had a house full of kids."

"Yeah." Bob stood up. "Thanks for your time. It was nice to meet you."

Monday, May 1, 1973, 0900 local time,
Naval Air Station North Island, CA

The conference room was the nicest one in the building that housed the staff of the Commander, Naval Air Forces, Pacific. COMNAVAIRPAC, AIRPAC for short, was an administrative command tasked with logistics support and training for the aircraft and helicopters flown by the Navy's Pacific Fleet squadrons. As was head of the department that reviewed purchase orders for fuel and other equipment bought outside the normal procurement process.

"Morning." The voice had a heavy New England accent. O'Reilly, who'd been looking out the window, turned to see a rear admiral wearing summer whites.

O'Reilly came to attention. The admiral dropped a folder on the table and pointed to a chair.

"Have a seat, Commander O'Reilly. I'm Rear Admiral Haggerty from the Navy's Judge Advocate General's office. The purpose of this meeting is to discuss your retirement. The Chief of Naval Operations, along with the Secretary of Defense, has determined that it is in the best interest of the Navy that you retire with the rank of commander as of the end of June. Your pension will reflect your years of service. You will not have exchange or commissary privileges or GI bill benefits. You will, however, be provided medical care at any military or VA facility and will have burial rights at any military cemetery except Arlington."

O'Reilly waited to make sure the admiral was finished. "Sir, Why? Maybe I don't want to retire?"

"The answer to your second question is you don't have a choice. And you know the answer to the first one."

"I'm not sure I follow." O'Reilly's gut churned as he resolved to play dumb and maintain his cool, calm-in-an-emergency Naval Aviator demeanor.

"Let me spell it out for you. Commander, we know you collaborated with the enemy. Your fellow POWs had their suspicions and described them in detail in their formal debriefings. The Navy now has proof. While you were in captivity, a Soviet colonel in their Air Defense Forces defected. He remembers reading a detailed description of the Standard ARM missile as given to a Soviet officer by an American POW who told them how it was tested, how it works and described our tactics. He used that information to write a treatise on the changes they needed to make to their tactics and missiles to make them more effective. That Soviet colonel was sent to Vietnam and used his ideas to shoot down at least sixty American airplanes before we put the base out of business."

Haggerty leaned forward. "Many American pilots died and or were captured because *you* spilled the beans. When we asked the Soviet colonel if the document gave the name of the American, he said yes. He didn't remember the exact name but said it had a funny spelling that started with the letter O, followed by an apostrophe. When given the name O'Reilly, he instantly confirmed it."

O'Reilly pursed his lips. "Admiral, I don't think you understand what I went through."

Haggerty took a breath to control his rising anger and stared at O'Reilly. *I want to say I'd like to have you stood up against a wall and shot, but can't. I promised my boss I would not get emotional, even though my younger brother died when his A-4 was hit by a surface-to-air missile.*

"Commander, I may not, but there are hundreds of POWs who do. You are one of three who are being forced to retire because of conduct unbecoming an officer while they were POWs. If you violate the terms of the letter that outlines the terms of your retirement, you will immediately be recalled to active duty and brought before a court martial. Or, if you refuse the retirement orders, we will immediately charge you and the court martial will go forward. On the board will be several of your fellow POWs. The charges will be, among others, treason, and the Navy will ask for the death penalty if you are found guilty."

The admiral held up his hand as if to say, "Let me finish." "As part of this agreement, you will not make or write a statement detrimental to the Navy. Nor will you participate in any former-POW activities unless specifically authorized in writing by the Chief of Naval Operations or the Secretary of the Navy or the Secretary of Defense."

Admiral Haggerty opened the folder in front of him. "In here are three copies of each document, which you will sign. One will go into your personnel record, one will go into a file in the DOD's MIA/POW office, and one you will keep for your files. I'll step outside for a few minutes so you can read them. When I come back, I'll sign for the Navy and AIRPAC will act as a witness."

Tuesday, January 17, 1978, 1959 local time, Buenos Aires

The apartment building did not have a guard or a locked front door. Residents stopped by the array of nickel-colored mailboxes near the elevator to collect their mail before going to their apartments. Janet entered the building carrying a shopping bag and stood off to one side as she pretended to sort through a small stack of envelopes. Her target, former SS-Oberstrurmbahnführer Hans Strausser of the 12th SS Panzer Hitler Jugend Division, had not arrived.

The background information from The Broker stated that Strausser arrived in Argentina in 1946 and immediately joined the Argentine Army as a major. When he retired, Brigadier General Strausser was commander of the Argentine Army's 2nd Armored Brigade.

Janet studied the walls, looking for any type of surveillance cameras. Seeing none, she sat on one of the chairs in the lobby and looked at her watch. Any moment, Strausser would arrive.

The glass door to the garage opened and Janet recognized Strausser's bodyguard—another former member of the Hitler Jugend Division. She stood up and walked toward the elevator. The bodyguard held out his hand as if to say stop. She stood back and watched as Strausser strode to the elevator.

The bodyguard followed Strausser and made sure the elevator door closed before anyone else got on. Janet watched the pointer over the elevator move until it stopped on the tenth floor, which, she guessed, gave Strausser a fabulous view of the neighborhood.

When the elevator returned, Janet got in and pressed the button for the tenth floor. When the door opened, she was confronted with a penthouse apartment's shiny steel door with two locks, each with cylinders that would be hard to pick. And according to her source, Strausser's bodyguards maintained a presence in the apartment at all times. Sneaking in during the day was probably not a good option.

Thursday, January 19, 1978, 1956 local time, Buenos Aires

Janet reviewed her plan. The SS officer's apartment on the top floor of the highest building in the neighborhood made a rifle shot impossible. Janet didn't like bombs; too many innocent people would die. So she had decided to stage the hit in the garage when Strausser had only the one bodyguard and the driver with him.

She had learned that Strausser arrived in the gated parking garage every night around eight. His bodyguard left the car and checked the hallway to the elevator. The Mercedes was left idling, with the general in the back seat, until his guard gave the all-clear. The driver didn't park the car until Strausser reached the elevator.

Janet knelt down on a folded newspaper so she could see under the parked cars that concealed her. Thin, latex gloves let her feel the cold steel of her pistol but kept fingerprints off anything she touched. At 19:58 the purr of a German-made engine sounded the approach of the General. She watched the feet of Strausser's bodyguard go into the apartment building before she popped up and brought her weapon to bear.

The long silencer made the Browning Hi-Power nose-heavy and out of balance. Janet had 14 rounds—one in the chamber and 13 in the magazine—ready to fire. It should be enough. She shot twice as soon as Strausser was clear of the car's door. He grunted loudly as he fell, clutching his bloody chest. The center of mass hits had destroyed his heart, and his brain was struggling to function as it used the last of the oxygen it would ever receive.

Hearing his charge fall, the bodyguard came running, pulling his pistol out from his shoulder holster. Another double tap sent him sprawling to the ground. As he fell, he fired two rounds into the concrete ceiling. The gun sounded like a cannon as the sound echoed off the concrete walls of the underground garage.

Janet came around the car she was using for cover—and saw two men carrying submachine guns running towards her. The leader spotted Janet holding the Hi-Power and started spraying nine-millimeter bullets in her direction in long bursts. His comrade held his trigger down until the thirty-two round magazine of his FMK-3 was empty.

Janet had dropped back behind a fifties era Chevrolet Bel Air and forced herself to fight panic. Nine-millimeter rounds whined past her on either side. Some clanged into the fender and engine compartment of the Chevy and adjacent Jaguar. Others sent chips of concrete flying off the wall behind her. She was cornered in a garage, and her two spare magazines were not enough for a long firefight.

The good news about submachine guns is that you can spray lots of bullets at a target in a few seconds. The bad news is that they empty their magazines quickly.

When she heard the clank of the empty bolts, Janet rose and fired at the one pulling the bolt back to charge his weapon. Her double tap caused the man to drop his weapon and use his hands to staunch the flow of blood from his abdomen and chest. Rounds seven and eight went into the second man as he rammed a fresh magazine into his *Fabricaciones Militares* FMK-3. He was still struggling to finish reloading despite two wounds in the chest when the ninth bullet from the Browning snapped his head back in a shower of brains and blood.

Janet ran forward, knelt and checked Strausser for a pulse. There was none. With her left hand, she pulled a printed card out of her pocket and placed it on the body as she had been instructed.

Su carrera en el SS y el apoyo de los nazis incluso en el Ejército Argentino finalmente han alcanzado a usted. Púdrase en el infierno. *Your career in the SS and support of the Nazis even in the Argentine Army has finally caught up with you. Rot in hell.*

The dying bodyguard weakly waved his pistol as he tried to aim it at Janet. A tenth round to the head ended his life. The first of the two men with the machine guns was still breathing, so she shot him between the eyes.

Janet unscrewed the suppressor, changed magazines and dropped the pistol, the partially used magazine, and the warm suppressor in her purse, then tore off her ski mask and latex gloves. Before opening the door to the street, she ran her hand through her hair and checked her reflection in the Mercedes' mirror. Janet took several deep breaths to try to calm herself.

The two-block walk to her rental car didn't help her nerves. Janet's shaking legs made it hard to push on the clutch, much less brake. Her foot slid off the gas pedal and the car abruptly slowed, leading to several horn blasts from the annoyed driver behind her. Ten blocks from the apartment, Janet pulled into an empty spot.

Her hands were shaking so badly that she had difficulty unscrewing the top of a bottle of sparkling water and splashed water on her clothes when she tried to drink. Janet got out of the car and walked down a block to make sure no one was following her. Then she dropped a paper bag with the empty bottle and the Browning's slide and barrel in a nearby trashcan. At a parking lot near her hotel, the suppressor and the rest of the pistol, gloves and masks went into three different trash bins.

This was her first real gunfight where the bullets went in both directions. In Cuba, instructors fired rounds that passed a few feet from her so she would know what it was like to be shot at. This time it had been different. The bullets were aimed at, not near, her.

She was lucky the men with sub-machine guns had "sprayed and prayed." If they had split up and pinned her down with coordinated fire, it might have ended badly for her.

Saturday, January 21, 1978, 1013 local time, Buenos Aires, Argentina
When Janet handed her boarding pass, passport, and departure card to the immigration agent at Ministro Pistarini International Airport, 22 miles south of Buenos Aires central business district, an immigration officer walked up to her and asked in English if she would come with him, saying that it would take only a few minutes for her to answer some routine questions. Janet forced

herself to be calm and respond politely.

Segundo Commandante Benjamin De Medina lead the way to a room with a long table and several chairs. He asked her to take a seat and to wait for his return. Janet glanced at her Rolex. She had two hours before her flight began boarding. She wondered if she would be on the plane when it lifted.

The door opened again and De Medina entered, along with another member of the *Gendarmería Nacional Argentina* carrying her suitcase. It was put on the other end of the table, next to her carry-on bag and briefcase. De Medina sat down opposite her and put a folder, along with her passport, on the table. "Do you prefer English or Spanish?"

"English. My Spanish is not that good."

"But you are carrying today's editions of two of Argentina's most widely read newspapers—*Clarín* and *Diario Democracia*. Do you intend to read them?"

"Yes. It is a way to improve my Spanish."

"The front desk manager at your hotel says your Spanish is excellent."

"He flatters me. Perhaps I make more effort than most travelers." *These compliments tell me they have already started checking on me.*

De Medina flipped open Janet's passport and pressed it flat. He then took several departure cards from the folder and laid them in a row next to her passport. "I see, Miss Symonds, that you have been to Argentina three times before in the past two years. Were these trips for business or pleasure?"

"Pleasure." *I enjoy killing people.*

"Why Argentina?"

"I like the people, the food, and its rich culture." *Compliment the man's country and you compliment him. Honey will get you more than feces.*

"What do you do for a living?"

"I don't work. I have a trust fund."

De Medina nodded, thinking, *That explains the first class*

ticket. "Besides Buenos Aires, where have you been in my country?"

"Bariloche, Mar del Plata, Mendoza, and Cordoba." *Keep the answers short. Focus, he may ask you about hotels.*

"Do you know why I pulled you out of line?"

"I assume it is a standard, random check." She smiled sweetly.

De Medina took a photo out of the folder and slid it across the table. "This is why." He searched her face for a reaction. He saw none, so he continued.

"Yesterday, a woman about 165 centimeters tall killed a retired general in the Argentine Army. She also killed his bodyguard and two security guards. This photo was taken by a security camera and shows the woman with a silenced pistol we believe to be a Browning Hi-Power. As you see, her face is concealed. Later, a woman dressed in gray was seen leaving the parking lot."

Then you don't have anything on me. How the fuck did I miss the security camera during my reconnaissance? The Cubans had taught her that when questioned, to answer with short answers. Don't give the police anything to use. *De Medina told me what happened, but didn't ask a question.*

By now, the other police officer had neatly laid out all her clothes on the table and had searched her purse and briefcase. He shook his head at De Medina, who nodded, and the man left the room.

"I see you like gray clothes."

"Oh, I do. Grays are in fashion now. And they go with anything. Plus, I look good in them."

"Miss Symonds, do you believe in coincidences?"

How do I answer that? "Well, they do happen."

"Let me share one with you. One or two days before you left on each of your prior three visits, a former member of the Nazi SS was assassinated. Each time the killer was, we believe, a woman about 165 centimeters tall and about 50 kilos in weight. No one has been arrested, and we don't have any suspects. After the second killing, we checked with Interpol. They had nothing other than a file on a female assassin known as *La Estrella Roja de la Muerte*. Many killings have been attributed to this woman, but no one has a picture of her face, and no one has seen her. The photo we have will go into their file, as well as ours, because we suspect that she killed these men."

Janet forced herself not to react.

De Medina laid down a row of photos of three men wearing SS uniforms. The twin lightning bolts collar tabs were clearly visible. She hoped he didn't notice that she recognized all them. They had been her marks. "These men, all senior officers in the SS, immigrated to Argentina after the war and were wanted for killing large numbers of Jews in the Soviet Union, along with other innocent civilians. May I ask you a personal question?"

"Sure."

"Are you Jewish, or are you married to a Jew?"

"No. I'm Catholic, and I'm a widow."

"I was curious. These men should have been tried, convicted, and shot for what they did. Whoever had these three killed did the world a favor. I'm Jewish, and my family has been in Argentina for almost a hundred years. We wish Perón hadn't let them in in the first place. Like Eichmann, they brought nothing but disgrace and trouble to my country."

De Medina stood up. "Ms. Symonds, you are free to go. After you repack your suitcase, I will escort you to the first-class lounge and personally deliver your suitcase to the plane. Thank you for your time."

The pleasant aroma of cilantro, garlic, parsley, and olive oil mixed with the smell of grilled meats greeted Janet as she entered the first-class lounge. Suddenly hungry, Janet was drawn to the buffet, where she filled a plate with strips of steak and chicken, pasta, and Caesar salad.

Once on the plane, Janet tilted her first class seat back, thinking, *Damn, that was close!* She closed her eyes and replayed the mission, her fourth in Argentina. What were her mistakes?

There were two that bothered her. The worst, the one that she could not get out of her mind, was not only had she missed the security camera in the garage, but also the two armed guards.

The *Clarín* and *Diario Democracia* had front-page stories about the general's death. *Diario Democracia* sourced its report with information provided by Simon Wiesenthal's Jewish Documentation Center, which had been pressuring the Argentinean government to extradite Hans Strausser to either Germany or Israel for trial as a war criminal. Janet wondered if the Israelis had paid her fee to kill Strausser. Or maybe the Argentinian generals running the government had determined Strausser's public and embarrassing pro-Nazi pronouncements could no longer be tolerated.

What Medina did not know was that this was not her third, but her sixth hit in Argentina.

As soon as Janet cleared customs and rechecked her bags to LA, she called her answering service. There were two messages. One was from Sandra Santorelli, asking her to call when she got back. The other was from a woman in the Pentagon's POW/MIA office whose name she didn't recognize. The operator at her answering service said the woman had called several times during the week. The message said she needed to talk to Janet as soon as possible.

Janet suspected the caller wanted to officially notify her that Randy was about to be declared dead. She'd already gotten the certified letter in December that told her that "in the event that Lieutenant Randall Pulaski was officially declared Missing in Action, Presumed Dead" she would get his Serviceman's Group Life Insurance, a death benefit of six months' pay and allowances, and would retain exchange and commissary privileges for the rest of her life.

Janet looked at the official notification as a "get out of jail free" card. When it arrived, she would be single. No divorce papers needed. She'd send the letter to the state government and the records would be changed to show that she was now a widow.

Even if Randy was alive someplace in Vietnam, in the eyes of the U.S. Government, he was dead.

Shortly after Brittney had introduced her to Sandra, Janet had hired the forty-two-year-old woman to be her CPA. Their professional sessions often ended with an invitation to dinner and spending the night at Sandra's house. After a quick call, Janet was smiling. Sandra had said dinner would be waiting.

The call to the POW/MIA office could wait until tomorrow.

Monday, June 23, 1980, 1423 local time, Hilton Head

Two men sat at a table in the clubhouse overlooking the 18th hole at the Sea Pines Country Club. Eighteen holes allowed the two friends to talk in the privacy of a golf cart, out of sight and hearing of anyone wanting to snoop on their conversation. Competition between the two men, one a former college sprinter, the other a former light heavyweight boxer on the Cuban Olympic team, was fierce, as was their betting on every hole and for the round.

Enrique counted out the dollar bills, one at a time. When eleven were on the table, he stopped. "You beat me badly this time. I need to spend more time playing golf."

"Yeah, well, if you didn't spend all your time in that communist paradise of yours, you might get in more practice rounds."

"You're right." Enrique Payà didn't mention that he was in Miami twice a month and played a round each time he was there. "So, you never told me. Do you like your new job?"

"It's O.K. I work in an office and don't have to ride around in rickety old airplanes, or keep looking over my shoulder as I play spy versus spy."

The longer Gary Savoy stayed at the CIA, the larger his pension became and the less he would have to rely on the millions stashed away in banks in the Seychelles and the Caymans. Unlike Lichtenstein and Switzerland, both were places where a wealthy man of color wouldn't stand out.

315

"So you have nothing to pass on to us?"

"Nope. I have a very narrow focus. Keep track of all the rumors and intelligence that come in the door. Then, take a look at them and provide monthly updates. It's pretty simple. Yes, its classified, primarily due to the sources, but there's nothing really valuable to sell. The POW/MIA organizations keep their Congressmen and Senators stirred up, and they call the CIA for verification."

"I understand. We'll keep in touch and maybe things will change so we can do business again."

"O.K." Gary didn't want to say that he'd read the documents describing Payà's brutal, sadistic treatment of American POWs in Vietnam. He debated if he wanted to let the DIA know that a senior Cuban intelligence officer who'd tortured U.S. POWs was in the country, but decided that the "How did you know that?" would lead to questions that had uncomfortable answers. *Enrique, you don't know it, but you are my get-out-of-jail-free card. You're also a threat to me. You and I both know if the FBI arrests you, you'll roll over on me to save your own skin. So the real question is, who will turn on whom first?*

Monday, June 30, 1980, 1956 local time, Chicago

From the balcony of his fifteenth floor condo, Richard O'Reilly had a clear view of Lake Michigan. His contacts in the city government had told him nothing would be built to obstruct his view because there were too many influential families in the building to allow that to happen. In the ruthless world of Chicago politics, if someone tried to develop the land, careers would end and people would die.

O'Reilly was now CEO of a thirty-million-dollar enterprise with vending machines, coffee, and beverage stations in Illinois, Indiana, Iowa, Michigan, and Wisconsin. O'Reilly smiled as he took a sip from a bottle of beer. Getting run out of the Navy on a rail, as he rationalized the Navy's actions, was the best thing that ever happened to him.

Yes, it had cost him his wife. At the time, she was very active in the POW/MIA movement. When she learned the real reason he was forced out of the Navy, divorce papers followed. The parting was agreeable—he kept his pension, they split their investments fifty-fifty, and she kept the house in Hanford.

Their two children were in high school at the time, and the price she extracted for visiting rights was that he had to tell them why he was forced to retire. Even though he didn't tell them the whole story, it made future visits and conversations difficult. During one visit, his son called him a traitor and told him never to come back. It was, he rationalized, the price of freedom.

After leaving the Navy, O'Reilly returned to his native Chicago and had dinner with his closest childhood friend, with whom he'd kept in touch. Rather than get drafted, Sean Finnegan had gone to officer candidate school and spent four years in the Army's Supply Corps.

After the plates were cleared, Sean had looked at his friend. "So, good buddy, what are you going to do for money?"

"I have my pension. It's not a lot, but if I am careful, I won't starve." O'Reilly didn't tell Sean that his half of their portfolio was just under five hundred thousand dollars.

"What do you want to do?"

"Not sure."

"Do you want to buy a business?"

"Sean, that takes a lot of cash I don't have. My preference is to come into a business and learn it from the bottom up, help build it, and, for that, get enough equity so that I can share in the profits."

"My friend, you're talking about 'sweat equity.' It means low salary, long hours, and, if you succeed, you get the promised equity after a few years. And then, if there is an initial public offering or a sale to a larger company, you get a lot of money. Are you really up for that?"

"I think so. I have the luxury of not having a family to support, so the hours won't be a problem. And, I'm arrogant enough to believe I can succeed."

"You test pilots are all alike. You think you can do anything."

"Maybe. But engineering and test flying does teach one how to analyze data and come up with a fact-based conclusion to make decisions. In business, I think that will be a handy skill."

Sean toyed with his glass of wine for a few seconds. "I think I have the perfect opportunity for you. I have a small company that provides vending machines to businesses and needs someone's attention to make it grow. If you're interested, I'll bring you in. You'll start by running routes where you place, repair, and stock the machines. Once you are good at that, then you can start helping me get more contracts and more machines. You can use your test-pilot experience to help me evaluate new technology. Vending machines are evolving very fast."

"How do I get paid?"

"Simple. You get a small salary and a percentage of what is sold in each machine on your routes. Help me get more routes and you get a piece of the new revenue. I'll give you some stock that will vest as you achieve specific goals. You'll also have the option of buying me out at some time in the future."

"Can I support myself doing it?"

"It won't keep you in Ferraris, but, with your pension, you can live on it."

"I'm in. When can I start?"

Five years after that July, 1973 conversation, after getting verbal notification that he'd won a contract for all of Cook County's buildings, O'Reilly had walked into Sean's office and told Sean he wanted to execute the buy/sell agreement. The agreement had three formulas for calculating the value of the business and required them to accept the average of all three or go to arbitration. It took them less than three days to do the paperwork. Sean didn't push back too hard because he had a quarter million invested and was about to get three million dollars.

In the process of winning the State of Illinois, Cook County, and City of Chicago contracts, O'Reilly became a large donor to the Daly political machine. Ten thousand dollar donations got him a meeting or a phone call. 50,000 and 100,000 dollar gifts got you access to the inner circle and introductions to procurement officers who decided which firm got which contract.

Arrangements were made over a series of expensive dinners and were always the same. The government would get a percentage of the revenue rebated, and if his firm was awarded the contract, the procurement officer got one percent of the sales deposited in a bank in Switzerland. The day before contract signing, an upfront goodwill payment was made to the procurement officer.

When O'Reilly took over managing the business, he'd gotten phone calls offering to sell him product at half the manufacturer's distributor price. O'Reilly knew exactly who was calling and became a regular customer. Now that the business was much larger, the question was, how much could these "suppliers" deliver from boxes that "fell off trucks" and was it worth the risk?

He told these "independent suppliers" that he would take a limited amount under three conditions:

1. the expiration date was at least six months from the date of delivery;
2. the product was not damaged; and
3. goods were still sealed in their original factory boxes.

The alternate supply operation became a two-way street. His machines went into businesses that were off limits, and machine vandalism dropped to almost zero. It was, in O'Reilly's mind, a "you scratch my back, I'll scratch yours" relationship that benefited both parties.

One of his "independent suppliers" told him one day over lunch that if he ever needed something taken care of, to let him know. The "something" was not defined.

Thursday, January 14, 1982, 0912 local time, North Vietnam
Pham didn't like his little camp anymore. It was his prison

nearly as much as it was the Americans'. His Barclay's accounts said he was a multi-millionaire, but he wasn't living like one. Living a triple life—one part defector, one part drug manufacturer, and one part North Vietnamese officer—was wearing on him, and he suspected time was running out. With the war over, sooner or later the North Vietnamese would demobilize, and his unit and source of supplies would be no more.

Pham rode the delivery truck to a small warehouse in Vinh where the bundles were nailed in a wooden box labeled "Rice." From there, he walked to the docks and, after showing his papers to the guards, walked on board the ship that was originally commissioned as the U.S. Army's *Samuel Jacob*.

This was the third time Pham had ridden on this ship built by the Albina Engine and Machine Works in Portland, Oregon, and launched in April 1946. Since then, it had been:

sold to the Dutch government in 1946;

purchased by a firm named KPM in 1951 and renamed the *MV Leti*;

resold in 1962 to Cathay Shipping Corporation and renamed *MV Bulan Mas*;

sold in 1965 to an unlisted owner and renamed *MV Juliet*;

renamed in 1968 by the unlisted owner as *MV Montes*;

sold in 1980 to an unlisted owner and renamed *MV Sri Bako*;

sold in 1981 to Crescent Shipping and renamed *MV Crescent Traveler*.

The *U.S.S. Samuel Jacob* had been based on the U.S. military's 381 design for FS or freighter supply boats during World War II to meet a requirement for ships that could get into smaller ports in the Atlantic and Pacific theaters. Twenty-five different shipyards had built three hundred and eighteen 381s. After the war, most were sold or abandoned. Over the years, Crescent Shipping had acquired many of them because they were cheap, reliable, and fit one of the niches they served.

The captain told Pham the sturdy, 180-foot-long, 555-ton

vessel was one of a dozen ships of this class owned by the Hong Kong-based shipping company his family used for legal and illegal shipments. What he didn't know was that the most famous 381-class ship was named the *U.S.S. Pueblo.*

From Vinh it was a short three-day trip to the British colony. Since the war had ended, Pham made this trip on a Crescent Shipping freighter every other month. Unless they were tipped off, Hong Kong customs officers didn't spend much time on such a small ship.

From where he stood on the wing of the bridge, well away from the captain and the helmsman, Pham watched as the *Crescent Traveler* passed within three hundred meters of an American carrier anchored out in the harbor, well away from the other ships and junks. A half an hour later, the harbor pilot directed the *Crescent Traveler* to anchor off Tsing Yi Island and wait for a berth to unload.

The customs official stamped Pham's passport and told him that he, along with the ship's other passenger, were free to go ashore. A waiting taxi boat took both passengers to a cabstand on the Kowloon side of the colony.

Pham felt he deserved a few nights in the five-star Peninsula Hotel. When it had opened in 1928, its owners, the Kadoorie family, had proclaimed the 170-room hotel to be "the best hotel east of Suez." It was across the street from the piers where ocean liner passengers came ashore, and a few blocks from the easternmost station on the Trans-Siberian Railroad. The Peninsula and the Mandarin were considered the two best hotels in the colony, which had many five-star hotels.

His stay at the Peninsula started with a bath and a massage. Back in his room, he called down to the concierge to let him know he was ready for his "guest." An attractive young woman, who had been waiting in the lobby, arrived ten minutes later.

She was, Pham noted, very patient and skillful. The woman used her hands, mouth and vagina, getting Pham to cum three times. As he watched her leave, he decided to ask for her again next time And, to show his gratitude, he would leave a nice tip for the concierge.

The next morning, Pham took the Star Ferry to Hong Kong Island and walked up the hill to the U.S. Consulate on Garden Road. After showing his Vietnamese passport, he told the Marine guard that he had information and pictures of POWs still alive and being held in Vietnam.

Pham was ushered into a room where the Marine, a Vietnam veteran, politely searched him and asked him to wait. Pham did not know an armed Marine was placed outside the door with orders not to let him leave the building.

Five minutes later, two men introduced themselves as Mr. Smith and Mr. Jones. Pham knew these were not their real names, but of course he went along with the fiction. Mr. Smith spoke first. "Mr. Pham, you say you have information on American POWs still being held in Vietnam. Please tell us what you know."

"Sure. Six American officers are still being held in Vietnam."

"Have you seen them?"

"Yes."

"When did you last see them personally?"

This was like fishing, and he'd just put the bait in the water. "Less than two weeks ago."

"You do know that the Vietnamese government, along with the Laotian and Cambodian governments, are adamant that there are no living POWs in Southeast Asia?"

"I am not surprised."

"So what you are telling us is that, nine years after the war, you know of not one, not two, but six POWs who are alive and being held in Vietnam. And you have seen all of them."

"Correct."

"Pardon us if we appear to be skeptical, but there have been many claims of Americans still being held. All turned out to be false."

"I am not surprised." Pham pointed at the sealed nine-by-twelve envelope he'd brought with him. "May I?"

"What's in there?"

"Photographs." Pham opened the envelope and spread twelve photographs out on the table. He had had the film and prints developed in a lab in Hong Kong the previous night.

After Mr. Smith looked at each photo, he handed it to Mr. Jones, who studied them before he put them down on the table. They were headshots of six Americans, as well as photos of them in twos and threes.

Pham sat calmly with his forearms resting on the table and his hands clasped. The chess game had begun, and his stomach churned with tension.

"When were these taken?"

"Less than two weeks ago." Pham wasn't lying. He'd taken them two days before he left.

"Do you know their names?"

"I can get them. But please understand that I risked my life taking these pictures. Going back will be even more risky." *More risk means more money.*

"Do you have any more photos?"

"No, these are the best I have."

"Where are the negatives?"

"In a safe place." They were in the Peninsula Hotel's jewelry safe.

"Can we have them so we can verify their originality?"

"Yes." Pham decided not to add, *If we come to some kind of agreement.*

"Let's assume these photos are real and the men are alive. How'd you come across the camp where they are held?"

"By accident."

"By accident?" Mr. Smith's tone was almost mocking. "Explain that."

"I'd rather not. It is complicated."

"Humor us, Mr. Pham. We have all day. Let's start with your background. You have a Vietnamese passport."

"I do. I am Vietnamese by birth. I lived in Saigon and served my time in the South Vietnamese military."

"Where did you learn English?"

"In a French school, and I graduated from U.S.C. You can check that out."

"What was your rank and your unit?"

"I was a major in the 22nd Division." Pham realized that neither of the Americans was taking notes. This session was being recorded! He forced himself not to look around for cameras.

"I presume that can be verified."

"Yes." What he didn't say was that just before the 22nd had been attacked, he'd surrendered his position to the People's Army's 203 Tank Regiment, opening a major hole in the line that turned out to be the 22nd's undoing. The deal he'd made with his uncle Dat was that he would be promoted to lieutenant colonel in the People's Army. He was brought to North Vietnam, where Senior Colonel Trung set him up in business.

"Give us an idea of where they are being held."

"In western Vietnam, along the Laotian border."

"The border between Vietnam and Laos is about a thousand miles long. Can you be more specific?"

"Yes, west of Vinh."

"That narrows it a bit. Can you be even more specific?"

"I can."

"Mr. Pham, in order to check this out, we need more details. I am sure that you understand this."

"I do."

"So where are they?" About thirty seconds of silence passed. Mr. Smith turned to Mr. Jones and made a palm-out gesture, as if to say "I give up." Mr. Jones took a step forward to the table and spoke for the first time.

"Mr. Pham, my guess is that you are a businessman. What do you want?"

Ahhhhhh, finally. "I am just that, a businessman. I want money for this valuable information. Two million U.S. dollars per POW seems fair. You pay me the money, I tell you exactly where they are."

Mr. Jones stepped back as if he'd been shoved. "You want twelve million dollars based on some photographs?!"

"Yes. Half now and half after you pick them up." *Let's see how valuable the CIA thinks they are.*

"We need to check this story out. How soon can you provide us with the negatives?"

"They will be delivered today."

"Where can we reach you?"

"I would prefer to contact you. I am leaving tomorrow."

Mr. Smith made a face. "I see. My guess is that for twelve million bucks, you will come back and talk to us."

Pham nodded. "How long do you need to check out my evidence?"

"A week or two."

"Good, it may be longer than two weeks before I can get back to Hong Kong. Is there a phone number I can call when I get back?"

Mr. Jones slid his business card across the table. "Call this number when you are back in town. We would prefer you to come visit us. The next time, we will have a list of questions. Then, if your story checks out, we will discuss the value of your information."

Pham knew that Mr. Smith had just signaled the end of the meeting. "Excellent." He stood up and they shook hands. Pham left the embassy thinking he was closer to getting out of Vietnam a very wealthy man than he had been when he'd entered the consulate.

Chapter 13
COBRA GOLD '82

Monday, February 1, 1982, 0639 local time, Thailand

Through his binoculars Marty Cabot could see soldiers snaking single file along the tree line. The intruders, a mix of Laotian People's Army and the People's Army of Vietnam, were headed toward the Hmong refugee camp.

Marty Cabot was in Thailand as part of the first Thai/U.S. exercise, named Cobra Gold. Starting in 1982, each year U.S. forces would deploy to Thailand to practice operating with Thai forces, in both command post and field exercises.

Not mentioned in the exercise announcement was the extended deployment of Navy SEALs and Army Green Berets to help train Thai units, which frequently skirmished with intruding Laotian, Vietnamese, and Cambodian troops. They had been entering Thailand every few months since 1979 at the rate of one intrusion with a company-sized force every quarter. When the Thai government provided proof to the U.N. and the attacking countries, the complaints were disregarded on the grounds that the units were in "hot pursuit" of rebels and drug smugglers.

The large weapons caches left by these units suggested they were trying to set up base camps for future guerrilla operations inside Thailand.

Marty had been assigned as the senior military advisor to the Royal Thai Marine regiment at the Nakhon Phanom Air Base. When the advisor assigned to this Marine recon team broke his leg, Marty had leapt at the chance to get out in the field.

The NKP base hadn't changed much since Marty had used it as a staging base for missions into Vietnam and the People's Republic of China. The Mekong River formed much of the border between Laos on the east bank and Thailand on the west. Nakhon Phanom was about a hundred miles north as the crow flies from where Marty lay on the ground.

Marty rolled on his side to face Lieutenant Mookjai, the Thai Marine Corps reconnaissance platoon commander. He was about six inches shorter and fifty pounds lighter than Cabot, who was six-foot-one and a lean and muscular two hundred pounds. "What's your plan, Lieutenant?"

Mookjai kept his binoculars on the enemy. He'd spent eighteen months in the U.S. going through the U.S. Marine Basic School and the Platoon Leader Course before going to the Marine Recon School, where he'd graduated at the top of the class. "I estimate that we are facing a company of two hundred or more, with a heavy weapons platoon. So, I am going to send one of our M-60 fire teams and four other men to get in position to take out their mortar and machine gun teams at the end of their column."

"Good idea. Are we cleared to engage?"

"My orders are clear. If we find any foreign soldiers on our land, we are to do what is necessary to force them to leave. So, yes, we will fire on them."

Mookjai rolled on his side and held his fist to his ear with his forefinger and pinky held out. It was the signal for his radioman to hand him the radio's handset.

"Who are you calling?" Marty was a fanatic about operational security. Radio communications that were not encrypted on frequencies that the enemy monitored had to be kept to a minimum. He knew from experience that the Pathet Lao and the People's Army of Vietnam had an excellent signals collection capability, developed during the Vietnam War.

"The Thai border station about a mile from here. They have a telephone link to our base. I am going to instruct them to have the regiment send the alert company as reinforcements and get us some air support."

Marty pointed in the direction of the enemy column. "Aren't you worried about them overhearing the conversation?"

"What are they going to do? If they turn back, then we follow them to the Mekong and make sure they leave. If they don't, then we attack and force them to go back. Either way, we accomplish our mission."

"Good. Ask them to pass the standard nine-line brief to the Joint Tactical Air Component Commander at the Cobra Gold exercise headquarters, and to the *U.S.S. Coral Sea* in the Gulf of Thailand. I am sure the air wing would prefer to drop real bombs on a real target, rather than practice bombs on a make-believe one."

Mookjai smiled. "Will do." When he finished, he handed the handset back to his radio operator and turned to Marty. "The reinforcements will be here in about ninety minutes. A Thai OV-10 will act as an airborne forward air controller and will be overhead in twenty minutes or less."

"Great."

The Thai Marine smiled. "The Laotians, Cambodians, and even the Vietnamese have been violating our territory for years. Sometimes we catch them, sometimes we don't. Today, we have a chance to give them a bloody nose. Let us go inspect my men's positions."

Mookjai gave instructions to his first sergeant, then turned to Marty and pointed to a mound about a hundred yards from their position. "I told him to move an M-60 team to that outcropping. When we start firing they are to concentrate on the two mortar teams we saw, then the machine guns. I also told him to have the two sniper teams concentrate on officers and the radio operator."

After checking that he was out of hearing from the other Thai

Marines, Mookjai continued in a quiet voice. "Lieutenant Commander Cabot, I know from seeing you in your khaki uniform that you are a veteran of many battles. I have a question."

"Let me guess. You are scared and are already second guessing your plan?"

"Yes, exactly."

"That tells me you are normal and a good leader. Lieutenant, you have a good plan. Execute it and see if works. If it does, press your advantage. If the enemy does something that forces you to change, then evaluate and make a decision. Don't hesitate. The first thing the enemy commander will do will be to determine who is attacking him and how best to defend. Then, based on his orders, he will decide to retreat or attack."

"To tell you the truth, Commander Cabot, I am both scared and excited. Are you going to join the firefight?"

"Our rules of engagement allow us to defend ourselves. So if bullets start flying, yes, the other SEAL and I will shoot."

The Thai Marine looked down the escarpment overlooking the trail the enemy was taking. "Good. I would like both of you to take up a position near the end of the line up there. I have passed the word that when I fire, it is the signal for everyone to start shooting."

Marty nodded and he and the other SEAL, a petty officer second class, picked up their M16A1 rifles. Each of them carried twelve 30-round magazines plus a thirteenth in the rifle, along with one smoke and two fragmentation grenades. Marty picked a large tree that would provide both concealment and cover.

For Marty, waiting was always the worst part: a time of self-doubt, wondering if his plan would work. Now it was worse. He wasn't in command, it wasn't his plan, and the platoon leader had never been in combat. Marty remembered the effort it had taken in his first firefight to force himself not to panic and to execute his plan. This would be much harder, because his life was in the young first lieutenant's hands.

329

The same day, 0816 local time, Thailand

Marty was studying the planned kill zone when he felt someone tap on his boot. It was Mookjai.

"The enemy has pulled off the trail. Do you think they know we are here?"

"Did they deploy into a defensive position or are they scouting the trail ahead of the column?" Marty knew that in Asia the answer to a direct question may reflect negatively on the person answering and, as a result, both men would lose face. While sensitive to the concept of face, he wanted to use their situation as a teaching point.

In Asia, giving someone higher up the chain of command bad news that was the result of the senior officer's decision could cause one to lose face. Mookjai decided that, technically, Marty was not in his chain of command and therefore no face was lost by either side. "We're not sure."

"We need to find out. I need two of your best men."

Mookjai turned and spoke in rapid Thai to his platoon sergeant who in turn, whispered to a nearby sergeant. Two men appeared and he spoke to them. The soldiers responded, and Mookjai spoke again. Both men nodded and Mookjai turned to Marty. "They have been told they are under your command. Use standard hand signals. These men are also very good with a knife. I also told them that you are a great warrior and during the Vietnam War killed many Pathet Lao and Vietnamese."

Marty smiled. "If you hear an M-16 fire, you start the ambush."

"Understood."

Marty led the two Thais and his fellow SEAL back into the jungle and down toward the trail in a game he called blind man's bluff. If they stumbled into the enemy scouts, the ambushers became the ambushed and one or more of them would die.

As they crept through the heavy brush and trees parallel to the trail, every twenty yards they stopped and listened. At a grassy area with just a few trees, Marty's sixth sense told him the enemy was watching. Behind a tree, he turned around and pointed in the direction from which they had come. Silently, the four men slid back into the foliage that bordered the clearing.

One of the Thai scouts pointed to his eyes and then held up four fingers and then four more. A patrol of eight enemy soldiers was moving from tree to tree along the edge of the trail.

Marty reached behind his head and pulled out the Gurkha knife he'd carried since the beginning of the Vietnam War. The last time he'd used it in combat had been to kill a Vietnamese colonel, in a fight to the death on a raid to destroy a secret missile base deep inside North Vietnam. He pointed to the two enemy soldiers on their side of the trail and drew his finger across his throat. The two Thai Marines nodded and shrugged off their packs before they drew their bayonets.

His plan was simple. Kill two of the enemy scouts with knives, then kill as many of the others as they could before withdrawing into the jungle. Aggressive action would make the enemy commander think twice before he decided to rush forward. If this didn't work, Mookjai would be outflanked and there would be nothing between the enemy and the refugee camp.

The first man in a Laotian uniform died quietly at the hands of the Thai Marine; his teammate came out from behind a tree and grabbed the second intruder. As the enemy soldier fought back, trying unsuccessfully to keep the Thai Marine from slitting his throat, one of the enemy scouts spotted the fight and shouted a warning. The remaining six began spraying the foliage around the clearing with their AK-47s. By laying on the ground and using trees as cover and concealment, the Thais cut down two more. The four survivors ran back toward the column. One of the Thais popped out into the clearing, kneeled, and squeezed off three quick shots that sent a fifth soldier sprawling face down in the grass.

In the distance, Marty heard Mookjai open fire on the main group of enemy soldiers. Long bursts from AK-47s were distinct from single .223 rounds from the Thai Marines, who were maintaining good fire discipline. The distinct rattling sound of two and three-second bursts from an M-60 machine gun fired by the Thais added another level to the noise.

Marty was repositioning his Thai marines when an artillery shell shrieked through the sky. It was followed by two more in rapid succession. He recognized them as ranging shots and, if the commander of the column still had radio contact with the batteries, within minutes the shells would be raining down on Mookjai's men.

He crouched next to the other SEAL. "Stay here as a gate guard. If they come at you, give them a bloody nose and disengage. You know the drill! I've got to make sure that we put the artillery out of action."

When Marty got to the Thai Marine position, Mookjai was calmly studying the enemy position. The shelling had stopped and the Thai marines were only shooting when they had clear targets.

"Lieutenant, any second we're going to get hit by artillery, so we've got to get out of here *now*! Let's move down to where we ambushed their scouts. If the Laotians advance, we can engage them there."

The urgency in Marty's voice convinced the lieutenant to move. As he started shouting instructions, the first eighty-five-millimeter shell exploded twenty-five meters in front of their position. A second one followed shortly, closer to their former position. The enemy gunners had begun walking their shells up the slope.

As shrapnel from the exploding shells whined overhead, Mookjai waited until all his men passed him before he followed the last man off the hill. Back near the clearing, Marty pulled the PRC-77 out of his backpack. When he heard a side tone, he keyed the mike, knowing that it was a long shot that any U.S. military aircraft was monitoring the frequency.

"Any U.S. aircraft on this frequency, this is Surfer Six actual, over." Marty repeated the transmission and waited. Anyone responding to the radio call would know he was commander of the unit Surfer Six. He stuck a finger in his other ear to block out the sound of the artillery shells pounding their former position.

"Surfer Six, this is Rector 95, over."

"Rector 95, this is Surfer Six Actual. We're engaged with a company-sized force of Pathet Lao and are taking artillery fire from the east side of the river, over."

"Surfer Six, Rector 95 is leading a flight of two OV-10s escorting the H-46s that just inserted the blocking force. Monitor this frequency and I'll see what I can do, over." Marty was sure that the voice on the radio was an American.

Marty spotted Mookjai about twenty yards away. He was directing his men to take up firing positions in an L-shaped ambush where the trail, which followed a large stream, turned a corner on the far side of the clearing. As he headed toward him, Mookjai handed Marty the handset.

"Sir, the blocking force is in position. They want us to move toward the enemy and keep up the pressure."

"Rather than go up the trail, why don't we leave some men here and move parallel to the trail until we make contact with the main body?"

"Good idea." Mookjai looked down at the ground and then at Marty. "Sir, thank you for warning us about the artillery. We would have all been killed up there. I was concentrating on the engagement and didn't think about anything else."

"That's O.K., Lieutenant. I was wondering why the enemy commander didn't react more aggressively to an ambush. The only answer I came up with was that he had something else to protect him, and that was artillery."

Five minutes later, the artillery abruptly stopped. Marty's radio crackled. "Surfer Six Actual, this is Rector 95. I don't think you will have a problem with the two batteries of eighty-fives on the Laotian side of the river. A mix of five hundred pounders and cluster bombs accidentally fell off the wings of two Navy A-6s from the *Coral Sea*. Have a good day. Call if you need us again."

Ten minutes later, Marty saw a waving white flag and

wondered if it was a trap. Mookjai turned to him. "That is typical. Rarely do the Laotians want to fight it out. We will take them prisoner; my government will hold them for a few weeks and then send them back."

The Thai Marines directed the surviving Laotians and their Vietnamese allies to gather in the clearing, the three officers separated from the men by a few meters. The surly political officer and his men sat alone, well away from the rest of the POWs.

Marty was looking at the pile of captured weapons when Mookjai ran up. "Sir, please come with me, it is important."

The same day, 1541 local time, Korat, Thailand

Adrenalin was keeping Marty awake. The mud he used to camouflage his face was streaked with sweat and matched his dirty, sweat-stained fatigues. He hadn't showered or shaved for four days. On the other side of the table was a Laotian Army colonel who was equally dirty and smelly. Arthur Reading, a U.S. Naval Intelligence officer, sat next to Marty. He gave no indication that the gamey odor from either officer bothered him.

Marty spoke first. "Colonel Kanthavong, please tell Commander Reading what you told me after you were captured."

The Laotian Colonel was the senior surviving officer of the two hundred members of the combined Laotian People's Army and Vietnamese People's Army raiding party. Kanthavong's experience during the Vietnam War had taught him that the Huey's distinctive wop-wop sound meant that they were surrounded, and trying to escape back across the Mekong would get most of his men killed. He'd surrendered, knowing he would be held for two weeks and then sent home.

Kanthavong took a drink from the glass of water that was given to him. He spoke in heavily accented English. "Commander, I am Colonel Makan Kanthavong from the Ministry of State Security, assigned to army intelligence. We entered Thailand to capture the leaders of a drug gang who have a base

334

near the Hmong refugee camp. My government wants to stop the illegal sale of opium, because every kilo that does not go to a pharmaceutical company ends up untaxed, on the black market. We buy as much as we can from the farmers, but the drug dealers always pay more. As a result, I recognize that we illegally entered Thailand. For that, I am prepared to accept whatever punishment comes my way. That is my karma."

Reading tossed his pen on his pad in a gesture of impatience and gave the Laotian a "don't waste my time" look. So far, other than writing down the man's name and rank, he hadn't made a note. "I'm not interested in the drug trade, Colonel. Is that all?"

"I told Lieutenant Commander Cabot that less than a month ago I was with a unit that followed a column of bearers carrying raw opium into Vietnam. We watched them enter a camp because we wanted to see if this was where they converted the raw opium into morphine base, or just a rest stop."

Kanthavong leaned forward. "In the morning, we saw five Americans in a separate compound, and another man who was either Vietnamese or an American of Asian descent. We watched them for two days and concluded they are prisoners who work in a factory which turns raw opium into morphine base."

Reading's jaw dropped. "How sure are you that they are Americans?"

"We heard them speaking English. Trust me, I know Americans when I see them. They are much taller than the Vietnamese and their skin, when they are tanned, is lighter. It appeared the men were in reasonable health."

"Do you know where this camp is?"

"I do. Give me a map of Vietnam and I can show you."

Reading nodded to Marty, who headed out the door.

"Do you know who runs it?"

"We are fairly sure. We know most of the families who run Vietnam's illegal drug business and are certain we saw a member of the Pham family. They were headquartered in Saigon. We suspected they were still in business, even though the head of the family left South Vietnam. We believe several family members are officials in the Vietnamese government."

"Has your government told the Vietnamese about the Americans?"

"I do not know. If they did, it would cause many to lose face."

Reading chewed on that answer for a few seconds. Yes, admitting there were Americans left alive in their country for so long would be a major embarrassment to the leaders of Vietnam.

"Why didn't you attack the camp and seize the drugs?"

"There were only eight of us and our mission was to track them, not arrest them. I wanted to see the route and how many kilos were transported. This way, when I briefed the minister, I could speak from personal experience. We counted twenty-five well-armed men at the camp."

Marty returned with a Tactical Pilotage Chart. Kanthavong studied it for two minutes. "Here." His finger rested on a spot west of Vinh in the mountains of North Vietnam along the border between the two countries.

Wednesday, February 3, 1982, 0900 local time, Hong Kong
In round two, Pham expected the CIA officers to ask for more details. This time there was a pitcher of water and four glasses on the table. He had just started reading the Hong Kong version of the *Herald Tribune* when Smith and Jones entered, followed by a third person, a black man.

The Americans sat on three sides of the rectangular table. As Mr. Smith poured a glass of water, he looked at Pham. "Thank you for coming, Mr. Pham. This is Mr. Apple. Shall we get down to business?"

A week before, Gary Savoy, a.k.a. Mr. Apple, had told the head of the CIA, who was preparing for a meeting with Congressional leaders and the President, that there was not one shred of credible evidence that there were any POWs left alive in Vietnam. Savoy had concluded his briefing with the statement, "Anyone claiming to have information on live American POWs is attempting to perpetrate a scam on the United States."

Pham expected it would take a lot of convincing to get the Americans to part with $12 million. So, he was ready with his evidence.

Mr. Smith continued. "We don't believe there is one, let alone six, POWs left in Vietnam. O.K., you sent us the negatives that match the photos, so we know the photos are genuine. But we need more to be convinced that this isn't a hoax. What else can you show us?"

Pham opened the clasp on a manila envelope and dumped out more photos. He spread them out and put the cellophane strip with the black and white negatives on the center of the table.

The Vietnamese officer watched Mr. Apple glance at two photos before tossing them on the table as if they were not worthy of his attention.

"How about if I give you three of their names? You can look up the date of their shoot-downs."

"Go ahead. Who's who?" Pham picked up a close-up photo. "This is Lieutenant Randall Pulaski, United States Navy." He slid the photo across the table to Mr. Smith, who took out a black government ballpoint pen and wrote the name down on the back of the photo in the upper right corner.

"This is Lieutenant Jeffrey Anderson, United States Navy." Smith noted the name in the same place in neat block printing.

"This is First Lieutenant Karl Kramer, United States Air Force." He stopped.

"How about the rest of the names, Mr. Pham?"

"No. Not until we have a deal."

Savoy tapped the table. "We're not anywhere close to making a deal. Twelve million is a lot of money."

"That's the price. Half when we make the deal and I give you the latitude and longitude of where they are being held. When you pick them up, I get the other half."

"You're pretty confident that you can make this happen, aren't you?"

"I am."

Savoy tossed the picture he was holding onto the table. "Too many people have tried this. I think you are scamming the United States."

"If the U.S. is not going to pay for their release, then they are of little use to the people who are holding them. The Vietnamese government will lose much face if they have to admit that these men have been in their country all these years. To prevent that, they will kill them instead. Life, as you know, is cheap in Vietnam."

"Are you suggesting they may be killed if we wait?"

"Yes. I can't guarantee how long they will be allowed to live."

Mr. Jones leaned forward. "Pham, are you telling us they are not being held by the Vietnamese government?"

"Yes."

"And, you are telling us that they will be murdered if the U.S. won't pay the twelve million."

Pham didn't hesitate. He needed to create a sense of urgency and up the pressure. "Yes. I might add that if it gets out that the U.S. Government made no attempt to get these men back and they were killed, it would be what you call a public relations mess." *I want the money, and if they are dead I get nothing, but neither do you. I just leave Vietnam with my secret.*

"When will you tell us where they are?"

"When I am paid the first six million. Then I tell you the rest of the names and the location." He held up a three-by-five card and slid it across the table. "This card has my bank account information."

"We would still pay you once we recovered the POWs."

"But not as much."

None of the CIA officers said anything for a few minutes. Then Mr. Jones leaned forward and picked up the photos of the men whose names Pham had not given them. "Can you bring us what is known as 'proof of life'?"

"What's that?"

"'Proof of life' is a picture of each one of them with something like a newspaper that has a date less than a week old."

Pham had not anticipated a "proof of life" demand. "I will try. The three names should enable you to verify who these men are and convince you that this is not what you called a scam."

"We need to get authorization."

"Then get it. How long will it take?"

"Come back in two weeks."

"I will come back with what you call a proof of life and the rest of the names. Make sure you have authorization to pay me. Again, time is of the essence. I cannot guarantee their safety. That is out of my hands."

The same day, 1300 local time, On Board the U.S.S. Coral Sea

The flag conference room on the last U.S. carrier built with a straight deck was a tiny eight-by-ten steel box just off the flag command center. To fill all the chairs, those sitting at the back of the room had to enter first. Once a chair was occupied, there was no room between the chair and the gray-painted steel bulkhead.

Marty had a chance to clean up, pack a bag, and change into a set of khakis before he boarded the C-2 cargo plane that flew him out to the *Coral Sea*. The helicopter propellers hadn't stopped turning when the admiral's aide boarded to lead Marty to the conference room to give his report. He arrived just before the admiral commanding Carrier Group One and his intelligence officer entered.

The admiral pushed the door closed. "Mr. Cabot, how good do you think this intelligence is?"

"Sir, good enough for reconnaissance. Colonel Kanthavong of the Laotian Army was pretty specific about the location, layout of the camp, number of guards, and make-up of the prisoners. We owe it to the Americans who are there to find out."

"I agree, but the intelligence community says there are no living POWs in Vietnam." The admiral, who had friends who'd been POWs, picked up the phone and dialed a two-digit number.

"This is the boss. I need to talk to CINCPAC himself. When you get his aide on the line, say that it's urgent."

The one-star admiral put the phone back on the cradle, knowing someone in his ship's communications center was dialing the satellite phone. When CINCPAC was on the phone, they would call the conference room. It took less than a minute.

The intelligence officer picked up the phone on the first ring. "Commander Carrier Group One. Commander Easting."

"Commander Easting, this is Admiral Hastings. What is so important that I had to be dragged out of a meeting?"

Easting pressed the speaker phone and nodded to the admiral.

"Sir, this is Rear Admiral Huntington. I've got some very interesting news." The Commander, Carrier Group One, told the Commander, Pacific Command, what he'd just heard. When he finished, he simply said, "I want permission to have an RF-8 make a pass or two over the site. If there are POWs there, we have some decisions to make."

"Is Mr. Cabot in the room?"

"Yes, sir, he's listening."

"Marty, how good do you think this intel is?"

"Sir, good enough for me to attempt a rescue once we confirm the location. I want to lead it."

Admiral Huntington made a mental note of the informal tone that a four-star-admiral shifted into when he spoke to the SEAL. That was a backstory he needed to understand.

"That's all I needed to hear. Marty, do you know where your partner in crime, Josh Haman, is?"

"Yes, sir. He's the assistant Air Ops officer on Admiral Huntington's staff."

"Perfect. The two of you get started on a rescue plan. Assuming the photos prove there are live POWs at the camp, I want you two to plan and execute the raid. In the meantime, I will get someone from NICPAC to bring the last five years of satellite photos of the area out to the *Coral Sea* as soon as I can get them there. Give me the latitude and longitude again?"

"Yes, sir." Marty recited the numbers.

"Admiral Huntington, as soon as I get off the phone, I will send you an operations-immediate message tasking the photo mission. The geography will be vague. Just don't fly an alpha strike to cover the photo mission. Do something that is deniable. Meanwhile, I'll run the political traps to cover our asses. Get good pictures and let's find out if this intel is real. If it is, I want to bring those guys home yesterday."

There were three "Aye, aye, sir"s and the call ended. Marty's face was grim. He'd been in that part of Vietnam before, and it was not a fun place to be.

"Lieutenant Commander Cabot, how do you know Admiral Hastings?"

Marty smiled. "Sir, he pinned a Navy Cross on my chest for a raid on a North Vietnamese missile base. At the time, he was CINCPAC's operations officer. He'd blessed the plan and gotten it approved."

"You led the raid?"

"Yes, sir. Josh Haman and his crew took my team in, shut their helicopter down, spent a night with us on the ground, and participated in the raid. He was the one who captured the Russian colonel missile expert."

"I... didn't know that." He'd never asked why a lieutenant commander helicopter pilot on his staff had been awarded two Navy Crosses and two Silver Stars.

He leaned back to open the door and called out, "Command duty officer!" His voice was loud enough to ensure that the officer, sitting in a chair at the far end of the command center, heard him. When the man appeared, the admiral stood up. "Get the air wing commander, the commanding officer of the RF-8 squadron, my operations officer, and Mr. Haman in here on the double."

Josh Haman's cheeks still showed the rings from wearing a helmet for four hours when he walked into the tiny conference room. His eyes opened wide with surprise. "Marty, what the fuck are you doing here?"

If there had been space, they would have given each other a bear hug. Instead, they shook hands across the table.

"To give you some honest work. We have a mission to plan."

"Where am I taking you this time?"

"Back into Vietnam along the Laotian border. West of Vinh."

"Oh, joy!" Josh's tone was sarcastic. Then he got serious. "Why?"

"We have accurate intel that six Americans are being held in the area, and if the photos verify it, we're going to go get them."

Thursday, February 4, 1982, 1209 local time, Langley

After telling his administrative assistant that he was going out to run an errand, the first thing Gary Savoy did was find a pay phone. The phone rang a dozen times, and Gary was ready to hang up when he heard a familiar voice. "'Lo."

"Bobbi, it's Gary."

"What's up, man?" Bobbi Wales' accent and style of speech depended on who he was talking with. Since he and Gary had grown up in the LA ghetto, he reverted to the way they spoke when they were childhood friends.

"What happened in Hong Kong? You said these guys could take out Pham before he got to the embassy. He showed up alive and well. Then they failed to kill him before he got on a boat back to Vietnam."

"I'll check with my guys. Is this goin' to be bad for you, bro'?"

"Could be." Gary looked around at the traffic and waited for a truck to pass. *I should have found my own off-the-book assets. Pham and his photos aren't just bad—they're a fucking disaster! It'll start an investigation and analysis of all the intelligence we've collected for the past nine years. Every briefing I've given on the topic of live POWs in SE Asia will come under scrutiny. This kind of fuck up spells END OF CAREER and maybe no pension!* "I want my money back. They took a job and didn't do it."

"That'll be hard, brother."

"Why?"

"'Cuz it went through three levels and each man took his cut. I'm guessin,' but what went to the shooters was probably about half of what you gave me."

"O.K., get me that half back."

"I don't think I can. They'll claim they got expenses, ya know."

"I don't care. They took a contract and didn't fulfill it."

"Look, Gary, I can pass the heat on down, but you are messin' with some pretty bad dudes. Them Chinese Tong gangs don't like being fucked with. They know they fucked up. Let them do their thing. You said you'll know when he comes back. They can finish it then."

Despite it having being "suggested" by higher ups that he was to bury any evidence of live POWs still held in Southeast Asia, there was nothing in writing to cover his ass. He had known that the day he took over the POW/MIA desk, but he'd figured that the chances of finding live Americans in Vietnam diminished every day. By now, the risk should have been minimal. Finding six live ones would open the whole can of worms, and he would be the fall guy. Worse, an investigation would almost certainly lead to his other activities, which he would prefer not be uncovered.

Gary looked up at the sky. He'd given Bobbi three hundred grand in cash and now was being told it was gone. He didn't have any contacts in the Far East, or he would have used them. If it were Africa or South America or the Middle East, he would have contracted directly with the shooters. They would have known that if they didn't do the job the first time, they were to keep trying until they finished it or were dead.

"O.K., let them know I want the job done right, and I'll let them know when Pham will be back in Hong Kong." He had no choice. *Fuck, fuck, fuck!*

343

Friday, February 5, 1982, 1034 local time, North Vietnam

Randy stopped weeding the row of corn when he thought he heard the sound of a jet. He used his hands to shield his eyes as he searched the clear blue sky. Nothing.

"Karl, did you hear that?"

"What?"

"I was pretty sure I heard the sound of a jet."

"I didn't hear it. Probably wishful thinking on your part."

No, dammit. I heard a jet. Not sure if it was theirs or ours, but I heard a goddamn jet.

The two men worked in silence, using their hands to pull out the weeds that were then dumped into a basket. When it was full, the basket was emptied on the compost pile. It took the five of them a week to weed the entire farm. When they were finished, it was time to start all over again.

Karl, despite his protests to the contrary, had a green thumb and got them to rotate crops so they didn't wear out the soil. Every few months, they expanded Pham's Phucking Pharm. By now, their trapezoidal-shaped field was nearly acres.

A sudden roar above caused all five to stop work and look toward the onrushing, growing sound. An RF-8G in dull, mottled gray flashed by about five-hundred feet above the ground. They waved with both arms as the plane streaked by, low enough so that they could clearly see the pilot's helmet and oxygen mask. The black letters "Navy" and the large letters "NK" on the rudder were easy to read.

Randy looked over at Jeff Anderson, several rows away. "What air wing is NK?"

Jeff thought for a few seconds. "Fourteen, I think. Dammit, I can't remember."

"Wonder what he was doing flying around here?"

"Don't know. I hope he was looking for us." It was what Randy wanted to think, but, deep inside, he didn't want to be disappointed.

FORGOTTEN

The same day, 1245 local time, On Board the U.S.S. Coral Sea

The photo interpreters studied the square black and white images and made tick marks with grease pencils on the negatives they wanted printed. Later, they studied the prints and marked the areas they wanted enlarged.

Overhead, the carrier continued flight operations. The last plane to land on the third cycle of takeoffs and landings was a twin-engine C-2 cargo plane. A lieutenant and a petty officer first class whose specialty was photo interpretation were met at the plane's ramp. Briefcases in hand, they were led down to the flag conference room that now was a planning center.

As they entered, Marty Cabot stood. "Everyone pay attention. This is Lieutenant Steven Henderson and Petty Officer Eric Rasmussen from the Naval Intelligence Center Pacific. They've been up all night, so let's see what they have, and then they can go get some shut-eye before we put them back to work."

The end of the table's green felt cover was cleared so all could see what the two officers brought in their locked briefcases. Henderson spoke first. "Gentlemen, what you are about to see are photos taken of the area of interest over the past two years by our KH-11 satellites, annotated on by date. In my bag I have the negatives, so we can enlarge them as needed."

Josh scrutinized the lieutenant, who was much older than the usual O-3. His ribbons indicated service during the Korean and Vietnam Wars. That told Josh that the lieutenant must have come up through the ranks before he was commissioned. In Navy parlance, he was a "mustang."

Rasmussen lined up three rows of six, eight-by-ten-inch photos. "The top row was taken two years ago. The middle shots were taken early last year. The bottom row was taken three months ago. If you look closely, you can see four different sets of letters and numbers in a field that changed over time."

On one photo, he'd circled the letters NF 302 and MY 04. In another photo, he'd drawn a line around the numbers NM 310 and NF 302. In the third, MY 04 and NL 515 were clearly visible.

Rasmussen gave the officers time to study the prints, then continued. "Those are tail numbers. It took us a while to figure them out because we had to match Navy and Air Force squadron numbers to these numbers and to losses. As Mr. Haman knows, aviators are told to lay out their tail letters and number as a recognition signal. We only went back two years. Back at Pearl Harbor, there is a team going back through every satellite photo of the area and we're confident we'll find more of these symbols."

Rasmussen pulled a sheet of paper out of the top of his briefcase and held it out. "Several airplanes with the same side numbers were shot down on different cruises, so that complicated our analysis. We came up with ten names, all of which are still on the MIA list and were known to have been taken prisoner."

Marty dropped the photo he was holding on the table. "This is great stuff. What we need now is proof that Americans are still being held there—" He was about to say "so we don't have another Son Tay" when the phone rang. The staff intelligence officer picked it up, listened for a few seconds and put it gently down on the table. "The RF-8 photos are ready. We have proof."

The same day, 1652 local time, On Board The U.S.S. Coral Sea
When all was ready, the call was placed to Admiral Hastings.

"Hastings here. Who's in the room?"

The admiral answered. "Commander Blakely, my staff intelligence officer; Lieutenant Commanders Cabot and Haman; Lieutenant Henderson and Petty Officer Rasmussen from the Naval Intelligence Center Pacific. That's it."

"Good. I know it is going to be hard to keep a secret, but you have to do your best."

"Yes, sir. Understood."

"Good. What do you have?" Huntington leaned forward to address the beige box that was the speakerphone. "Sir, let me put it in a nutshell. The photos taken this morning by our RF-8 confirm that there are Americans being held in Vietnam. We can clearly see the faces of five of the men. They are, pardon the expression, round-eyes."

"Henderson, do you concur with the analysis?"

"Yes, sir, I do. I'd bet my ass on it, sir."

There was silence for a few seconds before Admiral Hastings spoke. "That makes our world pretty complicated, doesn't it?"

The Commander of the Carrier Battle Group spoke for all of them. "Yes, sir."

"This is for your ears only. A CIA officer by the name of Gary Savoy was out here last week to meet with the Joint POW/ MIA Accounting Command. I asked for a briefing and spent over an hour with him. Apparently, a Vietnamese by the name of Trong Pham walked into the U.S. consulate in Hong Kong claiming he can deliver six Americans for twelve million bucks. Savoy is ninety percent sure it is a scam. However, I talked directly with the two CIA officers who met with Pham, and they believe him. There's too much detail in the photos to be a fake. They've asked for proof of life and Pham said he'd bring it. In the meantime, they've been given the task of stringing the guy along while the CIA figures out what to do."

Marty waved his hand and pointed at his chest. Admiral Huntington nodded him to go ahead. "Sir, this is Lieutenant Commander Cabot. Did you say the walk-in's name is Pham?"

"I did."

"Sir, that's the family name that was given to me by the Laotian colonel we captured. I'd bet the men in the photos and the ones he is trying to extort a ransom for are the same men."

The silence that followed seemed like an eternity.

"Gentlemen, here's what I want to do. I will run the traps to get approval for a Navy-led rescue mission. The Air Force will scream, but they don't have the assets in place and I can make a case that we do. Marty, Josh, what do you need?"

Marty spoke first. "Sir, I think an eight-man SEAL team can do it. We may need more but won't know until we get further into the planning. We've got one team here in Thailand and another in Okinawa if we need them. Sir, for security, we need to keep this out of message traffic. Josh?"

"Sir, we've got SH-3Gs on board the *Coral Sea*, but I would like to get one of the armor and weapon kits from the States. The reserve squadron HC-9 in San Diego should have them in deployable pack-ups. Also, a C-130 gunship would be helpful. Air Wing Fourteen on the *Coral Sea* should be able to provide all the close air support we need."

"Alright. I'll get JCS approval and this will go to the President. In the meantime, Marty and Josh, finish the plan. Call me if you need anything. Nothing about this goes in any kind of message traffic. I'll get the other stuff on the way. I will be in Cubi on Tuesday morning. Be ready to go through the plan. If we do the mission brief anywhere else in theater, it will turn it into a circus."

Admiral Huntington nodded. His mind raced, thinking that he was going to be in the center of a project that should get him a second star or even a third. Unless it got all fucked up. Since Haman and Cabot were Hastings' 'boys,' he'd be able to dodge the mud if this went south. "Aye, aye, sir."

"One more thing, Admiral Huntington. I want to say this in public so everyone in the room hears it. I have all the confidence in the world in Mr. Cabot and Mr. Haman. They're very, very good at this. In fact, I would say they are the best in the Navy and better than the Green Berets. Let them do their thing; the battle group and the Navy will provide them with what they need. Understood?"

"Aye, aye, sir." Huntington realized he had just been politely told to stay out of Cabot and Haman's hair and not make suggestions unless asked for them.

"Good. Anything else we need to cover?"

"No, sir."

Saturday, February 6, 1982, 1509 local time, Arizona
Janet woke blearily under a steady flow of cold air to the sound of the incessant clicking of a ceiling fan with a bad bearing.

She was shivering, with goose bumps on her bare arms and legs, and the throbbing pain in her head was far worse than a headache. Moving her head hurt, and the bright light coming through partially closed blinds forced her to squint. She could faintly smell the tangy odors of tacos, refried beans, and fresh salsa.

Where am I? Janet forced her brain to ignore the pounding and focus. *I remember lying on the ground observing a mobile home seven hundred yards away, waiting for my mark. I heard a footfall and turned around just before a black shape slammed into my head.*

Janet tried to move. Nothing responded.

Shit! Am I paralyzed? No. Taped to the chair. No wonder you're cold; those are your clothes piled in the corner. She had nothing on except her bra and panties.

Slowly, Janet examined the empty room. In the corner, her rifle rested next to her backpack and clothes. The door was closed and she sat on the only piece of furniture. In frustration, Janet jerked her body. The wooden chair creaked. Another violent movement and the frame cracked.

Janet paused, looked at the door. The knob didn't move. She could hear mariachi music and guessed it was probably from down the hall.

Another jerk as violent as she could make it caused one of the chair legs to fail with a loud crack. She fell on her back and her head hit the floor. The blow filled her eyes with stars. Janet took a deep breath and yanked her left arm. It, along with the armrest, came free.

With her left hand, she ripped the duct tape—hair and all—off her right arm. Then she pulled the tape off her legs and tried to stand up.

The room spun and Janet fell to a knee and started to giggle as she wound up in a sitting position. She realized that she hadn't removed the tape that held the back of the chair to her body.

Voices getting louder froze Janet. She picked up the broken legs of the chair, thinking they would be good weapons, and took a few wobbly steps to a position behind the door.

This has to be quick and quiet. I don't know how much strength or stamina I have. Focus, woman, focus, just like you were taught in the dojo. This is what all that training was for.

Through the crack between the door and the frame, she saw two men approaching. As soon as they stepped forward through the doorway, Janet slammed the door into one and lashed out with the leg of the chair at the other.

The first man staggered from the impact of the door hitting the side of his head. It gave Janet time to get to the second, who was pulling a gun out from his belt. Janet flipped the leg around and drove the splintered end into the man's throat as hard as she could. She was about to twist it when the first man bear-hugged her from behind. Janet slammed the back of her head into his face twice. The first time she got his chin; with the second she felt his nose break and he let her go, gasping with pain.

She whirled around on her left foot and kicked with her right leg. The strike landed perfectly in the man's crotch. As he bent over, groaning in pain, Janet grabbed the back of the man's head, twisted it to the side and slammed it down on the top of her left knee. The man's skull cracked loudly. For good measure, she twisted it far enough to feel his spine snap and let his limp body drop to the floor beside the bleeding corpse of the other.

Weapons! Both were carrying .45s with rounds in the chamber. She felt for spare magazines and found one on each body. She dumped the magazine out of one of the .45s and stuffed it, along with two spares, into the back of her panties and ventured out into the hallway. She took several deep breaths to get her head to stop spinning. It didn't work. Sudden movements of her head made her dizzy.

Do I get dressed and try to escape? Or do I clear the building and then decide what to do? Where would I go? Better to be the hunter than the hunted.

The mobile home was at the end of a two-mile long dirt road in the Arizona desert near the town of Ajo. When she had been watching the building, Janet had seen five men come and go. Two are dead. *How many more are here now?* Was her target still here?

The next room down the hall was a bedroom. The sheets were pulled off to the side of the bed, revealing the diamond pattern of the mattress. The next room was an empty bathroom. The Mexican music got louder and the smell of fresh spices got stronger as Janet neared what she assumed was the living room.

The hallway ended and Janet could see two men sitting in front of a TV set and one man getting something from a refrigerator. She recognized him as the mark from the photos sent by The Broker.

The mark turned from the fridge, beer in hand. His eyes widened at the sight of an attractive woman clad only in bra and panties pointing a pistol directly at him. From twenty feet away, the bore of the .45 looked like a small cannon.

As soon as the front sight was in the center of the man's chest, Janet squeezed the trigger.

The boom of the gun caused both heads watching the TV to turn around. Janet shifted aim and fired. Blood and brains from the first man's head was still in the air when the second man's head exploded.

Janet went around the kitchen counter and found her mark lying against the open door of the refrigerator. His hands were trying to staunch the pulse of blood pumped out by his damaged heart. A round to the forehead made sure his life was over.

Four down, and three rounds left. *Are there any more?* Janet crouched down and reloaded.

The front door slammed open, breaking the glass. Two men froze as they studied the room. Janet peered around the edge of the counter. One had a sawed-off pump shotgun, the other carried a large revolver, either a .357 or a .44 Magnum. She hoped that the counter gave her some concealment, but it wouldn't give much protection. Surprise and training were her best weapons.

Janet popped up with the .45 in both hands. She was still moving to a standing position when she squeezed off the first round. It caught the man with the shotgun squarely in the chest. The three-hundred-and-fifty-odd foot-pounds of energy shoved him into the man with the revolver. He never had a chance to bring his gun to bear before the first of two .230-grain slugs were entering his chest.

The man with the shotgun struggled to point it at Janet, who fired her eighth round into his head. Seven so far... How many more?

Before looking out the door, Janet reloaded and then topped off the magazine with the three rounds left from the first one. Peering into the parking lot, the bright sun momentarily blinded her, even though she shielded her eyes. No one. Two cars, one pick-up truck.

Janet stopped in the bathroom and saw the red bump on the side of her head. Even with an ice pack, in two or three days it would change to a huge black and blue mark.

Janet usually left the scene of a hit clean. No fingerprints, no weapons, and only occasionally an empty cartridge. This time, she didn't know what she had touched. A thorough investigator might find one of her prints. She got dressed and pulled on a pair of thin leather gloves from her backpack.

Using the keys she found in the men's pockets, she checked each of the cars, then started the pick-up truck because it was the only one with a full tank. With it running, Janet went back inside and crumpled up newspapers and placed them on the stove. Before she lit them, she pulled out the stove and used a kitchen knife to puncture the gas line in several places. She tossed a lit match onto the pile of paper, and the propane lit with a whump.

Half an hour later, Janet parked the green and white Chevy pickup in the same lot where she'd left the rental car two days before. She tossed the un-fired Springfield 1903 into the trunk. It was going home with her. At a gas station on the north side of Ajo, she tossed the disassembled .45 into the dumpster and called The Broker.

Before she pulled out onto I-15, Janet made an ice pack from a plastic bag. As she drove toward Phoenix, she held it on the side of her head.

The radio newscaster said that it was Saturday. *I got into my hide on Wednesday evening. That means I was out for two days. Did they rape me while I was unconscious? I haven't been on the pill since Randy was declared dead. If I'm pregnant, I'm getting an abortion.*

Chapter 14
REUNION

Monday, February 8, 1982, 2122 local time, Vietnam
Crescent Shipping's *MV Crescent Island* had docked at just after 0530 in Haiphong. The immigration agent had examined every page in Pham's Vietnamese passport before he stamped it. Still, Pham had had enough time to take the train to Hanoi to meet with Trung and get back before the ship finished unloading the canned goods in its hold and taking on cargo. Near Long Bien, the train had passed bomb craters and rusting trucks and surface-to-air missile launchers.

During their walk in a nearby park, Dat Trung warned him that the government was encouraging young officers to crack down on corruption. Their zeal was ending the old ways of family influence and "commissions." Trung said the Politburo had declared it would impose the death penalty for a long list of what it called "corruptive crimes."

Yes, Pham had reflected, *it is definitely time to wrap up projects and move on.*

Back in his camp, Pham stared at the ceiling in the pitch-black darkness of his camp headquarters, thinking about the CIA and the twelve million-dollar ransom.

Will the CIA pay me? If they do, I turn over the Americans and

354

leave Vietnam forever. Where shall I go? I could claim I'm a refugee from the Communists and emigrate to Australia or New Zealand, or even the U.S. I still have my South Vietnamese identity papers. They give me options.

If the CIA doesn't pay me, I kill the Americans and leave Vietnam. Or, I just leave them to their fate and never return to Vietnam. This way I won't have their deaths on my conscience.

What if the CIA believes me but doesn't want to pay? Will they torture me to get information? What if the Americans decide I am some sort of criminal and want to try me? My prisoners will identify me. Then what do I do?

Wherever I go, I'll have enough money. I already have almost ten million, so I can survive without the twelve. If the CIA doesn't pay me, I just won't have as much. One more trip to Hong Kong with the proof of life, and I'm free.

Pham liked his last thought the best.

Tuesday, February 9, 1982, 1146, the Philippines
A four-engine C-141B Starlifter sat on the transient ramp a few hundred humid yards from the terminal at the Naval Air Station at Cubi Point, a.k.a. Radford Field. It was named after the four-star admiral who'd had the foresight to have it built in the mid-1950s. The Air Force jet's dull gray and white paint scheme contrasted with the shiny, silver-white and blue Air Force special mission VC-140B JetStar parked nearby. The modified business jet had brought Admiral Hastings to the U.S.'s largest facility in the Philippines, the naval base and naval air station at Subic Bay. Josh hadn't been in this building since the Vietnam War.

Not much had changed, other than that the U.S. was at peace. The Vietnam War lingered in Josh's mind as unfinished business that left a bad taste in his mouth. Instead of fighting to win, a divided nation had walked away, leaving allies to a fate which all knew—but would never admit in public—would not be pleasant.

Hastings listened as his staff, a mix of SEALs and aviators, went over every detail in the plan. Changes were proposed and their merits discussed. The elephant in the room was the mission tasking. DC had approved a sneak-and-peek, not a rescue.

As they got toward the end, Hastings looked at the men at the table. "You all realize it will create a shit storm if we find Americans alive. Everybody from the former President on down has said that there are no POWs alive in Vietnam. Savoy's analyses have been taken as gospel by Congress. I'll brief the President and the national security advisor when I get back to Hawaii and recommend that we execute the mission as planned."

Marty looked the four-star admiral in the eye. "Sir, I don't think Josh or I, or any of the men who will be on the helicopter, give a fuck what Savoy says or thinks. Nor do I buy the State Department's doublespeak bullshit. If there are live POWs there, we're going to bring them home or die trying."

Admiral Hastings tented his hands under his chin. No one said a word as he stood up. "Gentleman, the mission goes as Marty and Josh have planned it. Formal authorization to execute the reconnaissance will be sent to the *Coral Sea* as soon as I get it. Get ready to go on a moment's notice. The code name I was given is *Express Ruby.* Admiral Huntington will be the on-scene commander. I'll brief Seventh Fleet on my way back to Hawaii. Marty, Josh, Godspeed and good luck. Bring our men home. If it causes a few people to get red faces, they'll have to get over it. If it costs me my career, so be it."

After shaking hands with Admiral Hastings, Marty and Josh were driven by jeep to the C-141 that would take them to Korat Air Base in Thailand. In the open rear cargo door they saw two familiar faces.

"What the hell are you guys doing here?" Josh dropped his bag, ran up the ramp and hugged Lieutenant Commander Jack D'Onofrio and Senior Chief Derek Van der Jagt. Marty did the same.

"Well, we got this operational-immediate message asking HC-9 for an armor pack-up for an H-3 to be shipped ASAP to the U.S.S. *Coral Sea.* It had a Brickbat priority rating that only the

President could authorize. As the squadron's operations officer, I started asking questions. No one had seen the kits in years. That's when I called Senior Chief Van der Jagt and asked him if he knew where they were. He said, yes, he'd helped put them in storage. We don't know the condition of the self-sealing fuel bladders, so I used the same Brickbat priority to get two more shipped to us in Thailand. They're for Air Force HH-3Es and have the same part number."

"O.K. So why did you come with the kit?"

D'Onofrio turned to Van der Jagt. "You tell them."

"Me, because I know how to install the kits. I got a call from retired Master Chief Gary Jenkins. He now works for CINCPAC as a civilian, supporting special operations planning. He told me, 'I'm arranging orders for you and Mr. D'Onofrio for an all-expenses paid government vacation in Thailand.' And D'Onofrio is here because Master Chief Jenkins believes you two need adult supervision. Then he said, 'Don't fuck it up.' That's all I know."

The whine of a jet engine starting made further conversation impossible. The C-141's loadmaster, standing a respectful distance away from the four men, shouted, "Gentlemen, we need you to take your seats or we're going to Thailand without you."

Thursday, February 11, 1982, 1358 local time, Thailand

What was supposed to take two days took four. One fuel bladder was cracked and couldn't be used. The other split when it was being unfolded. The two bladders for Air Force HH-3Es took 24 extra hours to show up, but didn't leak. On a two-hour test flight, everything on the modified SH-3G checked out.

While they were working on the helicopter, the rumor mill on the ship was running full steam. Navy enlisted men who'd been air crewman at one time or another in their careers as well as Marines knocked on Josh's stateroom door, wanting to go with him. Before politely turning them all down, he asked what they'd heard and why they were volunteering. Each one said the mission had to do with bringing some POWs or MIAs home. *So much for keeping a secret.*

Josh knew that mail was being held on the ship as a security measure until the mission was over. Admiral Huntington promised to make an announcement as soon as the helo left for Thailand with the two crewmen that Van der Jagt, D'Onofrio and he had picked. Both were experienced rescue air crewmen, but neither were combat veterans. One, Petty Officer First Class Joseph Martin, had spent a tour with the Marines as a corpsman. The other, Petty Officer Third Class Richard Acton, impressed them with his attitude.

When the modified SH-3G rolled to a stop on the ramp at Korat, they kept the large cargo door on the starboard side closed so no one could see the mini-gun. The mount for the M-60 and its boron epoxy shield was swung around inside so it was out of view. The M-60 was on the floor under the passenger seats.

As soon as the rotors stopped, Marty climbed on board and stuck his head and shoulders between the seats, grinning. "I like the side number."

"It magically appeared while the H-3 was being modified. We used 'Navy Helicopter 40' flying up here, but when we takeoff from Nakhon Phanom we'll be 'Big Mother 40'. If any of the Vietnamese signals intelligence people hear it, along with your call sign 'Gringo Six', and remember what happened during the war, it will give them chills. They will know The Ghost has returned."

Marty grew serious. "Our call signs were lucky back then. I hope they are this time."

Josh reached up and grabbed the handhold over the front cockpit window to pull himself up and out of the seat. "Me, too."

The SEAL stepped back into the cabin to give the two pilots room to get out. "You're four hours late. What happened?"

"It just took longer than we thought. The good news is that everything works."

"Good. How soon can we take off?"

"As soon as we finish fueling."

"The rest of the crew is in the hangar over there. Let's introduce everyone, do a quick brief, and get on our way."

The same day, 2144 local time, Vietnam

Randy lay on his back staring at the corrugated metal roof over the U-shaped cubbyhole he shared with Jeff Anderson. It was one of the three sleeping areas dubbed Air Force, Army, or Navy, based on the residents' service. According to Pham's rules, they were all to be in their beds at 2100. After telling them a rule, Pham always added, "Violators will be punished."

Randy wondered what had changed in the U.S. in the years he'd been gone. While he would like to believe that he was still married to Janet, he knew that was unrealistic. Randy suspected the restless woman whom he called "the horny one" had probably moved on. By now the Navy would have declared him dead and she was fucking the brains out of some lucky guy.

Each night, in the moments before Randy drifted off to sleep, he thought about the things he would do if and when he got back. Tonight he was wondering what Janet had done with his Shelby GT-350 Mustang.

He was remembering what it was like to drive it fast on deserted highways and windy-twisty roads, when a faint sound ended his reminiscing. Randy slowly sat up to get his ears closer to the source. Across the little room, Jeff Anderson was also sitting up. Then the faint sound went away.

"Was that what I thought it was?" Randy whispered.

"What did you think that was?"

"A helicopter."

"Me too."

"Jeff, maybe we're hearing things?"

"No, that was a helicopter."

"You sure?"

"Yeah."

"Do you think Pham and his guys heard it?"

"Probably."

Ashley whispered from his bunk across the narrow hall in the next cubbyhole. "I heard it, too. We execute our raid plan now. You two have the first watch. Wake me and Hank at midnight; we'll get Karl and Greg up for the last one."

Saturday, February 13, 1982, 0330 local time, Vietnam

The point man held up his fist and each man in the column of eight SEALs silently dropped to a knee. They were about two hours behind schedule. Marty had hoped they would be within a couple hundred yards of the camp by now, looking for a place to hide. But they weren't.

The SEALs waited until the voices disappeared into the jungle, heading toward Laos. According to the briefing, this was likely a column of bearers headed home for another load of raw opium. Marty thought about changing their route, but decided against it.

Forty-five minutes later, the point man again signaled a halt and passed the word for Marty, the number three man in the column, to come forward. They had found the farm.

Near the compound, they found a place to bed down for a few hours. Once settled, Marty transmitted the coded status at their designated reporting time: "Gringo Six is on the beach."

This wasn't the Vietnam War, and there weren't aircraft airborne twenty-four hours a day along the trail. The only radios they had were a Vietnam War-vintage PRC-77 and a PRC-90. The range of the PRC-77, on a good day, was five to ten miles. The PRC-90 was only for emergencies because it broadcast on the international guard frequencies and the military SAR frequency. The good news was that a plane above twenty-thousand feet could hear them from fifty miles away.

Hastings had promised to have a Navy EP-3, an anti-submarine warfare plane, converted to radio- and radar-signal collection, or to have an Air Force EC-135W Rivet Joint fly orbits within the range of the PRC-77. Theoretically, their sensitive communications collection equipment would pick up his signal.

Being a realist, Marty was not optimistic he would be heard. The lack of communication was a risk his team accepted. Bringing back POWs that had been held nine years longer than they should was much too important. None of his men had hesitated when he'd told them of the risks.

The one thing Marty knew for certain was that Josh would show up where the access road to Pham's camp fed into a wider dirt road, as planned. Until that time, they were on their own. It was time to get some rest.

The same day, 1448 local time, Vietnam

From his vantage point about two hundred feet from the factory, Marty didn't need binoculars to see the five Americans work at opium processing. Two men emptied backpacks and dumped plastic-wrapped bundles into a pile. Two others used a knife to slit open the plastic and drop the brown lumps into a fifty-five gallon drum, while a fifth stoked the fire. Marty forced himself not to interfere as he watched a diminutive Vietnamese overseer occasionally lash out with a switch made from bamboo.

While Marty and his fire teammate watched the camp, two other fire teams updated the map they'd made from the satellite photos. The fourth team conducted a reconnaissance of the area.

The camp was exactly as Kanthavong had described it. But where was the sixth American? There was no way they were going to do anything until he was found, or at least accounted for.

At a gentle tap on his shoulder, Marty turned around. His SEAL teammate pointed back toward the jungle. It took them about ten minutes to rejoin the other teams.

Marty shrugged off his pack to use as a makeshift desk, and Petty Officer Second Class Michael Murphy spread out a small sheet of paper. Before he'd become a SEAL, he'd been an electrician. It had taken Murphy two tries to get through Basic Underwater Demolition School, a.k.a. BUDS, because three weeks into his first try he broken his forearm and couldn't continue. He made it through the first class he could get into after it healed, and after he finished parachute training, the Navy had sent him to language school to learn Spanish. That made sense, since his platoon had originally been scheduled to go to Panama and Columbia, but since October 1991 his platoon had either been in the Philippines or Thailand.

Murphy smiled broadly. "Boss, all six Americans are here. The sixth one is back in the hut and I think he's injured, because he drags his left leg along when he walks. Anyway, he's of Asian descent."

"Outstanding!" Marty struggled to contain his excitement.

"Yes, sir. Security around the camp is almost non-existent, except for where the Americans are being held. There's two camouflaged and sandbagged machine gun positions with interlocking fields of fire about fifty meters from the end of the access road. Whoever put the guns there knew what he was doing. They will be tough to take out, even with a flanking movement. You come around the bend from the road and you're toast."

"Can they turn their guns around to defend the compound?"

"No, sir, but they will have to be put out of business, because the only place to land a helo is where the access road joins the main road, and that's in the heart of their killing zone."

"Go on."

"After that, there are the two guard towers. They have two men in each with a PK machine gun, and two sentries by the entrance to the fenced-in area where the Americans are held. Two other men walk around the fence when the Americans are in the compound."

"What's in the buildings?"

"Living quarters, a mess hall, and probably an armory of some sort. There are two GAZ light trucks and an old Army jeep."

"Anything else?"

"Behind the factory is a huge goddam hole. It had to be made by a bomb. Now it's a garbage pit full of burned-out pieces of metal. Nearby are two tanks with about a hundred gallons of diesel fuel each for the trucks and the generator. Boss, here's the really good news—I don't think they're expecting visitors."

Marty's heart said *Launch the raid, capture the Americans, and then call Josh.* His head said *He's missing something. Let's keep watching, and update the plan as needed to be ready for pick up when Josh arrives.*

"Good info. For the rest of the day we keep watching and taking notes. The problem, as I see it, is we only have one suppressed sniper rifle and we'll need it for the guards in the towers. We'll have to deal with the machine gun positions on the way out."

"Sir, what about the AC-130? It could blow them to hell in a hand basket, in a heartbeat."

"It could, but only if they can see the target. I'm not sure they have enough of a heat signature for the IR gear to detect them. And I don't want it raining death and destruction on the camp while we're trying to rescue the POWs."

Marty looked around. "Murphy, you and your teammate go back down the road and come up with a way to take those two gun positions out. When you do, give me a call on the radio. The rest of us will watch the camp in two-hour shifts. I'll make the next scheduled radio call at 1800. Call me before then."

The same day, 1800 local time, Vietnam

Marty moved another hundred feet up from where the six SEALs were positioned. The small clearing gave him a view of the darkening sky. He twisted the canon plug that held the antenna to the radio, to make sure it was as tight as he could get it in order to minimize signal loss, then pushed the lever from Off to On. As soon as the power light came on he keyed the mike. The side tone told him it was ready to transmit.

"Any station, any station, this is Gringo Six, over." Nothing. He tried again.

"Gringo Six, this is Aries 22."

Marty had been holding his breath; now her breathed again. Aries 22 was a Navy EP-3E. "Aries 22, Gringo Six. Pass to Red

Rider Actual and Big Mother 40 that the signal is pay dirt with six. Repeat, pay dirt with six. Pick-up at plus twelve. Copy?"

"Copy pay dirt with six and pick-up in twelve."

"Have the cavalry available starting thirty mikes before pick-up."

"Roger. We're excited. Good luck."

Marty looked at the handset for a few seconds before he hung it up. Pay dirt with a number was the code indicating they'd found the POWs and all six were alive. Twelve meant he wanted Josh to be in the area around 0600 the next day. Security must be shitty, because the operator knew what their mission was.

He wondered if someone in Hanoi was asking why an EP-3E was flying in this area. This mission track had to be raising some eyebrows. And the Vietnamese knew that the U.S. ground forces used FM as the preferred frequency band. It wouldn't take much of an imagination to guess why Gringo Six was where it was.

Marty leaned back against the tree and pushed his worry about the Vietnamese's electronic intelligence-gathering capabilities out of his mind. They'd taken precautions to minimize being detected, so he shifted to visualizing the camp and his raid plan before he dozed off.

On the other side of the wire, the prisoners were eating dinner. Through the open window, Ashley watched Pham have an animated conversation with two of his men. Pham seemed frustrated that the last shipment of opium wasn't already turned into morphine base. They had another day of work before the base could be ladled into "the bread baking pans."

The Green Beret looked around the table. Morale was up; they all thought they were about to be rescued. Ashley had been thinking all day about what they could do to maximize their chances. "We need to have our go bags ready," he told the others. "Hank, make extra rice balls. We're going to distribute the tinned food. If the shit hits the fan, keep down and see if we can make it to our bunker. If not, get down on the floor in the hooch. Clear?"

The bunker they'd built was eight feet deep and ten feet

square. It had steps that led down into the interior, and benches around three sides. The hole was covered with six-inch-diameter logs that were flush with the ground. Dirt from the hole went into two layers of large rice bags placed onto the logs. Ashley figured the bags would stop bullets and shrapnel, but a direct hit by a large artillery shell or a bomb would kill everyone inside.

Karl tossed his spoon onto the table. "Let's not get our hopes up. I've had as much disappointment as I can handle. Sometimes I wonder if I am losing it and hearing things, or just slowly going out of my mind."

Randy reached out and put his hand on Karl's forearm. "It's not your imagination. We don't know whose it was, but if it means another Son Tay, we need to be ready."

He looked at Ashley. "O.K. Green Beret, if you were to raid this camp, how and when would you attack?"

"Start sometime between two and four in the morning by killing the guards in the towers and out by the gate. Then neutralize Pham's men in the barracks."

Randy tilted his cup of tea toward Ashley. "Hank and you should have the watch at that time. You'll know what to listen for."

"Good idea. When on watch, we stay in our cubbyholes. Sit on the floor if you want, but don't let Pham or his men see you. Occasionally they shine a spotlight on our hooch. The Navy has watch from nine to midnight. The Army will assume the watch at midnight, and we'll take it to three because I think the attack will come during that time. Air Force, you take it from three to sunrise. Understood?" The Naval Aviators and Air Force pilots nodded.

Sunday, February 14, 1982, 0255 local time, Vietnam
Marty crouched just inside the tree line where the access road opened into the compound. With a bright full moon, he could see the entire camp. To his left, two SEALs aimed their MP-5s at the guards standing by the gate to the compound. Rather than expose

themselves by running across the compound to the gate, they were going to kill the guards, then cut the wire and come in from the side.

The bolt-action Remington 700 rifle known in the Navy as the M40 was aimed at the farthest guard tower, three hundred yards from where the SEAL sniper team lay. For the gun and the 7.62 by 51-millimeter NATO cartridge it was an easy shot. The 170-grain bullet came out of the barrel at about 2,550 feet per second, and even with the suppressor it wouldn't drop or slow much before it plowed into a sentry.

Once the sniper fired the first shot, the prison guards would be taken out by the two-man team assigned to free the Americans.

The remaining four would provide covering fire and shoot the guards coming out of their quarters. The two machine guns at the end of the access road would be dealt with during phase two.

Marty whispered into his throat mike, "Everybody in position?" He got four sets of two clicks. "On my mark.... Three.... Two.... One!"

Had there been a lot of ambient noise, the muted sound of the M40 would have gone unheard. In the stillness of the jungle night it sounded just like what it was, a suppressed rifle being fired. Marty saw the hands of the man standing in the farthest guard tower fly up. The sudden movement was seen by the guard in the other tower, who started swinging his PK machine gun as he searched for targets.

Marty imagined the sniper shifting aim from one tower to the other, holding his breath and, between heartbeats, squeezing the trigger. The guard disappeared and was replaced by his loader, who was also shot.

The PK in the first tower started spitting out tracers, fired by the guard's loader, in the general direction of where Marty and five of the SEALs were positioned. It abruptly stopped ringing mid-burst. The M40 had spoken a fourth time.

The two guards by the gate hunkered down and peeked around their little sheds. A three-round burst from a suppressed MP-5SD3 sent shards of wood flying. Several bursts later, the two guards were either dead or dying. With the guards down, the two SEALs assigned to rescue the POWs cut the wire and raced toward the hooch.

Lights came on in the building where Pham and his men bunked. Marty's radio operator fired the M-79 grenade launcher, which made its distinctive thunk. As soon as it discharged, the SEAL popped open the breach, stuffed another grenade in, and fired. He had nine more grenades in front of him and six more in his rucksack.

The first grenade entered the door of the guards' quarters and exploded. Number two went through the nearest window. The third punched a hole in the second building before exploding.

Marty didn't want this to degenerate into a firefight with the prisoners as hostages. He tapped the radio operator on the shoulder and pointed at the far end of the building. The radio operator nodded. Seconds later, the M-79 clunked and the anti-personnel grenade shredded the galvanized metal sides of the building.

Out of the corner of his eye Marty noticed a group of men with AK-47s. "On the right, guys, across the road." Then he saw another group running toward them. Two were already in the compound, and before they were shot down by the SEALs they tossed four grenades into the hooch.

His heart in his mouth, Marty lay there transfixed, thinking that instead of six live Americans he was about to bring back six dead ones because his plan had been too cautious. He saw flashes and heard two bangs, but not the third and fourth.

Furious, the two men tasked to get the POWs charged up the steps, yelling, "Navy SEALs! Keep your heads down!"

Marty saw a Vietnamese man crouched down, directing the remaining men. By now, there were bodies all over the compound, the work of the SEALs' marksmanship and the recklessness of the Vietnamese.

Marty took careful aim. At a hundred yards, his target was

almost at the maximum effective range for the nine-millimeter round. The German-made assault rifle bucked three times against his shoulder. In the dim light, Marty wasn't sure, but he thought the man staggered. He pulled the trigger again, and this time the man went down.

Another man appeared, urging a small group of guards forward. Marty let his MP-5 speak. The man staggered backwards and fell spread-eagled on the ground. Leaderless, the guards started to run. Marty and the other SEALs cut down as many as they could before emerging from their positions.

As suddenly as it had started, the shooting stopped. Marty keyed his throat mike. "Murphy, just make sure the eight bad guys down there with the PKs don't come back toward us."

Marty jogged over to the building where the Americans were kept, expecting to find six dead POWs. Instead, he found five live ones kneeling next to a mangled body.

"What happened?"

Ashley Smith stood up. The tears streaming down his face were clearly visible in the moonlight. "I'm Ashley Smith, Captain, United States Army. That's First Lieutenant Hank Cho, a fellow Green Beret. When the grenades came into the building, he tossed two out the window. Then, knowing there wasn't time to throw the other two out, he pulled them under his body. His last words to me were 'Enjoy being free again'."

Marty looked at the body. "We're bringing Lieutenant Cho home, too. We don't have a body bag, so we're going to carry him on a stretcher. Do you guys have anything we can use?"

Randy broke up one of the benches at their table. "We can use this and wrap him in a blanket. All we need is some rope to tie him to it."

A SEAL handed him a climbing rope. Marty nodded. "Do it, and let's get moving. We have a helo to catch."

The two SEALs who had gone into the headquarters building walked up to Marty. "Sir, we got these four books that look like diaries or ledgers, a tin cookie can with four different passports, a set of Army of the Republic of Vietnam identity tags, an ID card and pay book, a nice Nikon with several lenses, and four exposed rolls of film. Other than that, there's not much in the office."

"Good. We'll look at them later. Burn the place down." He keyed his throat mike. "Murphy, any movement on the gun positions?"

"No, they've been looking around, but are staying in their holes."

"We're on the way. Be there as fast as we can."

Marty waited until all the men were out of the compound before he jogged to his place as the third man in the column and signaled for everyone to move out. Four of the POWs carried the makeshift stretcher with Hank Cho's body.

Ten minutes later, Petty Officer Murphy stepped out of the shadows. "Sir, bad guys about fifty yards down the road. Follow me."

Marty motioned for his radio operator to follow him. Thirty paces later, Murphy motioned them to get down and they crawled forward. In the growing daylight, they could see the two mounds and the four men in each pit.

"Let's do this the easy way." Marty looked at his watch and motioned for the handset. It was 0438. "Big Mother 40, you up?"

"Gringo Six, we're about five miles out."

"The two bunkers on the access road are manned with machine guns. Need you to take them out."

"Where are you?"

"About fifty meters up the road toward the camp. We'll fire grenades at them, and if we don't take them out they'll fire back. You'll see the tracers."

Josh clicked the mike twice. Before he rotated it to the intercom position, Van der Jagt spoke up. By the sound of his muffled voice, Marty could tell he was wearing the modified oxygen mask and his head was outside the door looking for the target. "Sir, about five hundred feet or more above the terrain should be perfect."

"Ready to rock and roll!" Jack D'Onofrio called out. "There's the road and the junction. Come left about thirty degrees; then we can run in parallel to the access road and keep the ricochets from hitting our guys."

As Josh rolled the helicopter to the new heading, he keyed the intercom. "Good idea. It's nice to know that you remember some things after all these years as a reservist!"

Jack held up his middle finger. "Landing checklist done. I'll drop the gear as soon as you start the approach to land."

"Big Mother, Gringo Six. We've got you in sight and our heads down. Grenades on the way."

The M79 made a hollow, thunking sound as the grenade was fired. The radio operator released the catch, pulled out the empty brass case and stuffed a new round in, aimed and fired.

The flashes from the grenades highlighted the target. Van der Jagt's words "Going hot!" were drowned out by the humming sound from the mini-gun. Josh looked over his shoulder and down to the right. The stream of 7.62-millimeter bullets sent sand and wood flying as they chewed up the bunkers and the men inside.

To keep the target in sight and in range, Josh kept the H-3 in a 30-degree bank as he circled around for another pass at ninety knots. It gave Van der Jagt another chance to shred whatever was inside the bunkers. "Gringo Six, is that good enough?"

"We're checking."

Josh kept maneuvering the SH-3G erratically, not knowing what threats were below him. Marty's call "We're moving!" brought him back to a heading toward the road which, based on their analysis, should be big enough to land on. If needed, they could use it for a rolling takeoff; with eight SEALs and six POWs they'd be heavy. The good news was they were down to half fuel.

A gentle flare brought the helicopter to a ten-foot hover, the wind from the blades causing loose grass and twigs to fly all around. As the helicopter passed five feet, a string of explosions rippled past the right side, throwing shrapnel, chunks of dirt and rocks through the air. The helicopter shuddered from the concussion, and debris clanged into the fuselage. Out of the corner of his eye, Josh saw two large objects shatter as the main rotor blades hit them. Josh let the helicopter land.

Jack D'Onofrio pressed the intercom switch with his left foot. "What the fuck was that?"

Van der Jagt replied. "I saw us blow a dead branch around and it must have hit a trip wire, because I saw the explosions start someplace in the middle and then go in both directions. We took some shrapnel hits all along the side. I'm getting out to check."

"Van, you guys do a quick security check, then we're going to have to check all the blades."

"Yes sir, get them shut down and I'll figure out how to inspect them."

"Van, take your time. Jack, pull the engines back to idle and then I'll apply the rotor brake."

D'Onofrio reached up as he spoke. "Speed selectors coming back. Are you thinking what I am?"

Josh reached up and pulled on the red knob at the lever that applied the rotor brake. "Yeah. We need to make sure we don't have a crack in the leading edge of a blade."

About the time that the rotors stopped, Marty entered the passenger door. "Why are you shutting down?"

"We set off a bunch of mines and need to check the blades. Get everybody on board."

The radio crackled; encryption made it sound like the conversation was being held in a noisy tunnel. "Big Mother 40, this is Aries 72. Three pieces of bad news. One, Spectre 51 has a fuel leak, so they've headed back to base. Two, I've got four A-6s and four A-7s on the way, but they are about twenty minutes out. Three, we're picking up transmissions from Vietnamese Army units headed your way."

"Aries 72, how far away are they?"

"Big Mother 40, best guess from the guys listening to the conversations are ten to fifteen clicks. They're in trucks, so we estimate you have twenty minutes to get out of Dodge."

"Aries 72. Big Mother 40 copies."

"Big Mother 40, Aries 72. Red Rider wants a status update."

"Aries 72, tell Red Rider to stand-by."

Van der Jagt plugged his helmet into the intercom system. "Boss, good news so far. The helo has dents on the side and a few holes in the skin, but nothing major. All the blade indicators show a safe indication, which means that no nitrogen has leaked."

"I still want to visually check the blades."

"Sir, I knew you would say that. I need you to release the rotor brake. One of us is going to put a boot on a blade and pull it around. Then I'm going to look at it from the rotor head to the tip by sliding along the top of the fuselage."

"Van, how long do you think it will take?"

"Five minutes per blade."

Josh did the mental math. Five blades times five minutes equals twenty-five minutes. "We may not have that much time."

"I heard."

"Josh, this is Marty, I'll send a team a hundred yards down the road to at least slow them down. If nothing else, it'll make us feel better. As soon as we're ready to go airborne, they can run back."

No one said much as the first blade moved. Then the second, then the third. Then a long delay. Josh looked at the clock. Eighteen minutes had passed.

Finally, the fourth blade moved.

Due to the engine noise, no one heard the scream of the artillery shell that exploded a hundred yards behind the helicopter. The two SEALs came running back, twirling one hand over their heads as if to say, "Let's get going!" They'd spotted the armored scout car at the head of the convoy. The second shell landed a little closer.

Van der Jagt climbed up the passenger door two steps at a time and tapped Josh on the shoulder, who turned to see the air crewman spinning his hand over his head.

"Sir, there are dents in two blades. I had a Zyglo kit in my bag that was there in case we needed to check the blades when we arrived. I used it on all the dents on the blades. No cracks, so we should be good to go."

An explosion off to the right about a hundred feet away shook the helicopter as Josh released the rotor brake. D'Onofrio slammed the two engine speed selectors into the fly position. It seemed like an eternity, but it was probably only ten seconds before the rotor blades were spinning fast enough to take off.

"Boss, what are you waiting for? Everyone's on board and we're all buttoned up back here ."

Josh wasn't trying to be smooth as he took off, and he hoped a broken blade or an artillery shell wouldn't ruin their day. Once he had the SH-3G skimming the treetops at ninety knots, he turned over the flying to D'Onofrio. Now he had time to talk on the radio. "Aries 72, tell Red Rider that Big Mother 40 is on the way home with six former, repeat former POWs. Unfortunately, one died in the rescue saving the lives of the others."

Monday, February 15, 1982, 0900 local time, Langley
Gary Savoy was only told that the meeting was urgent. He was escorted into the director's private conference room, where he sat in one of the chairs on the side of the long table. with the polished mahogany top.

He carried a folder with his last briefing on POWs and MIAs, along with a notebook. If it was urgent, then clearly the director had a task for him.

According to the CIA officers in Hong Kong, Pham hadn't yet showed up with the promised proof of life, so Savoy had sent a memo up the chain of command that emphasized his doubts about the veracity of Pham's tale. He hadn't used the word extortion, but he'd alluded to false claims made in the past, and stated that it was unlikely, given the time that had passed, that Americans were still being held in North Vietnam. The only response he'd gotten back was "Keep leadership informed. A negotiated payment will only be authorized with proof of life."

Savoy's confidence was back. Time, longevity, and

connections were on his side. Over the years, he'd polished the tactics of dealing with people that he'd learned on the streets of LA. When he went into a meeting, he felt his street smarts and basic intelligence made the average IQ in the room go way up.

His swagger was backed by millions in his off-shore accounts, unreported to the CIA, and a Rolodex full of interesting characters he referred to as his "peeps." He kept in touch with them, so if and when needed, they responded. Many of his fellow citizens would call these individuals unsavory. Policemen and prosecutors would call them criminals. But they knew how to get a job done.

When the door opened and the white-haired director entered, he stood up.

"Gary, thank you for coming. Sit down."

Gary wasn't used to such harshness in the director's tone. This meeting wasn't starting off well.

"I just had a chat with the President of the United States. To be polite, he is not a happy camper. Do you know why?"

"No, sir." Gary never volunteered anything until he knew which way the wind was blowing.

"As part of the transition, I gave him a briefing on POWs and MIAs based on your team's work. This morning, he informs me that the Navy rescued six POWs being held in Vietnam. *You* told me there were none, and that's what I told members of Congress *and the President* just over a week ago. I need an explanation and I need it *NOW!*"

The director's palm slammed down on the table hard enough to cause Savoy's diary to jump. He didn't have an answer.

The director opened his folder and slid a photo across the table. "Ever see this photo?"

Savoy studied the photo. It was a farmer's field. He let it drop on the table. "No."

"Bullshit. It was in one of your briefings five years ago. Look at it again."

Savoy picked the photo up again as if it had some strange, fatal disease. He wasn't a photo interpreter, but he studied it for about thirty seconds.

The director let his impatience show. "Let me give you the answer. This is just one of many photos taken of western Vietnam. Like many others, this one has the call signs of Americans who were shot down. Since the end of the war, a quick review of these photos has found at least a dozen like it from the same location. They were rotating them every month in an attempt to signal us and *YOUR TEAM* wasn't smart enough to notice."

"Sir, I'm sure there is a logical explanation."

"Humor me. Six Americans spent nine extra years in captivity because you and your team weren't paying attention."

When he'd first started in this job, he'd been told the "right" answer to the "POWs left behind" question was that there weren't any. Therefore, he hadn't encouraged the team to dig deeply into the intelligence the CIA and the NSA collected. Savoy knew that answer would fly now.

"Here's what I think. Your people got lazy. No one took a serious look at these photos, much less compared one-year's take to the prior year. You just put them in a file. Then you filled out reports and said the same thing every year—'There are no credible signs of POW activity in North Vietnam.' Am I close?"

"No sir—we looked at everything."

"Yeah, but for what? It took a twenty-three-year-old Navy photo interpreter less than thirty seconds to find those call signs. When he went into the archives, he found a history of them. What's worse, he found analysis and reports sent to the DIA and to your office strongly recommending that the CIA look into them. And what did you do? Nothing. *Not... a... fucking... thing!"*

Savoy realized defending his team was pointless. Throwing them under the bus wouldn't work. Silence was best.

"Right now, the President wants a public hanging and the arrow is pointed at you. I don't like lynchings, but, Gary, the only thing between you and a seat in the personnel department being processed out of the agency is your stellar track record in Africa. So here's the deal. A joint CIA/DIA task force is being set up to look at every shred of intelligence we have on POWs and MIAs. It is going to be run out of DIA's facilities in Arlington and you, my friend, will give them, without reservation or modification, every piece of intelligence, both raw and evaluated, that you have. If they ask you to shit, you ask where, how much and what color and odor. You with me so far?"

"Yes, sir."

"Good. This team will be briefing the Joint Chiefs, the President, the National Security Advisor, and me on a regular basis on its progress. If you have any problems you can't solve, come to me. If you or any member of your team screws up, I will run that person *and you* out of this agency on a wooden rail shoved so far up your asses you will think you are trees." The director took a deep breath. "Do I make myself clear?"

"Yes, sir."

"Good. Get out of here. My administrative assistant will call you with details of who you will report to at DIA later today."

Savoy left the room, relieved that, as of the moment, he wasn't fired. But once the investigation began, it would be hard for him to leave the country because he would be taken to a facility to be "debriefed." *It is time to save my ass!*

The same day, 1700 local time, Stallion Springs

Janet had the TV on in what she called the "great room" more as noise than to listen to the news. From where she stood in the kitchen, the dining room table was between her and the floor-to-ceiling windows in the living room that gave her an unobstructed view of the ridge and valley.

The clouds outside told her that a front was bringing snow tomorrow. She hoped the weatherman would say how much and when it would end. Janet was half listening when a different voice interrupted the broadcast.

We are interrupting this broadcast because the President of the United States has a very important announcement.

The screen flickered, and she saw a man sitting at a desk in

376

what everyone knew was the Oval Office. Janet stopped slicing celery stalks, wondering what the former governor of California was going to say.

My fellow Americans, yesterday Navy SEALs rescued six American POWs who were being held against their will in Vietnam. These men were captured in 1970, and in 1978 they were declared 'missing in action, presumed dead.' At the time, we knew four of them, two Air Force and two Naval Aviators, had been captured alive. The two Green Berets were listed as missing in action.

Since the end of the Vietnam War, there have been rumors about POWs still alive in Vietnam, Cambodia, and Laos, yet no one could confirm their existence. For years, all three countries denied they were holding American prisoners in their respective countries.

We now know that is not true, because just a few days ago we found proof. We knew who they were and where they were imprisoned.

When I was shown photos taken by their captor and by a Navy reconnaissance plane, I immediately ordered the Chairman of the Joint Chiefs to get these men back as soon as possible. I did not want to wait hours or days or months for the diplomatic niceties to follow their course and give the Vietnamese time to move them, or worse, kill them.

During the rescue, the Vietnamese tried to kill the six Americans. One, a first lieutenant and a Green Beret, sacrificed his life to save his comrades from grenades. His actions helped ensure that his fellow POWs would come home safely. He will be posthumously awarded the Medal of Honor for his heroic actions.

At this moment, the Americans are at a Naval Base in the Pacific undergoing medical exams. After that, they will undergo a debriefing and get assistance in re-adjusting to life in America. My administration is notifying their next of kin and arranging for them to be reunited with their loved ones. Once that is done, we will release the names of the rescued men.

I have ordered the Director of the Central Intelligence Agency to review all intelligence about any American who we know was captured alive and not returned to us at the end of the war. I pledge to you that I will increase the pressure on Vietnam, Cambodia, and Laos to come clean about any Americans who may have died there since the end of the war, or who may be still alive.

Thank you and good night. God bless America.

Janet stood there, knife in hand, frozen. Randy! One of them had to be Randy! She realized that if anyone was trying to contact her, they might be having difficulty. Since telling the POW/MIA office to remove her name from the list of members when he was declared dead, she'd changed her phone number and post office boxes twice.

She poured four fingers of scotch and sat down in her favorite chair. Until this moment, Randy and their marriage had been shoved into a little locked compartment in the back of her mind. *Now what?*

Chapter 15
THE ROAD TO NOWHERE

Wednesday, February 17, 1982, 0736 local time, Chicago
Richard O'Reilly stared at Randy's Pulaski's photo on the front page of the *Chicago Tribune*. In the row of six, he was the third from the left. It was too early in the morning for a glass of bourbon, but he poured one anyway. *"Oh, shit!"* repeated over and over in his mind like a broken record.

The same day, 1030 local time, Honolulu
The Naval Hospital at the Pearl Harbor base was originally built in the 1930s. It was expanded during World War II, modernized during the Korean War, and updated again during the Vietnam War. Since the end of the Southeast Asian conflict, it had been the premier military hospital west of San Diego.

Randy's parents had arrived the day before and, like other family members, had been picked up by Admiral Hastings' driver and brought to the Navy Lodge's cottages on the Barbers Point Naval Air Station. Each of the two-bedroom buildings was just a few hundred feet from a private beach. On the counter of each cottage were keys to cars provided free of charge, along with cards that gave the families access to the Naval Exchange and the commissary. A letter, signed by Admiral Hastings, said they were guests of a grateful nation and the United States Navy. They were to present the cards and Pacific Command would be billed.

Ladislaw Pulaski held his wife Sandy's hand as they were escorted to their son's private room. They had not seen him since the week before he'd departed for Vietnam. It had taken them years to accept the reality that Randy was missing and presumed dead. Every October 22, the anniversary date of Randy's capture, they'd lit a candle and prayed that Randy would come home alive. Like Janet, they'd believed he would turn up, sooner or later.

When the President of the United States had called immediately after his speech, Ladislaw had thought it was a hoax. The couple were well known in the POW/MIA movement and had often received prank calls, starting in 1973 after the Pulaskis were interviewed by a local TV station on the POW/MIA issue. Threatening and obscene messages were left on their answering machine. On the anniversary of the release of the POWs in 1977, anti-war protestors had thrown eggs and verbally assaulted veterans and their families. So it had taken several minutes before Ladislaw was convinced he was actually talking to the President.

During the conversation, Ladislaw held the handset so his wife could hear. The President said Randy was fine, and United Airlines had two first-class seats waiting for them at O'Hare to fly them to Honolulu. After they hung up, the Pulaskis hugged as the tears flowed. Randy's return was proof of the power of prayer and that God was looking out for the Pulaski family.

When they entered the room, Randy was looking at the ships in the harbor/ He was wearing a set of khakis, and on his collar were the silver oak leaves of a Commander, United States Navy. The Department of Defense had promoted each of the six returned POWs for all the time they were eligible.

"Randy? His mother's voice caused him to whip around and smile. The three of them hugged, and no one said a word until his mother looked him in the face and asked tremulously, "How come you are so tanned?"

"I spent a lot of time out in the sun working on a farm."

"You look very thin."

"I am. For the last ten years, I've been eating mostly vegetables. The doctors told me I need to put on about twenty pounds."

"Did they torture you?"

"Mom, yes. In the beginning they did. But since the war ended, the bastard who kept us prisoner was hoping to ransom us, so he didn't."

Randy looked around and asked the obvious question. "Where's Janet?"

His mom looked at his father, who returned the look. Both were uncomfortable. "We don't know. When you were declared missing, she came to see us a few times, then drifted away. After you were declared dead, she shipped us your things. She brought your Rolex and class ring when she came for the funeral. I haven't heard from her in years."

"Don't you have her address or a phone number?"

"No. Oh, that reminds me..." Sandy Pulaski opened her purse and rummaged around until she found a sealed envelope hand-addressed to Lieutenant Randy Pulaski. Randy immediately recognized his wife's neat script.

"She said to give this to you if you ever turned up, or for us to read it twenty years after the day you were shot down."

Randy sat on the bed and ripped the envelope down the edge. In it were two sheets of paper. The top one was a hand-written note, neatly printed.

My Dearest Randy,

It is my fervent hope that you are the one reading this letter. I gave it to your parents after you were declared dead. Since then, I have moved on and chosen not to associate with any of my fellow MIA widows. It is just too painful.

If you are reading this, fantastic! I started working right after you were shot down, and since then every dollar of your pay, along with the payout from your Serviceman's

Group Life Insurance, went into a trust fund. Along the way, I added money. It should give you a nice nest egg with which to restart your life.

The second sheet has the contact details, account numbers, and a special ID that you or your parents need to use to gain access to this trust fund.

The only things I kept were a few pictures of us together, my engagement ring, the Rolex that you bought for me, and the Shelby. As you know, I love driving fast, and it is a constant reminder of the fun times we spent blasting around the California countryside. Your brothers and I made an agreement that I would never sell it and would make sure that it was kept in pristine condition. And, if I couldn't drive it, I would give it to them.

If you are not reading this letter and it is the twentieth anniversary of your shoot down, I want your parents to use the money to establish a LT Randall Pulaski scholarship at Purdue for men or women who want to go into aviation. This will keep your memory alive long past our time on this earth.

All my love,
Janet

Randy couldn't stop the tears from flowing down his face. His voice choked from a combination of joy and sadness as he handed the letter to his mother. "This sounds just like Janet."

"Are you going to try to find her, son?"

"Honestly, Dad, I don't know."

Thursday, February 18, 1982, 0803 local time, Washington, DC

There were only three people in the Oval Office: the President, the Secretary of State, and the Director of the CIA. The President, resplendent in a dark charcoal-gray suit and red and blue-striped tie, came around from his side of the desk and faced the Secretary of State.

"Thank you for coming on such short notice. Tell the Vietnamese that we want a full accounting of our POWs, and we want it now. That starts with those that were killed after they were captured, and includes looking for any that may still be alive and returning them to us immediately. Deliver this message to their foreign minister in person in the next twenty-four hours. They look like fools, and they know it. Use their loss of face as leverage."

The President turned to the head of the CIA. "We have to see if we can find any ourselves. I want a full briefing in ten days that gives our best estimate on whether or not there are any more POWs alive. The last analysis was crap."

Monday, March 8, 1982, 0803 local time, Hanoi

Major General Trung sat in his office, wondering whether members of the People's Public Security would come here or to his apartment. He'd read the report about the rescue operation.

Along with photos of the destroyed opium processing facility, there were pictures of each of the thirty-six men who'd been killed. The photo of Pham's bullet-riddled body made Trung cringe. To the investigators, the purpose of the facility was clear —use the Americans as slaves, and turn raw opium into morphine base.

The report said that the People's Army had been alerted by unusual American airplane activity in the area. Two infantry companies and a battery of 85-millimeter guns had been dispatched with orders to kill or capture any invaders. They'd arrived ten minutes after the Americans had departed. The last paragraph stated that the country had been embarrassed and recommended that all those who'd known about or assisted this operation should be prosecuted.

For those accused, this most likely meant a quick trial before facing a firing squad. Theoretically, after a conviction, a lawyer could file an appeal, which would only make sure that none of the legal steps were skipped before the accused was executed. Trung went over his options for the umpteenth time.

Flee the country. *As the head of the logistical department, I report to the Minister of Defense. While I'm not watched, getting on a flight run by an airline of a non-Communist country or a ship would be difficult, if not impossible.*

Defect. *Probably my best option. Getting to the door of a foreign embassy of a non-Communist country will be difficult but doable. But which one? Defection works only if I can convince them to hand me over to the Americans who would see me as an intelligence bonanza.*

Suicide. *That is the coward's way out. I've taken the Makarov out of my desk several times, but I will not pull the trigger.*

Wait and see. *Maybe the investigation wouldn't get to me. I haven't had contact with the customs officials in Vinh in years. Most, if not all of those who know about my brother are dead and I do not mention him at all. There isn't anything that ties me to Pham, other than requisitions for matériel, and they were legitimate. They will find goats to sacrifice, and once they have saved face it will be back to business as usual.*

He could see the Argentine embassy from his flat; he could be there when it opened at 0900. *I think I will wait and let this play out. If I went, I would have to get my wife, and the two of us would have to approach the embassy, which has Vietnamese policemen guarding the entrance. And, there is no guarantee that the Argentinians will give me asylum. They do not want to put their exports to Vietnam at risk. There is a fifty-fifty chance they will turn me over to the authorities, and then I will be killed. No, it is better to wait this out.*

Thursday, March 25, 1982, 0803 local time, San Diego

Randy's temporary billet while he adjusted to life in the U.S. was on the staff of Commander, Naval Air Forces, Pacific on Naval Air Station, North Island. The base took up the entire northern tip of the peninsula forming the westernmost boundary of San Diego harbor, and its long piers were home to the carriers of the Pacific Fleet. After completing a series of taped interviews on his experience as a POW, Randy went to work in the shop that oversaw transition training to the A-7.

When he'd made it clear to the Commander that he wanted to resume flying, Randy had been told that when a flight surgeon gave him an "up chit," the Navy would send him to Pensacola for a familiarization course. The flights would determine whether or not he would get a flying billet.

If he didn't pass the check ride, Randy decided that he would leave active duty and join the reserves until he was eligible for retirement. His options had been made sweeter by the size of the nest egg Janet had created for him. At first, he thought the $1.8 million number a type-o, or a cruel joke, but the list of deposits to a bank in Liechtenstein had convinced him otherwise.

Randy was so engrossed in reading a report that he didn't react to the first knock on his office door. The second, louder knock got his attention. Without looking up, he said, "Come in."

Josh Haman walked up to the desk and held out his hand. "Welcome home, Randy. I'm Josh Haman. The last time we met, I was busy flying the helicopter out of Vietnam, and the medics were in such a hurry to get you on the C-141 I never got a chance to welcome you home. The *Coral Sea* got back two days ago."

"Thank you, and thanks for picking us up. Please sit down. May I get you a cup of coffee? It pours like jet fuel, but it smells like coffee."

"No, thanks. Do you have a minute?"

"I do, I do. I'd love a break." Randy looked at the man across the table and was surprised to see his decorations. There weren't many men walking around with two Navy Crosses, two Silver Stars, and three Distinguished Flying Crosses, and that was just the first of five rows of ribbons.

Josh decided to skip pleasantries and say what he'd thought about almost every day since October 22, 1970. "Commander, when we picked you up in Vietnam, it was actually the second time I had a chance to rescue you from Indian country."

"Whaaaaaaat do you mean by that?"

"Sir, I was the co-pilot of the H-2 that left you in the water back in '70. And, the chief petty officer, the one in the back of the H-3 when we picked you all up, was the rescue swimmer."

Seeing Randy's confused look, Josh continued. "Let me explain. In 1970, I was a nugget who had been in country just over a month. It was my first combat rescue. I couldn't get the aircraft commander to go back to pick you up. There wasn't any doubt in my mind, or the crew's mind, that if Higgins—the aircraft commander—had had any balls, we could have picked you up. If Higgins had let us do what we were supposed to do, you wouldn't have spent twelve years in captivity. I'm here to apologize."

Randy didn't know what to say. He had to admire the man's courage. Haman had just confirmed that his being a POW had been preventable, which had eaten at him for twelve years. Lying on his bed in Vietnam, he'd played out scenarios of what he would do to the helicopter pilots to exact revenge for leaving him. He nodded slowly.

Being a prisoner had taught him many things. One was to control what you can, and try to influence what you can't control. Beyond that, you're in God's hands. Maybe this was one of the things he couldn't control or influence. *Talk to this man before you do something stupid.*

"Apology accepted. I admire your courage in coming to see me."

"Thank you. Not a day has gone by that I haven't thought about that in some way."

"It would bug the hell out of me, too." Randy spun his coffee mug around. "What happened to Higgins?"

"Sir, it is a long story. The *Readers Digest* version is that about six months later, Higgins was run out of the Navy for being a coward. You were the last of four he allowed to get captured. I'd be happy to tell you the whole story, but only as my family's guest at dinner this Saturday night. Several of us would like to honor you. And, in a quiet moment after a glass or two of wine, we'll tell you the whole story."

"Who's the 'we'?"

"Commander Gary Nash, Judge Advocate Corps. Gary is a reservist now, but at the time he was one of the attorneys who put the case together against Higgins. He also helped me get through a pilot disposition board. That's another story related to Higgins. Now Gary has a private law practice and is my attorney, as well the lawyer for the other gentlemen whom you've already met— Jack D'Onofrio, the copilot in the H-3, and Marty Cabot, the SEAL who led the rescue team. We all worked together in Vietnam. They're good people, and you won't be the only bachelor. Marty will bring his latest flame, and he knows all the watering holes where eligible, willing women hang out. Anyway, I'll grill some steaks, if that's O.K. with you. You'll enjoy talking to our wives as well. Think of it as the start of a social life."

"Accepted. Steak sounds wonderful."

"Excellent." Josh took a piece of paper out of the breast pocket of his khakis. "Here's the address. Plan on being at our house around six-thirty. You will be the guest of honor, but don't dress up."

Saturday, April 3, 1982, 0900 local time, San Diego

Gary Nash saw Randy Pulaski enter the small suite of offices that the Navy Judge Advocate Corps Reserve Unit 1063 used on its drill weekends. He put down his coffee cup and watched as one of the enlisted men pointed to where he was sitting.

After shaking hands, Gary spoke first. "I'm glad to see that you decided to take me up on my offer."

"Well, as Vito Corleone said, "You made me an offer I couldn't refuse.'"

"Have a seat here in my palatial office. As I told you at dinner, you can read until your eyeballs bleed, but you can't copy anything."

"No problem. I'm getting good at that at AIRPAC."

Gary went over to an open four-drawer safe and pulled out five large folders and a bound book from the bottom drawer. He put the book on the table first. "This is a copy of the pilot disposition board report that evaluated the actions of Josh Haman and his crew. In it, you will find the interviews of Josh and the members of the detachment that led to the investigation and charges against Higgins. These two folders contain the complete transcript of the board's sessions, and transcripts of all the tapes given to the board."

He put down a third folder. "This contains the charges that the Navy was prepared to file against Lieutenant Higgins for cowardice in the face of the enemy. In it, you'll find your CO's and air wing commander's reports and cover letters. Also, there are letters and reports from others that confirmed that Higgins was a coward."

The fourth folder he put down bulged with papers. It was the thickest. "This folder has the results from the investigation that led us to charge Higgins with filing fraudulent reports on the readiness of his helicopter and its availability to fly rescue missions."

Gary held on to the fifth folder. "You with me so far?"

"Sure am."

"And these are copies of the Navy's case files from when Higgins, who is now an attorney, tried to sue the Navy and Commander Haman in Federal court for libel. Higgins claimed that Commander Haman, who had been a Lieutenant Junior Grade at the time, led a mutiny, and gave false testimony at the board. I was Josh's civilian attorney and worked with other JAG officers to build a 'friend of the court' briefing supporting Josh's defense. The head of the Navy's JAG corps took the judge out to lunch and gave her the evidence the Navy would make available. Two days later, the judge threw out the lawsuit as baseless and did so with prejudice. That means Higgins can't file a lawsuit against Josh ever again in any U.S. court."

"Wow! I'll start with the board's report."

"Good choice. Just read away, and if you have any questions, either I'll answer them or we can call Josh. I've known him since 1970. Leaving you in the raft really gnawed at him over the years. He felt guilty and believes he owes you for all the years you were in captivity."

"I gathered that much."

"I hope you won't do anything stupid with regard to Steve Higgins. If I were in your shoes, I'd want to beat the shit out of him before I castrated him with a very dull, serrated knife. And then, I'd want to skin him alive and enjoy his suffering."

"My plan was to introduce him to the bamboo pole and see how he likes that, along with being beaten by canvas hoses."

"Don't. Here are two good reasons why. One, he is not worth it. Two, if Higgins does anything that the Navy, Josh, or I don't like, we hammer him over his actions in Vietnam. He can never escape the fact that he was given a general discharge with no benefits for disciplinary reasons in lieu of being hauled in front of a court martial. The Navy can always change its mind, because there is no statute of limitations for cowardice in the face of the enemy."

"Got it."

"Promise me you won't do something stupid."

"I promise."

"Excellent. Now let me get to the heart of the matter. The 'find Randy Pulaski a good woman' fan club talks every day. The members are Rebekah Haman; Jack's wife, Mary Lou; and my wife, Sandy. They like you a lot and think you are a good man who needs a good woman. Trust me, they don't take no for an answer; but they'll ask both of you before they make introductions, which will happen at dinners at one of our houses."

"I... can fend for myself."

"You tell them that. They know who's who in the zoo amongst eligible women, and once your story gets around, you'll have to fight them off."

Randy held up his hands in surrender. "O.K., I give in." He

knew a good deal when he heard one. He'd already tried the bar scene and didn't like it. He was tired of answering the question, "What have you been doing for the past twelve years?"

"Good. The fan club and their spouses are meeting at my house this Saturday night. There may be an extra woman or two, because they are trying to get Marty married off as well."

Tuesday, April 6, 1982, 0900 local time, McLean

Gary wanted no one around when he made his call, so he waited for the man using the center pay phone to finish his conversation and leave before he stepped up to the bank of phones in a hotel five miles from CIA headquarters As he picked up the handset, he made sure the man was gone, then dropped a quarter into the slot.

"'Lo."

"It's the man from LA." Since the attempted hit on Pham, they'd agreed not to use their names.

"It's been a while. Whazzup, man?"

"I got another project for you. It's local."

"Cool."

"I want someone taken out to send a message"

"That's heavy, man. Who is he?"

"I'll send you his name and address along with a photo."

"How do you want it done?"

"I don't care. Just take him out quickly."

"You owe him money?"

"No. He's a co-worker." *Shit, he shouldn't have said that.*

"He agency?"

"Yeah."

"That drives up the price, man."

In Africa and South America, hits were political targets and the locals were cheap. The price depended on the risk to the assassin. Gary looked at his watch. He didn't want the call to run longer than three minutes. "How much?"

There was silence for a few seconds. "Twenty-five large."

Gary guessed the hit man would get fifteen and Bobby Wales would pocket ten. Wales had gotten out of the ghetto by going into the Army. After he got out, he wound up in DC, where he was, as he would often say, a facilitator. He put people in touch with other people and took a cut. His connections made him rich, so he could afford a good lawyer when he was "interviewed" by the police.

In the past, Gary had used him for "off the book" agency work when a trail led to the U.S. "Half now and half when it is done."

"Fifteen and ten. Tomorrow, usual way."

"Done."

Wednesday, April 7, 1982, 1046 local time, Chicago

Air hissed out of the Peterbilt 352H's brake system as the driver set the brakes. Quiet returned to the residential street when the 375-horsepower Caterpillar diesel engine pulling the eighteen-wheeler rattled to a stop.

The matching metallic silver paint with red stripes on the tractor and the forty-foot-long enclosed trailer gleamed in the sunlight. Three-inch block letters—"GT Car Transport, Inc." and a permit number on the driver and passenger's doors were the only markings on the truck or the trailer.

Randy was the first one out of the door of his parent's house to watch the truck be unloaded. He'd flown to Chicago after his parents had called him, saying that a representative of GT Car Transport had called to arrange delivery of a 1966 GT 350.

The driver asked for identification and had Randy sign several forms before he opened the back of the tractor-trailer. From his spot on the lawn, Randy's excitement grew as the back of the car slowly revealed itself as the ramp came down.

While the truck driver unhooked the tie-downs, Randy bounded up the ramp.

"Sir, I have to drive it off the truck. Then you and I walk around the vehicle to make sure it hasn't been damaged in any way. If everything is O.K., I'll give you the acceptance form to sign, and the keys."

Randy nodded and got down from the truck. The GT350 rumbled into life. The driver eased the car into reverse and, once it was clear of the ramp, shut it down. The Shelby gleamed in the sunlight.

As Randy was signing the acceptance form, the truck driver handed him two thick manila envelopes, one of which had a letter taped to the top. "Sir, these came with the car. One has the owner's manual and title, and the other all the maintenance records."

Randy sat in the car and put his hands on the wood-rim steering wheel. Memories of driving the car flooded back. For a few seconds, he imagined Janet sitting next to him as they drove up to Yosemite for the day, or on the mountain roads. Each excursion had led to a picnic and wonderful sex in a secluded spot.

By sending the car back, Janet was talking to him. With that in mind, he ripped open the envelope and started reading the typewritten note.

Randy,

I wanted to return the car to you so you can enjoy driving it again. Five years ago, I took it to a restoration shop in LA that specializes in Cobras and GT350s and they went through it with a fine-tooth comb. Everything that needed to be replaced was done so with genuine Shelby parts. It runs like a top and is fast as hell!

All the papers are in order. After you were declared dead, I probated your will and the title was transferred to me. The title is signed over to you along with a notarized bill of sale for $1 from the State of California. All the maintenance records you had along with those since you left are in the Manila envelope labeled with the #1, with the registration. #2 has the owner's manual.

All you need to do is register it in your name and

get it insured. Now that you are back safe, you should enjoy this wonderful car. All the best.

Janet

Randy's head dropped. There was no address. *On one hand, Janet gives me gifts and, on the other, she hurts me by staying away. Finding her is the only way to get closure. But how? And why? What could come of it other than pain for both of us?*

Thursday, April 8, 1982, 0725 local time, Evanston, IL
Other than a fresh coat of paint and some new bushes in the front, the house hadn't changed in the fourteen years since her parents had told her to leave. Janet suspected the heated greenhouse in the back, her mother's pride and joy, was still there, and that, inside, the house was as immaculate as ever.

A Volvo 245 wagon sat on her parent's driveway. Her mom and dad liked Volvos, and every five years they bought a new one and retired the old.

She bet their routine hadn't changed. Her father would drop her mother off at work and then go to his job. The hospital where her mother worked as an administrator was a block from the offices of the small law firm where her father was a partner.

Her parents were the perfect middle-class, second generation Americans who made the world a better place for their children. Both sets of grandparents had come from the wreckage of the Austro-Hungarian Empire right after World War I and settled in the Irving Park area of Chicago. Her father had spent World War II in the turret of a Sherman tank in the Second Armored Division. After being wounded in Sicily, he'd rejoined the unit just before the Normandy invasion. By the end of the war he was a tank company commander looking at Soviet troops on the other side of the Elbe River.

As a teenager, Janet had started questioning everything. In college, her social and political views, already thought to be extreme by her parents, went farther left. At first, her parents thought Janet was just rebelling, but soon realized that her beliefs were not the same as theirs. Discussions turned to shouting matches.

The worst one had been the day before she graduated. Janet said hurtful things. Her parents said hurtful things. At a pause in the shouting, her father said in a quiet, firm voice, "Janet, you will pack your belongings and put them in your car. After the graduation ceremony, do not come back here. Go wherever you want, but this house is no longer your home. We don't want to see or hear from you until you change your radical views."

She'd turned to her mother, whose face was a pale death-mask. "Neither your father nor I can take your radical political rants and insults anymore. We love you, but you are destroying our family, so get out and stay away. In our minds, the Janet who grew up here died when she went to college. We'll try to remember the younger Janet, not the one who is here now."

When Janet walked out of the auditorium the next day, her father and mother hugged her one last time, then walked away. She'd realized they'd planned this painful separation. Graduation was the right time because, in their minds, they had done their job, i.e. raised her and paid for a good education, so she was starting life debt free.

Right at 7:30, her parents came out of the door. They looked older and grayer, but her father was still the proud, erect man she remembered. Her mother, despite the graying hair, still had a trim, attractive figure. From where she sat, they looked great.

Janet wondered how the rest of her family were. Neither of her brothers were listed as KIA or MIA, and she hoped they, along with her baby sister, they were healthy, married, and had children.

Janet followed the route she knew so well. The red light gave her a chance to wipe the tears from her eyes.

She *had* changed, but not in the way her parents hoped. She giggled as she played the conversation in her mind.

Mom or Dad—"Janet, have you changed?"

Janet—"Yes, I have. Now I am a millionaire capitalist with a five-hundred-acre ranch in California."

Mom or Dad—"Are you married?"

Janet—"No, not anymore. I married a Naval Aviator because the Weather Underground wanted me to infiltrate the U.S. military. I also fell in love with him. Then he got shot down and was MIA and presumed dead for twelve years, until he showed up a few months ago."

Mom or Dad—"Oh that's wonderful, when can we meet him?"

Janet—"You can't. We don't live together. When he was declared dead, I became a widow. I never remarried because now I am a lesbian."

Mom or Dad—"What have you been doing all these years?" *In other words, "How'd you make all that money to afford a five-hundred-acre ranch in California?"*

Janet—"The Weather Underground arranged for me to spend four months in Cuba, where I was taught to be an assassin. Being the opportunistic capitalist that I am, I now am a freelancer and travel all over the world. I've killed people in Chile, Argentina, Italy, England, Australia, and Canada, as well as the U.S. I'll kill anyone, anywhere for someone willing to pay my fee. And, I'm good enough to be very selective."

Mom or Dad—"Do you like being an assassin?"

Janet—"Oh, yes. It's a rush and it turns me on."

The light turned green and Janet drove away, giggling. She had work to do. The Broker had called with another assignment. She assumed it was from one of the Chicago Mafia families. Sometimes they had their own hit men make it bloody and messy to send a message. Other times, they wanted to use an "outsider." For those jobs they called The Broker, and, most of the time, The Broker called Janet.

Janet was dressed warmly enough to ward off the dampness and the chill from the forty-five degree air coming off Lake Michigan. The ski hat was light gray, the turtleneck sweater a

395

medium gray, and the jeans charcoal. The comfortable hiking boots and purse were dull black.

From reconnaissance she knew that the man left his third-floor apartment at ten and walked down the stairs on his way to work. An area of shadow on each landing was perfect for hiding.

At 0945, Janet wedged herself into a stairway corner with a suppressed Browning BDA held at her side. She liked the ninety-five-grain .380 round for close-in work like this because, with a suppressor, it didn't sound like a gunshot. The BDA had just come on the market, and after practicing with this one at a nearby gun range, she'd decided to buy one when she got home. It was about the size of a Makarov and the Walther PPK/S, but had a fatter grip to house a double-stack, twelve-round magazine.

Footsteps sounded. In the dim light, she could see a man's shoes and pants legs through the bannister. Right on cue, the man matching the photos she'd been sent appeared. "Godfrey Bannister?"

"Yes, who are...?" The man raised his hands when he saw the gun in hers. Janet fired once. Bannister collapsed, sprawled on the last three steps. Stepping around the growing pool of blood flowing from where his left eye used to be, Janet checked for a pulse. Bannister had none.

After picking up the empty brass cartridge, Janet unscrewed the suppressor and, along with the pistol, both went in her purse before she entered the lobby. Two minutes after pulling the trigger, Janet started her rental car. She felt her heart rate begin to slow down as she pulled out of the parking lot, thinking that, in a day or two, she would be $300,000 richer.

Monday, April 12, 1982, 0725 local time, McLean
When the door opened to the director's conference room, Gary Savoy stood up. In front of him were three thick folders. "Good morning, sir."

"Good morning, Savoy. Where's Gus Grenholm?" The head of the CIA was not smiling.

"Don't know, sir. I haven't seen him since Friday. If you are pressed for time, we can go through what I brought."

"Where's Lieutenant Colonel White?"

"No idea, sir—why?" *I deliberately didn't invite White because, like Grenholm, I can't control what he will say.*

"Lieutenant Colonel White and the other four surviving POWs are supposed to be helping the team look at the possible locations where Americans might still be kept. Next time, I want White here."

"Yes, sir. I don't know why he didn't show up."

The director glared at Savoy, not liking what he heard. He was stuck with Savoy for the time being. Since the rescue, he'd remembered Savoy's debunking an analysis of statements by POWs corroborated by Cuban defectors claiming the North Vietnamese had sent at least 17 Americans to Cuba. All were now assumed to be dead. All the reports referred to a Cuban Colonel Hernandez. No one in the CIA knew his real name, but from the POWs they had a description of what he looked like.

"Give me the *Reader's Digest* version while we are waiting for Grenholm."

"Sir, we divided all the possible sites where POWS might still be held into three categories—highly possible, possible, and unlikely. Each has its own criteria for being placed in its category."

"What's the punch line?"

"There are only two sites out of about a hundred that make the possible category and just one in the highly possible group."

"Is that your conclusion, or Gus's or Ashley's?"

"They would agree to that assessment." He knew they wouldn't, but that problem was being solved.

"Neither of them are here, which is very disappointing. Quite frankly, Savoy, I don't trust your judgment." The director opened the smallest folder. "Have you read the debriefs of the guys who were just freed?"

"No, sir, I've not read all of them." He let the others read them and give him the highlights. His agency experience told him that this bureaucratic crisis would pass, and he would continue as an agency employee until he retired. The government looked after its own, because the only thing worse than a FUBAR situation was to make it public. That was why known traitors were allowed to retire and lead comfortable, well-lubricated lives. He was just a bureaucrat, and he'd only done what he'd been told to do.

"Savoy, did you tell the analysts to go through them with a fine-tooth comb and compare them to the debriefs of the guys who came back in 1973?"

"I did. I can re-emphasize that when I get back to Arlington." It was a bald-faced lie. He'd told them it was a make-work, cover-your-ass project. More than ever he was sure there were no Americans left alive in Vietnam. If there had been, they were dead now, so they couldn't further embarrass the People's Republic of Vietnam.

Back in Africa, Savoy had never trusted anyone to keep quiet. If there was any doubt, they were shut up permanently. This way, there was only one side of the story, his.

The director's eyes bored into Savoy. "Do that. All five of the people we just got back were held at different camps along the Ho Chi Minh trail at different times. I want the five to look at what your team has. In their debriefings, they drew sketches of the interim camps and provided very detailed descriptions."

"Yes, sir."

"I'm surprised that you haven't taken a look at them."

"Mr. Director," an administrative assistant, a bespectacled, balding man with a fringe of white hair, entered the room. "Sir, you need to take this call."

"Savoy, wait here."

After taking the call in his office, the director stood still, processing what he'd just heard.

When he returned, his face was grim.

"That was the head of the FBI. Gus Grenholm was murdered last night. Some asshole pulled alongside his car and damn near blew his head off with a .357 Magnum. It was a hit."

Gary Nash looked up from the court filing he was reviewing to see his administrative assistant standing in the doorway. "Daphne, what's up?" She knew not to interrupt him when he was prepping for a court appearance unless it was really serious. "Gary, a Randy Pulaski is here. He says it is important."

"Send him in."

After shaking hands, Gary pointed to a worn, brown leather couch in his office. He plopped himself down in the easy chair alongside. "What's up?"

"I gather you are well connected in the Navy's legal community."

"Thanks for the compliment. I like to think I am. Why?"

"I want to talk to you about one of my fellow POW's who I believe became a collaborator, if not a traitor. He needs to be prosecuted. Whom should I talk to?"

"Did you cover this in your debriefing?"

"I did, in gory detail. My de-briefers listened carefully. I was told to forget about it because it was investigated when they came home in 1973. This guy is like a bad dream."

"Who was he, and what did he do?"

"His name is Richard O'Reilly." Randy spent five minutes summarizing what he'd told his de-briefers. He ended by saying, "I heard every fucking word he told Major Gorov before they took him to Hanoi."

"How well do you remember this?"

"Like it happened yesterday. I've been stewing on this for twelve long years. Right after my debriefing, I wrote down everything I remember. Here it is." He put a folder on the table.

Nash reached forward, opened the folder, and picked up the first page. It was double-spaced and neatly typed. "Is this the only copy?"

"Nope, I've got the original and two more stashed away."

Randy stood up. "I found out that Stockdale wanted to court-martial this guy but was told they didn't have a witness to what O'Reilly told the Vietnamese. It was all hearsay. Now the Navy has a witness—me. Is there anything I can do?"

"Short answer is, I don't know, but I do know who to call. Let me read this and get back to you."

The same day, 2036 local time, Washington, DC

For dinner, the five former POWs went into Crystal City. It was a way to celebrate their freedom and, again, toast the bravery of Hank Cho. Over the years of their imprisonment, they had all watched him deteriorate physically. Randy thought that, in a way, his brave act had been a way to end his suffering. They were walking toward the parking lot when two men, clad in jeans, black turtlenecks, and ski masks, appeared in the twilight.

Ashley screamed, "Everyone down!" and shoved Jeff into a doorway. Randy, seeing the Uzis, dove between two cars before the train of bullets could find him. Karl Kramer took two bullets in the chest before he flattened himself on the sidewalk. Ashley got hit with one in the side and one in his left leg. The men reloaded and sprayed the area again before jumping into a panel van. As they drove away, the two men emptied two more magazines in their direction. Two more nine-millimeter rounds struck Karl. Randy memorized the license plate, along with the make and model of the blue and white vehicle.

Karl was still alive when they loaded him into the first ambulance that arrived ten minutes after the attack. Ashley, less seriously wounded, went in the second.

Surrounded by police officers, Randy sat next to Greg and Jeff on the step of the doorway with his arms around his friends' shoulders.

"Holy fuck, I survived twelve years in a goddamn prisoner of war camp and damn near get killed on the streets of Crystal City, Virginia. Is this fate's version of Catch 44? I want to know what the fuck is going on!"

FORGOTTEN

Wednesday April 14, 1982, 0621 local time, Washington, DC

Trying to block out the noise of the district's rush hour traffic, an angry Gary pressed the handset of the pay phone against his right ear and stuck his index finger into his left. As soon as he heard Bobby Wales' voice, he started yelling. "What the fuck were those guys thinking? The incompetent idiots opened up with automatic weapons on a street in Arlington! They fired 192 rounds at five targets and didn't manage to kill anyone!"

"They'll finish the job, dude, or they don't get their money." Gary tried to contain his frustration. "No, they won't. Call them off."

"Why?"

"Because they're incompetent morons. They'll expose us all."

"No way, man. They won't roll over on us."

Gary hoped his voice conveyed the importance of what he was saying. "I DON'T TRUST THEM. The feds got a license plate."

"I'll tell the brothers to lay low."

"Tell them to get out of town and stay out. If they start talking, I'll hunt them down and kill them myself."

Bobbi knew Gary would do what he said he would do. "Yes, boss."

Gary wasn't sure if Wales was mocking him or being subservient. He banged the phone down. Before he dialed another number, he pulled out a piece of paper with ten digits written in groups of two. He knew the man from his days in Africa.

"Raul. It's Gary."

"Hey, long time no speak. Where the hell are you? There's a lot of background noise."

"Yeah, I'm at a gas station pay phone. Look, I heard you have contacts that do wet work."

"I do. Is this on the books or a private party?"

"Private."

"What do you need done?"

"Some people taken out."

401

"Define some."

"Five."

"That's a bunch. Where are they located?"

"For the time being, DC."

"I need more info. What can you tell me?"

The traffic noise seemed to get lower as he described the five men. Gary looked around and saw there was someone waiting behind him. It was time to go.

"Do you have the talent?"

"Yeah, but it won't be cheap."

"I guessed that much. Find out and I'll call you tomorrow at the same time."

The same day, 0646 local time, Chicago

The ringing phone jarred O'Reilly into wakefulness. He looked at his Rolex and immediately thought *"You only get bad news at this hour."* He tried to force the sleep from his voice. "Morning."

"Is this Richard A. O'Reilly, the former POW?"

"Yes." It was a reflex answer, one he didn't consider before responding. "Who is this?"

"You don't know me, but I work in the Defense MIA/POW Office and wanted to give you a heads up."

"About what?" O'Reilly was now fully awake.

"The Navy Judge Advocate General office is seriously considering reopening Stockdale's original request to have you court martialed for treason. They have new evidence."

O'Reilly felt as if he'd been punched in the gut. *It had to be Pulaski. He was the only one around when I was interrogated by Gorov.* "Do you know what evidence?"

"No. All I can tell you is that a high-priority request for records, debriefings and other documents signed by the Chief of Naval Operations, the Chairman of the Joint Chiefs, and the Secretary of Defense landed on my desk."

"Why are you calling me?"

"Look, I think the political leadership fucked the military during the Vietnam War. They had a bad strategy, and then they tied one hand behind your backs. Guys got killed, wounded, and, like you, taken prisoner. I don't want to see old wounds reopened. You need to get a good lawyer who knows the Uniform Code of Military Justice and general court martial procedures inside and out. My guess is that they are coming after you and want a large piece of your ass."

"What else can you tell me?"

"Isn't that enough? Look, man, I've gotta go. Just making this call puts me at risk."

The dial tone told O'Reilly the caller had hung up. The next time he looked at his watch, he realized he'd been staring at the wall for ten minutes. When he finished shaving, he knew what he had to do.

The same day, 1347 local time, Arlington

According to the writing in the lower right-hand corner, the photo had been taken on November 12, 1970, by an RF-8G from the *Oriskany.* Each time Randy studied the eight-by-ten photo with a loupe, his eyes were drawn to the middle of the compound. Taken from about a 30-degree angle above the horizon, he was sure this was Duong's compound and he was the shape in the cage. The thought made him shudder.

The intercom buzzed and Jeff Anderson pushed the button. "Commander Pulaski, it's the hospital. They want to speak to you."

Randy pushed the button activating the speakerphone. "Commander Pulaski."

"Sir, this is Doctor McDowell. I'm sorry to have to tell you this, but Major Kramer passed away We did what we could, but three bullets did irreparable damage to his heart and lungs. His parents, brother and sister were at his bedside when he died. Again, I am so sorry. The Chief of Stagg of the Air Force told me that if Major Kramer's parents agree, he will be buried at

Arlington a week from this Saturday, with full military honors."

Shit, fuck, piss, and corruption! Karl survives twelve years in a hellhole and gets gunned down in Virginia. I am going to find the fuckers who did this if it is the last thing I do.

"Thank you, Doctor. What about Colonel Smith?"

"He's awake and out of surgery. Colonel Smith will recover, but he will need many months of rehab, and possibly more surgery."

"We'll be over to see him later today."

"Please bring your ID cards. We're limiting visitors to that wing, and the military is providing security."

Randy, Jeff and Greg were looking at each other in stunned silence when Gary Savoy came into the room. Most of the time he stayed in his office and emerged only when summoned because the former POWs needed more information.

"I'm going to a meeting. Is there anything I can do for you?"

"Yeah, Find Karl Kramer's killer."

"What do you mean?"

"Karl died about an hour ago."

"Oh."

Randy looked at him. *No "Oh, I'm sorry to hear that." No "He was a good man." No "I hope they find the killer." No emotion, nothing.* A cold feeling settled in the bottom of his gut.

Savoy felt as if he was an unwelcome intruder as he stood in the doorway. Hearing no requests, he left.

Thursday, April 15, 1982, 0646 local time, Forest Heights, Maryland

Gary found a strip mall off Maryland Route 210 a mile north of Interstate 95 where it was quiet. Three dollars and twenty-five cents in quarters demanded by the operator went into the phone before the operator connected the call. A man's voice announced, "Intercontinental Logistics."

"Raul?"

"Yeah, who's this?"

"Gary."

"Sorry, I didn't recognize your voice."

"No problem. What do you have for me?"

"Two independent contractors. One I use when you don't care if it is messy. The other is the best in the business. This person does it quietly with no mess, no fuss, just a confused bunch of cops. However, the individual is expensive and very picky."

"What's the damage?"

"The first is a group of guys. They said they'd do it for three hundred and fifty thousand, including expenses. The other is a lady known as *"la estrella roja de la muerte."* Assuming she takes the project, she'll want two hundred and fifty thousand per target. Once she understands the project, she may want more."

"I'm not paying that kind of bread."

"So you want the other guys."

"Yeah."

"Before I take this, let me tell you that if you are planning on waxing who I think you are, you're out of your fucking mind. I heard about the botched hit in Arlington. Special forces guys don't take to this kindly. They don't care about the law and will stop at nothing until they find the killers. If they show up on my doorstep, I'm warning you, I'll point them in your direction. You were good to me and now I'm returning the favor. I want to warn you that this kind of hit will probably create a shit storm the likes of which you've never scene. You'll have every police agency looking for the shooters, who may roll over. I'm only saying this because you and I go back a ways."

"I appreciate the warning, but I want this. These guys are ruining my career."

"So retire and do something else. Take my advice and don't do this."

"My idea is to make this look like the work of anti-war terrorists. There are still plenty of radicals who blame vets, especially bombers and so-called 'war heroes'. The FBI and the CIA will be so busy with the usual suspects they won't give give anyone else a second thought. How do you want the money?"

"Got a pencil? Write this number down. It's an off-shore bank in the Seychelles."

"Go." Raul rattled off the name of the bank and a twelve-digit number that Gary repeated back.

"They want half and the expense money up front, so I'll let them know they have the job when one hundred and seventy-five thousand is deposited in the bank. When the job is finished, I expect the remaining one seventy-five within twenty-four hours. If it is later than that, they come after you to collect."

"Yeah, yeah, yeah. I'm good for it."

"I hope you know what you are doing, because once I call these guys, there's no going back."

Gary answered by pressing the lever to disconnect the call.

The same day, 1303 local time, Chicago

Two men sat in the corner in a small four-star Italian restaurant on South Morgan Street in what was officially known as University Village. Locals called it Little Italy.

Out of respect, and to meet the Mafia chieftain's need for privacy, the maître d' made sure that none of the tables around the two men were occupied. People who knew Vincenzo DeLuca nodded respectfully as they came and went.

Now that all that remained were cups of coffee, it was time for business. "So, Richard, what is so urgent that we couldn't cover in a phone call?"

"A while ago, you told me that if I ever needed 'something done' to call you. Well, that time is now."

"What is the something?"

"A hit."

DeLuca didn't say anything for a few seconds. Anything he said from this point on made him a co-conspirator. "For what reason?"

"His testimony could put me in jail for a very long time." O'Reilly didn't mention that a conviction could have him facing a firing squad, or standing on a platform with a noose around his neck.

"And you are sure you want to do this?"

"Yes."

"I see." DeLuca took a sip of his coffee. "Is this person local?"

"No."

Another sip of coffee. Even in the Mafia, hits were not authorized on whims. The fact that it would take place outside of Chicago gave him an out; he didn't have to risk his own people. "For this type of work, we like to use an outsider who negotiates the contract with one of his resources. All we do is agree to the fee and transfer money from one offshore bank to another." DeLuca tented his hands. "We've used him before. He has talent who don't leave a mess, if you know what I mean."

"What are we looking at?"

"That depends on the work involved and the risk. Plan on spending three hundred to five hundred grand."

"You've got to be shitting me. In the news, you read that you can buy a hit for five thousand dollars."

"True. And the next thing you know, the police are knocking on your door."

"Point taken." DeLuca made the writing gesture and a pad was quickly brought to the table by a waiter. He tore off the top sheet and precisely folded it so the sheet was one quarter its original size. With a fountain pen, he wrote down two ten-digit numbers. He preferred a fountain pen because, unlike a ballpoint, it didn't dent the paper. "We call him The Broker. Memorize these numbers, then destroy the sheet of paper."

The same day, 1842 local time, Dulles Airport

The last group of passengers from the flight from Toronto had picked up their bags and left, leaving Gary Savoy alone at the last phone in the line of six. He stood with his back to the wall as he surveyed the world around him and dropped change into the slot.

"Hola."

"Gary here. Got a minute?"

"*Sí.*"

"The shit is hitting the fan over the guys we just rescued from Vietnam. I am sure the subject of the seventeen Americans pilots taken to Cuba will come up again."

"*No estoy preocupado.*" I am not worried. "*No hay nada que los CIA pueda hacer. Además, todos están muertos.*" There is nothing the CIA can do. Besides, they are all dead.

"I just thought you'd like to know, for old time's sake."

"*Gracias por llamar.*" Thanks for calling.

Gary could tell the man on the other end of the phone didn't want to continue the conversation. "Be careful, *amigo.*"

"*Gracias, yo siempre soy.*" Thank you. I always am.

Gary wasn't surprised that the Cuban intelligence officer's words were followed by a dial tone.

The same day, 0732 local time, Palmdale

The message "Call your boss, it's important" which the answering service relayed to Janet was unusual. Normally, the message was "I have a new customer for you, please give me a call at such and such time and a number." That was a signal to call from a pay phone to get the number of the pay phone he would use.

The next day, she opened a package from The Broker and found herself looking at a picture of Randy. Her stomach churned as she read the notes that included his apartment address and phone number. There were also three phone numbers, along with times and dates to call each one.

It took her a few minutes to find a bank of pay phones in a hotel in Palmdale. The Broker answered with his standard "Allo."

"Who's the buyer?"

"One of his fellow POWs."

"What the fuck is going on?"

"Here's what I know. There were three POWs who the Department of Defense wanted to court martial after they were released, but Nixon wouldn't approve it. Rumor has it that now the guy you are looking at can testify that he saw the buyer commit treason. Without the mark, the government doesn't have a case and the buyer knows it."

"That's ugly." Janet's voice hardened. "Will the buyer pay my fee?"

"Yes."

Raul was used to Janet firing questions at him. This time there was silence, so he asked what he suspected. "This is personal, isn't it?"

The only way that Raul would have known she knew Randy was if someone had told him. She suspected he knew more about her background than she'd provided. The most likely source would have been either someone in SDS or Cuban Intelligence. Based on his background, she ruled out SDS. "Yeah."

"You going to take the contract? I told him three-fifty, including expenses."

Scenarios ran through her mind. "You know the name of the buyer?"

"Yeah. He was really nervous. He got my name from one of your very satisfied customers in Chicago."

"Do you know how to reach him?"

"I do."

"Send what you have on him to me."

"Are you thinking of doing what I think you are planning?"

"Yeah."

"I love it. Neither the guy who sent him to me nor I like traitors. They're bad for business. I'll get the entire fee up front. Call me when it's done and I'll give you air cover with the people in Chicago. They'll understand."

Friday, April 16, 1982, 2122 local time, McLean

Gary had dropped the third of three large plastic bags into the garbage can when he heard the phone ring. The extension was in the kitchen, just inside the door to the garage. "Hello."

"Hey, dude. Whazzup?"

Savoy recognized the voice of Bobby Wales. "I'm glad you called. Things are getting hot."

"You don't need to tell me that, dude. Everywhere I go there's a cop looking for those shooters."

"Yeah, well, you need to get out of town and lay real low. I found out the shooters gave the cops your name, and now there is a national all-points bulletin out for you." Right after he said that, he realized that if his phone was tapped, he'd just confirmed that he was a co-conspirator to murder. It didn't matter.

"That explains a lot. Thanks, man. See you around."

The dial tone told Gary that he needed to finish packing and get out of town.

Chapter 16
REVELATIONS

A sign in the lobby said "Condo Open House 1-8 p.m. 10th floor." Perfect! Janet read the smaller print and looked around to get a feel for the building. She was in California rancher mode, complete with the appropriate IDs.

Signage on the tenth floor directed her toward an open door at the end of the hall. An unobstructed view of Lake Michigan drew her to the floor-to-ceiling windows that separated the living room from the balcony.

"Good afternoon, thanks for coming. I'm Estelle Cone." Janet turned around and looked up at the much taller woman. "Janis Goodrich." The squeeze at the end of the handshake was almost a caress, which Janet returned without thinking. "May I get you something to drink? Coffee, tea, hot chocolate, or something stronger? It's still a bit chilly out there."

"It is." Janet unzipped the charcoal-gray down vest she wore over a cream-colored turtleneck sweater and shoved the black beret into a pocket. The sweater, vest and hat, along with fashionable, expensive jeans and comfortable, worn, thick-soled cowboy boots, contrasted with Estelle's dark charcoal-gray pinstriped suit, white blouse, and stylish red tie. It was expensive,

411

fashionable, and screamed lesbian. Estelle took the vest and headed for a nearby closet.

"Stronger, as in…?"

"Wine. We have a nice Shiraz, merlot, and a chardonnay. All from numbered bottles from Mondavi's private collections."

"Shiraz or merlot would be fine." Janet took a plate from the living room side of the see-through counter to the kitchen. On it went chunks of brie, cheddar, and what she thought was gruyère, along with several baguette slices.

A smiling Estelle handed her a glass of wine. "Cheers."

"Cheers."

"What brings you to Chicago? I hear a long lost local accent."

"I grew up on the north side and left after graduating from college…."

Janet let her voice trail off. Estelle put her hand gestured in the direction of the couch, as if to say, "Let's sit and talk." "Where do you live now?"

Janet sat at one end of the couch, leaving a cushion between herself and Estelle. "California. I have a small ranch near Palmdale."

"How small?" Estelle was qualifying the visitor to see if she had the wherewithal to pay for a condo that started at half a million.

"It's about 500 acres."

"I know nothing about ranching, so I'll ask the obvious, stupid question. Do you raise cattle?"

"No. I let my neighbors use about half of the land for grazing and growing hay. The rest is hilly and wooded. My house is at four-thousand feet above sea level."

"So what brings you to this open house?"

"As my parents get older, I want a place nearby." It wasn't a total lie.

"What kind of business are you in?"

"I'm retired. I lucked into a lot of money, so I do what I want." Janet loved saying that.

Estelle's eyebrow rose a millimeter or two. The woman had just qualified herself as a buyer. "Good for you." Estelle stood up and held out her hand. "Let's take a tour of the condo." She gave a knowing smile, and Janet felt her loins stir.

In one bedroom, decorated as an office, Estelle pointed to a section of concrete on a stand. "That's a model of how we prevent you hearing your neighbors, no matter how much noise they make. In addition to the concrete, there's three inches of foam. You could fire a gun next door and, unless it was a cannon, we wouldn't hear it."

That means a .380 with a suppressor would work nicely.

Estelle continued with her spiel. "We have video cameras in the elevators, halls, and lobby. Future residents are very interested in our security center. If you'd like, I can take you down there."

"Yes, I'd like to see that." *And what they can see.* Estelle told her associate where they were going and turned to Janet.

"Follow me." In the spacious security center, Estelle stood directly behind Janet and let her breasts press against Janet. Janet took it as deliberately sexual and responded by tilting her head back to intensify the pressure.

The security surveillance was good enough that Janet realized a disguise would be needed. After the security manager showed her the locks, however, she knew that picking them would be easy.

After the tour, Estelle smiled as she looked at Janet, and her eyes asked the question her mouth wouldn't speak. Janet's eyes sparkled. Neither woman said anything on the elevator ride back to the tenth floor and the condo where the open house was being held. "So, what do you think?"

"Very nice." It was meant, and taken, as a double entendre. Estelle looked at her gold Rolex President with diamonds around the bezel. "How about a drink and then maybe dinner?"

We'll never make it to a restaurant. I want to make love to this woman!

"Don't you have to stay for the open house?"

"No. I'm the president of the real estate company. I have more associates here to meet with prospects."

"What time?"

"How about now?"

Janet's eyes gave Estelle the answer.

Two hours later, Estelle was still breathing heavily as she propped herself on her elbow. She traced the scars on Janet's leg and then moved to the ones on her hip and bicep. "You've got some interesting scars."

"They came from an auto accident. A wealthy producer ran a red light and I got a nice settlement. My turn."

"I'm all answers."

"Are you always this aggressive with strangers?"

"Yes, when I see something I want. Look, I just turned fifty, and I like to get to the bottom line quickly." Estelle ran her fingers around Janet's breasts and then down to her wet crotch. "When you came into the room, you interested me. You're clothes screamed butch, but you could have been femme. When you responded, I couldn't wait to get you into bed."

Janet shifted so she could lick Estelle's clitoris. The older woman moaned and put both her hands on Janet's head. "OHHHHHHHH!" Estelle gasped and shook with pleasure. "Stop, please stop...."

"O.K. So tell me, were you always lez? When did you know?" Janet was genuinely curious. What had it been like, before the decade of free love?

"Mmmm. I didn't date much before college. In high school, girls who liked girls were pariahs, and nice Jewish girls definitely aren't supposed to be lesbians. But I wasn't very interested in boys, so I focused on my studies. After my parents got divorced, home just wasn't the same, so I decided to go to a college out of state. I went to Bennington College, which should be called Lesbian College." Estelle laughed quietly. "My first roommate went to Bennington solely so she could be a lesbian in public, not because it was a good school—which it is. Anyway, within a week, she was teaching me. I was a virgin, and she took my virginity. But... she was more interested in sex than school work and flunked out after one semester."

"And then?"

"Ah." She smiled. "During my first spring semester, a professor took me under her wing. God, that was an education. She really knew what she was doing when she made love to me."

Estelle sat up against the headboard and caressed Janet's hair as her head lay on her upper thigh. She could feel Janet's breath on her vagina as her new lover's fingers caressed her. The waves of pleasure made it hard to talk.

"Hmmmmm, Janis, you're really good at this..."

"Thanks. So are you."

Estelle moved her hand to caress Janet's rear and her sex. "Where was I?"

"Bennington."

"Oh, yeah. As soon as I got back for my sophomore year, this professor introduced me to bondage. She wanted me to be a slave and help her train other slaves. During the Christmas break, she was fired. The word was that she violated some morality clause in her contract—OHHHHH!" Estelle shuddered as Janet found her sweet spot and an orgasm consumed her.

When the waves of pleasure subsided, Janet wanted to pick up the conversation. "What did you tell your mother?"

Estelle smiled. "This is the really cool thing. We were having one of those mother-daughter talks when I told her that I was a lesbian. She said she'd known it all along because of the way I looked at other women. Then she dropped a bombshell on me by saying she was bi. Her desire to be with other women was what led to the divorce. My dad couldn't live with it."

"Were you surprised?"

"Oh, yeah. Big time. Here's the great part. We started going to lesbian bars together to find lovers. We even shared a woman on more than one occasion."

"That's a great story!"

Estelle cupped Janet's chin in her hand. "Your turn."

"Mine is not so interesting. I've had both men and women, and I prefer women." Janet told her about her first college roommate and the parties she went to where group sex was the norm.

Janet stopped as memories of those days ran through her head. Estelle asked, "Do you like sex with men?"

"Short answer is, rarely. I haven't in years. Longer answer is, if you can get a man who likes pleasing a woman and you both come together, there's nothing like it. I found only one."

"And who was he?"

"My husband."

"Are you divorced?"

"Technically, I'm a widow. My husband was a POW who never came home." *Well, he's home now, and I want to, but don't want to, see him again. There's way too much water under the bridge.*

"Oh, shit, I'm sorry I asked."

"No big deal. Anyway, I became a lesbian full time after he was shot down."

Tuesday, April 20, 1982, 1700 local time, Chicago

Janet had learned to trust The Broker's "resources." All the firearms his contacts provided were zeroed in and either brand new or barely used, and the information he provided was always accurate. Even so, she followed Reagan's motto of trusting but verifying through her own reconnaissance.

Before going to the Harbor Point Condominium complex, Janet pretended to read a book in the hotel lobby to see who delivered the envelope that contained a locker key, and if anyone arrived or stayed to see who picked it up. After sitting in the lobby for two hours after it arrived, Janet went to her room and called the front desk to have it delivered.

Today was no different. After two hours of waiting in Union Station, other than a bag lady with two carts of junk, no one had been in the area longer than thirty minutes. A trip to the bathroom gave her another scan of the area before she got the bag out of the locker.

Back in her hotel room, Janet field-stripped the Browning and examined each cartridge before slipping it into the barrel to make sure it fit. Satisfied that the rounds would not jam, she loaded the four twelve-round magazines.

Next, she screwed on the suppressor, and with a loaded magazine aimed at "targets" in her room. Satisfied that she had the feel of the weapon, Janet dropped a round in the chamber.

Her tour of the security center had showed her that the stairwells of the fifty-four-story building were not monitored. From the underground parking lot, she entered the stairwell, knowing that to exit onto any floor but the lobby she was going to have to jimmy the door open.

Latex gloves made it a bit harder to work the picks, but once she had the door to the 12th floor unlocked, Janet pulled a floppy hat down over the shoulder-length blonde wig and walked to O'Reilly's door. Her plan was simple. Ring the doorbell and, if he answered, smack him in the face and get into the apartment. Or, pick the lock and wait for him.

Janet pushed the doorbell and waited. Not hearing a voice, she slipped the picks into the lock and easily opened it.

Inside, Janet put down her purse and the camera bag she was carrying on the tile floor and listened. Out came the BDA with its suppressor.

She cleared the condo, then closed the living room's floor-to-ceiling curtains. On the large, glass-topped coffee table in front of a couch she mounted a small video camera on a tripod.

Now that she was ready, Janet thought about Estelle's invitation for tonight. When she'd told the realtor that she was having dinner with an old friend, the older woman had smiled and said, "Great. Come over when you're done and we can pick up where left off. I have some special toys we can play with." When Janet asked what that meant, Estelle laughed and said, "Come and find out."

Janet moved to a position behind the door when she heard a key turn in the lock. After O'Reilly closed the door, she sent him sprawling with a blow to his neck, followed by a kick to the back of his knees.

O'Reilly was trying to get up when she kicked him in the ribs. The blow knocked him on his back. He gasped for breath as he as he looked up at his assailant. "Who are you?"

Janet pointed the BDA at the center of O'Reilly's chest. "Stand up."

When O'Reilly paused on his knees, Janet bitch-slapped him on each cheek. He held up a hand. "Just let me get up. Don't hit me!"

Janet kept the gun leveled at him as she stepped back. O'Reilly stood, bent over with his hands on his knees. Janet hit him again on the side of the head.

O'Reilly staggered but managed to say upright. He held up both hands, palms out in front of him. "Please, don't hit me anymore. Tell Vincenzo, or whoever sent you, that I will make it right no matter what he wants."

"Vincenzo didn't send me. And you can never make right what you did."

Janet shifted the gun to her left hand and punched O'Reilly as hard as she could in the solar plexus. She felt the softness of his muscles give way. *The man doesn't work out.* O'Reilly's mouth opened but no words came out. He put his hand on the back of the chair to keep from falling over as he gasped for breath.

"I said, don't hit me!"

Janet ignored him. "Sit on the couch, in front of the camera."

As O'Reilly moved gingerly toward the sofa, Janet's tone became more imperious. "Is this how long you resisted before you spilled your guts to the North Vietnamese?"

"You have no idea what I went through!"

"Oh, yes, I do." *Don't let your emotions get involved. Keep focused.* "You are going to do what you are good at, which is confess. This time, however, you are going to tell the truth about what you told the North Vietnamese."

"I told them a fairy tale. Nothing they could ever use."

"Bullshit. That's a lie and you know it."

`"They beat me."

"Like I did?"

"Worse."

"You should have been court martialed for collaborating with the enemy."

"The government doesn't have any witnesses, or enough evidence."

"They do now. A birdie told me that you were about to be recalled and tried. The government wouldn't do it unless they knew they could win. You're going to be stood up against a wall and shot."

"I doubt it." He actually smirked.

Janet fired a round into the couch two inches from O'Reilly's torso.

"Start talking. Name, rank and what you told the North Vietnamese. Tell the truth, or this is going to be very, very painful." She turned the camera on.

"You can't make me talk."

Janet fired a second round because she didn't want her voice on the tape. This one slammed into the concrete an inch from O'Reilly's ear. A chip opened a wound on his cheek. He flinched and paled. Slowly and deliberately, Janet aimed the gun at his crotch. He recoiled, and started talking.

"I'm Richard Aloysius O'Reilly, Commander United States Navy, retired. I was a prisoner of the North Vietnamese. During the first six months of my captivity, I told them everything I knew about the Standard Arm Missile, the Navy and Air Forces electronic warfare tactics and anything else the North Vietnamese and their Soviet allies wanted to know. I was debriefed extensively by a Soviet officer by the name of Nikolai Gorov, who was an expert in surface-to-air missile tactics, and others who were experts in electronic warfare…."

According to the camera's counter, O'Reilly talked for fifty-three minutes. At the end, he leaned back and spread both arms on the couch. "There, I confessed. And you can never use that tape in court, because it was obtained by coercion. No judge would admit it as evidence. Now you know. Are you happy? Now, go fuck yourself and get out of my life."

Janet pulled the VHS cassette out of the tape recorder and slid it in her backpack.

"What's this to you, anyway? Who are you?"

"Randy Pulaski's wife. You put a hit out on him. Except you became the mark. Rot in hell." Janet watched O'Reilly's jaw drop as his brain processed that he'd been double-crossed. It was his last thought as a .380 hollow-point bullet between his eyeballs ended his life.

Janet left the camera and tripod. She'd wiped it clean before she left O'Reilly's apartment. On went a different wig and hat. She pulled off her jeans, rolled and stuffed them into the pack, along with the running shoes. On came a mid-calf skirt, and a pair of heels and a floppy hat that was pulled down over her eyes.

The gun and suppressor went into separate bags in her purse. She left the same way she entered—through the stairwell.

On the way back to her hotel, the latex gloves went into a trash bin in front of a coffee shop. She dropped another bag into a trashcan on East Lower Wacker, and the third in the Metro station at Wabash and Randolph.

It was 1939 by her Rolex when Janet pulled off the wig. She had enough time to change into a dress, clean her hands with bleach to remove any gunshot residue, rub lotion over her hands, and still make it to Estelle's apartment by around eight-thirty. On the way t, her clothes and wigs went into another trashcan.

"Excuse me, ma'am, are you a resident?" The security guard approached Janet as she headed for the elevator.

"No, I am not. I'm going up to Ms. Estelle Cone's condo. She's expecting me."

"Would you please wait until I call her? May I give her your name?"

On the tour, she'd been told the security policy required that all visitors sign in, and residents had to approve their entry. "Sure, tell her Janis Goodrich is on the way up."

The guard came over to the elevator smiling. "She's expecting you." With that, he slid his magnetic card key into the slot and pushed the button that would send the elevator to the fortieth floor, where Estelle had two two-bedroom condos combined in a single unit. It gave her almost twenty-five hundred square feet of prime real estate. Out of habit, Janet stood on the side of the door.

The door opened and Estelle smiled at the sight of her guest. "So glad you could come. My, you're all dressed up."

"Jeans weren't appropriate for Spiaggia."

"How was dinner?"

"Very good and outrageously expensive."

"Care for wine?"

"Sure. What are you having?"

"You."

"Perfect."

A wave of the arm directed Janet to the couch. Estelle's tight black leather skirt came only half way down her thighs. Her four-inch heels had straps that wound up to her knees. Janet could see the black leather bra. After she sat down, Estelle curled one leg up under herself and smiled. "Let's talk about what we want to do tonight. We've got some exciting choices."

Janet let their fingers intertwine. "How about you surprising me?" *I would like to really get to know this woman, but there is no way I could have a long-term relationship without revealing my past. Any evasion would make her suspicious, and she would never trust me. Damn, damn, damn. I need a new life!*

"That's an open book?"

"I'll let you know if I'm uncomfortable."

"And if I don't stop immediately, you'll karate chop me?"

Janet laughed. "Something like that."

Estelle gently tugged on Janet's hand and both women moved to the center of the couch so they could kiss. The taller women spoke first. "That's a great way to get started."

Thursday, April 22, 1982, 1358 local time, Washington, DC

An opened box sat in the center of Admiral Haggerty's desk. Standing in front of his desk was the young lieutenant commander in charge of building the case against O'Reilly.

"So, Wellington, tell me what is sitting on my desk?"

"Admiral, sir.... The tape and the note arrived today by courier. The security people examined it and made sure it was not a bomb. The note, I am told, could have been printed on any computer printer. It says, '*Here is O'Reilly's confession. There is no need to court martial him because justice has been served.'* There's no name on the note, and the return address on the package is bogus."

"Do we know where O'Reilly is?"

"We do, sir. He's in the Chicago city morgue, the victim of what the police told me was a professional hit. There's no evidence of a struggle. The lock was picked and there are no unusual fingerprints on either the video camera, the tripod, or anywhere in the apartment. The only prints they found were either O'Reilly's or the prints of the girls he dated. So far, all their alibis check out."

"Have you watched this tape?"

"No, sir."

"Then let's have a look. When we're done, we'll decide what to do next."

Thursday, April 29, 1982, 2112 local time, Cologne, West Germany

The 142-room Grand Hotel Excelsior Hotel Ernst was one of the oldest in Cologne. Having barely survived World War II, it had being rebuilt in the 1950s, and was run by the same family that had bought it from the original owners in 1871.

After completing an assignment in Antwerp, Janet drove to

Cologne. Dressed in clothes she'd bought in Brussels, Janet leaned over the concierge's ornate desk. "Do you know which is the best club to meet people my age?"

The man nodded and responded in accented English. "Are you looking for a man or a woman?"

Janet wasn't surprised by the man's question. She'd decided to visit Cologne for a few days because she'd heard it had one of Germany's largest gay communities. "Woman."

The concierge opened a drawer and pulled out a stack of cards. Several went into a pile on the desk before he found the one he wanted. He scribbled a note on the back that to Janet was unintelligible. "Tonight is a good night to go to the Blue Ox. Take this card and they will give you a fifty percent discount on their cover charge. Try their pretzels—they are the best in the city— and drink a sweet dessert wine called *spätlese*. It is served cold and is very good. If you don't like wine, any of the beers on tap are excellent." He bobbed his head and smiled. "The pretzels are in special shapes."

"Danke." Janet had executed several hits in Germany and knew the word for "Thanks."

In one of the hotel's clothing boutique windows she saw a short leather mini-skirt that she had to have. She'd always wanted one, and the soft, black leather fit her like a glove. As she tried it on, she thought of Estelle.

When she left the hotel, she wore the skirt and a tight-fitting, light gray sweater. Janet thought the outfit was sexy, even provocative. Her black pumps were not the usual stilettos, however; she hated wearing high heels.

At the Blue Ox, the card worked its magic. Janet picked a chair near the end of the bar on the second floor, so she could watch the dance floor and listen to the soft, romantic music.

Even in the dim light, the shapes of the pretzels in the sampler made her smile. Several were penises. Others looked like a woman's breast. One was shaped to look like a woman's vagina.

Her glass of Schloss Leiser Rhein *Spätlese* was just as

advertised—clear, light, ice cold, and refreshing. Janet was on her second glass when a woman eased herself onto the bar stool next to her and ordered Kölsch, Cologne's unique beer.

The blonde picked up the beer in her left hand, took a sip, and turned to look at the dance floor. It gave Janet time to admire the woman's stylish off-white cashmere sweater and black leather pants, which glistened in the overhead lights.

After watching couples move around the dance floor, the woman slowly turned back and stared at Janet for a few seconds. "Luna?"

Janet hadn't heard that name since the last time she'd talked to Enrique in Miami. That had been ten years before. The only other time she'd used the name had been in Cuba. "Monika?"

"Yes, it is I." Her English was clear, even less accented than when they'd shared a cabin in the Escambray Mountains. "This is a pleasant surprise. At first I thought it was you, and then I thought, 'No, impossible.' Then I decided to take a chance. You look wonderful."

Janet reached out and touched the forearm that was holding the beer. Monika put the glass down. "Thank you. The years have been kind to you, too."

"Are you in Cologne for a vacation, or working?" Monika kept her voice even, but she'd had steeled herself to start this conversation. *Luna, what I really want to know is if you are here to kill me. The Cubans told me that if I ever revealed any details about my training, they would hunt me down and kill me. I haven't told my parents much about my Cuban "vacation" and they haven't asked.*

Janet shook her head. "Vacation. I had some work in Belgium and came to see Cologne. What are you doing these days?"

"I never finished my training. I am done with the Cubans and the revolutionaries. If you can believe it, I joined the capitalists!"

"What happened?" Janet knew that failing the course meant you might wind up in the bottom of a dirt-covered pit. Few, if any, were sent back to their home countries early.

"Well, about a month after you left, I was on that insane rope climbing exercise where you climb up that thick, fifty-meter-long rope, get to the top, hold on while you take something out of your pack and put it on the bar, then slide down."

"Yeah, I remember that. You weren't the only one who had trouble getting to the top."

"It took me a while to learn the technique, but I finally managed."

Janet nodded, as if to say "Continue."

"That day, something happened. They never told me what, but I think the bolts holding the beam broke, and I dropped fifteen meters. The only thing keeping me from falling was the rope looped around my right wrist. When I came to an abrupt stop, I felt bones in my arm snap as my arm was ripped out of my shoulder joint. I was screaming and flailing around, trying to get my left hand back onto the rope. I couldn't, and I dropped another ten meters or so."

"Oh, my God." It was all Janet could say.

Monika looked down. "Later, they told me I hung there for nearly fifteen minutes. I don't remember it; I kept fading in and out of consciousness. As they loaded me in the ambulance, I could see my right hand was black. I woke up the next morning with bandages up and down my arm. The Cuban doctor told me that my arm was permanently paralyzed."

Monika turned to let Janet see that her arm was hanging straight down. "My shoulder, elbow and wrist joints were completely dislocated, and all the nerves and ligaments were severed in several places. They said that if I had hung much longer, the arm would have been ripped off. If that had happened, I would have fallen to the rocky ground and probably died."

Janet stood up and wrapped her arms around Monika. "I am so, so sorry."

The German woman pushed her away gently. "Don't be. Actually, I think it turned out to be a good thing."

"Why?"

"They kept me in the hospital for four weeks, until they were sure there was no infection, and then they took the cast off. They didn't even attempt to help me adapt to having only one usable arm. Instead, they sent me back to Germany with two-hundred fifty-thousand deutschmark as a settlement and medical records saying I had been in a rope climbing accident at an adventure park. After all, you can't be a forger with only one working hand."

Monika picked up her right hand and placed it on her lap. "I am very lucky. They could have killed me. Instead, they said someone would contact me when I am back in Germany, where I could help recruit more students."

"That's very unlike the Cubans."

"I know. At first I was scared and expected a bullet in my back any day, but nothing happened. Twice they asked me to talk to a fellow student, and I did. After that, I got one or two calls to remind me that I was not to divulge anything about my training in Cuba. I haven't been contacted in years, but I am still afraid that one day, it will resurface."

"Me too. I worry about it all the time."

Monika stopped to take a sip of her beer. "I am sorry if I am distressing you."

Janet put her hand on Monika's arm. "Oh, no, trust me, you are not. Please go on."

"My parents let me stay at home while I took an advanced degree in physical therapy. I promised them I would abandon my radical views. Now, I work with patients who have been injured in an accident or lost limbs to cancer. I like the work very much." Monika giggled and took another sip of her beer. "Imagine me as a member of the bourgeoisie!"

Paranoia made Janet suspicious. *Was Monika here by chance? Or is something sinister about to happen? The Cubans may have blackmailed her into setting me up because they don't like the idea I went freelance even though they are contacting me through The Broker? Or, it could be another one of The Broker's clients who see me as a loose end?*

Janet wanted to finish what started in Cuba. She wanted to make love to this woman and her desire for sex pushed her fear out of her mind. Her gut also said it was O.K. and it was never wrong. She looked into Monika's intense blue eyes. "So, do you have a lover?"

"No. I broke up with my last one almost a year ago. We'd been together for three years. Nothing since, other than one night stands. You?"

"No. I've not been in a relationship for many years."

Monika leaned forward. Slowly, she extended her left hand to touch Janet' hair, then slid her fingers behind the back of Janet's head. They kissed, and the kiss deepened as their tongues touched and danced.

"I have been waiting a very long twelve years to do that. When I thought I recognized you, the first thing that went through my mind was *'Is it really you? If it is, you are not getting away this time.* I have dreamed of what it would be like to make love to you. At odd moments, I would find myself wondering what you were doing."

Janet rested her forehead on Monika's. "I'm here, and I want to make love to you. Back in Cuba, when you had your hands up my shorts, it was all I could do to ask you to stop. I wanted more, so much more."

"I remember that night very clearly."

Janet reached for her purse and took out two hundred Deutsche mark notes. It was more than enough to cover a beer, two glasses of *spätlese* and a pretzel sampler. As she placed it on the counter, Janet caressed Monika's cheek and kissed her softly on her lips. "Let's make up for the past twelve years."

Friday, April 30, 1982, 0924 local time, Cologne

Janet propped herself up on the pillows and basked in the sun streaming through the window. When Monika rolled over, Janet guided her head so that her cheek rested on her right thigh, and watched Monika's chest move slowly as she breathed. Her fingers

427

went up and down Monika's side before caressing her right breast, bringing it to life. Monika moaned softly.

Not since Helen and she were lovers, had Janet felt this relaxed and at peace. Even the longer, on and off again relationships with Brittney and Sandra were mostly about sex. This was different, because she didn't have to be guarded about what she did for a living. Monika knew about the training and could guess the rest.

Janet's hand caressed Monika's vulva. Her fingers went inside the vagina and, as they slid out, they gently touched Monika's clit. A soft, dreamy voice encouraged her. "Keep doing that."

It was time to repay the favor of last night, when each orgasm Janet had was stronger than the one before. Her body had shook with pleasure that was so intense it bordered on pain. Janet gently pushed on Monika's knees. Instead of opening them to let Janet continue, the German girl rolled on her side and pushed Janet on her back.

Janet didn't resist and let her mind and body submit to the pleasure until she couldn't take it anymore. Just before she felt she was going to pass out, she begged Monika to stop, but all she got was a grin and more pleasure. "Oh, my God..." were the only words she could speak.

Monika stopped long enough to kiss her lover's face. "I love the taste of you."

Janet's chest was still heaving from her last orgasm and she struggled to get out the words, "I love what you do to me!"

The German sat next to Janet, gently stroking her stomach while she waited for Janet to come down from her pleasure high. After Janet pushed herself into a sitting potion, Monika straddled her thighs and pulled her right arm into her lap. "Being with you again makes me happy, very happy."

Janet smiled, not knowing what to say. She squeezed her lover's hand.

"Luna, I need to tell you something."

Janet lay on her side with her head propped up on a pillow.

"What is it?"

Monika lifted her paralyzed hand. "My arm is dying. Some of the bones are just about dead, and they cause infections. Each one is worse than the other. I've had two surgeries already to correct the problem, and they bought me some time. But if the condition is allowed to continue, it could be fatal. So, I am faced with two choices. One is to have another operation, in which they open up the arm from shoulder to wrist to try to repair the damage to the arteries. The doctors say, depending on what they find, it has a fifty to sixty percent chance of fixing the circulation permanently. But, more likely, in a few years, the condition will return. My other choice is to have the arm amputated, which really doesn't change anything because I have been living one-handed ever since the accident."

Janet took both Monika's hands in her own.

"After going back and forth many times, I decided to have my arm removed at the shoulder, because it is a permanent fix. The day we met, I'd had a blood test. If the infection is gone, they'll schedule surgery as soon as they can."

"Monika, if that's what you want to do, it's fine with me. I'll like you either way."

"I was hoping you would say that." Monika nodded and pushed her right arm off to the side as if she was done talking about it. "Luna, if we are going to have a future together, we need to know who we really are. Let's start with our real names. Can you do that?"

Janet got into the same position facing Monika. The movement gave her time to think. When she'd gotten to Cologne, she'd called The Broker from a Bundespost office to tell him that she was taking some time off. So, it was now or never. "You want to know my born name, or the name that I use when I am home, or the one I use in my..." Janet searched for a word and came up with one she knew Monika would understand, "...work?"

"Let's start with our born names. I'll go first to make it easy." Monika took a deep breath. "I was born Karin Egger. Egger means digger in German. Monika Arndorfer is dead."

"You said no one has contacted you since you were in college?"

"No. Well, I am not sure. Back in 1976, a crazy person by the name of Dieter Stiglitz led a terrorist group called Red Hand. One day, a student I knew from before I went to Cuba sat down next to me. We had been to meetings that denounced the West German government and capitalism. He asked if I was interested in learning more about Red Hand. I told him no, and I never heard from him again."

"Do you think he knew about Cuba?"

"I don't know. I was pretty far left in those days, and not the only student who believed that if the government didn't become more socialist it should be overthrown by revolutionary means. There still are many German students who think that way. My *vati* —my dad—told me a couple of years after I came back that he wasn't worried, because most young people grow out of wanting to be revolutionaries. He said as long as it didn't result in someone like Stalin or Hitler, it was more or less normal. Now the only associations I am a member of are related to my profession. Now I believe that pure socialism will never work. It doesn't allow for individuals to do what they want and chase their dreams. Everything is programmed, like, well, like a computer. So now I like capitalism and its freedoms." Karin paused. "Your turn."

"It is great that the Cubans left you alone." Janet took a deep breath. "My parents named me Julia Amy, and their last name was Lucas." This was not only going to be hard, it was going to be very risky. But if she wanted to have a relationship with this beautiful woman, she had to trust her. "When I moved to California, I changed my name to Janet Williams, and then I married and became Janet Williams Pulaski."

"Why did you change your name?"

"I wanted to get away from my family. They kicked me out of the house because I was so radical. It was a way of disassociating myself from them, so let's use Janet Williams for now. As you can imagine, I have several identities."

"O.K., Janet. I understand." Karin changed the subject. "Are you divorced?"

"No. It is a long story." Janet told her about Randy.

"Now that he is back, why don't you go back to him?"

"I can't. I just can't." Janet's voice tailed off.

"Why not?"

There it was, the question that she asked herself often. "I'm a lesbian. And, I'm butch, if you know what I mean. I haven't had sex with a man in years. I don't want to. I need a woman like you to satisfy me." *There is a second reason. It is called my profession.*

Monika took Janet's hand. "The more masculine my lover is, the better I like her."

"What about in Cuba?"

Karin took a deep breath as her mind brought back details she had not thought about in years. "Cuba. One of the female instructors came up to me one Saturday after you left and whispered in my ear that she had the same needs as I did and to meet her in cabin two."

"I thought that homosexuality was forbidden in the camp."

"It was, but she had strong desires like I did, and we needed to satisfy them. We were only together five or six times. It wasn't enough."

"I had trouble going without sex for that long."

Karin took Janet's hand and pressed it on her right breast. Janet obliged with a few caresses that caused Karin to sigh with pleasure.

"When I was growing up, I never let a boy touch me. I would look at other girls and dream about having sex with them. When I started at the University of Cologne, I was looking for an apartment. I found a landlady who had several reasonably priced furnished flats. Greta Scholz was in her late fifties, and she insisted on interviewing every student who rented from her. We were sitting in her living room and I noticed a picture of a young woman wearing prison clothes. So, I asked if that was her mother. Greta said 'No, that was me. My parents took it after the Nazis imprisoned me because of my sexual preferences. They let me out in 1944 only if I agreed to marry an SS officer and bear him children.' He was killed during what you Americans called the Battle of the Bulge. By then, she was pregnant with twin girls. The Nazis jailed lesbians and transsexuals early in the war. In 1943, they let out the gay men because they needed soldiers."

"I never knew that. What happened then?"

"I told her I loved the apartment."

Janet leaned over and French kissed her lover. "And then?"

Karin giggled. "It is very boring."

"Karin, there is nothing about you that is dull."

The German girl shifted position so that she was sitting on her folded up legs. "Greta asked me if I wanted to look at the apartment again, just to make sure. I said yes. I was looking out the window when she came up behind me and put her hands on my arms and kissed the back of my neck. My knees buckled and she caught me. She turned me around and asked me, 'Is this your first time with a woman?' I told her I was a virgin. She kissed me and said, 'Wonderful. I will teach you.' After I moved in, we would make love in her apartment or my flat. She was a wonderful teacher!"

"Did your parents know?"

"Oh, yes. When my brother and I were in school, he would introduce me to women he thought were lesbians. Most of the time he was wrong!" Karin reached out and touched Janet's cheek with her finger tips. "Your turn."

"How I became a lesbian is certainly not as interesting as yours." Karin waved her hand as if to say "Come on, tell me," and smiled. "Let me be the judge of that."

"O.K., here goes." Janet paused to gather her thoughts. "I was a tomboy. In America, that means I did a lot of boy things like hunting, and camping, and I played sports with my dad, two brothers, and my sister. In college, I tried threesomes and group sex with guys, and was never satisfied. One night, my roommate Gracie put her arms around my shoulders and said she could help me. A couple of hours later, I couldn't believe what I had experienced. It was great, but I still believed that I wanted to have sex with men." Janet made a face that said, "How stupid of me to think that." She told Karin about Randy, and then Helen.

"Did Helen's husband come home?"

"Yes. We had split up before then. She is now a lawyer and, among other things, a champion of gay and lesbian rights. Helen divorced her husband soon after he came home."

"Do you still keep in touch with her?"

"No. Helen and I have very different sexual interests. She is very much into bondage and discipline."

"Have you tried it? It is big here in Germany."

Janet's mind raced back to her second night with Estelle, who had tied her up in several different positions. The orgasms had been intense. "Yes, once. It is certainly different."

"I haven't, although, with the right partner, I might try it." Karin looked at Janet as if to say, "With you, I would consider it."

"After Helen, I wandered around in the sexual wilderness. I had lovers, but nothing steady or long lasting."

Karin looked down and began to stroke Janet's thigh. "Are you lonely?"

Janet looked at Karin as if she had been stabbed with a knife. She shuddered, not from pleasure or pain, but from the release of emotion. Tears flooded down her cheeks. The dam broke. "Yes. I am tired of being alone."

Karin awkwardly shifted positions so she could pull Janet on top of her. "You're not alone anymore." She could feel Janet's tears wet her breasts.

Saturday, May 1, 1982, 1100 local time, Arlington
DIA's headquarters complex had started out as an all-girls school, until 1942 when the buildings were taken over by the Army's Security Agency under the War Powers Act. When the

433

DIA was created in 1961, the four-story buildings known as Arlington Station Buildings A and B became its headquarters.

Randy plunked a stack of six coffee cups and an unopened bottle of Balvenie DoubleWood twelve-year-old scotch on the table. "Every year, on the anniversary of the fall of Poland, the creation of the Free Polish Army, and the end of World War II, my father drinks a glass of whiskey in one swallow and then throws it into the fireplace, cursing the Germans first and then the Russians."

No one said anything while Randy finished opening the bottle and poured at least two fingers into each cup. "Today, and every year on the anniversary date of our freedom and the anniversary of Karl's death, we will get together. Josh, if you and Marty want to come, we will be honored to have you. At this gathering, we toast Karl and Hank, our freedom, and this great country."

The four others nodded. "Gentleman, unfortunately we don't have a fireplace in this room, so we will have to dispense with that part of the ritual, but the next time, we will damn the Vietnamese and whomever killed Karl."

He handed a cup to each of the others present and held up his. "To Hank Cho, may he never be forgotten, and may he rest in peace."

The men touched their cups. "Here, here. To Hank Cho. May he rest in peace."

Hidden in the single malt scotch was a faintly sweet flavor; Josh thought he smelled honey or and vanilla, along with a faint taste of sherry. Later, when he read the label, he'd learn that the whiskey was aged in traditional oak casks before being transferred to Oloroso sherry casks.

"To Karl Kramer, may he rest in peace." Again, they touched cups and drank. No other words were spoken for a minute or two, then Josh asked, "What's the latest on the shooting?"

"Jeff, you tell them. You had the last conversation with the FBI." Josh was surprised, thinking that the Virginia police would be in charge. "FBI?"

"Yes, FBI, and since automatic weapons were used, the Bureau of Alcohol, Tobacco and Firearms is also involved. The shooters used Israeli-made nine-millimeter Uzi submachine guns. The Feds tracked down the license plate we gave them and raided a warehouse. In the shootout, one gang member was killed and three arrested. They found the two guns used to attack us, among many other illegal weapons. One of the gang member gave up the low-life middleman who hired him. His name is Bobby Wales. They raided his house and storefront, but he was long gone. There is a nationwide manhunt for him. The Feds want to know who hired the contract. They think it is a very short list."

Josh asked what he thought was an obvious question. "Why?"

Randy answered that one. "Well, only a very few people knew we were here in DC. At the top of the list is Gary Reginald Savoy. Ever meet him?"

When Josh shook his head, Randy went on grimly. "He's the bastard who ignored the evidence that we, and others, were still alive in Southeast Asia. Having us show up alive and well after he missed or ignored the intelligence for the past nine years is probably career threatening. Here's where it gets ugly. The first DIA officer to lead the review team was assassinated shortly after the project started. I'm betting the Feds will find the gun that killed him among the ones they just captured. Now the Feds want to talk to Savoy, but they can't find him."

No one said anything, so Jeff continued. "Just so you know, Ashley has been moved to a secure location, and we've been told to make ourselves scarce."

"What are you guys planning to do?" As he spoke, Josh looked at Marty, who nodded ever so slightly.

Randy answered. "We are scheduled for an award ceremony at the White House. After that, Greg will go back to his family farm. It's in the middle of nowhere, and any strangers will be immediately noticed. The rest of us are not sure."

Josh leaned forward and put his hands on the table. "Randy, do you want to hide or flush the murderers out?"

"I don't like hiding. Jeff?"

"I prefer to be on the offensive and be in the driver's seat."

Josh's mind was in high gear as he nodded. "Good, I think Marty and I can come up with a plan that will work."

"You're going to have to sell it to the Feds."

"Randy, does the FBI know for sure that there is still a contract out on you guys?"

"They believe there is still an unfinished contract. Now that the first set of shooters have been captured, the price will go up and there will be more takers, assuming the buyer is still willing to pay, or if he hired more than one team."

Marty watched his friend. When Josh's mind was racing, Marty's job was to make sure whatever came out was practical. Josh kept going. "I don't like going to funerals, particularly ones that put the good guys in the ground before they've reached a ripe old age."

Randy waved the bottle of scotch. "Amen to that."

"Good, let's have a quiet dinner and figure out what to do. I've got some ideas."

The same day, 1832 local time, London

Staying at a small hotel in the Bayswater neighborhood appealed to Gary, because it was trendy and off the beaten track. Black men weren't uncommon in London, and his Canadian passport explained his lack of a British accent.

Everything Savoy valued was in a single suitcase and briefcase. Clothes he could buy anywhere. His collection of valid passports, driver's licenses, and credit cards, along with the bank account numbers and passwords, committed to memory, were the keys to his new life.

Gary estimated he had twenty-four to forty-eight hours to get off the grid. London was a convenient stopping point because there were flights to everywhere. Once he left London, the long hands of the CIA and its friends became weaker and weaker.

Savoy had the outline of an escape plan just in case he ever got wind of the CIA or FBI beginning to dig into his activities in Africa, or his relationship with Payá. He executed his departure from the land of his birth the as soon as it became clear that the agency might decide to scapegoat him. And, if CIA accountants began digging into his past, they'd learn that he'd skimmed millions. But he'd been careful. Dummy and now-defunct businesses and destroyed records would make it difficult, if not impossible, for them to find the ten million in bank accounts in Switzerland and Liechtenstein. It was money for a rainy day—and the thunderstorms had blown in.

He'd already researched possible destinations and settled on Brazil and South Africa, in that order. His valid South African passport made that country a real possibility. Did he want to use it? Or should he fly to Brazil as a Canadian and apply for residency as someone who'd recently retired and wanted to party for the rest of his life? Choices, choices, choices.

Sunday May 2, 1982, 0812 local time, Cologne

Janet sat naked at the small table in Karin's eighth floor apartment, sipping a cup of coffee. In the background, she could hear Karin showering.

The 250-square-meter apartment felt like her place in California—home. For the first time in years Janet felt totally relaxed, sexually satisfied, and mentally at peace. She liked the feeling.

Over the years, she'd become emotionally numb to the act of killing. Early on, she'd realized the killing was not the most important part of her job. Getting away clean and leaving little or no trace of her presence was number one, followed by pre-hit surveillance. Over time, to keep from being caught or killed, she'd become suspicious of everyone, and it was wearing her down. *Maybe this is my chance to have a normal life and a lasting relationship?*

Their common experience in Cuba made Karin the perfect candidate, and there was already the desire to be together. Karin had changed. She had changed. Neither no longer wanted to change the world.

Could we make it work?

Monday, May 3, 1982, 1400 local time, Hanoi

At precisely, ten—the scheduled time for the interview—Major General Dat Trung walked into the small conference room down the hall from his office. Protocol dictated that, as the senior man in the meeting, he should arrive last. It was also a matter of power, even though the visitors were not from the People's Army. While he let the men wait and drink tea and eat *bánh cáy*—a rectangular cake made by grinding, then baking a mix of sticky rice, sesame, sugar, carrots, and orange peel—Trung's administrative assistant informed him that there were four men waiting, not the two that he'd been told when the interview was scheduled.

The four men stood and bowed their heads slightly when Trung entered. As the most senior visitor, Senior Colonel Diem from the People's Border Force introduced himself first. He immediately pointed out that he was not related to the former general who'd led the rebellious south. Senior Colonel Phó said he worked for the office of People's Public Security. When introduced by their senior officers, the other two captains nodded. Each of the four had a pad of paper in front of him.

Senior Colonel Diem began. "General Trung, thank you for making time for us today. We would like to ask you some questions so we can complete our investigation on this bandit drug dealer Pham. We will try to be brief."

Translation. We already know the answers to the questions and want to hear what you have to say. Hopefully it will confirm what we know. If it doesn't, then we will be here for a long time.

"I serve the People, so, please, let's start."

The two captains produced identical Sony cassette tape recorders from their briefcases. On cue, Senior Colonel Diem pointed to them. "General, do you mind if we tape your

438

responses? We will give you one copy for your records, if you wish."

"Thank you, I will take one for my records." *This way, I can hide it and, if needed, compare it to what they play at my court martial. They do not have anything on me.*

Diem crossed his hands on the pad. "Excellent. General, would you like a summary of what we have learned so far?"

"Yes, that will be very helpful." *It will help me determine how far my head is in the noose. And, if it is, then I can decide what to do. By then, I will be watched and it will be hard for me to escape. So it may be my karma to die in Vietnam.*

"Good. We know that Pham surrendered his firebase and his unit in return for a commission in the People's Army. After that, it gets a bit shadowy. He was given command of the 329th Special Reconnaissance battalion that was supposed to hunt American Special Forces patrols in the area where Cambodia, Laos, and Vietnam meet. We know he worked with a Major Thai who was developing tactics to more effectively find and destroy these American units. We also know that he set up a patrol base near where the Americans were kept."

Trung nodded. "That is true."

"General, we cannot find any patrol reports from Colonel Pham. Have you seen them?"

Pham was supposed to submit them. Maybe he got lazy thinking that I would protect him forever. "No, and nor should I. Operationally Lieutenant Colonel Pham did not report to me."

Diem asked his next question. "At the time he built his first camp, he was in the Fourth Military District and, I believe, in those days you were its commander."

Trung nodded in agreement.

"As military district commander, you provided supplies to Pham. Is this true?"

"Yes. There was nothing unusual about his requisitions." Trung had seen them all. Some he'd signed, most he hadn't.

"Did you ever inspect his base?"

"Yes, I did. I went there several times." *The official records of the Fourth Military District say I went there every year.*

"Did you find anything out of the ordinary?"

"No. I believe the inspection reports are in the district's files."

"Yes. We have read them."

"Good. Then you know the reports and my inspections showed that Lieutenant Colonel Pham's unit was under strength, but carrying out its mission. After the war, his unit was supposed to patrol the border. On average, he had about half his men deployed in the jungle and half at the camp." *That is accurate to a point. They went into the jungle to escort drug shipments from Laos and Cambodia.*

Diem looked down his list of questions and checked off more than one. "One last question, General... How are you related to Pham?"

Not if, but how. There's no harm in telling the truth. "His father is my brother. When given the choice, I moved to Haiphong and I joined the People's Army. My brother stayed in the south." He'd almost said Saigon, but caught himself in time.

"Pham decided to join the winning side. I do not know what happened to my brother or his family since I moved to Hanoi almost thirty years ago." *That's not entirely true. I know my brother and his two surviving children are in the United States.* Trung waited a few seconds. "Do you have any further questions?"

"No general, that sums it up."

"Well, Senior Colonel Diem. I have a question for both of you."

Trung waited until both men were looking at him. "What are your conclusions? I need to report this meeting to my superiors."

Diem looked back at the general. "Sir, so far nothing you have told me contradicts what we know. However, our report will say that there are many irregularities in the records of the Fourth Military District during your command and under your successor. Much can be explained by the contingencies of the war. Others can be covered by the fact that the command was manned at about fifty percent, which meant that shortcuts had to be taken. Due to our losses in the war, our leaders redirected where men were assigned. Preference was given to manning combat units, not military districts. This is a long way to getting to the answer. There is nothing in our investigation that says you committed criminal acts."

I got wealthy from my commissions for facilitating the drug shipments. I never touched the bribes given to the customs agents or forged any documents, but I know who did. "Excellent." Trung started to stand up to signal the meeting was over.

Senior Colonel Phó spoke up for the first time in the meeting. "Excuse me, General, but, before we leave, I would like to ask one more question. It is a simple one."

Trung settled back down in his chair, somewhat annoyed that Phó was using this simple interrogation technique to try to catch the subject off guard. "What do you want to ask?"

"My question has three parts. Did you know about Pham's trips to Hong Kong since the war ended? Did he tell you why he went? And did you know whom he met with in Hong Kong?

Trung smiled to hide his fear. "To answer your three questions, I signed Pham's application as required by regulations and it was reviewed and approved by the Ministry of People's Security and the Foreign Ministry. Two, I don't remember what he put on his passport application as a reason for his travel. He didn't confide in me. And, three, I don't know who he saw or where he went."

"That brings up an interesting question."

"Which is?"

"He was recently seen entering and leaving the U.S. consulate. Any idea why?"

"No." Pham had never told him, but he suspected he knew the reason.

"We think that he was trying to negotiate a ransom for the Americans."

"Really? Why do you suspect that?"

"We followed Pham on one of his visits to Hong Kong. A lab technician sold our agent a set of prints. General, we believe he approached the Americans, and when they learned where their servicemen were being held, they rescued them. They burned the compound to cover their tracks."

"That is an interesting theory. Besides the pictures, do you have any other facts?"

"No, it is just a hypothesis based on what we know."

The less said about Pham, the better. I had no control over his actions. I could, however, have shut down his camp easily and had him arrested, but I didn't because I was making a lot of money.

"Did you have any conversations with Pham about his Americans? The records show that you were there several times when, we would presume, the Americans were being held in his camp."

Ahhhhh, now we get to the real purpose of the meeting. They want to know if I knew about the Americans. Well, unless you start torturing me, the answer is no.

"No, I never saw any Americans." *Technically that is not a lie. The Americans were kept either in the field or in their building with the rain shields down, so I never saw them.*

"Sir, are you sure?"

"Yes. I saw military supplies and soldiers on guard or returning from patrol. There was a garden of sorts, and I commended Pham on his frugality in growing his own food. He explained that the garden was tended by soldiers who were temporarily off patrol duty due to illness or injury, until they recovered. It seemed a reasonable, even commendable use of manpower."

"Thank you, General. Those are all our questions."

The same day, 0913 local time, Los Angeles

As soon as Janet had gotten her luggage and cleared customs in JFK's special line for first-class passengers, she found a pay phone. Her answering service had three messages. One was from Sandra, saying that her tax return was ready and needed to be sent off with a check. The other two were from The Broker. Two calls in the space of a few days meant it was urgent.

The plane from Frankfurt had been late, leaving her little time for conversations before boarding the flight to LA. She told Sandra's assistant that she would stop by in the morning, sign the return, and mail the check to the IRS. She declined Sandra's invitation to join her for dinner. Desire to have sex with anyone but Karin just wasn't in the cards.

When no one else was using any of the other phones in the bank of six, she called The Broker. "Good morning."

"Who is this?"

"One of your favorite assets."

"Ahhhhh, Red Star of Death, how are you?" Normally, he used the words "my friend"; on rare occasions he used the name he gave her.

"I'm fine. I told you I needed some time off. You left two messages. What's up?"

"Two things. One, I have work for you when you are ready. Two, I was recently contacted by a former colleague who was putting out a contract on the five American POWs who were just rescued."

Is he telling me this because he wants me to protect Randy? "Is the buyer with your former employer?"

"Yes..." The Broker hesitated for a second. "He is, or, more than likely, was."

That's an interesting answer. A CIA agent gone rogue. "Is it sanctioned?"

"No, it wasn't. I gather it didn't make the European papers, but someone tried to kill all five of the returned POWs. One, Karl Kramer, was killed. Another, Ashley Smith, was hit several times. The other three, Greg Christiansen, Jeff Anderson and Randy Pulaski, escaped unharmed. The Feds already have the shooters and are looking for the man who hired them. My customer had me put out a contract to do the job right. At the time I took the commission I didn't know who the targets were. I offered him two options, you and a group of other men. He took the cheap way out. So now there's a second contract out on the former POWs. It's a mess."

Janet wondered why The Broker was more chatty than usual. *What is he trying to tell me? He knows the buyer and he's scared.* "Where's the buyer?"

"I don't know. He transferred the first half of the money. My guess is he's flown the coop, if you know what I mean. If the guys fulfill their contract, I'll be on the hook for the balance if I can't get him to pay. But it is not the money, it is the principle. I'm guessing he is trying to off these guys to cover his own ass."

The phone bonged three times and the operator told Janet she had thirty seconds left; if she wanted to continue the call, she had to deposit another four dollars. The Broker interrupted. "Give me the pay-phone number and I'll call you back."

Janet rattled off the number and hung up. Thirty seconds later, the phone rang and she yanked it off the cradle. "Where were we?"

"You're someplace in New York."

"I am. You just told me that you had a mess on your hands. You've got a deadbeat buyer and wanted me to know you let a contract that bothers your conscience."

"Something like that...."

Yeah, you can't warn the targets because it would be a violation of your contract. Silence is your mantra. But I could, if I wanted to, take care of the problem for The Broker. So, if I volunteered to fix the problem, he would pay me.

That leads to two questions. One, am I willing to put my future at risk to save Randy's life? And, two, if the CIA come looking for The Broker, how much will they learn about the work I've done for his customers?

"Raul, what do you want from me?" Rarely had they ever used each other's names.

"Help would be nice."

"You know my fees?"

"I do. Is there a chance of a discount?"

"How many of them are there?"

"I am not sure how big their team is. Probably six, but it could be more. They've only done work for me outside the U.S. They are probably going to go in heavy when they think they can get them all together. That makes it very messy."

"Are they Americans?"

"No. My contact is an ex-Spetsnaz officer who recruits his former comrades. They are a nasty combination of cruel, brutal, and ruthless. Most of the time, they work for the Russian *mafiya* who let them do freelance work outside the Soviet Union. I first met them in Angola."

"How fast do you need an answer?"

"Tomorrow or the next day. I don't think the shooters have arrived in the U.S. yet."

"I need to think about it. This is not what I do. I'm happy to eliminate targets over a period of days or even a week or more, no problem. Getting into a shoot-out with a bunch of ex-Russian special forces guys is not my cup of tea. It's impossible to control events and I'm liable to get shot." *If I could take them on one or two at a time, it might work.*

"I understand."

"What kind of info on them can you get for me?"

"Not very much."

"How about photos, travel plans?"

"I don't know what I can get."

"Look, I don't think this is something I want to take on. My suggestion is that you talk to your friends in the CIA and let them figure out who should be involved." Janet let that statement sink in for a few seconds before she continued. "If that doesn't work,. call me the usual way and we can set up another conversation."

Scenarios ran through her head on the flight to LA and during the two-hour drive from her accountant's office in Burbank to

Palmdale. She didn't want Randy murdered just because some lousy desk jockey with a dubious past was upset that his career might be ruined because five POWs showed up alive when they were supposed to be dead. To cheer herself up, she thought about the wonderful four days she'd just spent with Karin.

When they'd stopped during a walk in a park on the bank of the Rhine River, not far from Karin's apartment, Janet had put her hands on Karin's face. "I'd like to fly you to the U.S. to spend a week or so with me."

Karin looked at her new lover. "Are you serious?"

"Yes. I very much want to be with you. You said you were planning a ten-day holiday, so why not come to the U.S. and spend it with me?"

"The flights are very expensive." It was Karin's way of saying that the airfare would make a big dent in her limited savings.

"Don't worry, I'll pay for everything." Karin stopped and faced Janet and looked into her eyes, studying the face of the woman who had just re-entered her life and brought her so much happiness. Karin caressed Janet's cheek before kissing her. "In my heart, I know we both want to live together someplace, but I don't want to be hurt. So I will come on one condition."

"And that is?"

"The killing must stop. You have to promise me that when we see each other again, you are retired. You said you are ready. So retire. End it."

"It is not that easy, but, yes, I will be retired. It is time to stop."

"You promise?"

"Yes, I promise—" Janet couldn't say another word because Karin's lips pressed against hers and her tongue slipped into her mouth, searching. They split after a few seconds. "I accept. I will come."

The day they'd picked for Karin's arrival was Friday, June 4. Since boarding the plane in Frankfurt, Janet had been running different scenarios on how to get out of the business of being a hit woman. The words "Wrap up loose ends" kept popping into her head. She didn't want to be anybody else's "loose end."

Her conversation with The Broker added a new complication. Instinct said "Stay away." Her heart and long lost feelings, even her duty to Randy, said "Help out." It was a conundrum that she had to resolve.

By comparison to how she felt about Karin, her feelings for Helen had been puppy love. Janet smiled about a conversation they'd had during breakfast the previous Sunday. "My love, if we're to be together, you'll have to get used to the fact that there are things I just can't do."

"Like what?"

"I can't clap my hands."

"O.K., that's no big deal except at a concert. What else?"

"I can't use a knife and fork, so I can't cut a steak, which is the American classic. If you were paying attention to what I eat, you noticed that everything I eat can be cut by a fork or eaten with a spoon."

"I can cut it for you if you will let me. Name another."

Karin's eyes sparkled with a mischievous look. "I can't caress both your breasts at the same time, or hold one breast with one hand and stroke your clitoris with the other. I will have to choose between one or the other."

"You have a dirty mind. I like it. So far, it hasn't seem to make any difference to me." Janet was so engrossed in thinking about Karin that she passed the Palmdale exit for both the post office and the dojo.

Cursing, she got off at the next exit and went back west. She needed a workout desperately, to change the flow of chemicals in her body from hormones to adrenalin. And she had to check her mail.

Tuesday, May 4, 1982, 1430 local time, Washington DC

The four former POWs were ushered—or, in the case of Ashley, wheeled—into the Oval Office, ostensibly for a photo opportunity with the President, who would pin medals on their chests. Each man was presented with the POW medal and given the nation's third highest award for bravery—the Silver Star.

Once the ceremony was over, the four were led to a conference room. In it were the Vice President, the Chairman of the Joint Chiefs of Staff, the Secretary of State, the National Security Advisor, and the Secretary of Defense.

The President sat and everyone followed. "Good afternoon, gentlemen. Let's get started."

Ashley nodded to Randy, who stood up and went to the end of the room where an 80-inch projection screen was set up. Even though Ashley was the senior man and had been in captivity the longest, he wanted Randy and Jeff to present their findings, because they'd done most of the work while he lay in a hospital bed. "Mr. President, we had a team of photo interpreters study photos of North and South Vietnam, Laos and Cambodia for possible POW camps. We also went through all the POW debriefs to identify where they had been held. When necessary, we flew them to DC to show them photos to help identify other potential POW camps."

Randy had been told the President liked a short summary and then the punch line. Ashley replaced the slide displaying the categories with the map of Southeast Asia with dots showing all the sites studied. "We divided potential POW camps within the past twelve years into three categories. The blue stars are the sites with an 80 per cent chance or higher that POWs were kept there after the war. The yellow dots represent a forty to sixty per cent chance. The black dots are those that have some indication Americans were there after the war, but odds are very low, less than twenty percent. In all, we looked at eighty-six sites.

Randy pointed to each of the blue stars. "Our analysis led us to these six sites where we think Americans were kept after the Vietnam War."

Another slide appeared on the screen. "This is a picture of where we were held a year ago. It was taken two years ago by a

KH-11 satellite. We are showing this to show you what we think might indicate live POWs."

Randy pointed out the key attributes—either an SOS or a call sign, and a nearby compound and signs of activity, cars, guards, etc. He nodded to Ashley who clicked on the next slide.

"We named the six sites after baseball teams. We are going to show a fraction of the photos that support our conclusions. This is the site we call 'Twins'." In this photo, taken in 1977, you can clearly see the letters NG 102A made by boulders. In places, there are stones missing, but if you trace the letters, it is very clear. We're ninety percent sure that NG 102A is from a VF-96 F-4 with the side number 102. Alpha tells us the pilot, not the back-seater or radar intercept officer, was held captive here. In 1983, we found a photo that had SOS in the same field. The Navy's records note that in 1977, a VF-96 F-4 was shot down and the pilot was seen being captured. He did not come home and was declared 'missing in action, presumed dead' in 1978."

Randy looked around the room and saw nothing but grim faces. He hoped they were as angry as he was at the probability that others had been left behind and no one had done anything about it. He was sure the Vice President was.

Randy covered the other five sites. "So the answer to the question is simple. Yes, I am sure we left men behind. The six of us are living proof of that. Were there any more? Probably. Are they alive today? We don't know. It is up to you gentlemen to determine if we should find out. If you take that course of action, every one of us, as well as the team that brought *us* home, will volunteer to be on that task force to do whatever is necessary to bring *them* home. That concludes my brief."

The President rested his clasped hands on the table and looked around the room. After a long, stony, tense silence, he spoke. "I don't know whether I am more angry or horrified. For years, our government has been telling the American people no POWs were left alive in Vietnam. We now know that is not true. I am not going to get into a discussion about whether it was a deliberate lie or ignorance or incompetence, but *this* administration is going to get to the bottom of this."

After writing three lines on the pad, the President put the cover back on his fountain pen. "I want three things done. One, we again tell the Vietnamese and their allies that we want our men back. I know we just had that conversation with them. This time, show them the evidence and tell them we are prepared to go public. Give them forty-eight hours to answer. Two, we start flying over their territory looking for more sites. If they shoot at our planes, all hell will break loose. Don't define hell, but move two aircraft carriers into the South China Sea, and move B-52 and fighter-bomber squadrons into Thailand, and they can figure out what it means. Now, sometimes a carrot works better than a large stick, so offer them some aid, but do not—*do not*—make it look like a ransom. Nixon promised aid if the North Vietnamese adhered to the terms of the treaty, but since they didn't keep their side of the bargain with regard to South Vietnam and becoming more forthcoming about American MIAs, it was never delivered."

He turned to the Director of the CIA. "Three, I want some housecleaning done at the agency. Anyone who saw these photos and was responsible for the reports that ignored the evidence needs to be fired. I want those people out of the agency, and yesterday is not soon enough. I don't care if they have been there fifty years, get them out, and if it has to be done publicly, so be it. Make it so that they cannot take advantage of their service to make money or work in the intelligence community again. This will send a message that this level of incompetence will not be tolerated. The American people will side with my administration."

The CIA director spoke up. "Mr. President, do you want us to send in recon teams?"

"Let's wait to see what we find and how the Vietnamese react before we risk more men." The President stood up and nodded. "Gentlemen."

Each man came to attention as the President left. The CIA director motioned with the palm of his hand to the four former

POWs as if to say "Stay." He turned to the aide waiting to escort them out of the White House. "I'll walk them out."

When it was just the five of them, the head of the CIA sighed and said, "This is a great start, but our work is not done. I need you to make sure everything is indexed so an idiot can understand what they are looking at. Then, I need you to write down everything you ever discussed with Savoy. I don't care how small a detail you think it is."

Four "Yes, sirs" acknowledged his instructions. Randy spoke first. "It's already done, but we can go through it one more time and have it wrapped up in a day or two."

"Great. Next, here's the latest about Savoy. The Director of the FBI told me this morning that Savoy has fled the country. Now that he is outside the U.S., the CIA can go after him. I will bring his ass back, but don't count on it being alive."

"Did he put a contract out on us?"

"The FBI think so, and we concur. We don't know if it is still active. However, there may be other players, such as the Vietnamese, who want you dead as well."

"What about this Wales character?"

"The FBI and every police force in the U.S. are looking for Wales. We'll find him, but it may take time."

As the informal spokesman, Randy asked the obvious question. "What do you want us to do?"

"Go to ground. If you want, I can arrange to move you to a CIA safe house. It's your choice. Ashley is on his way to one now." Randy looked at the others. "We have a plan."

"Care to tell me about it?"

"No, sir. The fewer people who know the plan, the better. However, a cover-our-ass letter would help."

"What does it have to say?"

Randy thought for a few seconds, then wrote on the pad in front him. He showed it to the other POWs, who nodded in agreement. He spun the pad around and slid it to the Director of the CIA.

"Sir, we need something like this signed."

THE PRESIDENT OF THE UNITED STATES
    AUTHORIZES THE FOLLOWING SIX OFFICERS:
(1) LTC ASHLEY WHITE
(2) CDR RANDALL PULASKI
(3) CDR JEFFREY ANDERSON
(4) LTC GREG CHRISTIANSEN
(5) LCDR MARTY CABOT
(6) LCDR JOSH HAMAN
AND OTHERS INVOLVED TO USE WHATEVER
    MEANS AND U.S. MILITARY RESOURCES
    NECESSARY TO STOP AN ASSASSINATION
    ATTEMPT ON ANY ONE OR ALL OF THEIR
    LIVES.

"That's pretty ballsy."

"Yes, sir, we just don't want to be hung out to dry if we have to take the law into our own hands. We think whoever Savoy hired isn't going to play by any set of rules. All they care about is killing us and getting their money. We want to do what is necessary to protect ourselves and not go to jail. It's what we would call a Catch 44 letter."

"What's Catch 44?"

"It's a long story."

"I'm listening."

Randy gave him a *Reader's Digest* version of Hank Cho's explanation of numerology, which had been expanded over their years in captivity.

The director smiled. "I'll add a phone number for any doubting Thomas's to call, and have copies signed by the President for you tomorrow."

"Thank you, sir. Please make sure that the heads of our respective services have copies as well, to put into our service records."

"Yeah, yeah, yeah. I know—CYA."

"Yes, sir, that's what DC is all about."

The letter was in Randy's hand the next morning. That evening, news coverage of the award ceremony included a description of the sailing trip the POWs planned to take to celebrate their return.

Chapter 17
PROTECTION DETAIL

Friday, May 7, 1982, 1746 local time, Hanoi

Major General Trung came out of the building to see his driver standing at attention in front of Senior Colonels Phó and Diem. The young man saluted both men, then marched away.

Senior Colonel Diem motioned to the open car door. "Major General Dat Trung, please come with us."

Trung, as was his custom, got in the back seat on the right side. Senior Colonel Diem bent over and looked at the general. "Sir, move over." His tone was commanding and bordering on rude. Senior Colonel Phó was already in the passenger seat, next to a driver whose face Trung could not see.

As soon as the staff car pulled out into traffic, Diem turned to the general. "Trung, the politburo has decided that by not reporting you knew six Americans were being held by the bandit Pham, you caused the People's Democratic Republic of Vietnam to lose much face. Our country is embarrassed. My investigation concluded that you knew he was keeping them prisoner. Therefore, you are to be executed."

"What proof do you have?"

"The politburo doesn't need proof. Your careful answer that you did not see the Americans is very different from a denial.

454

One, you should have taken the time to inspect the building in which they were kept, which looked like a prison compound, but you didn't; none of your reports said you did. If you had, we believe you'd have seen the Americans. Furthermore, it is not normal to have the rain shields down when it is sunny. The fact that they were down was the bandit Pham's way of hiding the Americans from you. Senior Colonel Pho and I visited the camp after our interview. It is obvious that Pham kept prisoners in what was not an authorized prison."

Trung didn't say anything.

"You are to be shot as a Major General, but you will be buried in a private's grave."

"What about my wife? Has she been told?"

"This morning she was removed from her position as a physician and is being taken to a re-education camp. Her sentence is five years."

"And my remaining son?"

"His career in the Army will not be affected. We are sure he knew nothing of your crimes. The navy memorial of your other son who died gloriously in 1970 for his country in a torpedo boat that was attacked by an American helicopter will also not be changed."

"Do I get a trial?"

"No. One is not necessary."

Trung remained quiet, looking out at the city for the last time. *They have not said anything about my third son. Anh hated Communism and became a South Vietnamese Marine officer. His unit was never defeated in battle. After Saigon fell in 1975, Anh stole two fishing boats and got the 120 men in his company and their families out of South Vietnam. They were picked up by a U.S. Navy ship. He is now a U.S. citizen living in Southern California.*

Trusted friends had smuggled letters and pictures from America about once a year. These were studied and committed to memory, then burned.

After the first letter had arrived, Trung had sent one back.

More recently, they'd managed to smuggle two or three letters a year in and out of Vietnam. The last one Trung had sent contained references to his money in Swiss bank accounts. Now Anh had the account numbers and codes, so even if Dat was not able to get out of Vietnam, Anh could access the money. The accounts held close to ten million U.S. dollars. Maybe Anh would use some of the money to get his mother out of the re-education camp, where Trung was sure she would otherwise slowly die.

The staff car braked to a stop well outside the city. Diem pushed on Trung's side. "Out."

Trung opened the door and started to stand up realizing that it was his karma to die in Vietnam. He never saw the Makarov in the hand of the driver, he only heard the shot that put a bullet in the back of his head. Nor did he feel Senior Colonel Diem rip off his general's insignia.

The same day, 1630 local time, Santa Catalina Island, CA

The wind off the California coast was its usual ten to fifteen knots from the west-northwest. With the #2 Genoa jib and the mainsail on the 60-foot mast pulled tight, Josh's 40-foot C&C sloop *Impuls* heeled over on a port tack. The downwind gunwale was ten inches above the water as the sloop sailed as close to the wind as possible.

Before they'd left, Josh had told several people at the marina that he was taking two of the former POWs out for a weekend guy's trip to Catalina Island. He needed more ice than usual, and asked the dock boys to help him carry the ice chests, food and beer to the boat.

The Canadian-built sailboat was designed for the Great Lakes and the Atlantic Ocean. It had seventy-nine hundred pounds of lead molded into its fin keel, which gave it a stable ride in the long Pacific swells. Its spec sheet said that the sloop's maximum hull speed in smooth water was twelve knots. According to Josh's calculations, based on bearings from points on the coast, *Impuls* was making eight.

In the cockpit, Josh stood next to Randy, who was at the wheel. Both enjoyed the salty spray splashing on their faces. To Josh, this was the type sailing *Impuls* was designed for.

Satisfied he was where he wanted to change course, Josh put the binoculars he used to study the shoreline into a bin mounted on the front of the binnacle before speaking to his two passengers. "Randy, Jeff, stand by to come about."

Randy, at the helm, and Jeff, sitting by the port winch, acknowledged the command. Their only sailing experience had been in the ROTC summer sailing summer course. Josh had been sailing off and on his entire life and loved to be out on the water. Along with his 1965 Porsche SC Coupe, *Impuls* was his pride and joy.

The helicopter pilot popped the main sheet out of the cleat and felt the rope pull against his grip. "Hard a-lee.... Steady up on a course of two-five-zero."

Randy turned the wheel to the left to change from a starboard to a port tack. As the bow of the sailboat started its turn, Jeff released the line tied to the foot of the sail, known as a sheet, so the wind could push the sail around the forward side of the mast to the port side. Once the foot of the sail was clear of the mainmast, Jeff shifted to the starboard side. He looped the half-inch-thick line around the winch three times and began turning the winch handle. The ratcheting sound told Josh what he needed to know without looking, and he pulled the main sheet through a clamp so that the boom holding the bottom of the mainsail stayed about five degrees to the starboard of the boat's centerline.

Randy glanced down at the compass and steadied *Impuls* on its new heading. String tattletales on the big jib and mainsail stood straight out, parallel to the deck, telling Josh the sails were trimmed properly. He looked over the starboard side; the gunwale was ten inches above the water. *Perfect. Let her rip!*

Impuls made landfall just south of Moonstone Cove on Santa Catalina Island. Just before they entered the cove, Josh started the diesel and dropped the sails. He headed for a vacant mooring, the southernmost one in the row closest to the open ocean.

Impuls was riding gently at the end of a mooring line when an Islander 40 sloop with a dark blue hull, named *Pane,* picked up the buoy next to Josh's sloop. The name of the boat was not about windows. Instead, it was Jack D'Onofrio's tribute to his late father, who'd been a baker. *Pane*—pronounced "pan-nay"—is the Italian word for bread. "And, yes," Jack often said, it takes a lot of bread to afford this boat."

Later, a Columbia 45 sailed into the cove and picked up a mooring near the middle of the arc of buoys. *Tortman's* owner and captain was a large black man whose shaved head glistened in the fading sunlight. Once tied to a mooring, Gary Nash dropped a ladder over the starboard side to make it easier for the six visitors —three from the *Impuls* and three from the *Pane*—to come aboard and join the five on board *Tortman.*

Cans of beer were handed out. After a quick toast, the lawyer stood in the center of his boat's cockpit. "O.K. everyone listen up." Nash, by his sheer size, was a presence to be reckoned with, and he didn't have to speak loudly to be heard. "When we left, there were some people in the marina's store asking where you"— he pointed at Josh—"were going. I stood back in line and listened. Their Russian accent told me the bad guys are here. All they have to figure out is how to get to Catalina Island."

Josh turned to Marty. "They've taken the bait. Let's eat and then get everything ready. Tonight the island will be a madhouse of tourists, with lots of boats in the cove. On Saturday, it just gets more crowded and noisier. They'll probably make their move in the wee hours of Saturday night, when there is less risk of collateral damage—or witnesses—and plan to leave early Sunday morning. My guess is that they'll try to be quiet, so they have a head start before someone reports us missing or finds our bodies."

Randy piped up. "Jeff and I tried the missing thing before. Neither of us liked it...."

Saturday, May 8, 1982, 1349 local time, Stallion Springs

FORGOTTEN

The thermometer in the shade of her porch said it was a pleasant seventy-eight. Out in the sun, it was ten degrees warmer, and the wind was gusting between fifteen and twenty-five miles an hour. Janet sat on the shaded deck sipping a cup of coffee after lunch. A glint in the field across Banducci Road caught her eye.

Paranoia sent possibilities racing through her mind. *Was someone watching her? If so, how long had the observer been there?*

She estimated the flash was 1,500 yards away, and the top lip of a creek bed was a perfect place for a sniper to hide. Slowly, Janet scanned the area, looking for something that didn't belong.

Experience told her there were too many variables standing in the way of a first shot hit at that distance. In the time it takes a bullet to travel almost a mile, the earth's rotation moves a stationary target a few feet. Bullet ballistics and atmospheric conditions add more variables and increase the chance of missing.

Was he observing before moving in closer?

She tucked the book under her arm, picked up the plate, and turned sideways to the glint to make herself a smaller target. Once inside, she grabbed the "go bag" she kept in the house. In this small pack there was a shoulder holster with a Browning BDA and six full magazines, a wallet with a set of unused IDs and credit cards, and ten thousand dollars in cash.

It was enough, she hoped, to get to her safe deposit boxes in Palmdale, LA, or Bakersfield, where she had more cash and IDs. From the gun case in the living room, Janet unlocked her Model 1903 Springfield with a ten-power scope and grabbed the three boxes of twenty 30-06 rounds from the top drawer.

In the cave, she took the small passageway that led up the rock formations to a ledge about a hundred feet above her house. It was a perfect overwatch position for just such a contingency. Freeze-dried food and water were stored in a steel box at the back of the ledge, along with powerful binoculars. On top, there were several sandbags on which she could rest the rifle. Behind her, there was a path up through the rocks to the top of the ridge that would let her escape into the San Joaquin Valley.

In position, Janet felt the coolness of the stone against her hips and abdomen. A glance at her watch told her that it had taken her just four minutes to get from being a target to being the hunter.

Slowly, she scanned the field with her Nikon 10 X 50 binoculars. She often used the ledge to practice observation skills, and she knew the area around her like the back of her hand.

After about ten minutes, Janet rolled out the foam pad that was part of the stash. It made lying on the granite more comfortable, but it still didn't change the result. She saw nothing. Nada.

There was only one way to make sure. In the garage, she hung towels from the passenger's sun visor and the driver's side window to create a very narrow slit through which Janet could see the road. They would obscure her outline, making it harder for anyone in from or on the side to aim at her.

Janet put the bolt-action Model 1903 rifle back in the gun cabinet and pulled down a lever-action Winchester 94. The saddle carbine was smaller, easier to handle, and the lever-action rifle could be fired faster. One at a time, she slid six 150-grain, 30-30 rounds into the magazine, then levered one into the chamber before sliding in another round. The remaining 13 bullets from the box went into her front pocket. In the car, she wedged the rifle barrel down between the passenger's seat and the center console.

Driving down the access road, Janet pressed the remote so that she didn't have to wait twenty seconds for the gate to open. Seeing no traffic, she floored the Blazer's gas pedal and skidded to a stop on the shoulder of the road, a hundred yards from the creek.

Ducking as she got out of the car, Janet peered around the front fender. Still nothing. The cows in the field ignored her. With the Winchester in hand, Janet went to the back of the Blazer and peered around the rear tire. Still nothing.

Taking a deep breath to try to calm her heart rate, Janet jumped across the drainage ditch along the side road, put her foot on the middle strand of barbed wire, and vaulted the barbed fence. Several nearby cows mooed, either in approval or annoyance. Other than the wind in the grass, the only sound was a passing car.

Sure that she was within a hundred feet of where she'd seen the glint, Janet studied the grass, the Winchester pressed into her shoulder, safety off and ready to shoot. Her heart was pounding out of her chest and her brain expected that she would be hit by a bullet any second. She didn't like being the target!

When she got to the creek, Janet found a weather-faded, empty beer can wedged against a rock. The sun had reflected off it. Weak-kneed and shaking, she leaned on the rifle and sobbed.

Am I losing it? Can I ever get away? Am I going to spend the rest of my life looking over my shoulder?

Sunday, May 9, 1982, 0037 local time, Moonstone Cove

The soft glow from the half moon and pinpricks of light from the stars made it a perfect night for night vision goggles. Under the *Impuls,* two waterproof lights turned the bay water around the sloop a translucent yellow-green. Josh, sitting on the steps to the darkened cabin with a suppressed MP-5SD on his lap, remembered Rebekah had bought the lights, saying they added romantic touch to a night tied up at a mooring. In the cabin behind him, Randy and Jeff were supposed to be asleep.

Marty, on the dinette bench seat, whispered, "Didn't some movie star drown out here a couple of years ago?"

"Yeah. Last year, in a town farther up the island called Two Harbors, Natalie Wood fell off the pier. There was a big stink about it, because some believe she was pushed by someone who knew that she couldn't swim."

"Oh, yeah. What a waste. She was good looking."

In the stillness, it was a perfect time for one's mind to wander. And to be scared. Their plan counted on the assassins' desire to be discreet and not pull alongside and blast away with machine guns.

Nash stood at the base of the ladder that led down into *Tortman's* cabin. By standing a step inside the door, he could see the back end of a sport fisherman with the naked eye and, with a pair of night-vision binoculars, watch what was happening. He keyed the microphone plugged into a short range radio. "Listen up, guys. Game is on. Three in a small Zodiac just left the Bertram sport fisherman *Rusty Hook*. I also saw two more slip into the water. That leaves four on the cabin cruiser." The voice of Gary Nash started Josh's adrenalin flowing. On *Impuls,* Josh slid back to check on Jeff and Randy, who were now sitting up holding their .45s. Both gave him a thumbs-up.

On *Pane,* two SEALs slipped over the side and headed toward *Impuls.* Their re-breathers didn't leave a trail of bubbles. In seconds, they were twenty-five feet below Josh's boat and in position to stop attackers from attaching a bomb to the bottom of Josh's sailboat.

From *Tortman,* two more SEALs slid into the water, headed toward the sport fisherman. When it had arrived Saturday morning, one of the SEALs noticed it was towing a 15-foot Zodiac with a heavily muffled outboard motor. By the afternoon, they had seen nine men on board. Close-cropped hair and a Spetsnaz logo tattoo on the bicep of one man told them all they needed to know.

Everyone on the *Impuls* heard a soft thump, and the sailboat gently rocked. Josh peered over the lip of the hatch and saw a hand grab the jib sheet pulley track. A black shape, then another, rose over the deck edge.

Josh aimed at the larger shape's head and shoulders. The HK MP-5SD rattled and three 115-grain nine-millimeter rounds spat out the short barrel. Shifting fire to the second target, he squeezed the trigger. The man's hands flew up as he fell backwards into the water. The splash was much louder than the noise of the suppressed MP-5.

Under the *Impuls,* one of the SEALs tapped his swim mate and pointed to two approaching divers. Both had spear guns, and one had a large bag hanging from his belt. When the attackers were overhead, the SEALs rose from their hiding place a few feet above the black rocks.

At five yards from the man with the bag, one SEAL fired his own spear gun. The arrow went straight into the man's belly and he headed for the surface, streaming blood. The other man turned and fired his spear. It shot past. The second SEAL fired, but his spear bounced off the swimmer's air tank.

The two drew knives and grappled, slicing at each other. Blood streamed from cuts and billowed in the water around the fighting swimmers, eerily illuminated by the green light. The second SEAL slashed this opponent's air hose and ripped off his mask. Frantic to get air, the man surfaced, followed by the first SEAL, who grabbed him from behind and put his knife to his throat. The man surrendered.

On the *Impuls,* Josh pointed his HK at the remaining man in the Zodiac, who dropped his suppressed pistol and put his hands up. "Do you speak English?"

The man shook his head. "*Nyet.*" Josh told him in Russian to get on board the *Impuls* and then directed him to kneel down. Marty tied the man's hands behind his back, then pulled his elbows together with rope.

In the Zodiac, Josh saw the inert shape of a man. Then he heard a gentle thump and saw a corpse bumping up against the hull of the *Impuls,* oozing blood.

Marty turned to the two former POWs in the cabin. "Jeff, Randy, give me a hand getting this body on board the Zodiac."

They quickly pulled the corpse into the Zodiac where it lay next to the body with a bloody chest caused by three nine-millimeter bullets less than two inches apart.

The first SEAL surfaced, holding a knife to the throat of a man who was bleeding from a knife wound.

Marty pointed to the bleeding man. "Jeff, Randy, bring him on and tie him up. Then we'll get the guy in the water, the one with the spear in his gut."

When the SEALs were all on board, the Russian with a spear protruding from his stomach was stretched out on the fiberglass bench seat on the port side of the *Impuls'* cockpit. Blood oozed out between his fingers and dripped down the side of the bench seat and into the scuppers.

Josh took stock. The older SEAL a guy by the name of Nick, turned to him. "Do you have a first-aid kit?"

"Sure, why?"

"I got cut a bit." Without saying another word, Nick passed out.

Randy helped Josh lay him out on the starboard bench seat. They could see where he was gashed in the side and arm. The other SEAL peeled off his mask, flippers, and tank and went to work. "I'm a medic. He's lost lots of blood. My medical kit is on *Tortman.* Please get it over here ASAP and I can treat both men."

After he told Gary what had happened on the *Impuls,* the lawyer said, "I'll be there as soon as I can with the medical kit. *Rusty Hook* has been taken by our guys. One of the two Russians on board is worse for wear, and there are two live locals. One we think is the boat's captain and maybe the owner, the other is his helper. Both decided discretion was the better part of valor. Those who are still alive are being tied up."

Josh prodded the unhurt Russian with the barrel of his MP-5. "Who's in charge?"

The man looked at him blankly. Josh repeated his question in Russian. No answer. "Look, we're not the police. We don't have to play by the rules. If we want, we can feed you to the sharks.

The man responded in Russian. "Bullshit."

"Oh, really!" Josh grabbed the unwounded Russian by the back of his wet suit. He didn't offer any resistance as Josh shoved his head over the railing so he could see the black silhouettes of at least a dozen sharks that were swimming around under the sailboat, looking for the source of the blood. "They're waiting for a meal. Do you want to be their dinner?"

The man's head shook violently as he tried to push himself up from the gunwale. Josh shoved his head back down. "Take a really good look."

With the help of Randy, Josh pulled him into a sitting position. The man's eyes were wide with fear.

Josh put his face close. "Now, who is your leader?"

"He's dead."

"I don't believe you." Josh grabbed the man again and started to push his head toward the rail. "*Stoi, stoi!* I will tell you!" This he yelled in English.

"Oh, so you speak English?"

"*Da.* Not very good, but I speak."

Josh let him sit back down. The man vomited and the smell made Josh's stomach churn. "Who is he, and where is he?"

"On other boat."

"What's your name?"

"Maxim Startsev."

"O.K., Maxim, what is your leader's name?"

"Viktor Mulkov. He Spetznaz colonel, now *mafiya*."

"Are you Spetsnaz?"

"*Nyet.* GRU. "

"What rank were you?"

"Captain."

"Why did you leave?"

"I like to drink and fuck. Got in way of work. *Mafiya* pay better. You know *mafiya*?"

"Yeah. Russian mob."

"Not understand mob."

"Mob as in gangsters."

"*Da,* like Al Capone."

Josh turned away as he struggled to keep from laughing. Here he was off Santa Catalina Island interrogating a former Russian GRU officer who'd just tried to kill him, who knew about Al Capone. He keyed the throat mike and said, "Gary, find out which one is Viktor Mulkov."

Josh turned back to Startsev. "How much are you being paid?"

"Twenty-five thousand each man."

"Rubles or dollars?"

"Dollars. Russian rubles not worth shit."

"Who hired you?"

"I don't know. Viktor knows."

Josh smiled as he asked his next question. "Does Viktor like swimming with sharks?"

"*Nyet,* you crazy bastard."

"Not crazy. I want you to talk."

"You still one crazy bastard."

Josh laughed, taking the Russian's words as a compliment.

Startsev waved in the direction of the others. "You American military?"

"Yes. We are all Navy."

"You obey rules, no?"

"Tonight, Maxim, there are no rules. You tried to kill my friends and me, and I suspect that you entered the country illegally. We will turn you over to the FBI later."

"You knew we were coming, no?" Josh didn't answer.

"We have traitor. Only way you ambush us." The Russian was speaking but no one was listening, for just then Gary was coming alongside the *Impuls* in a dinghy. With one hand, Gary swung the heavy medical kit over the gunwale. The SEAL medic opened the kit and began assembling equipment. He looked up and demanded, "Who here is O positive?"

Marty and Jeff raised their hands. "Good. Line up, guys. One of you are going to give my shipmate a transfusion."

Marty stepped forward. He, too, was a SEAL.

Josh took this all in, thinking quickly. "Gary and I are going ashore to make a call. Randy and Jeff, if the Russians do something you don't like, shoot them."

Randy waved the MP-5SD in the direction of the two Russians. "I'm Polish. I'd like to shoot Russians and feed them to the sharks while they are still alive."

The GRU officer pushed himself as far away from Randy as he could. Both Americans smiled at Startsev's reaction.

Thirty minutes later, Josh got off the pay phone at the end of the pier and Gary put a hand on his shoulder. "Did you do anything that violated that Russian's rights?"

Josh shook his head. "I didn't torture him, but I did scare him enough to cause him to puke."

"How'd you do that?"

"By threatening to feed him to the sharks. We could see them below."

"Really?"

"Yeah, there were at least a dozen, and some were pretty big."

"Remind me not to drag my hand in the water."

"Yeah.... Gary, we have about thirty minutes before the Coast Guard helicopter wakes everyone up. In the meantime, I want to chat with Viktor Mulkov. Counselor, you can be my witness that I am on my best behavior."

"Right. The only thing between all of us and Fort Leavenworth is that piece of paper signed by the President."

Josh looked up at his friend and lawyer. "Look, Gary we're in the world of special operations. If we have to, we bend and sometimes break the rules, because if we don't, we die or, worse, we fail. If we die, who cares? If we fail and live, we get our asses handed to us by armchair experts who have never been shot at. On the other hand, it is hard to argue with success. Today we succeeded. The Feds will make some arrests, the Coasties will take great delight in going through the books of the company that charters the *Rusty Nail*, the immigration folks will be very interested in their passports, and the CIA helped foil a plot to kill former American POWs. What's not to like?"

Gary looked at his friend for a few seconds. "When you retire, you should go into politics."

Josh laughed. "No way, José!"

Monday, May 10, 0953 local time, Miami

Between now and the time Karin arrived in the U.S., Janet had to find a way to end her career that didn't put her in a box six feet underground. Miami was her next stop in her effort to tie up what she now called her "loose ends."

Before leaving Stallion Springs for Los Angles and a non-stop flight to Miami, she'd worn latex gloves to wrap gun parts and ammunition in aluminum foil and cookie tins so they could be mailed by overnight express to her hotel. Then she'd dressed in a in a stylish women's business suit that allowed her to wear gloves before handling the prepared boxes and a letter for Enrique Payá.

At the Federal Express office, she asked the clerk for an envelope and inserted the letter, adding several centerfolds from the latest issues of *Playboy, Penthouse,* and *Hustler.* The young man at the counter of the convenience store where she's purchased the magazines had asked her, "Are these for your boyfriend?"

Janet had looked him in the eye as she put a twenty-dollar bill on the counter. "Nope, they're for me. I like looking at beautiful women. They turn me on." Her answer had caused the young man's jaw to drop.

American Airlines' redeye to Miami left just after midnight. By the time she collected her checked bag, picked up the rental car, and wove her way to the hotel on Miami Beach, it was almost 10 in the morning. On the way to the hotel, she stopped at the National Gun Store on West Flagler to buy two extra magazines for the BDA and one hundred rounds of ammunition.

A brief nap ended when a clerk at the front desk called to tell her that her packages had arrived. Right after the bellman left with a five-dollar tip, Janet examined the boxes to make sure they hadn't been opened. The assembled and loaded Browning went into a holster that Janet dropped in her purse along with three spare magazines.

After shopping at a grocery store, she headed for Little Havana and a two-building complex on 6th Street between 10th and 11th Avenues. One building was L-shaped and the other a long rectangle; together they formed a U around the parking lot. Apartment 309's numbered parking spot was vacant.

On the door, a FedEx tag said there was an envelope waiting

for Enrique in the mailroom. She lifted the tag and pretended to read it as she studied the locks. Convinced she could pick them easily, it was time for her next move.

Back in the car, she pulled on a set of latex gloves and carried the two paper sacks of groceries to Payá's apartment. It took her longer to pull on the gloves than it did to pick the lock. As she pushed down on the lever, she moved the door less than a sixteenth of an inch. A small piece of paper uttered toward the floor.

Ahhhh, the oldest telltale in the book. With her heart pounding, Janet checked the edge of the door, looking for an alarm or a trip wire. Finding none, she went inside.

The two paper bags went on the kitchen counter, then Janet replaced the telltale and took a quick tour of the two-bedroom apartment. Next, she looked behind the pictures on the wall, in the lamps, and on the furniture for hidden microphones, cameras, and anything else that would record her presence. Frustrated at finding nothing when she was sure there ought to be something, Janet stood in the center of the living room with her hands on her hips.

The Broker had given her Payá's address and the information that Enrique arrived home late on Monday afternoons. Payá's latest invoice was seriously overdue, and Raul was tired of paying off contractors. Then there was a small matter of Payá having double-crossed him on several occasions. It was time to send a message. Raul said that it was up to her as to what she wanted to do.

Nevertheless, Janet wondered. *Did Raul lie to me? Is this a set-up? On the other hand, taking care of him for The Broker makes one less person who knows about Luna. It's worth the risk.*

Before she'd left LA, she'd picked up copies of published airline timetables and quickly determined that the logical and easiest way to get from Havana to Miami was through Mexico City. It had the most flights.

Unless he spent Sunday night in Mexico City, the first flight from Havana to Mexico City to Miami would arrive around three.

Knowing how long it took to clear customs, get a rental car, and drive here, Janet estimated that he would be unlocking the door around four.

Janet glanced at her Rolex. It was three-fifteen. She resumed searching.

In the desk in the second bedroom, set up as an office, Janet found a six-by-nine envelope taped to the bottom of the top right hand drawer. She dumped out the contents, and Argentine, Peruvian, U.S., and Canadian passports cascaded out, along with credit cards, driver's licenses, and national identity cards to match the passports. They went back into the envelope, and she put it on top of the desk.

In the kitchen, Janet found a loaded Makarov in the back of the silverware drawer. Its threaded barrel told her that there was a suppressor someplace in the house. In another drawer, she found three loaded magazines and two boxes of Soviet-made ammunition. Amongst the cooking utensils, she found the suppressor wrapped in a cloth held in place by rubber bands. *Perfect!*

Janet removed the Makarov's magazine, along with the round in the chamber, and field stripped it. Once it was reassembled, Janet dry fired it several times to make sure it would work. Satisfied, she spun the silencer onto the threads and tightened it before she slid in the loaded magazine. The slide came back easily and she let it slam forward, loading the pistol before she dropped out the magazine and topped it off.

Satisfied that she was ready, Janet moved a living room chair so it was not in the direct line of sight for anyone coming into the living room. The Makarov sat on the end table by her right hand, next to a bottle of water. The Browning, now with the suppressor screwed on, was in her lap.

The wait gave Janet time to skim through the diary she'd found hidden under a loose floor molding. She flipped through it to the the time when she had been in Cuba and started reading. Once she'd read enough, Janet closed her eyes and rehearsed the questions she was going to ask Enrique. The two unknowns were his answers, and whether he arrived with someone.

The sound of a key being inserted in the lock brought Janet into the moment. Enrique, heavier and grayer than the last time she'd seen him, entered the apartment and dropped the Federal Express envelope on the kitchen counter. The door behind him closed with a soft thunk.

"*Buenos días, Enrique.*" Janet's voice was soft and friendly, as if she were talking to a lover.

Enrique moved to the other side of the kitchen counter to put space between the stranger and himself. "*Quién es usted?*" Who are you?

"*¿No se acuerda de mí?*" Don't you remember me?

"*No.*" His hands dropped to below the counter.

Janet waived the Makarov and spoke in Spanish. "Don't bother. I already have it."

When Enrique spoke this time, Janet could sense he was afraid. *He should be. He is in the presence of the monster that he created.*

"*Quién es ustéd?*"

Janet made a moue and pursed her lips. "*Me siento halagada de que no me reconozca. Soy Luna. Luna Serrano.*" I am flattered that you do not recognize me. I am Luna. Luna Serrano."

"Ahhhhhh, Luna Serrano."

Janet could tell he was stalling, trying to remember. "*Deja que le ayude. Yo soy la que ustedes llaman la estrella roja de la muerte.*" Let me help you. I am the one named the Red Star of Death.

Enrique's eyes widened. He came around the counter with his hands out to his sides. "*Lo siento mucho. Se ve tan diferente, y a la vez tan hermosa.*" I am so sorry, you look so different, and yet you are still so beautiful.

The Cuban's charm had no effect. Janet waved the Makarov and switched to English. "Sit down at the end of the couch. I am going to ask you questions and you will provide truthful answers."

"*Sí, sí.* You look so..." The Cuban struggled for a word. "I don't know, different."

Janet took it is as a compliment. The brunette wig concealed her mannish hairstyle that screamed she was butch, and her mix of gray, androgynous-looking clothes made her inconspicuous.

"First question. What do the Soviets—and by that I mean the GRU and KGB—know about me?"

Enrique leaned back. "I can't tell you that."

"Yes you can, and you will. If you don't do it here in the comfort of your living room, we can go to the Everglades and have this conversation."

"You came to kill me?"

"I haven't decided that yet." It was a lie. She was the only one who was going to walk out of this room. Enrique was a loose end.

"So you have turned on the people who made you into one of the best assassins in the world and paid you well. Knowing you, you probably invested it and are now rich."

Janet ignored him. "What do the Russians know about me?"

"They only know we trained assassins and a woman by the name of Luna Serrano killed Uglov in a fight. We had to tell them that because we gave them Uglov's body, and any medical examiner worth his salt would find the broken temple bone."

"What else?"

"I know they hired you several times because they went through me, but I don't remember the details. We were just a cut out." Payá figured that the more he talked and the more information he gave this woman, the greater his chance of walking out of the apartment.

"Ahhhhh." Her hand moved so the barrel of the Makarov was pointed at Enrique's chest. "What else?"

"Other than that, nothing. Honestly, I do not know what they know about you now."

Janet decided to change the subject. "Do you remember a German woman by the name of Monika, who was my roommate?

The last name on her passport was Arndorfer."

"You mean the very good looking, naïve blonde with long hair that everyone wanted to fuck, including me?"

"Yes. Her. What happened to Monika?"

"Why?"

"Right now, just curiosity. What you tell me will fit some pieces into a puzzle."

Enrique leaned back, and crossed his legs. He appeared to relax a bit. "It has been a long time. If I remember correctly, she hurt her arm in an accident. We sent her home with a modest sum of money and a stern warning not to tell anyone about her time in Cuba."

"Why?"

"The East Germans interviewed her after you left. We didn't want to lose credibility as an organization that could train effective revolutionaries. They had wanted her as a forger, but she wasn't very good, even with with two arms. With one..." Enrique shrugged. "The accident was a good reason to send her home. We could have killed her, but thought she might, under the right circumstances, become an asset. One way or another."

Right circumstances meant that the Cubans would blackmail Karin to get her to do what they want, and if she didn't, they'd kill her. This was Karin's nightmare.

"Why are you suddenly interested in Monika after all these years?"

"We bumped into each other in West Germany."

Enrique looked surprised. "She recognized you?"

"Apparently, I made an unforgettable impression. Maybe it was the hand-to-hand combat." Janet took a sip from the bottle of water and decided to change the subject. "How do you know Raul Moya?"

Enrique tried, but was not able to hide his reaction. "How do you know that name?"

"I'm asking the questions." Janet waved the Makarov. "Don't try to bullshit me, Enrique."

473

The Cuban decided to tell the truth, thinking it would go to keeping him alive. "Are we talking about the Raul Moya who owns International Logistics?"

"The one and the same."

"It is complicated."

"Humor me."

"We are related by marriage. His mother's sister is married to my father. That makes us cousins. We have different views about the future of Cuba. But it gives us a reason to communicate. I am lucky in that my work takes me to the United States and all over the world. When I am here, I am free to talk with my relatives, and I bring news back to those who are loyal to Cuba."

"Tell me about your business relationship with Raul."

"After your first dozen or so missions, we were sure that you were not going to get killed or arrested. So, I sold the idea to my superiors that we could still hire you out, but not do it directly. This would reduce the risk of any of your missions being tied back to Cuba. And, I heard that Raul is in that business, so I suggested that he contact you. I gave him the details on how you could be reached. We talk every few months or so when I am in the U.S.. He told me that you are his favorite and thinks you are one of the best."

He's trying to be charming. "When was the last time you talked to Raul?"

"Two months ago. We met for dinner at a cousin's house here in Miami. There was a wedding, and I represented the Cuban side of the family."

"Did you talk about me?"

"No. He said he was thinking about retiring and had enough money. I think Raul will shut down his business at the end of the year and disappear. He knows how to do that."

So do I. I will live quietly on my ranch or someplace else, and enjoy Karin's company and my money.

"So, Luna, what are you going to do next?" Enrique leaned back in the chair. He'd answered all of Luna's questions. She had come with questions, not hired for a hit. She would depart, and he would soon be in the arms of his mistress.

Janet's hand with the Makarov moved in one swift motion and when she squeezed the trigger, it sounded like someone spitting. Enrique's expression of surprise ended when his head snapped back as the bullet slammed into his forehead.

The answer is, kill you. Sorry, you are a threat to Karin and me.

Chapter 18
RETRIBUTION

Tuesday, May 11, 1982, 0812 local time, Newark

Before starting on a bowl of yogurt and fresh fruit at the Marriott Hotel, Janet folded the *New York Times* in half so she could read the top half of the front page. In the center, the headline told her that the nationwide manhunt for Bobby Wales was over. His body had been found floating in the Delaware River just south of Philadelphia.

The writer summarized a second attempt on the POWs in California in which five Soviet citizens were killed and three arrested, along with two Americans. All the Soviets, the writer noted, were ex-GRU or Spetsnaz and were currently members of the Russian *mafiya*. The article ended with a paragraph stating the FBI was still investigating to see if the two incidents were related.

Janet leaned back after reading the story. *Thank God Randy and the others are safe. This must have been the hit that Raul said went to the other players. I am so glad they are O.K.*

Wednesday, May 12, 1982, 1312 local time, Newark

By the time Janet got back to the Marriott Hotel at Newark Airport from a quick trip to Stroudsburg, Pennsylvania, to get ammo for the BDA, the boxes she'd shipped from Miami had

476

arrived. They were packed the same way she'd shipped the Browning to Miami from LA. The indicator on the dental X-ray sensor she'd left inside the box showed that it had not been exposed.

From her room, Janet dialed a number she'd memorized, and a familiar, lilting voice answered. She could tell there was an air of expectancy. "Hello?"

"Karin."

"Hi! I am so glad you called. I went to the Lufthansa office today to pick up the ticket. There must be a mistake. It was for a first class seat. It is a very expensive ticket."

"It is not a mistake. Get used to it, because we will never travel coach, unless it is the only type of seat available."

"Are you sure?"

"I told you, I can afford it. I am what you Germans call a rich American."

Karin laughed, then became serious. "I miss you."

"I miss you too, love. Only twenty-three days until we see each other again."

"I can't wait."

"Me, neither." Janet paused for a second. "I already have one big surprise planned for you."

"Wonderful. Any hints?"

"Not now, but maybe in a few days I will give you a hint."

There was silence for a few seconds. Karin's hesitant tone gave away what she was thinking. "Are you O.K.?"

"I'm fine. I'm doing just what I told you, making sure I can retire so we can be together and not worry."

"Great. I have a date for my surgery. It is this Friday, so I should be able to travel without any problems. My *muti* and *vati* will be here to take care of me."

"Wonderful." Janet could hear the excitement in Karin's voice. She wanted to say, "Should I come and be with you?" But it would be an empty offer she thought better not to make. She had to be fully retired the next time they met.

The two women talked for another twenty minutes before the call ended. Janet lay back on the pillow and closed her eyes. *In just over three weeks, I will be done, finished, and I can spend the rest of my life with Karin.*

Her hand slid between her thighs and she couldn't believe how wet she was. A few minutes later, she was shuddering with pleasure. It was good, but not as good as what Karin could do to her.

As she lay on the bed, letting the feeling of pleasure subside, Janet looked at her watch. It was a woman's version of one of Seiko's many chronographs, not the Rolex Randy had given her. The Rolex was in her home gun safe, and under it there was a note instructing the reader to send it to Karin if she was killed.

Thursday, May 13, 1982, 0926 local time, Newark
The next morning, Janet placed the other call.

"International Logistics."

"Hi."

Raul's voice brightened. "Janis, how are you?"

"I'm fine. I took care of your collection problem in Miami. Hopefully, others will learn from his mistakes."

"Can we meet? I have material that I would like to show you for a major project that will pay you extremely well. I could use your help now to figure out what else we need, and I don't want to send it."

This is the first time he's ever asked to meet me. Why? Usually, everything is sent by mail. Is this a trap, or does he really need help? Is he, too, planning to retire? "Where and when?"

"My place. Tomorrow would be fine. How about right after lunch, say about one?"

Janet read aloud the address she'd copied from the White Pages in the hotel room.

"Yes. That's it. Where did you find it?"

"International Logistics is listed in the Newark White Pages, but it has a different phone number."

478

"That number goes directly to an answering machine. I check it every few hours, but the only people who use it are my banker, accountant, lawyer, and the manager of my property management company."

Why did he volunteer all that? There was something about his tone that was unsettling. He was not the usual cheerful-but-all-business man Janet knew. "What's wrong?"

"I've had better weeks."

"Tell me."

"Tomorrow I will tell you everything. I'll see you at one. Be careful."

He always says that. Like a father to a daughter. But what is going on? Maybe Enrique was right about Raul retiring, but his timing is off. Something is wrong.

Thursday, May 20, 1982, 1102 local time, Newark

Even though Janet had agreed to show up at one, paranoia and instincts drove her to begin canvassing the neighborhood around the address at eight in the morning. From her vantage point across the street, Janet could see a ten-foot-high chain-link fence, topped by three strands of barbed wire that went around the building. The windows on the eighth floor were the only ones tinted gold, suggesting that Raul had the entire floor. She suspected the tinting did more than keep out the sun and bet the glass would stop high-powered, armor-piercing rifle rounds, like the 30-06 bullets she had.

At eleven, Janet walked into the lobby. It resembled other apartment lobbies in the neighborhood. A door led down to the basement, where she found a locked steel door with a "Do not enter" sign opposite rows of chain-link storage cages with numbers and letters denoting apartment numbers. Some were fuller than others.

In the elevator, she pushed number 7. Nothing happened. Looking again at the panel, she noticed a red button next to the one for eight under what was a small speaker. There was also a slot for a card that allowed the elevator to go to eight. Janet pushed five and the elevator began to rise.

There was nothing unusual on five. She went into the stairwell that was marked as a fire escape and climbed past the sixth floor, only to find a steel panel with a cipher lock that prevented access to the seventh floor. The lack of a handle, hinges or keyhole told her the door could be opened only from the inside. This meant there was only one way into Raul's apartment, and that was by the elevator. She wasn't about to try to rappel down the side and crash through what she believed were probably bullet proof windows.

Janet toyed with the idea of showing up an hour-and-a-half early and rejected it. Instead, she decided to see who came and went. After picking up a sandwich and a Coke at a nearby deli, Janet sat down on a bench in the park across the street.

It was, she noted, 1133 when a black Suburban with blacked-out windows parked in the no-parking zone in front of the building. Four men got out and went into the building, and the driver, clad in a windbreaker and black turtleneck, leaned against the hood and lit a cigarette. They looked military, but she would bet they were not American. Curiosity and fear for Raul's safety drew her to the building.

By crossing at the intersection, Janet had a chance to walk past the Suburban. The man in the windbreaker gave her the once over and went back to watching the street. His close-cropped hair and burly appearance screamed bully, ex-military, or police. An older man whom she guessed was in his sixties approached the building as she did and held the door for her.

Inside, Janet dallied in front of the mailboxes, ostensibly fishing for a key. By the clock in the lobby it was 1140 when she got in the elevator.

Swallowing her fear, Janet pushed the white button by the number eight and then the red one. When the elevator didn't move, she pushed the buttons again.

"Yes." The voice sounded like Raul, but she wasn't sure.

"Hi, it's Janis. I'm here early. Traffic was lighter than

expected. Can we meet now?"

Janet counted one thousand one, one thousand two, one thousand three. When she got to five, alarm bells in her brain were ringing, warning her he had company and wasn't calling the shots.

The elevator moved up and stopped. Its doors opened, revealing another shiny steel door at the end of a short, four-foot-wide landing. A button on the side just under another slot suggested that she push it. *Whomever designed this entry knew what he was doing. There is no place to hide and I feel very exposed.*

Janet heard an electric motor and the door slid open, revealing a combination of living room, conference room, and office. Silhouetted against the window, Janet saw a man sitting at the desk waving at her to come in. No one else what in sight. *Why doesn't he get out of the chair?*

As she stepped into the room, a cold cylinder pushed into the side of her neck caused Janet to freeze.

"Come in, come in. Please join us..." The speaker walked toward her from another room, and a familiar shape—a Makarov with a suppressor—came out from behind his back. Its country of origin matched his accent.

"I apologize, but my comrade must search you. We don't want any extra guns in this room. Please put your hands on top of your head."

Janet nodded dumbly. The man ran his hand up and down her sides, taking the opportunity to make sure he got a good feel of each breast before he turned his attention to her legs. He focused on the inside of her thighs and made a point to push the palm of his hand against her vulva to cop a feel.

He stepped off to the side and said something in Russian. Janet interpreted it as "inspection complete." *You incompetent bastard, you missed the BDA in the small of my back, and the throwing knives under each forearm.*

Janet acted as if she was cowed. "Who are you?"

481

"Oh, I am so sorry. I am Vasily Uglov. The names of my comrades are of no interest to you. What you may find interesting is that I used to be GRU. Now I am independent contractor. I came to find out from your friend Raul why eight of my men were either killed or arrested in California. He hired us, but I think he also told CIA or maybe FBI. To me, that is logical conclusion, no?"

Uglov paused as he took a step forward. "Did you know about this assignment?"

Janet shook her head. "I don't know what you're talking about. Raul is just a friend, and we had a date for lunch. I called a few minutes ago to let Raul know I was here early." The few seconds gave her time to scan the room. There was one man coming toward her, another to the side and one standing in a doorway across the living room. The speaker was standing next to the man in the chair, who must be Raul.

"We shall see." The speaker motioned with the Makarov. "Sit!" Janet heard a chair being banged down behind her. There was no way she was going to let herself be tied to a chair. When the man who'd felt her up grabbed her wrist, she twisted violently. She moved behind him to turn him into a shield. Out came the BDA and, as the man tried to break free, Janet pressed the muzzle into his back between the shoulder blades and pulled the trigger. The muzzle blast had nowhere to go and the pistol jumped back so hard it almost came out of her hand. As he jolted forward, she fired another round into the back of his head.

She heard the rattle of two different suppressed Makarovs. One round hissed past her. Several thudded into the body of the dead man.

Before Janet dove between the couches, she shot at the man standing in the corner. Both rounds hit him in the chest. Two down, two to go. Janet felt fear in the pit of her stomach because she knew she only had nine rounds left, no spare magazines, and hated gun fights.

The fourth man came out of the bedroom firing. He emptied

seven rounds into the sofa, sending foam, shards of wood and fabric flying through the air. She felt a searing pain in her left side. Instinctively, her left hand went to the area above her hip. She felt warm blood.

I'll worry about the wound later. Janet popped up and fired a double tap as the man ducked behind the doorframe to reload his Makarov. Both her bullets struck the molding less than an inch apart. She knew that the diminutive 95-grain .380 copper-jacketed round was not going to go through a wall unless it was just two layers of sheet rock. Time to find out.

Janet crawled to another position and sent two bullets in the direction of where Uglov was kneeling behind the desk. Then two more, aimed about six inches inside the doorframe. Two little black holes appeared in the wall about an inch apart and were followed by a grunt.

Her target came around the door, bleeding from a wound in his upper arm and another in his chest. From her prone position alongside the edge of the couch, her next bullet was a kill shot, and the man's head snapped back.

Uglov stood up and fired two more rounds at her. Neither was close. She returned the favor, but neither hit the target as Ugly ducked behind Raul's big desk. Janet looked down. The slide was locked back; the BDA was empty.

The Russian stood up and put two rounds into Raul, who was pushing himself back away from the firefight. Janet threw one of the knives at Uglov and charged. Uglov twisted his upper body to get out of the knife's deadly path and threw his empty Makarov at Janet.

Uglov managed to parry Janet's first series of blows. A punch that sank into the Russian's stomach told her that he wasn't in as good a shape or as fast as she was.

Vasily narrowed his eyes at Janet. "You are wounded. It weakens you." Janet kept her focus on Uglov's face and hips so she could take in her opponent's intent and all of his movements. She did not glance down, which was probably what he wanted her do. The wound hurt, but she was running on adrenalin. So he wanted to play mind games, did he? She could play, too. "I knew a Pavel Uglov, once, in Cuba. Any relation of yours?" Vasily dodged Janet's kick aimed at his chest. It wasn't her best, but she wanted to retain the initiative.

"*Da,* my brother. So you knew him? Were you one of his whores?" Vasily struck, Janet parried. He launched a flurry of feints and blows. One hammered Janet on the left side of her head, and then he landed another one on her cheek. Janet staggered backward, seeing stars. *Is it the wound or the blow?* To give herself time, she moved around the chair in the center of the room.

With her head clearing, she moved toward the GRU officer. "He was good at hand-to-hand combat, *nyet*?"

"The best. He was instructor. Also Olympic boxer."

Janet's chest heaved as she took a deep breath to clear her head and get oxygen into her lungs. She glared at Vasily, who was sweating heavily and wheezing. He had to be in his fifties, twenty to thirty pounds heavier than he should be, and he smelled like a smoker.

The five D's of hand-to-hand combat—distract, disarm, deny, disable and destroy—flashed through her mind.

Janet came forward as she spoke. "He wasn't that good. I killed him in a sparring match."

"Bullshit. My brother died of heart attack."

"That's what the Cubans wanted you to think. I hit him in the head and drove his temple bone into his brain. He was dead before he hit the floor."

Vasily gave her a defiant stare. "No woman could beat my brother."

"I killed him, just like I am going to kill you."

The D's were out of sequence. Uglov was disarmed, and she'd already parried his first set of blows to deny his attack. While he reacted to her comments about his brother was the time to disable.

Janet faked a series of strikes to the head to get Vasily's hands up, then used a sidekick to drive her heel into his solar plexus. He gasped audibly and staggered back as the air went out of his lungs. Another kick to his right leg dislocated his knee. He screamed in pain, limping as he tried to tackle Janet, who spun to the side and stomped on the side of the Russian's lower leg with the bottom of her foot and felt the tibia break in two. Vasily howled and put his hand on the desk for support. His right leg was bent at an odd angle. Blood was starting to soak his pant leg.

Focus, focus, focus. That's what her instructors in the dojo pounded into Janet's head when she sparred. Every little movement of your opponent means something.

I've denied his attacks. I've distracted him and made the fight emotional for him. I've disarmed him. I've disabled him. Now, it is time to destroy him.

Janet bobbed and weaved under Uglov's weakening parries before she hammered him with a series of blows to the face that ended with simultaneous palm strikes to both sides of his head. Stunned, the former GRU officer's head hung down. Blood and snot dripped onto the desk. He tried to hop at Janet, who kicked him in the balls. He bent over, screaming curse words in Russian.

It was time to end it. The second throwing knife came out of its hiding place. Janet grabbed Uglov's chin from behind and pulled his head back as she shoved the knife into his throat and twisted. Warm blood spurted out of his jugular vein and ran down her arm. Vasily gurgled for a few seconds, and died.

Janet now saw that the Russians had taped Raul to the chair, and blood was leaking from two bullet wounds in his abdomen. His face was swollen and one eye was almost closed.

She ran into the bathroom and grabbed two towels and pressed them to his midsection. "Hang on, Raul. I'll get you to a doctor."

"No, don't bother. I'm done for. This only speeds up the process. I… I have incurable lung cancer. Too many Cuban cigars. Let me die in peace."

"No, you can't die yet."

"Why not?"

"Because we need to talk."

"You sound like the wife I never had. Women always want to talk. What do you want?"

"How much do your customers know about me?"

"Nothing. They only know your fees, and those are paid to me. That's it. Once I have the information, I add to it and arrange for the weapons."

"Is anyone looking for me?"

"Are you asking me if you are under surveillance, or if there a contract out on you?"

"Yes to both."

"No. None of my customers are looking for you. About five years ago, one of my contacts at the CIA passed on some photos they got from the FBI. Then two years ago they sent me another set. Apparently, you turned up on one of their stakeouts in which the target was killed. I told them I didn't know who the woman was. They have no name, and you look different now."

"So, no one in the CIA or KGB or GRU or the Italian or Russian *mafias* knows the names I use?"

"No. I don't think the Cubans ever gave it to the Soviets. They only know that there is a freelance female assassin known as *la estrella roja de la muerte* they can hire.

"Good. Where is your file on me?"

"Why?"

"I'm retiring and I don't want any records. What did the Cubans give you?"

"What they gave me is in your file. It is their analysis of your background, and I know about your husband because they know. Farthest file cabinet, top drawer. It's open." Raul waved weakly.

Janet saw the row of file cabinets when she came in.

Raul wheezed and spoke. "You talked to Enrique?"

"I did. What do you know about a woman you may know as Monika Arndorfer?" Raul grimaced from the pain. "Never heard of her."

"Good." She could tell Raul was weakening. The towels were

red with blood. Raul reached out with a bloody hand. "Don't worry about the police. The floor below us is unoccupied and there is a steel plate and extra soundproofing around the apartment. Trust me, no one heard a thing. I want you to do me two favors when you leave."

"What are they?"

"At the top of each of the file cabinets, there is a red toggle. Pull them and they will set off the thermite grenades that will destroy all my paper files. If I am lucky, the fire will burn the place down and incinerate me."

"I can do that. What is the second favor?"

"Janis, or whatever your name is.... You made me an awful lot of money. I have one last assignment for you, and if you promise me that you will do it, I will give you everything that is in my offshore accounts."

"What is it?" One of Raul's hands fell away from his stomach. Janet gently placed it back on top of the wound. She could tell he wasn't going to last much longer. "Kill Gary Savoy. The CIA is looking for him. They want him dead because he ignored all the signs that the POWs were alive. He put out the contract on the American POWs. Because of that, the Russians showed up and were pissed because their men got caught or killed. They wanted to know where Savoy was so they could get the rest of their money before they killed him. After we met, I was going to give you the job to take out Savoy. Do it, and you'll get my money."

Raul coughed up some blood. His voice was getting weaker and his breathing shallower. "Yesterday, I got a call from a friend telling me he knew where Savoy was in Rio. The details are on my desk in the yellow folder. The Russians never looked in it." He stopped for a few seconds.

"Kill the fucking bastard who got me killed. That is my revenge."

Janet picked up the folder. It had an address in Rio, and a name along with two phone numbers.

"Savoy is arrogant. To cover his mistakes, he kills the people who work with him. He got many of my friends killed with his treachery. Go to Rio, call the phone number, and the man will provide weapons and show you the condo where Savoy is staying. It is not a trap."

"And if I promise to do this?"

"I will tell you where the files on my offshore bank accounts are. A few weeks ago, I added Janis Goodrich to the list of signatories, using the name from the passport I set up for you. I was going to ask if you wanted to come in out of the cold, and this was a way of showing good faith."

Raul winced in pain and more blood flowed from his mouth.

"And if I say I will, but don't, how will you know?"

"Because if you don't hunt Savoy down and kill him, I will come up from hell and make your life miserable until the day you die." Janet smiled and Raul tried to laugh, but just coughed up more blood.

"I'll do it as soon as I can."

"Thank you. The file with all the bank accounts is in the bottom file drawer of the one closest to me. It is a green folder. In the drawer above it, there is a red file. It has a list of doctors all over the world who provide 'off the books' medical care. It looks like you'll need one, and they come to hotel rooms. They only take cash. My safe at the back of my bedroom closet. there's at least ten grand in there. Take it. Write down the combination."

Janet copied the numbers as Raul recited them: "Four times past zero to the right to 56, left three times past zero to 12, right two times past zero to 26, left once past zero to 19, then to zero before you spin the handle."

The red folder could wait, so she pulled out the green one and brought it over to Raul. She opened it in front of him. He nodded. "That's it.

Raul was struggling to talk. "All the passwords and codes are in there. Use it to give Rafael some money. That's my guy in Rio."

Janet had seen enough men and women die to know Raul was

near the end. "He is a very, very good man who was my mechanic in Africa and Laos. I trusted him with my life, and you can trust him. He is expecting a call from you."

"You knew I would go after Savoy?"

"I was pretty sure, once you found out that he ordered the hit on your husband."

Janet smiled. "I didn't realize I was that predictable."

"You're not when you are working, but I suspected you have a softer side."

Thank you. I am sorry this has to end this way."

"Me, too." Raul fell silent, and his eyes rolled back into his head. Janet checked for a pulse. Nothing.

Janet stood in the middle of the room, silent. Then she put the green and red files into Raul's briefcase that was sitting on the credenza behind his desk. She pulled the knife out of Vasily, rinsed it in the kitchen sink, retrieved the other knife and returned both to their holsters. In the safe, she found stacks of 9mm, .380 and .45 ammunition. Reloading the BDA would come later, once she took care of her wound.

In the bathroom, she glowered at the image in the mirror. She looked like she'd been in a barroom brawl, and tomorrow it would be worse. She didn't want Karin to see her like this. After washing her hands, she gently pulled off her turtleneck sweater. In the fleshy area just above her hip, in the front, there was a small hole and a deep gash where the bullet had exited.

She gently wiped the blood away with a damp washcloth and looked at the raw, bloody flesh. She opened a bottle of hydrogen peroxide and steeled herself, knowing it was going to burn. Holding the washcloth beneath the wound, she poured as best as she could from one end of the gash to the other. She gritted her teeth as the clear liquid bubbled, cauterizing the wound. Before applying adhesive tape and gauze to close it, she used her finger to press bacitracin ointment into the wound. It still oozed blood, and she knew in a day or so it would get infected.

In the chest of drawers, Janet found a gray sweatshirt that

would give her a baggy look. She got the cash from the safe and put it a small duffle bag she found in the closet. Janet put two boxes of .380 ammo into the briefcase and dumped out a third. Twelve rounds went into the magazine and a thirteenth went into the chamber before she put the gun back in its holster.

Next, she went through the file cabinets and found three more files of interest before she pulled the toggles on the thermite grenades. When she could see flames, she took the elevator down to the first floor. The man by the Suburban was talking to a good-looking woman and didn't give her a second glance. Getting away was more important than killing him, so she turned her back and walked on. He would find out later what happened to his comrades. It was, according to her watch, exactly one-fifteen.

Friday, May 21, 1982, 0730 local time, San Diego

The first row of chairs was reserved for the admiral, chief of station, the operations officer, and the intelligence officer. As the air operations officer, Josh had a reserved seat in the second row. He waited for the meeting to start by going through the ever-renewing stack of messages. Even if they didn't require action on his part, he needed to know their contents.

"Attention on deck." The words brought everyone in the room to their feet. When Admiral Huntington walked in, he didn't take his seat. Instead, he went to the podium and nodded. "Seats, gentlemen."

The admiral opened a folder. "Gentlemen, we are going to deviate from the normal morning staff meeting agenda because we have to deal with a serious legal issue. One of our officers has committed a serious breach of Naval Regulations that we must deal with immediately. This event was brought to my attention yesterday afternoon by the staff's admin officer, who, in conjunction with our legal officer, has recommended the proper course of action for me as Commander, Carrier Group One."

Josh looked at Admiral Huntington's grim face and wondered who had fucked up big time. Navy carrier group staffs have less

490

than fifteen officers and thirty enlisted men, and something this ugly would be hard to keep secret.

"Lieutenant Commander Joshua Jonathan Haman, stand at attention." It was spoken harshly, as if the admiral had disdain for the conduct of the individual.

Josh carefully put his message board down on the chair before he came to the position of attention—heels together, back straight, palms at rest against his thighs with his thumb along the seam of his trousers, eyes focused straight ahead, but unseeing. He could sense the eyes of his fellow officers on him. Like them, he was wondering, "What the fuck did I do now?!"

To let Josh stew, the admiral made a show of putting his reading glasses on and adjusting them as he studied the paper in front of him. Josh's brain raced, playing back tasking after tasking he'd been given by the admiral or the chief of staff or the operations officer. There was no red flag that he'd screwed up something.

The guttural sound of a man clearing his throat focused the eyes of the fourteen officers in the room at the front. "I won't read all the gobbledygook of Navy rules and regulations, so here goes. From Commander Carrier Group One to Lieutenant Commander Joshua Jonathan Haman, subject, not wearing the proper insignia for an officer in the United States Navy."

The admiral looked at Josh, who had a blank look on his face.

"In accordance with Navy regulations, a message received on Wednesday, May 19, 1982, from the Chief of the Bureau of Naval Personnel and the authority granted to me, as Commander Carrier Group One, you, Lieutenant Commander Haman, are out of uniform."

For the first time since he'd walked in the room, Admiral Huntington smiled. "Mr. Haman, you need to be wearing these." He took a small red box with a Vanguard label out of his pocket and tossed it to Josh. In it was a pair of the silver oak leaves worn by Navy commanders. "Congratulations, Commander Haman, and well done. This letter that authorizes you to wear the rank of commander will go in your jacket. At the end of the day, you will let us know the date of your wetting down."

Josh stood there, shaking his head and smiling as the others in the staff clapped and offered their congratulations. The Admiral raised his hand. "The detailer called me the other day and asked when you could be detached to go to CO/XO school, so, Commander Haman, there is a command in your future. My aide has the detailer's name and phone number, so sometime in the next day or so you can work that out. Again, may I be the first to congratulate you. Now sit your ass down and don't let the silver oak leaves go to your head, because now someone will think that you know what you are doing and everyone around here knows that isn't the case."

Saturday, May 22, 1982, 1433 local time, Dallas

After Janet had described the wound, the first doctor from the list had said he would come to her hotel room. If needed, he would drive her back to his office.

She was, Dr. Jaime Gomez said, lucky that nothing vital had been hit. He numbed up the area, cleaned and stitched it together, then handed her two bottles of drugs. One was for pain and the other was an antibiotic. He also gave her instructions for cleaning the stitches, and how to remove them when the wound healed. They both knew that, had she shown up in an emergency room, the police would have been called because she had a gunshot wound. Dr. Gomez never asked for her name and left with three thousand dollars of the money she'd taken from Raul's safe.

Janet spent two days in her hotel room, trying to keep the swelling on her face down and following Dr. Gomez's instructions on how to keep the gunshot wound from getting infected. Room service provided food, and she only went out to go to a drug store for medical supplies.

Despite using ice packs, the side of her face was swollen and starting to turn yellow and black. Several times Janet gently pressed on her cheekbone and wondered if it was cracked or possibly broken. Without an x-ray, she would never know.

As she applied enough makeup to minimize the discoloration, Janet debated about what she would say if someone asked her what had happened. Saying she'd fallen or walked into a door just wasn't believable. Telling the person that she'd been beaten up by an abusive husband would raise too many follow-up questions. She settled on a car accident, and that her head had slammed into the window.

She'd flown to Dallas for two reasons. One, there were non-stops to Rio every day. And, two, she didn't want to connect through Miami in case the Cubans were looking for her.

On the bed, Janet spread out the documents she'd collected from The Broker's apartment. It was the first time she'd had the time and energy to study them. In the payment file was the customer's name, which appeared to be some sort of code, next to the fee and payment dates. It became clear that most of the hits were for the British, West Germans, Israelis, and Americans, as well as a smattering from other country's intelligence organizations. There were two or three for the Soviets, and a dozen or so from the New York and Chicago mafia families.

She started to count, and then stopped. She didn't want to know how many people she'd killed, or for whom. *One more and I am DONE!*

Before she'd pulled the tabs on the thermal grenades, Janet had done a quick search of the file cabinets. Taped to the bottom of the top drawer of the cabinet closest to the door, she'd found a #10 envelope. In it was a key and a business card for a storage unit on which Raul had written the unit number and entrance code, along with a receipt saying the rent was paid through the end of the year. As she looked at the card, Janet debated wither or not to go there first and then to Rio, or vice versa. She decided Rio first, storage unit later.

The green folder with the bank information was the most interesting. She wasn't surprised to discover that one of his banks was one of hers. There was also a sheet with the names of an attorney in Liechtenstein and another in Berne. When she opened the sealed envelope, she found the letter with the instructions to use and the code words that would authorize the attorney and bank officers to give the bearer—Janis Goodrich—access to his funds.

Janet sat back. Raul had been telling the truth about planning to retire. The dates on the letters showed they'd been sent earlier this year. *Maybe, just maybe, the reason he wanted to see me was to give all this to me.*

But the Russians had shown up. She suspected he would have eventually told them all he knew about Savoy. If she hadn't shown up when she did, who knows what would have happened.

Gary Savoy's folder was the last one Janet studied. In it, there were a dozen recent black and white photos of the man and a glassine sheet with the negatives. The handwritten date on the negatives said they'd been taken the week before. What surprised Janet the most was the color photo from his CIA credentials—that had to have come from the agency that also wanted him dead.

Janet picked up the push-button phone and dialed 8, got a second dial tone and entered 011. Then she pushed the buttons for 55—the country code for Brazil—followed by the number 21 and then the eight-digit number. It rang twice.

"*Olá.*"

"Rafael?"

"*Sí.*"

"Raul Moya said I should call you. Do you speak English or Spanish?"

"Both."

"Good. English then."

"Who's this?"

"*La estrella roja de la muerte.*"

"Raul mentioned your name. Are you coming to Brazil?"

"Yes."

"When do you arrive?"

"Not sure yet. I will call you when I get there. Can you print pictures?"

"Are you talking about the ones I sent to Raul?"

"Yes."

"You don't have to bring them, I have newer ones and will make prints in my lab. If you know where to look, Savoy is easy to find."

"Rafael, please don't take any more. I don't want him alerted or to put you in danger. When we talk the next time, I will give you specific instructions."

"O.K. But do not worry about me. I have worked for Raul for many years. I haven't heard from him. Is he O.K.?"

Janet swallowed hard. "Yes. I just saw him two days ago." *I will tell him the truth later. Well, at least what he needs to know. I have to figure out how to do this without meeting him.*

"Tell him the money for the first payment arrived and thank you."

"I will." *What payment?*

Monday, May 24, 1982, 2030 local time, San Diego

Only a pink glow from the sun was left on the horizon, and both Rebekah and Josh could feel the temperature start to drop. He put down his wine glass and pulled his wife of eight years against his chest.

"The kids are supposedly getting ready for bed," she said, snuggling in.

"Good. Soon we'll have a little quiet."

"Yes. Do you have a date yet for the CO/XO course?"

"Yes, first week of October. The detailer did say he would keep us in San Diego so we won't have to move to either Norfolk or Mayport. I may not have a choice of squadrons, though. Why?"

"I was going to buy the tickets for our trip to Israel this summer. We wanted to leave right after the kids get out of school and spend a month or so with them at Ginosar. I want to make sure that you still can take the four weeks of leave the Admiral promised you could have."

Ginosar was the kibbutz on the Sea of Galilee where Leah, Rebekah's mother, had grown up. "Is Leah planning to come?" He knew his workaholic father-in-law would never take more than a week off.

"Oh yes."

Josh took a sip of his wine to give him time to think. It was a big deal, not because of the cost of the tickets, but because of the commitment to his children. "Give me the dates and I'll file the leave papers in the morning. As soon as the admiral approves them, buy the tickets."

Rebekah wrapped her arms around her husband's neck and French kissed him. "Good decision. If you play your cards right and the kids go to sleep when they are supposed to, you'll get really lucky tonight."

Wednesday, May 26, 1982, 1241 local time, Rio De Janeiro

The weather, which had been pleasantly warm when Janet arrived the day before, had changed to crashing thunder and heavy rain. According to the sheet slid under her door the rain was supposed to end before lunch, and the rest of the day would be partly cloudy with highs in the upper seventies.

The forecast was wrong and the rain never stopped. By the time Janet got back to her hotel after an initial surveillance of Savoy's building, she was wet from the waist down, and her soaked shoes squished as she walked Only the brochure of the condominium apartments, which she'd wrapped in three plastic bags, was dry.

After she dried off and changed clothes, Janet dialed a local number.

"*Olá.*"

"Rafael?"

"*Si.*"

"I am Raul's friend."

"*Ahhhhhh, señora...* I was beginning to think that you changed your mind and were not coming to Rio."

"I'm here."

"When can we meet so I can give you the pictures?"

"Raphael, we're not going to meet, at least not yet. That's to protect us both."

"*Señora,* please listen for a minute. I understand your concern, but Raul is one of my closest friends. We are both Cubans and hate what the Castros are doing to our country. Since 1973, I have been one of Raul's agents in South America. He has been very good to me. I will die before I do anything to harm him or his family. There is much I can do to help you."

Spoken bravely, but there are people in my line of work who will torture you to get a description of me before they put a bullet in your head. I don't want that to happen.

"Rafael, thank you, but, for the time being, I still prefer that we don't meet." *Let me give him some hope.*

"How do you want me to deliver the pictures?" Janet gave him an address of an American Express office near the hotel. She told him to put the photos in a sealed envelope inside a sealed envelope and deliver them this afternoon. Waiting for him would be a list of the "tools" she would need. Rafael repeated the address and Janet said she would call him tomorrow morning to arrange the next step.

On her second trip to the complex where Savoy rented a condo, Janet sat on a bench by the fenced-in pool and pulled out Nancy Garden's novel *Annie on My Mind.* It was easy to read a few paragraphs at a time. From where Janet sat in the shade, she could watch the comings and goings of the residents, hoping she would spot Savoy.

Janet's sixth sense said she was being watched. A study of the complex didn't turn up a tail, so she walked up and down the street and around the complex. Nothing looked out of place or unusual, yet the feeling didn't go away. Back by the pool, she picked another bench; as she sat down, she made eye contact with a man. *Not Savoy.* When she returned his smile, he approached.

"Hi, I don't mean to be forward, but I saw you sitting here

from the balcony of my condo. I am Gunther Schmelling."

Janet could see he wasn't wearing a wedding ring. "Hi, I'm Janis."

He stood awkwardly in front of her. Janet guessed he was six-one or two and about 190 pounds. His long blond hair was neatly trimmed.

"Oh, please sit down."

"Thank you."

She turned to face him and the two chatted for a few minutes before he asked the dinner question she'd known was coming.

"Thanks, but no thanks. I am leaving Rio tomorrow. I'm just taking a break before I finish packing."

Gunther was not upset with the no. He wished her safe travels and moved on. His departure didn't end the "being watched" feeling.

On the way back to the hotel in a taxi, Janet concluded everyone driving a car, truck, or bus in Brazil thought he or she was either Emerson Fittipaldi or Nelson Piquet in a Formula One race car. There were only two positions for the gas or brake pedals —full throttle to get maximum acceleration and speed, or hard on the brakes to avoid hitting another car. Blasts of the horn accompanied by weaving in and out were part of the favored driving style.

Janet didn't like the uncomfortable feeling that she was a target. Paranoia in her line of work was healthy, but unchecked, it could drive you insane. She rationalized that she was just being careful when she wedged a chair under the door handle. Between it and the lock, it gave her a feeling of security.

The next morning, Janet checked into a hotel two blocks away as JayLynn Nance. Her valid U.S. passport and credit cards said she was from Chicago, Illinois. From her new room, she called Rafael.

"Buenos dias, Rafael."

"Good morning, *señora.* I have what you need. It is your third choice."

"Good enough. Here's where I want you to deliver it this afternoon. Have it wrapped in a plain box." She gave the name of her current hotel.

"Do you not think it would be better for me to give this to you in person?"

"No, I do not. It is better that the two of us do not meet." She hoped he would get the point.

"I tried to call Raul to report that we have made contact and he did not answer, nor has he returned my call. I did not leave a message. Has anything happened?"

Shit. The Newark Fire Department would have found the bodies and called the FBI, who may or may not have called the CIA. My assumption is that the CIA and the FBI are keeping the phone lines open as part of their investigation. By now, the CIA and the FBI know Rafael called, and that means Rafael is in danger. I have to keep him focused.

"Has he transferred your fee?"

"Not yet. I am not worried."

"I will see if I can reach him. How much does he owe you?"

"Ten thousand dollars."

"Does it go to the usual accounts?" Raul's file had Rafael's bank account numbers. All she had to do was make a call to transfer it, along with a nice tip.

"*Sí.*" She decided to tell him; his reaction would tell her if he was as close to Raul as he claimed. "Tomorrow, let's talk tomorrow. Hopefully, by then I will have talked to Raul and will know the status of the money transfer."

"*Gracias, señora.*" Right after she hung up, Janet walked to Savoy's apartment complex. The feeling that she was being watched came and went. *But by whom?*

Later, she picked up a note at the front desk of her hotel which said that a box had arrived. She sat at a chair and watched the front desk clerk and the empty lobby for over an hour before she had it delivered to her room.

Raul had provided a Browning Hi-Power with Brazilian

military markings and a threaded barrel. Someone had ground off the serial numbers. Wearing a set of tight-fitting latex gloves, Janet disassembled the weapon and made sure that the firing pin would strike the cartridge primer. Satisfied the gun would work, she screwed on the eight-inch-long suppressor and slipped an empty magazine into the butt. For the next ten minutes Janet practiced pointing and aiming at targets around her hotel room to get the feel for the pistol.

With the magazines loaded and stashed in her backpack, Janet tried to take a nap. She couldn't get the thought out of her mind that she was being tailed.

Was this a trap? Was she going to die? *I'll be ready for him this evening. I know his routine. This will all be over in a few more hours.*

The same day, 1945 local time, Rio de Janeiro

Gary Savoy came out of the elevator in his apartment and gave Janet, who was standing off to the side, the professional paranoid's once-over eyeball. He tried to disguise the look as that of a single man making a quick evaluation of a woman with a smile and a nod, then went on his way.

Is he going to come back with a date or alone? Rafael said he likes to go out to dinner around seven-thirty in the evening and come back at nine or so. He left late.

The lock of Savoy's apartment gave way to the picks in her latex-gloved hands. With the door cracked less than a sixteenth of an inch, a piece of yellow paper fell away from the lower side of the door and slipped to the floor. *Simple, but effective.* The two grocery bags that she'd brought with her to make it look as if she was a resident, and which held her gear, went on the kitchen counter before she replaced the telltale.

Savoy had left a light on in the living room. The faint sound of the air conditioning fan was the only noise.

Janet went through the bedroom first and noticed something odd about the clothes hanging in the closet. Before touching them,

Janet took a step back and stared. She went through the little alcove off the living room that had a built-in desk and drawers and found a six-inch ruler. The hangars were spaced exactly four inches apart.

It's another way for Savoy to know if the apartment had been searched. What else am I missing?

Indirect light from the street and the lamp in the corner created soft shadows in the living room and dining area. She studied the heavy outer curtain, designed to keep out all the light, and the sheer inner one to let light in and keep prying eyes out. Both were open.

Something in her brain told her to look up, and she saw a glint on the rooftop across the street. Instinct told her to spin and get down. A twinkle of breaking glass was followed by a smack as a bullet spent itself on the arm of the chair.

The first bullet was followed by a second one, a few inches lower than where her chest had been. This round sent shards of wood splinters from the leg of the chair next to the couch. A third and a fourth smacked loudly into the concrete floor and ricocheted into the cement wall.

Janet peeked out the window just in time to see a man on the roof of the building across the street pick up a rifle with a scope. *That's stupid. Never break concealment.*

Goddamn, that was close. But was I the target, or was Gary? Or was it Gary doing his own wet work? Whoever it is should be coming to this apartment to make sure I am dead. Or, if Gary was the target, to see if I killed him. Whoever it is, they need proof that either Gary or I am dead, and that means pictures. They can't rely on newspapers for the proof they need to get paid.

Who are these guys? I know from Raul that the CIA wants Gary dead. Or is it the Russian mafiya wanting their money, retribution, or both?

Janet pulled the blackout curtain closed and felt a stab of pain from the wound above her hip. *Would they enter quietly, or kick the door down and come in with guns blazing?*

The best cover was behind the kitchen counter, which made the living room a perfect killing zone. But anyone who'd studied the floor plan would know that. Oh, well!

Janet didn't have to wait long. The clicking sound of a lock being picked started less than ten minutes after the first bullet sailed through the glass.

From her hiding spot on the floor of the kitchen, the widening band of light on the kitchen wall told her the door was being opened slowly. The door closed with a soft click, and the kitchen was dark again. Surprise was Janet's ally as she popped up with the Browning at the ready. *"Hola, soltas sus armas!" Drop your weapons, now!* Janet hoped they would pause to identify themselves. She really did not want to kill CIA agents. Both men froze for a second, then the one with a submachine gun that looked like a Beretta M12 with a huge silencer turned toward her. Janet was on autopilot. Two rounds went into his chest. Then two more went into the second man. He staggered back, trying to bring his M12 to bear. She aimed and put a bullet into his head.

Janet came around the counter and found the first target was moaning. Blood was oozing from a hole in his upper chest and one in the center of his breastbone. He was trying to prop himself up with one hand.

"Who hired you?"

"No one. We're freelancers." The man wheezed and blood oozed from the hole in his right lung.

"Why did you try to kill me?"

"We didn't want you to get the reward."

"What reward?"

"The CIA wants Gary Savoy dead and is willing to pay one hundred thousand U.S. dollars. We didn't want you in the way."

Janet was about to raise her pistol when the man's head flopped over. She touched his neck—no pulse. *Now what?*

After finding nothing that would tell her who they were, Janet dragged the bleeding bodies into the bedroom. *Was there a third or a fourth man?* The answer to that would have to wait until after

Savoy showed up, if he did. A no-show by Savoy would tell Janet that she was the target and Rafael was not the friend Raul thought him to be.

Thankfully, the polished, hardwood floor made it easy to mop up the blood, and in the dim light the stain didn't show. The bloody towels she tossed into the shower stall. What glass she could sweep up went into the trash. Janet looked at her watch before replacing the tattletale. It was just before eight; she spent the next thirty minutes searching the apartment. In the freezer, she found Gary's stash of passports. He had Canadian, Australian, and South African passports—all with different names. The picture in his U.S. passport was missing.

Taped to the bottom of the two drawers in the kitchen, she found more envelopes. One had a sheet with numbers she recognized as bank accounts. The other had two familiar blue folding wallets. Each had ten thousand dollars in American Express traveler's checks.

Satisfied she wasn't going to find anything else, Janet dug the bullet out of the couch with a kitchen knife. Its tungsten tip explained why it had penetrated the glass without deforming. *They didn't get the ballistics right, and that saved me!*

At 8:50 Janet heard a key enter the lock. Gary flipped on the light as he stepped inside, and Janet stood up with the Browning pointed at his chest.

"Gary Savoy, I presume?"

He spread out his arms in a non-threatening move. "And you are…?"

"Doesn't matter. Sit down in that chair. You're very high on several shit lists."

Gary looked around and saw the bullet holes and torn up couch. Anger colored his tone of voice. "Who the fuck are you?"

"I'm asking the questions. *YOU* sit the fuck down."

"To answer your question, I'm Arnold Fleming, and I'm South African."

"Nice try." Janet held up his CIA badge and then tossed his

503

American passport at him. "Tell me why you ordered the hit on the American POWs who were just rescued."

Gary settled on the chair next to the couch and sighed. "Lady, you've got the wrong guy in your sights. Senior officials in the State Department made it clear that it would be very inconvenient and politically explosive if live POWs were found. For years, I told anyone who asked that there were no Americans left alive. Those five needed to die to prevent several powerful politicians from being embarrassed. If more POWs were found, the political shit storm would ruin many more careers, not just mine. I was set up to be the agency's fall guy."

"But it was you who put out a contract on the POWs."

Gary nodded. "You don't understand. Where I grew up in the ghetto, it was either you or me. I preferred that it be the other guy. The first was on Gus Grenholm, the CIA officer sent to review my work. A couple other analysts, who could have told investigators that I told them to ignore the evidence, were also killed. Look, what are you getting for killing me—a hundred, two hundred and fifty, maybe three hundred grand?"

Janet shook her head. "Nope, more."

Gary tried not to sound desperate. "I'll offer you twice as much as what you are getting."

Janet shook her head again. "I'm not interested."

"What? Don't you want more money?"

"This is not about money."

"Everything is about money. How much do you want?"

"Not a dime." *I have enough money. Raul's millions are icing on the cake.*

Gary Savoy now knew he was not going to leave this room alive, yet the intelligence officer in him forced the question. "What's it about, then?"

"Getting even. Tying up loose ends. Doing a favor for a good friend. One of the former POWs you tried to have killed is my ex-husband. Call it protection, or even revenge. Pick one, I don't care."

"No shit, I can give you much more."

"Yeah, no shit." Janet was tiring of the give and take. If she was going to spend time with Savoy, she wanted something that made the risk worth taking. "What's the more?"

"Back when I was in Angola and West Africa, I started passing information to the Cubans, because I wasn't a fan of U.S. policy. It's a black-white thing, just like Vietnam. I was tired of seeing black men die for their white governments. I wanted the South Africans to bleed, so I sold the Cubans information on the South Africans and the help they were getting from us."

"Then when you suspected some people were going to turn you in, you eliminated them."

"You got it."

"Were you afraid Raul Moya would turn you in?"

"No, Raul was cool, man. He just got my shit to wherever it needed to go. No muss, no fuss. He didn't ask questions other than when and where. He just wanted the money."

"Who was your Cuban contact?"

Savoy swallowed hard. "It started out as a guy by the name of Enrique Payá, and then he left Angola. About five years ago, he surfaced again and left a note at my place in Fort Lauderdale. At the time, I was working in covert operations planning and I sold him information on CIA undercover agents in Latin America and the addresses of some of the safe houses. Then, I got the POW/MIA gig and it didn't give me access to anything that was of use to him. But when I could, I gave him stuff."

"Interesting."

"Yeah, I knew what I gave him allowed the Cubans and the Russians to make life difficult for the CIA."

"Who's after you?"

"Could be a lot of people besides the CIA. The Cubans might be pissed at me because I turned down their offer to defect. They may be afraid I'll spill the beans to get back into the good graces of the CIA. Or it could be the Soviets. It's been years since I ripped them off, but they have long memories."

Gary eyed her, taking in the way she held the weapon. "Who trained you?"

Janet decided the answer didn't matter. "The Cubans, with help from the KGB and GRU."

"You know Payá?"

Janet nodded. "Yeah. I killed him a week ago."

Gary's eyes got wide with surprise. "You killed Payá?"

"I did. I have his diary. Bet you're in it."

"Probably." Gary slowly unbuttoned his shirt, yanked a key off a chain and put it on the table. "Here, this is worth letting me go. This is for a safe deposit box at the Bank of America branch on Herndon Parkway in Reston. In it, you'll find a treasure trove of info. You can make good use of it."

"Like what?"

"Stuff I never passed on to the agency, such as the list of POWs taken to Cuba and the Soviet Union. And, the code name of the Soviet's source in the FBI and where he works."

"What else?"

"The names of the Cubans who were infiltrated into South Africa and the U.S. as illegals."

"Who gave you this info?"

"Payá, among others."

Janet didn't move for a few seconds. "Just for your information, I'm known as *La estrella roja de la muerte.*"

Gary's eyes flickered as his brain processed the information. "'The red star of death'... Enrique told me that there was a hit woman with that name. He said she was really, really good because she was focused, ruthless, and unemotional."

"All true. And, now you've met her." The Browning spoke once and Gary's head snapped back as the bullet sprayed bits of his brain and skull all over the wall. Janet put the pistol on the table and said thanks to the corpse as she picked up the key. She knew there were no fingerprints on the pistol. It would be just one more piece of the puzzle.

Chapter 19
PARTY TIME

Thursday, May 27, 1982, 0900 local time, Rio De Janeiro

The tall, lean, athletic man escorted to her table by the maître d' didn't look at all like what Janet had expected. He didn't look Cuban. He looked Nordic. "JayLynn, hi. I'm Rafael."

Janet gestured with her hand as if to say "Sit down." The Cuban pulled his chair close to the table and spoke in a soft voice. "It is nice to meet you. I can tell by the expression on your face you were surprised that I am not short and dark-haired with a dark complexion. Well, I hate to tell you, but there are many Cubans who look like me. Many have American or European parents. My mother and father escaped from Germany before the war to avoid being thrown into one of the concentration camps. Cuba was one of the few countries that would take German Jews."

"O.K., I'll adjust my future expectations." On to business. "Is it done?"

"Yes."

"Good."

They waited until the waiter took their order. Rafael leaned forward with his palms at on the table and whispered, "What happened to you?"

Janet touched the large bandage on the side of her face that covered the large black and blue mark. She made it larger than necessary to make it hard for Rafael to recognize her in the future. Her dark sunglasses made it impossible to tell the color of her eyes.

"I was in a fight."

"I am sorry to hear that. Are you O.K.?"

"Yes. My opponent is worse off."

The answer satisfied Rafael. "*Señora,* there must have been a terrible mistake with the money transfer."

"How so?"

"My fee was ten thousand U.S. dollars. Two million was transferred. Not two million Brazilian Reals, but two million U.S. dollars."

"It was not a mistake. It is a present from Raul. He instructed me to make the transfer."

"I must talk to him and say thank you."

"You can't. I am sorry to be the one to tell you, but he is dead."

Rafael looked at her and tears started to come out of his eyes. He was visibly stunned.

"I was with him when he died." She summarized what had happened. "He made me promise to take care of Savoy."

"So you are now going to take care of me the same way you took care of Savoy and the Russians."

"No, Rafael. I am going to get on a plane and leave Brazil. I did Savoy for Raul, who was very, very good to me. I could not let Raul's killers and betrayers go unpunished, but it was my last project. I am now retired."

"It is over, then."

"Yes. And we never met."

"I understand. I am going to retire as well. Thanks to Raul, I have more than enough money." Rafael held up his glass of freshly squeezed orange juice. "*Salud.* To my friend Raul. He was a good man, and may he rest in peace."

Janet did the same before she took a sip of her juice. "To Raul.

He was very good to both of us. May he rest in peace."

The same day, 1140 local time, San Diego

Every outdoor table in the patio restaurant at the Hotel Del Coronado gave the diners a view of the ocean. When Josh walked up, his wife was flipping through her Day Timer, checking future appointments.

Rather than a peck on the cheek, she French kissed him for a few seconds before Josh sat down. Rebekah liked to do that because she knew it made Josh uncomfortable when he was in uniform.

"So, Rebekah, what's so exciting?"

"Randy has a girlfriend."

"So soon...." *I haven't talked to him in a few days.*

"Well, they've gone on several dates, and from all reports, sparks—you know, the good ones—are flying."

"So the yentas have a success story?"

"Yes, indeed. The first time he was at our house, he confided in Sandy and me that the singles bar scene turned him off. To make a long story short, Sandy works with a woman who is an engineer, believe it or not, with Raytheon here in San Diego. Her first name is Zofia and her maiden name is one of those Polish ones with more consonants than vowels. It is spelled P R Z Y B Y S Z N K I. Just before Randy went to DC, Sandy and I met with Zofia. She's widowed—her husband had a heart attack and left her with two boys who need a father. We made the introductions, they had a lunch, then another lunch, and then started dating seriously. Zofia really likes him. Anyway, the two of them are coming to your wetting down this Saturday. I just thought you would like to know. Be surprised."

"Okay, I will be. How about Jeff? He needs a good woman, too."

"Trust me—Sandy, Mary Lou, and I are working on it."

"Any other exciting news?"

"Yeah, I'm not pregnant. I just came from the doctor's office and the tests are conclusively negative. But I'm going back on the pill. We don't need a fourth."

Josh made an exaggerated wipe of his forehead. "Amen to that!"

Friday, May 28, 1982 1845 local time, Cologne

It was all Janet could do to stay awake as the taxi climbed the hill to the Dolder Grand Hotel in Zurich. She felt as if the stress from the last two weeks had sucked all the energy out of her body. She was in a fatigued fog as she numbly followed the bellman to her room.

After breakfast with Rafael, Janet had flown to London and caught a connection to Zurich. She got the energy to keep going from a call to Karin from the British Airways first-class lounge in London.

Karin again asked what her second surprise was. Janet giggled and said, "You'll like it and you'll get it soon."

After sleeping for ten hours, Janet stood in the shower with her hands on the tiles and let the hot, steamy water cascade over her head. It was as if she was washing off the dirt she'd collected for the past twelve years.

Before she went out, Janet looked through Payá's diary while she wondered what was in Savoy's safe deposit box in DC. She concluded that with whatever was there and the diary, she had a bullet proof set of "get out of jail free" cards.

Refreshed, she spent Saturday and Sunday exploring Zurich's Old Town as a tourist. Long runs on Saturday and Sunday along the shores of Lake Zurich helped her relax. Each day she had a long, pornographic call with Karin, during which they described how they would please each other.

By Monday, Janet was well into what she called the "decompression process." After each hit, she reviewed every detail in her mind and filed away lessons learned before the details were pushed back into a compartment in her brain that was closed forever. This was, she hoped, the last time she would ever visit this memory bank.

Her appointment at Raul's bank—Lombard Odier—on Talstrasse was at nine on Monday morning. It was where all his accounts were. She arrived fifteen minutes early, carrying the letter from Raul, as well as the access codes and documents saying she was Janis Amy Goodrich.

This meeting was the first step in getting Raul's money transferred to her. She suggested to the Lombard Odier bank officer to contact Erich Imboden—her bank officer at Pictet & Cie —to verify her identity. It turned out that the two were friends, and after a short conversation Imboden and Lombard Odier agreed to close Raul's accounts and transfer $22,562,301 to her.

After a long lunch, Janet stopped by Pictet & Cie to set up a monthly transfer of thirty thousand to her Wells Fargo checking account in California. For tax purposes, Janet's income came from managing the assets of a trust fund held at Pictet & Cie.

With Raul's money, Janet now had $35,629,189 in her banking and brokerage accounts. It was more than enough to live comfortably for the rest of her and, hopefully, Karin's lives.

The Swissair flight from Zurich to Cologne arrived around six, and by the time Janet got out of the cab in front of Karin's apartment it was almost seven. Perfect.

Janet pushed the bell in the lobby. A familiar voice responded on the scratchy intercom. *"Wer ist da?"* Who's there?

In her most authoritative voice, Janet responded. *"Blumen für Fraulein Egger."* Flowers for Miss Egger.

"Bitte kommen hoch." Please come up.

Janet rapped on the door twice. She heard the deadbolt being released and the door opened. Karin's eyes opened wide at the sight of her lover. *"Oh, mein gott!"*

"Surprise!"

Janet no sooner got the word out of her mouth than Karin threw her arm around her and kissed her deeply and passionately before pulling her into the apartment.

Breathless, Janet pushed back and blurted out, "Karin, I am

finished. Done. Retired. It is over."

"I am so glad." Karin pushed back. "How do I look?"

Janet had forgotten. Now there was an empty sleeve dangling where a paralyzed arm used to be.

Karin unbuttoned her blouse and pulled off the right side. "See, it is gone. It is still tender around the incision, but I am so happy. I couldn't believe how much better I feel without that useless thing hanging down. No more infections."

"I'm so glad." It was all Janet could say, and more might sound insincere given what she'd gone through the past month, so she changed the subject. "In five days, we'll fly to Los Angeles together."

"Are you sure?"

"Oh, yes. Our seats are next to each other."

"How long have you known this?"

"Since I bought the tickets!"

Karin hugged her lover. "I'm so excited. What are you going to do until we leave on Friday?"

Janet put her hands on the sides of Karin's face and drew it to hers as she spoke softly. "Rest, sleep, and make mad, passionate love to you."

"Hmmmmm." Karin kissed her lover and used her hand to put Janet's on her mound. "Let's start now."

Friday, June 4, 1982, 1835 local time San Diego

Friday night dinner at the Haman's was a family affair. All three children were expected to attend and engage in conversation with their parents.

Their three children—Sasha, Sara, and Sol, keen observers of their parent's behavior—saw their parents talking in hushed tones while preparing dinner. Sara, the most vocal of the three, was the first to broach the subject on all three kids' minds. "O.K., Dad, when are we moving?"

Josh looked at his six-year-old daughter. "We're not going anywhere. We're all going to Israel for a month. When we come back, I am going to a several Navy schools."

"To teach you how to be a commander?" Sara giggled. She liked to poke fun at the Navy.

"Not exactly. I have to go learn how to hunt submarines, and then go to a special commanding officer school."

Sasha, the oldest at eight, piped in, "Will you have homework?"

"Yup, lots, just like you."

"Will mom ask to see it before you turn it in?"

Rebekah turned away to keep from laughing.

Josh leaned forward. "If she wants to see it, she can."

"Dad, you didn't answer my question. Are we moving?" Sara was insistent.

"No. We are not moving. My next unit will be a helicopter squadron based right here in San Diego."

"You promise?"

"Yes. I just found out today. I can't promise because it could change, but I'm pretty sure we're staying in San Diego.

Sara, shot both fists in the air. "*YES! None of us wanted to move again.*"

Friday, June 11, 1938 local time, Stallion Springs

Both women were enjoying the warmth of the setting sun hanging over the Tehachapi Mountains that ringed the valley. The highest peak reached just under eight thousand feet and looked as if an arrow was sticking in the sun. Once the sun disappeared behind the mountains, the temperature would quickly drop from the mid-seventies to an overnight low in the fifties. Soon, if they stayed outside, they'd need light jackets.

Before she stood up, Janet emptied the bottle of wine into Karin's glass. "I'll go get another bottle."

Janet had been waiting for this moment all week. It wasn't just the lovemaking, it was the companionship. She'd never felt this way about another person before.

She re-emerged with a bottle of Henkell Trocken on which

condensation was beginning to form, and two new glasses. "I thought we would enjoy some champagne instead of wine."

Karin swung her legs around and grinned at Janet, who put the green bottle on the table. "Ohhhh, Henkell. Very nice."

Karin had no idea of what was coming next in what had been a wonderful week.

The first night had been spent at the Wilshire Hotel in Beverly Hills. They'd spent the next day visiting shops on Rodeo Drive. When they'd been getting ready for dinner, Karin had stood in front of the mirror, drying her hair with a towel, when Janet came up from behind and cupped her breasts with her hands. Softly, she used the palms to caress her lover's mounds. "They are so beautiful. I love them."

Karin had leaned back against her equally naked lover. "Mmmmm. I'm glad." She'd closed her eyes while she enjoyed the feeling, before pulling one of Janet's hands off. "Please stop... I'm hungry, and we have a reservation."

Dinner had been at Spago, where Karin saw three movie stars. The next day had been spent at Venice Beach before driving to Stallion Springs.

Now Janet poured the champagne and took Karin's hand. "Before we take another drink, I have something to say to you, my love."

Karin looked at Janet quizzically, not knowing what was coming. In a fluid movement, Janet dropped to her knees. "Karin, I want to give you a token of my love for you to wear from this day and forever." Janet slid onto her finger a ring with a six-carat, Asscher-cut diamond in the center of a solitaire setting. "Will you live with me for the rest of your life?"

Karin's eyes got wide and she smiled. She put her hand under Janet's chin. "Is this the third surprise?"

"Yes."

"Then let me give you my answer in the best way I know how." A gentle pull on Janet's hand brought their faces together. For the next minute or so, Karin's tongue explored Janet's mouth.

She stopped to take a breath, then led Janet to the bedroom.

Karin put her finger on Janet's lips as if to say, "Do not say a word" as she undressed her lover and gently pushed a willing Janet on her back. Karin gently pushed her lover's legs apart and buried her face in Janet's crotch.

The German girl stopped licking Janet's clitoris when Janet started moaning as she orgasmed. Karin straddled Janet's hips. Her shoulder-length blond hair framed her face as she looked into Janet's eyes. "I think what I just did is a better answer than the simple word yes. I can't imagine life without you."

Friday, June 25, 1982, 1006 local time, Bonn, Germany
A nine-by-eleven-inch envelope sat on the edge of the desk of the receptionist in the entrance foyer of the U.S. embassy. The bulge in the middle was about four inches thick, and there was a number ten envelope taped to the top.

The embassy staffer, a man in his early fifties, stared at the envelope. "Miss Radford, one more time, what did the woman say?"

"Sir, she said it was for the CIA's chief of station. In it, she said, he will find the diary of a high ranking Cuban intelligence officer and a key to a safe deposit box in Herndon, Virginia, leased by Gary Savoy. She said, 'Tell him to read the letter in the white envelope first.' She then paused and looked at me as if to say, 'Do you understand?' I said I would see to it, and she turned and walked out. The woman was in front of me for all of thirty seconds."

"Describe her."

I'd say early to mid-thirties, maybe 120 pounds, not much of a figure. She was dressed in jeans and wore a floppy sun hat and had a bandage on the side of her face. She had sunglasses on. Oh, and her long brown hair was a wig."

"How do you know?"

"I could see blonde hair peeking out behind one ear."

"Do you know if she signed in?"

"No, Mr. Cochrane, I don't."

Cochrane paused for a few seconds while he debated whether or not the envelope was likely to contain a bomb. He decided it wasn't and took the offered letter opener.

> To whom it may concern:
>
> In the manila envelope you will find the working diary and professional notes of the late Enrique Payá, who was a director in Cuban intelligence. The diary covers fifteen years. Payá ran agents in the U.S., one of whom was Gary Savoy, whom he met in Angola.
>
> The smaller envelope contains the key to Gary Savoy's safe deposit box in Herndon, VA and the address of the bank. These documents are being provided with no strings attached. Please do not waste your time trying to find or identify me or guess how they came into my possession. I have copies of the photos and the diary and can assure you that my fingerprints are not on any of the documents.
>
> A concerned citizen.

The words "Hmmmmmm, very interesting," slipped out of Jason Cochrane's mouth.

"Sir, what is so interesting?"

"Sorry, I can't tell you. It's classified." With that, Jason Cochrane, the CIA's counter-intelligence specialist, picked up the package and headed to his office.

THE END

EPILOGUE

Josh Haman

While at CO/XO school, Josh received orders as the Executive Officer of HS-2 that was deploying ten weeks after the school finished. The current executive officer of the squadron had failed his annual flight physical due to diabetes and high blood pressure and would be medically retired. Josh's orders included a brief stop at the HS-10 where he had been an instructor and where he would be given a short transition course to the SH-3D and a NATOPS check. While there, he would also attend the two-week Helicopter Anti-Submarine course. Later in his career, he would serve on the Seventh Fleet staff as chief of staff for operations and plans, and command a 39,500-ton *Tarawa* class landing ship dock and a carrier battle group before retiring as a rear admiral.

CDRs Jeff Anderson And Randy Pulaski

Randy Pulaski married Zofia Przybysznki a year to the day after they met. By then, he'd already plunged into the role of being the father to Zofia's children.

Jeff, on the other hand, chose to remain a bachelor. He accepted, but never got over the fact that his wife had remarried and the man had adopted his son. It took a year of legal maneuvering before his ex-wife Marjorie and her husband Steve allowed him to have his son for a weekend a month so he could be a part of the life of the boy he'd sired.

Both Jeff Anderson and Randy Pulaski received orders to report to the Naval Air Medical Institute in Pensacola, Florida. After passing thorough physicals, they were given a series of familiarization flights at VT-4. The flights started with four hours of dual before they were turned loose to fly solo. It was the first time either had been in a cockpit since they'd been shot down.

Besides practicing takeoffs, landings and instrument flying, the two men flew the T-2Cs off the *U.S.S. Lexington* as part of a contingent of flight students making their first carrier landings. Both passed the informal three-week course with flying colors and joined Josh Haman in the prospective commanding/executive officer class that began that October.

Pulaski and Anderson became COs of light attack squadrons flying F/A-18As. After their XO and CO tours, Jeff Anderson and Randy Pulaski were both promoted to captain. In 1990, once he received his date of rank as a captain, Jeff retired and began flying for American Airlines. Randy stayed in the Navy and retired as a rear admiral.

LTC Ashley Smith

Ashley wasn't surprised when his parents told him his that his fiancée hadn't waited for him to come home. While he was in captivity, his grandmother told everyone who would listen that Ashley was never returning. Every Friday night until she died, a week before the six MIAs were declared dead, she went to temple to say Kaddish for her grandson.

While he was in the hospital, Ashley was told he was going to be medically retired and asked if he would be an instructor at the Army's Special Forces School at Fort Bragg. Right after he reported to the school for Green Berets, Ashley walked into Fayetteville's oldest synagogue, Beth Shalom.

Rachel Cohen was sitting in for her friend when Ashley limped into the office and introduced himself. Her first reaction after talking to him for ten minutes was *"Oh my God, the man of my dreams just walked into my life."*

They were married about eight months later and now live in Fayetteville. As soon as he could, Ashley used his GI Bill to pay for a master's degree at the University of North Carolina in Fayetteville and then a doctorate in history at Duke. Dr. Ashley Smith is a visiting professor at the United States Military Academy as well as an instructor at the Army's school for Green Berets.

LTC Greg Christiansen

Greg Christiansen also returned to flight status. The Air Force granted his request to become a full-time Air National Guardsman flying the C-130. As soon as he completed his twentieth year in the Air Force he retired from the guard and joined Northwest Airlines.

Karin Egger and Janet Williams

Janet returned to Cologne, Germany, to spend several weeks living with Karin. While there, she met with her lover's parents, who welcomed her as a new member of the family. In September, Karin resigned her position and moved to Stallion Springs, where she now lives with Janis Amy Goodrich, and became a U.S. citizen.

GLOSSARY

A-26K Counter Invader—The B-26 Invader was originally designed as a high-speed medium bomber to replace the Douglas B-25 Mitchell and the Martin B-26 Marauder. The "bomber" version had a glass nose for a bombardier/navigator and the "attack" variant had a "solid" nose with eight fifty-caliber machine guns. 2,505 B models and 1,091 C models were built. The airplanes with the solid nose were originally flown by a single pilot, with a loader/navigator for the guns in the nose, and a gunner in a glassed-in area in the rear fuselage. The gunner controlled two turrets, one on the top and the other in the bottom of the fuselage. Each turret had two fifty-caliber guns.

In 1948 the airplane was re-designated by the newly independent Air Force as the A-26 and it was used as a night intruder during the Korean War. Early in the Vietnam War, the Air Force wanted to use the airplane for interdiction missions along the Ho Chi Minh and forty Cs were taken out of mothballs and converted to the K model. The rear turrets were removed along with the wing guns. Four ordnance stations on each wing were added. The avionics were upgraded and the cockpit layout changed to allow for a pilot and a co-pilot.

Historically, this airplane is very significant for two reasons. First, it is one of only two airplanes in U.S. military history that have been flown on combat missions in three major wars—World War II, Korea and Vietnam. The other is the C-47.

Second, its designers—Ed Heinemann and Ted Smith—created many of the best military and civilian aircraft ever built. Before the B-26, Heinemann designed the A-20 and the Navy's SBD Dauntless dive bomber. Later, he would lead the design team for the A-1, A-3, A-4 and other successful aircraft. One of the young engineers working for Heinemann was Ted Smith who would, after the war, design the Aero Commander twin-engine business aircraft and found the Aerostar Corporation.

Beretta M12—A light, very concealable light machine gun that Beretta started manufacturing in 1962. The weapon has a distinctive silhouette with a pistol looking handle under the barrel as well as one with the trigger. It fires 9mm rounds at roughly 550 rounds per minute. Normally, it is loaded with a 32-round magazine, but 20- and 40-round ones can be used. It is available with a folding stop and the weapon is made in Italy and under license in Brazil and Indonesia.

Call Signs, Squadron Names and Tail Codes—They're all different. Call signs can change from mission to mission. Squadron names are given when the squadron is established and tail codes represent the command to which the squadron is assigned. Unless a specific mission call signs are assigned, a publication called JANAP 119 (Joint Army, Navy Air Force Publication) that lists all the "standard" unit call signs. Over time these change; however, for the purpose of *Forgotten*, the following unit/squadron/tail codes were used for the six POWs:

Pilot	Squadron	Squadron Name	Call Sign	Tail Code	Side Number
Pulaski	VA-153	Blue Tail Flies	Power House	NM	310
Anderson	VA-22	Redcocks	Beefeater	NF	302
Kramer	23rd Tactical Air Support Squadron		Nail	NF	515
Christiansen	Detachment 1 of the 416th Tactical Fighter Squadron	Operated under the name Commando Sabre	Misty	SE	04

Code of Conduct—After the Korean War the U.S. military created a code of conduct that governed the actions of any U.S. soldier captured by the enemy. It was enacted in 1955 by President Eisenhower via presidential directive. The code has evolved over the years and it can be found in its entirety on Wikipedia at *h t t p : / / e n . w i k i p e d i a . o r g / w i k i / Code_of_the_United_States_Fighting_Force.*

Dragunov—The semi-automatic rifle was designed in 1963 and has a distinctive-looking stock. It is usually fitted with a four-power scope and weighs about nine and a half pounds. The weapon fires a 7.62 X 54mm round and is fed with a 10-round box magazine. It has a maximum effective range of about 800 meters.

Exercise Cobra Gold '82—Cobra Gold began in 1982 as an annual, joint bilateral, Thailand/U.S. exercise. Today, participation in the exercise is still controlled by the two founding countries. If a country wants to join, it must first be granted observer status before it is allowed to participate. In 2014, over 16,000 men and women from Indonesia, Japan, Korea, Malaysia, Singapore, Thailand and the U.S. conducted joint field and command post exercises. In addition, in order to foster international cooperation among other nations, the participating armed forces often participate in humanitarian and civic assistance projects designed to improve the quality of life and Thailand's infrastructure.

Homestead Act Of 1862—This piece of legislation was a continuation of the U.S. government policy that fostered Jefferson's egalitarian ideal of the "individual farmer" who improved the land and fed his fellow citizens. To encourage farming, people needed land and the federal government had lots of it in the less populated regions of the U.S. Lincoln signed this particular act. It granted any U.S. citizen or immigrant who was twenty-one or older and who had not taken up arms against the federal government 160 acres if he agreed to settle, work and "improve" the land for five years. This law and those that followed outlined a three-step process to get the land—(1) apply; (2) sign an affidavit saying you will improve the land; and (3) file for the deed and title. It was this act and the ones that followed that opened the floodgates of immigration that began after the Civil War because in Europe most of the land was already taken and expanding an existing farm was very difficult.

Il-62M—This is an improved version of the IL-62 long-range transport. One hundred ninety-three of these four-engine aircraft were built. The four engines were located in two in pods at the aft end of the fuselage. It had a range of about 5,400 miles at a cruising speed of about 430 knots. The cockpit crew for international operations included a pilot, co-pilot, flight engineer and navigator plus four to five flight attendants to serve the 174 passengers.

Karate gi—A karate gi is the garment worn by students of karate. It is similar to a judo gi as it shares a common origin. It is a combination of a white robe that is worn with loose-fitting white pants. The robe is worn with a colored belt called an obi that shows the "rank" or skill level of the wearer.

Makarov—Designed by Nikolay Fyodorovich Makarov, the compact semi-automatic pistol was the standard-issue side arm for the Soviet military and police from 1951 to 1991. It is still widely used today by police forces and military units all over the world. Factories in the Soviet Union, East Germany, the People's Republic of China and Bulgaria have manufactured millions of Makarovs. The weapon has an eight-shot magazine and fires the 9mm x 18mm cartridge whose dimensions are between those of the 9mm x 19 Luger and the .380-round in size. The pistol is similar in size and weight to the Walther PPK and PPK/S.

Misty—"Misty" was the call sign of a group of combat-experienced fighter pilot volunteers who formed a top-secret squadron based in South Viet Nam. By design, they flew low and fast, looking for targets on the Ho Chi Minh trail, carrying only ammo for their four 20mm-cannons and marking rockets. Their CO, Colonel Bud Day, was shot down and became a POW in the Hanoi Hilton. The squadron spawned two Air Force Chiefs of Staff, five other generals, two astronauts, several industry CEOs, and the first man to fly around the world unrefueled in a light aircraft.

Nail—Call sign of the 23rd Tactical Air Support Squadron that flew out of Nakhon Phanom Airbase in Thailand. The squadron flew O-1 Bird Dogs and OV-10s.

Nunchuks—Nunchuks are a traditional Okinawan martial arts weapon made from two hardwood or bamboo sticks connected by a short length of rope or chain. They are widely used in karate and are effective in a fight as long as the other individual does not have a long weapon such as a sword. Nunchuku, the Japanese word for the weapon, were made popular by actor and martial arts expert Bruce Lee and his fellow expert Don Inosanto.

PSSF—PSSF stands for "People's Public Security Force." This references the group of agencies within the government of Vietnam that include the Public Security Ministry; Public Security Departments of provinces and centrally run cities; Public Security Offices of rural districts, urban districts, provincial towns and provincially run cities; and Public Security Offices of communes, wards and townships.

U.S.S. *Coral Sea* (CV-43)—The *Coral Sea* was the last of the three *Midway*-class aircraft carriers built. Her keel was laid in 1944 and the ship was commissioned in 1947. The *Coral Sea* was assigned to the Atlantic Fleet until she was decommissioned for a major refit in May 1957. Three years later, in September 1960, the carrier emerged from the Puget Sound Naval Shipyard with a new angled deck and was assigned to the Pacific Fleet. In 1985 *Coral Sea* returned the Atlantic Fleet and her air wing participated in the bombing of the terrorist training camps in Libya in 1986 in Operation El Dorado Canyon. The *Coral Sea* was decommissioned in 1990 and scrapped.

The actual deployment referenced in *Forgotten* took the *Coral Sea* into the Indian Ocean and the North Arabian Sea during the hostage crisis in Iran. As part of the cruise, the ship made two port calls in Thailand. For this reason, the carrier and its battle group are used to support the plot.

During the cruise, the *Coral Sea* left Alameda, CA, in August 1981 and returned in March 1982. At the time, Carrier Air Fourteen with tail letters NK was on board and the ship was part of Carrier Group Five. The deployment included 98 continuous days at sea on Gonzo Station in the North Arabian Sea. The air wing's squadrons and airplanes were:

VF-21—Black Knights NK 100—F-4N
VF-154—Freelancers NK 200—F-4N
VA-97—Warhawks—NK 300—A-7E
VA-27—Royal Maces—NK 400—A-7E
VA-196—Main Battery—NK500—A-6E/KA-6D
VAW-113—Black Eagles—NK 600—E-2B
VFP-63 Det. 2—Eyes of the Fleet—NK 115—117—RF-8G
HC-1—Pacific Fleet Angels—NK 610—614—SH-3G

Vietnamese Military Districts—The Vietnamese People's Army divided the unified country into nine military regions. The 4th Military Region or Military District covers an area south of Hanoi/Haiphong to what used to be the DMZ that separated North and South Vietnam. Its headquarters is in Vinh. Commanders of Vietnamese Military Districts are usually also members of the Central Committee of the Communist Party of Vietnam.

Zuni—The Zuni is a five-inch, air-to-ground rocket fired from the LAU-10 launcher. The rocket weighs 110 pounds, forty of which consists of the weight of the warhead, and the remaining 70 pounds is made up by the rocket motor and fuselage. It has a range of about five miles, although it is rarely shot that far and is normally delivered in a diving attack. The rockets can be fired singly with each pull of the trigger, or all at once in a salvo. The most common method is "ripple" fire in which the pilot selects the interval between rocket launches. For example, if he sets "one second," when the pilot pulls the trigger the rockets leave the pod at one-second intervals.

About the Author

Marc Liebman

Marc retired as a Captain after twenty-four years in the Navy and is a combat veteran of Vietnam, the Tanker Wars of the 1980s and Desert Shield/Storm. He is a Naval Aviator with just under 6,000 hours of flight time in helicopters and fixed-wing aircraft. Captain Liebman has worked with the armed forces of Australia, Canada, Japan, Thailand, the Republic of Korea, the Philippines and the U.K.

He has been a partner in two different consulting firms advising clients on business and operational strategy, business process re-engineering, sales and marketing. Marc has also been the CEO of an aerospace and defense manufacturing company as well as an associate editor of a national magazine and a copywriter for an advertising agency.

Marc's latest career is as a novelist and six of his books—*Cherubs 2, Big Mother 40, Render Harmless, Forgotten, Inner Look* and *Moscow Airlift* have been published. A seventh—*The Simushir Island Incident*—will be released in 2019. *Big Mother 40* was ranked by the readers who buy books on Amazon as one of the top 100 war novels. *Forgotten* was a 2017 Finalist in Historical

Fiction in the Next Generation Indie Book Awards, a Finalist in Fiction in the 2017 Literary Excellence Awards, and was rated as Five Star by Readers Favorites. *Inner Look* was also rated Five Star by Readers Favorites.

The Liebmans live near Aubrey, Texas. Marc is married to Betty, his lovely wife of 49+ years. They spend a lot of time in their RV and visiting their four grandchildren.

If You Enjoyed This Book
Please write a review.
This is important to the author and helps to get the word out to others
Visit

PENMORE PRESS
www.penmorepress.com

BIG MOTHER

BY
MARC LIEBMAN

Big Mother 40 is a story well told and one in which aviation and special warfare veterans of the Vietnam conflict will identify, and about which they will tell their friends. Younger readers will enjoy the book simply as a great adventure.
— Michael Field, Captain USN (retired) Wings of Gold, Winter 2012 issue

Liebman skips macho combat images to plunk us into the deeper connections of war, from fear and courage to the truer realms of human relationships. His detail is authentic, and he lends even greater validity to the operations he describes with valuable author notes at the back of the book including a historic analysis of the time, military glossary and roster of characters. Despite the book's intensity and detail, the story is fast-paced. For a book you won't forget, you have to read BIG MOTHER 40.
Bonnie Toews, Military Writers Society of America, January 2013

PENMORE PRESS
www.penmorepress.com

CHERUBS 2

BY

MARC LIEBMAN

In combat, there is a fine line between being overly cautious and cowardice. It's Josh Haman's first tour in Vietnam and he's fresh out of the training command - a "nugget" in Naval Aviator parlance. Josh Haman has to figure out on which side of the line the combat search and rescue detachment's officer-in-charge stands. Untested and without a lot of experience, he has to make a career and life and death decision and live with the consequences.

Josh gets his first taste of the unpredictability of Naval operations when he is picked to be a pioneer in flying helicopters in Navy special operations. He, and Marty Cabot, a Navy SEAL, become pawns in inter-service politics. The two of them are ordered to fly missions that could, if not carried out successfully, have international consequences

PENMORE PRESS
www.penmorepress.com

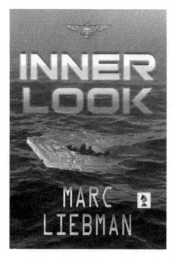

INNER LOOK
BY
MARC LIEBMAN

International Espionage, NKV Russian Intelligence , US Intelligence, CIA, Argentina spy story, Peril at Sea , Helicopter stories , Sea stories,

After John Walker and Jerry Whitworth are arrested for passing top-secret information to the Soviet Union, the project Inner Look is initiated to determine if there are any other spies operating within the government intelligence agencies. Navy SEAL Marty Cabot and naval aviator Josh Haman are assigned to the project in the hopes that their unconventional approach and out-of-the-box thinking will yield more answers.

Cabot and Haman discover that the security leaks go higher up than anyone imagined. Furthermore, the leaks have compromised many of their missions.   For Josh and Marty, it's not just about national security, it's personal.

Their pursuit turns international, taking them into dangerous waters. Nothing but their skills will keep them alive when the KBG sends assassins to silence the traitor and neutralize the threat they pose.

PENMORE PRESS
www.penmorepress.com

RENDER HARMLESS

BY

MARC LIEBMAN

Car bombs set by a group called Red Hand are going off all over West Germany, killing American, British and German citizens. Red Hand's manifesto reads as if it was copied from Nazi propaganda. Now, just four years after the 1972 Olympics massacre of Israeli athletes and three decades after the Holocaust, the West German government is facing its worst political nightmare: Germans are once again killing Jews – and former Nazis who want to create the Fourth Reich may somehow be involved.

The West German police can't find the shadowy members of Red Hand, so the American and British governments decide to act covertly. Josh Haman, part way through an exchange tour with the Royal Navy's Fleet Air Arm, joins the team led by his friend and SEAL Team Six member Marty Cabot. The hunt takes their team into East Germany to execute their written orders, which tell them "to find, neutralize and render harmless to the United States and her allies the members of Red Hand."

PENMORE PRESS
www.penmorepress.com

Penmore Press

Challenging, Intriguing, Adventurous, Historical and Imaginative

www.penmorepress.com